Strangers
in Our Midst

Strangers
in Our Midst

Kathleen Vellenga

40
PRESS

Strangers in Our Midst
Copyright © 2013 by Kathleen Vellenga. All rights reserved. No part of this publication may be reproduced, distributed, or transmitted in any form or by any means, including photocopying, recording, or other electronic or mechanical methods, without the prior written permission of the publisher, except in the case of brief quotations embodied in critical reviews and certain other noncommercial uses permitted by copyright law. For permission requests, write to the publisher, addressed "Attention: Permissions Coordinator," at the address below.

Design: John Toren

Library of Congress Cataloging-in-Publications Data
Library of Congress Control Number: 2013943029
Vellenga, Kathleen
Strangers in Our Midst/Kathleen Vellenga
First Edition: October 2013
10 9 8 7 6 5 4 3 2 1

Forty Press, LLC
427 Van Buren Street
Anoka, MN 55303
www.fortypress.com

ISBN 978-1-938473-09-8

To my husband Jim and our marvelous family

1

Mayflower, mid-Atlantic
October, 1620

Elisabeth Tilley

For days the ship groaned as the wind shrieked against the closed portholes and hatches. Sails were furled to prevent them from ripping to shreds as the Mayflower floundered up then down into the trough of the waves, then up again as if God were pulling us toward redemption, our ship's hull resting in His protective palm, only to dash us back toward eternal damnation.

Lightning illuminated the hundred souls crammed into the 'tweendecks. Children clung to their mothers. Men shouted useless warnings to their families. There would be no escape if the ship broke apart; death waited in the water. I had long prayed to escape the dull life of a cloth-maker's daughter but I had not imagined I'd be praying to escape an ocean grave.

Darkness returned with each crash of thunder, but truth be told, the terrifying storm relieved the dreariness of being confined to the 'tweendecks for six weeks.

The need for fresh air drew me from my bed. Flinging my covers off, I wrapped my shawl about me and placed my feet on the shifting floor. Feeling a warmth there, I reached down to find Rogue and felt the thrum of her barking beneath the cacophony of wind and goats' bleating. Each time lightning flashed, I could see her creep toward the hatch. I got down on my hands and knees and found I too could keep my balance on all fours. At last I touched the ladder and pulled myself to my feet. I hung on desperately as the ship pitched and heaved. An enormous spasm within the ship threw me hard. The floor rose up and struck me. A howl of fearful cries crashed through the darkness.

I repeated the Psalm that Father read at evening prayers, *I am poured out like water and all my bones are out of joint. My heart is like wax, it has melted within me.* Never in my thirteen years had I prayed with such fervor. Taking a deep breath, I gagged from the reek of puke, sweat, and overflowing piss pots. My thigh muscles strained as I grabbed a rung and pulled myself up once more, my ribs protesting each breath.

God will lead safely His people, Father often reminded us. At the moment, most of His people on the Mayflower were wailing and crying. If God preserved me, 'twould be a tale to capture any listener. As the sea pounded against the ship, I sucked in the fresh smell of the salty air seeping through the hatch, clearing my nose of foul odor. Turning to Rogue, I let go of the ladder only to be knocked down again. This time by a man.

"What are you doing up and about in the storm?" he yelled above the wind as he picked me up. "You should be in bed."

The hard muscles in his arms pushed against my sore ribs as he set me on my feet. I gasped for air and caught the scents of sweat and the rope tar and ink on his hands.

"Stay back!" he commanded. "We're going up to discover what happened to the ship." He climbed the ladder and struggled to open the hatch. The light from above revealed him to be John Howland, Master John Carver's clerk.

"I'm coming, Howland," Master Carver called to his manservant. John Howland held the hatch open for his master, then it closed and only faint light came through the cracks.

"Elisabeth! Elisabeth Tilley!" cried a familiar voice. 'Twas so dark I only saw a shape lurching toward me until it touched my shoulder. I flinched in pain but did not cry out.

"What are ye doing out of bed? Thy mother is afraid ye've been knocked about the head. She sent me to find thee."

Bracing herself against the ladder, Aunt Agnes wrapped her warm green shawl about me, pulling it gently around my shoulders. With light fingers, she traced my nose and cheekbones.

"Nothing broken, praise God, but ye feel swollen." Aunt paused with her fingers on my mouth, and then sniffed. "Bleeding, but not much." I hadn't noticed.

A faint light told me the sun was rising. The fierce wind calmed to low moans, and the dog skulked away.

Aunt Agnes bent her head to look into my face in the dim light. "God in Heaven preserve thee! Thy cheeks look like a cabbage!"

"Bide a moment while I gather my strength," I said weakly.

"Must ye be carried?" she asked.

I had not yet depended on anyone to carry me about like a lost sheep and did not intend to start now. The Promised Land was no place for helpless lambs. Straightening, I took a step.

"Elisabeth!" she cried.

I staggered and sank to the floor.

Attitash

The rank odor stopped me. My eyes strained to locate the sour smell. A few paces ahead, near the little waterfall, a tangled lump moved. Stepping closer I saw the yellow hair of a Stranger. His chest rose and fell, but he made no sound. I heard only the three-note bird warbling and the brook splashing over the rocks above the pool.

My dog, Suki, sniffed the man's cloth shirt. He must have been left behind when the big wind-canoe sailed back across the Big Salt Water. This Stranger looked like he'd been sick a long time or fell into boiling water. His cold blue eyes opened; his lips moved silently. My skin felt as if a snake had slithered across my neck.

I pulled my furs tighter and backed up a step. He raised his hand; it dropped. Suki barked. Her legs were straight, the hair on her neck stiff.

"L'eau..." He uttered in a hoarse voice.

I remained still.

Raising up on one arm, he tried again. "Nee-pee."

I gestured to the pool. "Nipi?" I asked suspiciously.

"Oui...Ahhe." Moving his arm slowly, he waved toward the pool, and then slumped, a faint grin on his sickly face.

I watched him as he reached toward his leg. Wrapped around it at the knee was a noose similar to those our men spread to catch deer. I looked to a nearby tree where a rope dangled, its end frayed.

"Nee-pee," he said again.

He was too weak to attack me. I would get him water.

I went to the stream and filled the beaker, and then returned and set it just within his arm's reach. He drank, spilling some. "Merci," he uttered. His voice was so low I wondered if he dreamed aloud. Holding his bad leg with one hand, he grimaced and gestured toward the thick bushes beyond the path. He strained to speak, "Mat-chan-ni." He spoke so slowly I had to repeat the sounds in my head before I understood. Matchanni—our word for 'filled with bad spirits.' I raised my eyes but could see nothing. He pointed again to the bushes. "Nan-com-pees." He paused to see if I understood our word for boy. When I nodded, he smiled and relaxed a little.

I moved toward the bushes slowly as a new smell assaulted my nose—not the peculiar stink of Strangers, but the thick, sharp smell of bad spirits when they claim our bodies. Taking short breaths to keep the smell from entering me, I followed the scent until its strong power stopped me. A few paces ahead of me, curled on his side in the tall grass lay a young boy. He looked as though he'd lived for four or five circles-of-seasons. My breath came faster. He might harbor the Strangers' evil spirits which attacked our bodies and sucked away the life of our Wampanoag People! I began chanting to keep the bad spirits away.

Cautiously, I pushed aside the tall grass. The child's black hair was still long and not pulled back. Wampanoag beads were strung around his legs and arms. Creeping closer, I knelt to put my hand near his mouth and felt a faint breath. He was sick, but still alive.

Hearing a bird-whistle, I looked up. My father was moving slowly toward the yellow-haired Stranger. Papa signaled for me to keep quiet. Once upon the Stranger, he put his spear against Yellow Hair's neck.

"Stay back, Attitash," my father commanded.

"His leg's badly hurt," I called. Papa looked down at the Stranger's damaged leg.

Following Papa's brave refusal to fear the Strangers' evil spirits, I picked up the thin little boy. Yellow Hair tried to gesture, but the spear point on his throat kept him silent. I laid the boy next to him and stood near Papa. His arm muscles tensed as he held the spear against Yellow Hair's throat then moved it slowly down to his chest.

"Look for his knife," he said.

My throat seized. I had given him water without checking for a weapon!

"Look in his belt pouch."

Singing a chant to repel the Spirits, I probed with trembling fingers and pulled out a small knife. Handing it to Papa, I returned to the little boy and stroked his hot cheek. The child opened his eyes, confusion filled them. Then he saw Yellow Hair and reached out his hand. Yellow Hair's face became so pained it hurt my heart. As Papa fashioned a tree limb to support Yellow Hair's broken leg, I poured water in my hands and smoothed it over the boy's face. He looked as my brother might, once he grows out of the cradleboard.

"How do you know this Stranger?" I asked the boy.

His voice was the merest whisper. "He carried me."

I felt the child's heart turn to the Stranger.

"I'm taking him home," I told Papa and lifted him onto my back.

Papa kept his eye on Yellow Hair.

When I reached our home, Grandmother asked if I'd brought the water I'd gone to fetch. Before I could answer, her nostrils flared. Singing the prayer with me, she took the child in her arms. His eyes darted fearfully from Grandmother to me.

Papa soon followed with Yellow Hair. Grandmother strode toward him.

"Wait, Hopamoch." Her voice was low, but stern. "Do not think you can bring a Cloth-man into our house."

"He's injured and will not harm us, wife's mother." Papa kept his eyes down respectfully, but his voice was firm. "He was taken captive by our people and speaks our tongue."

Grandmother's voice sounded like the first crack of the sky-fire god. "Our people took captives because his people killed our men!"

The boy was too young to remember, but I did. Strangers had let our men come onto their big wind-canoe to trade. Before the talk could begin, their firesticks killed all our men.

"Put him by the fire," Grandmother said as she shoved a basket aside and spat on Yellow Hair. "He is nothing but another Do-Evil trying to possess us! If I could, I would send the bad spirits across the Big Salt Water forever." She folded her arms across her sagging breasts. "At least we won't have any more like *him* here until the cold moons are gone and warm moons bring soft winds." The Stranger was laid in a small shelter hastily built from branches and woven mats. He was not given prayers and poultices; only the sick child received Grandmother's healing.

During the night, the storm gods shook the trees and made Big Salt Water dance as if bad dreams filled it. No one else in our three-fire neeshwetu seemed to hear. My family was asleep by one fire, Grandmother piled high with furs at the honored end; aunt and uncle were asleep by another. I heard a stirring and noticed it was Uncle Seekonk's clan nephew building up the fire. Uncle had recently brought Black Whale to our home to prepare him for his Vision Quest. He was tall for an almost-grown man and I had noticed how his wide eyes sparked with pleasure when our elders told stories. He did not seem to notice as I watched him now.

Elisabeth Tilley

"Why were ye out in the storm?" Aunt demanded.

"I thought to follow the dog to where I could get a breath of air." I paused to draw one. "But I was knocked down twice. First by the storm, then by John Howland."

A beam of sunlight broke through the port-hole crack, and Aunt peered into my face. "Elisabeth, John Howland is not the sort to knock a young maid down. Ye must have been dreaming."

"Nay, he did not intend to. He was rushing up the ladder, he and Master Carver—"

Just then the hatch opened and Master Carver climbed down without looking at us. John Howland followed. He closed the hatch and came to me.

"Are you injured?"

"Nay." I tried to shrug, but my ribs hurt.

"What did you find out?" Aunt Agnes interjected.

He grimaced. "Naught but the ship's master telling us nothing. Master Carver went to the great cabin on the top deck and spoke to Captain Jones himself. Something has gone awry, but he won't say."

He again turned to me. "My apologies for knocking you down," he said and strode off.

Aunt Agnes led me slowly back to the space allotted to our household. Families attempted to shield themselves from the others—a feeble effort, like everything on this mad ship, affording only the façade of privacy. Most families, like ours, had curtains hung round the beds. The few who'd brought servants also partitioned their area with boards from the dismantled shallop, as the small sail boat would not be needed until we reached the colony of Virginia.

Mother's face, looking older than her fifty-some years, sagged with relief when she saw me. "Elisabeth, why do ye not stay where it's safe when the wind is blowing so fiercely?" Her hands clenched with fury, but relief prevailed.

She turned to her sister-in-law. "What happened, Agnes? I had to cling to the bed and it felt like the ship split in two!"

"No one knows, sister." Aunt Agnes took her shawl back from me. "I'm going back to bed," she said and left.

I touched Mother's hand, offering a silent appeasement for her worry.

"I'm sorry," I said. "The stench was so strong I had to find fresh air."

"Could ye not just pull the covers over thy nose?"

"I tried, but they stink, Mother."

She could not dispute this. Earlier, she had opened the hatches all round to bring fresh air, but the increasing wind and rising waves washed seawater into our crowded space instead. It had soaked us, and all the bedding as well. Still, she had no patience for a trifle like moldy covers. Naught was to be done but to seal the hatches and endure the vile smell of moldy seawater until such time as God would bring fair weather.

"When will ye learn to endure the trials God gives us, Elisabeth?"

I changed the subject. "Do you need me to fetch something, Mother?"

"Yea, thank ye. A bit of ale, Elisabeth."

I found our small jar for her, then returned to bed and pulled the putrid covers over my nose. I tried to think of the rosemary and thyme kept near our hearth in Bedfordshire, but the smell of rope tar, ink and sea salt on John Howland's hands captured my thoughts.

2

Attitash

When Nippa'uus rose large and yellow over the Big Salt Water next morning, the storm was gone but the child's face was still hot, his breath too fast.

All day, Grandmother sang prayers for the boy. She sharpened her tools for scraping deer hides, and for the first time I noticed her hands. The skin was stretched taut over the bones and her knuckles were big bumps. She did not pause to rest. Mama stood next to her, her own hands worked quickly, husking and grating the weachimin kernels. Mother's skin was smooth like mine, but her fingers were round with muscles. Grandmother stopped singing as she caught me watching. "Keep working, Attitash. Your fingers won't get strong if you don't use them."

Mama handed me bundled purple flowers that looked like little fingers. "We need more wallwort pulp for the poultices." I pounded the flowers' black roots until the sticky white juice oozed out, then brewed tea with the emptied leaves.

When night pushed Nippa'uus behind the trees, we took turns watching the child. He struggled to breathe. I answered when he cried out, just as the first light of a new day came through our smoke hole. He barely opened his eyes, calling pitifully for Yellow Hair. My throat ached with his longing. Desperate to comfort him, I moved him closer to Yellow Hair, who sat up to cradle the little head, painfully shifting to keep his injured leg propped on a pile of sphagnum moss. The leg had turned green; red streaks showed the bad spirits' path running up his thigh toward his heart. I watched as his eyes lingered on the boy.

"Attitash, what are you doing here?" Mama demanded.

I thought she would tell me to leave, but she did not.

I spoke quietly. "I think this Stranger tried to save the child; he wants to say farewell."

Yellow Hair raised his head higher, clearing his throat as he looked at the boy. "Je vou…" his voice cracked and he tried to get a deep breath to speak our tongue. His chest heaved and his arms twitched.

Mama did not look at Yellow Hair. Her attention was on the little boy. She said, "The child's body is giving up."

Just then the boy's eyes opened and turned inward, as if watching his spirit prepare for its journey. I sang louder. He moaned and his mouth fell open.

Yellow Hair buried his face in his hands and wept.

I looked to Mama. "Why couldn't we save him?" I asked.

"The cloth-men's gods are too strong," Mama told me, stroking the child's body. "They have killed so many of our People, Attitash. This is just one more."

"But why couldn't Yellow Hair make his gods spare this child?" My shoulders tightened with the effort to keep my sobs inside. "He tried to save him."

"Why do you believe that?" Mama's voice was flat, weary with explaining something I already knew. "The Strangers are full of deceit."

"Maybe with his injured leg, he did not have enough strength to pray to his gods," I said.

Yellow Hair moaned; his face contorted as his lips moved silently. I could not tell if he understood our words or was saying his own prayer for the child. Mama paid no attention to the gurgling sounds coming from him.

Tisquantum, our chief sachem's servant, arrived and with a quick nod to Mama spoke to Yellow Hair in sharp sounds—the tongue Tisquantum had learned while held captive.

"Come, Attitash," said Mama, "we must prepare one of our own for his spirit-world journey." She carried the boy's body back to our fire, where Grandmother wrapped him in soft deerskin and poured red ochre to preserve his body for the spirit journey.

My little sister, White Flower, helped me choose white wampum shells. As we put them in a bowl for the boy's spirit to use, Black Whale turned to me as if we had spoken to each other before.

"Have you prepared everything for the boy's spirit journey?" he asked.

"Almost." I kept my voice as even as his.

He removed the fur he wore over his shoulders. His body was slick with the pungent bear grease that kept him warm. He set a little bow and arrow by the child

"I made this for the spirit journey," he said. His craftsmanship was hasty, I could tell.

My father entered, carrying his quahog-shell tools to dig the grave. "We will bury the child where you found him, Attitash."

I closed my eyes to shut out the memory.

Papa lifted the small bundle, and we all walked towards the pool. When we arrived, Papa and Black Whale began digging. My sister and I arranged the wampum and food in little bowls.

I asked my father where Yellow Hair would be buried.

"Tisquantum will take Yellow Hair's body to the sand and the animals will take care of it," Papa said.

"He will be forever lost without a journey to the Spirit World!" I tried to keep my voice respectful, but my distress showed.

"None of us could change Tisquantum's mind. He cares nothing for a Cloth-man lost forever. Everyone in

Tisquantum's village was lost while the Strangers held him captive. When he returned to Patuxet, all our people were dead from the Cloth-men's bad spirits."

The muscles in Papa's jaw clenched as he pushed his quahog shell shovel. Our home along the shore of the Big Salt Water was our pride. Wampanoag means *people of the dawn*, since our people receive the first light of morning. But living with the first light became our despair as it meant we were the first to receive the Strangers' bad spirits when they came in their big wind canoes. It meant we were the first to die.

I kept my distress inside my throat as Mama helped Grandmother lay woven reed mats over the body. During the prayers for the spirit journey, my mind fixed on how to let Yellow Hair's spirit join the child's.

When our prayers were finished, I walked alone along the stream.

Nearby, someone crashed heavily through the thickets where the stream runs towards the Big Salt Water. Parting tall reeds, I saw Tisquantum, his face flushed, dragging a deerskin which held Yellow Hair's body.

"Stop!" I called out.

Tisquantum paused and then continued dragging his burden. I pushed aside sharp reeds and blackberry bushes and with one long stride threw myself onto Tisquantum's back. His breath blew out in a whoosh and I could feel his ribs. Twisting to dislodge me, he let go of the rope. "Get off me! You little *whoresdaughter*!" It had a mean sound. It was a Strangers' word.

"Yellow Hair must be buried with the little boy!" I hissed into his ear, as I grabbed his topknot and pulled hard.

Tisquantum twisted and I fell to the ground. "Do you know what they do to girls like you?" He shook me so hard my teeth cut into my lips. Fear of his strength surged and

I stepped back so I could run. My foot bumped against Yellow Hair's body and I jumped.

Tisquantum laughed and picked up the deerskin again.

I willed my voice to stay low so I wouldn't sound like a little girl. "This Yellow Hair carried the little boy a long way to find water."

"He helped the boy because he had to! He'd lost his own people and was captive."

My mind scrambled to remember what I'd heard about Tisquantum.

"Didn't a Stranger help you escape?" I asked.

"No!" he said angrily. "He provided the means for my escape without intending to." Tisquantum's eyes narrowed. "He brought me as a slave from across the Big Salt Water. He needed my tongue to get more beaver from our People."

"Yellow Hair learned our tongue, or tried to."

"They all still talk with two hearts and two tongues." Tisquantum picked up the deerskin. "These cloth-men kill our people with firesticks and bad spirits, just to get the beaver pelts and useless yellow rocks."

I rubbed my neck at the soft spot under my hair, struggling to find convincing words.

"When I first saw this Stranger," I began, "I wanted to knock him in the head with a rock. Then I saw how the little boy trusted him. Yellow Hair brought him to us, risking his own life to save the child!" Tears of frustration burned the backs of my eyes. "I held the little boy when his spirit left him. The Yellow Hair wept. We buried the boy just a few paces from here." I pleaded, "No one would know we buried Yellow Hair with him."

He did not answer.

"You've become like your captors! You are a Stranger!" I said angrily.

The lines by Tisquantum's mouth and eyes deepened.

He dropped the deerskin and spat. "You don't know what you say! You don't know what they're like!" Tisquantum turned his face from me; holding his arms tight against his body.

Was Papa right that no one could convince Tisquantum? I struggled to keep my voice even. "I'm sorry. I don't really know what they're like." His shoulders sagged just enough to let me know some of his anger eased. "The Spirits would not be pleased if we do not show respect, even to those cruel to us. It is taboo to leave anyone—even an enemy—to be torn apart by animals."

Turning back at last, Tisquantum's eyes revealed nothing. "I will do what you want, Attitash." I smiled and started to thank him. "Wait..." he silenced me. "On two conditions. First, never tell anyone what we have done." I nodded, keeping my eyes down to show respect.

"And second?" I asked.

Tisquantum gripped my arm. "You must never, ever say I am like the Cloth-men; never say I am a Stranger! I am not!" When I did not answer he tightened his grip on me. "Promise or the yellow hair lies above ground."

My heart twisted as if it too was in his grasp. "I will not tell anyone. I will never say you are like the Strangers." But I knew he was too much a Stranger. Only fear kept him from following their ways completely.

He let go of my arm and directed me to help drag the body. As we stumbled with our burden, my hands shook nervously so I could hardly hold onto the deerskin.

Elisabeth

"Elisabeth, put the needle in thy proper hand!"

I had been trying to hold the torn edges of Father's shirt with my left hand and stitch with my right. Neither hand would work, the left wanting the needle and the right refusing to sew. An unusual sound in the shifting of the Mayflower's boards had caught Mother's attention. She seemed so distracted that I'd shifted the needle to my left hand. But Mother's faded blue eyes missed nothing.

"My right hand is gammy, Mother!" I pleaded.

Mother's face flushed. "Do ye want Satan to possess the rest of thee, and not just thy hand?" Her fingers passed over her eyes, as if to control tears. "Ye must not yield to temptation, Elisabeth. Take out those left-hand stitches."

The fingers of my right hand felt numb, like the cold lump in my chest. Please, God, I prayed, release Satan's power over my left hand.

While pulling out stitches, I calmed myself by imagining we were already in Virginia—the scent of freshly mown hay, the taste of fresh water, the sight of a little house all our own with thatched roof and a tall chimney. Where did the barbarians live? Hopefully, their caves were not close to our settlement. I tried to picture a real heathen maid. She would have very dark eyes. Feathers and paint would obscure her face, but her hair would be exposed. She could not possibly have a civilized countenance like the heathen in my dream. It was a dream that came to me in England, followed me to Holland, and remained stowed in my thoughts as I sailed to the New World.

Far above me the surface of the water is shimmering with light. I glide through the shallow depths as effortlessly as the fish that swim alongside and gently brush against me. Beneath are ancient sands that once were mountaintops but have since been washed into the deep waters carrying their secrets with them.

I follow a little black whale, rising through the water toward the light. Brown hands break the surface. They might be a gypsy's, but there are no rings on the fingers. Muscled brown arms dissolve into distant and unfocused images.

A face breaks the surface, leaning to drink; a gypsy maid's face with long, black hair, free of nightcap or coif. Her dress is made of skins, as is the large pack resting against her exposed shoulder. She is no gypsy. She is a savage of the Promised Land!

I surge above the water. The heathen fills her hands and holds them out to me. When I refuse, she laughs, throwing the cold water in my face. I rub it out of my eyes and nose, sputtering. Her laughter subsides as she reaches again into the water and offers me a small fish and an eel. I take the fish.

I hear chanting and look to the shore. Naked children are dancing on the wet sand. The maid begins to swim toward them as they run into the water. A large wave swallows them.

I sink beneath the surface but see no children. Only the boots of our own men, marching in the water as the tide pushes us toward shore.

At last the stitches were out, and I painstakingly began new ones with my right hand. A sudden heave in the ship made me poke my finger instead of the shirt and I touched my tongue to the tiny spot of blood to suck out the stain.

"How can the Captain steer the Mayflower toward Virginia if we're not going forward? Are we lost, Mother?"

"The wind's still so strong it would tear the sails," she said without looking up from her work. "And Captain Jones cannot steer with the sails furled." She said confidently, "God's hands hold us."

My vision of Virginia was lost in the heaving sea. "Will we be here 'til the ship sinks?"

"Nay. That could not be God's will." Mother ran her needle through her hair to grease its slide through the cloth.

My fingers stopped. "But if we can't go forward, would

we go home?"

"Elisabeth, God would not send us back to England where King James has hanged some of our saintly people."

"Being hanged could not be any worse than drowning in these depths," I said, feeling as if I truly meant it.

Mother looked at me gravely. "What do ye know of either? God made ready the Promised Land for us by sending a great plague. The barbarians have been greatly reduced in number, so that we might dwell there and tame the wilderness."

She examined my sewing.

"Make thy stitches closer together."

Attitash

Mama held Little Fish at her breast and handed me the water pot to fill. Everyone else still slept and I hurried to the pool, relishing the early morning quiet.

As I dipped the wooden pot in the pool, the face of a young woman appeared in the water. But it was not my face. Her face looked more like the yellow-haired Stranger's. Her eyes were quiet water—gray, with many colors reflected. Her hair, hanging beneath a cloth on her head, was the color of deer and curled like wood shavings. The Strangers had been coming in their big wind-canoes since long before my grandmother's grandmother was in her cradleboard. But never young women like me. Never any women.

The water began to seethe as if hot rocks were thrown into it, and her face distorted, then disappeared. The three-note bird was no longer singing. My chest constricted as though I'd taken a breath of air during the coldest moon. The water quieted and the strange girl's face reappeared. This time, her eyes showed fear and her mouth was open, as if calling for help. The wind wrinkled the water and again her face disappeared. Drawing a deep breath to calm my spirit, I picked up the water pot and started home.

I was deciding what I should tell Mama, when I saw Black Whale standing by the fire. He greeted me with a silent nod.

"What are you doing here?" I said, setting the water pot on its three sticks.

"You don't want me?" Black Whale picked up an ear of weachimin from the basket, broke off a few kernels and cockily popped them in his mouth.

"Did you want me to think you were a Narragansett?" I asked, sitting on the cold ground.

He laughed.

"I've seen enough of you to know you would draw your knife if you thought that," he said. "You would try to be the one young woman who could drive off our enemy." He settled himself near me, tucking his breechcloth between his leggings. "Uncle told me you are very strong. I'm sure any Narragansett who tried to take you would suffer."

I let my eyes seek his. Black Whale resembled his clan-uncle Seekonk; both had broad cheekbones, a slight groove between their eyebrows and the curve of high foreheads.

"Is that what he is teaching you for your vision quest?" I added sticks to my fire. "I thought you were learning how to survive alone in deep snow and cold."

Black Whale grinned. "Uncle taught me that a strong woman—even a young one—has helped many a warrior survive winter."

"Did Uncle teach you that strong is better than pretty?"

Black Whale shifted his legs. "He told me to find a woman who's both."

Acutely aware of the nearness of his leg, my mouth babbled on. "Mama is."

"Ahhe, your mother is both." Black Whale's eyes were back on the fire. "And your cousin Seafoam too."

So, he favored my pretty cousin.

"Seafoam will choose a husband strong enough to complete his vision quest and handsome enough to give her children," I said. I waited for his response, but he did not answer.

"Is that how your mother chose your father?" I asked.

"I don't know what my mother wanted in a husband." Black Whale's voice was heavy, his jaw muscle tensed. "I was still a baby when the Strangers' bad spirits sent Papa to the Spirit World. She does not talk about him."

My eyes wandered to his full lips and firm chin. "You must be like him."

He took more kernels and gnashed them with his teeth. "The Cloth-men's bad spirits have killed too many of our People."

"And the Narragansett?" I asked.

"They live inland and few have been caught by the Cloth-men's bad spirits." He paused, acknowledging that threats came from many directions. "The Narragansett are capturing our crops, our strong warriors, and taking our women."

He lightly touched the muscle in my arm. "You are strong, Attitash, but be careful. We have many enemies." He picked up his bow and tested the string. "You must be on guard all the time."

I leaned forward and blew fiercely on the fire. "I have my knife. And I know how to use it."

3

Elisabeth

When shrieking gales brought another ferocious storm, we maids and women were confined to the stifling 'tweendecks. We prayed to influence God; the menfolk made the decisions.

"Elisabeth, I'll do some mending if ye take Humility away," Aunt Agnes offered. "The babe is as weary of me as I of her."

A fussy child was a welcome relief from trying to use my right hand, with the ship lurching at every stitch. Snatches of worried conversation pelted me as I carried Humility slowly through baggage and people to the Carver household. Mistress Carver's fine linen bed curtains were tied shut. No one answered my *halloo*, though they had three servants in addition to John Howland.

Before I could call out again, one of the Billington brothers bumped against me, nearly knocking Humility from her position on my hip.

It was troubling enough to have tender new swelling around my nipples, and curly new hair itching in my secret place. To have these loathsome Billington boys coming so close they might smell my new scents was more than I could bear. John Billington, his hair so fair the dirt showed, laughed and ran off, followed by his younger brother Francis.

The swaying bed curtains parted and the Carvers' ward, Desire Minter, smiled at me. She had removed her white coif, and her slender fingers pulled the wooden comb through the tangles of her heavy dark hair. I sat on the embroidered coverlet.

"At home I would not be forced to endure boys like the Billingtons," I complained.

"They are not the only problem." Desire tucked her hair back into her coif. "Men always crowd around. Sometimes they seem to be just bold eyes." She leaned in close. "Did ye wish this journey, Elisabeth?"

"'Twould be an adventure, I thought, getting away from the hard work of Father's cloth making." My voice caught as the ship trembled, hung on a swell, then slid down so fast Humility cried out. I quieted her and then looked back at Desire. "I'm young and had no choice. But surely you could have stayed in Holland if you wanted to. You are from a family with means, a grown maid."

"According to my mother, I'm too pretty to stay in her new husband's house," Desire said sadly. Her long lashes fluttered over her dark blue eyes. She was five years older than I and still unmarried. "Mother thinks I should be grateful that Mistress Carver was willing to bring me."

"Did you want to stay in Holland with them?" I asked.

"I would have left Holland and returned to England if I'd had a choice."

She took little Humility from my arms and wrapped her fingers round the babe's curly hair. "Where's thy mama?" she said softly. She arched a delicate eyebrow at me. "The child's father died?"

I nodded. "Aunt Agnes agreed to take in her little niece."

"I had no more say than this babe." She handed Humility back to me. "Look at this Elisabeth." Desire held her hands out for me to inspect. "My fingers look like I'm a servant!"

"Your hands are lovely, just like you." The ship's shudder swallowed my words.

"Torn nails and grimy hands are not lovely," she sighed. "But then, if I had been considered un-lovely, I would not be here in this reeking, crowded ship, would I?"

"What do you mean?"

"Oh, my dear! How could ye understand?"

We hung onto the bedposts as the Mayflower heaved up and up, then slid helplessly down the waves. Desire shot me a silencing look as the maidservant arrived. One of her muscled, red hands gripped a basket of dried biscuits, and the other clung to the boards for balance. She could no doubt plunge her hands into scalding water without flinching. I hid my own rough hands under my apron as Humility reached her little fingers for a biscuit.

Thanking Desire, I carried Humility past the Carvers' fine leather trunks. When we stepped away from the household, I shoved my elbow against Francis Billington's back so he'd let me through. He was a bit taller than I, hair the color of carrots fresh from the ground. Francis's freckles bounced as he stuck out his tongue at me. John Howland arrived, cuffed Francis, and made a place for me to stand.

Humility started to wail, reaching for a now-absent biscuit. I feared John would tell me to keep her quiet, but his summer-green eyes crinkled. The sudden warmth in my throat confused me.

"What's the babe want?" Howland asked. He gave Humility his strong finger to grasp and she did so.

"Nothing we can give her. She's not the only one weary of this voyage. So many storms, so little food, so crowded I can't move without bumping into someone." Humility gave up struggling and I leaned against the boards with her head cradled on my shoulder. "Do you think it's more dangerous to go forward to the new world or return home?"

"Life is always dangerous." John flexed his arms, the

muscles straining the sleeves of his jacket. "Besides, the king signed our patent to get rid of us. He does not want us back."

"Desire hopes we'll go home to England."

"No!" His vehemence startled me. "We have nothing if we return, even if we escape persecution." John gestured westerly. "In the new land, we will have our own law and plenty of land. Back home, I would be a servant the rest of my life."

Without conscious effort, my left hand started to reach out for John Howland's, to feel the hope he carried. I pulled it back just in time to spare embarrassment. Hot faced, I cradled Humility close and struggled back to our household.

Attitash

"Stay close to me, White Flower," I warned.

The storm, which had kept us by our fires, had finally fled. We could now collect fresh water and my younger sister and I were eager to do so. White Flower held her water jug against her belly. She still had skinny hips and would not be able to balance her jug on them for another circle of Nippa'uus.

Pepe'warr, the white frost moon, had skimmed the pond's surface, and the ice at the edge of the stream crackled underfoot as we bent to dip our jars. A crow's warning cry startled me. As I lifted my jar, a twig broke along the path. I gripped my knife and parted the bushes. A flash of legging and breechcloth brought chills to my legs. A man's head came into view. Instead of the three black stripes our men wear, he had Narragansett smudge designs on his face.

I pushed White Flower to the ground, whispering, "enemy." Her eyes widened but she kept her body quiet. Creeping silently, I threw a rock to hit a tree ahead. He

was not close enough for me to hear his breathing, but I
caught his scent. Holding my knife steady, I moved slowly
in a circle—ears straining as I silently prayed bad medicine
to make his legs cramp.

Suddenly, my hands were yanked behind me. My knife
was twisted from my hand and a leather strip tied over my
eyes. White Flower cried out as I felt a rope loop around
my body, securing my arms. "Run!" I desperately called to
White Flower. I could hear her gasping for breath between
sobs. From the tug on my rope, I knew she was also tied
up, our ropes connecting us.

Sharp voices silenced us both. A man with a Narragansett accent said, "Canonicus," which I knew was the Narragansett's chief sachem. Another man answered in Wampanoag accent, talking about wampum. I was sure I knew
the voice. Then I heard footsteps running away. I would
never forget how that voice said, "Wampum," as if he were
speaking of a great spirit, instead of trading shells.

A club poked us forward. When I tried to move my
hands, the rope was jerked hard, pulling us both down.
My enemy grabbed me around the ribs, his hands digging
into my breasts as he pulled me and White Flower to our
feet. He shoved us again, and I matched my sister's steps
to keep us on our feet. Just one set of footsteps seemed to
follow us.

I tried to get my bearings by listening, but could not
tell which path we were on. Finally, the rope jerked us to
a stop and the blindfolds were pulled off. Only the Narragansett was with us. Stealing a glance at his face, I realized our kidnapper was not much older than Black Whale.
White Flower's face was streaked with tears, her eyes swollen. My belly churned from the effort to shut out the
thought of our enemy's hands preying on my little sister,
and on me. Even if we escaped this man, others of his na-
tion might be waiting.

He pushed us forward all morning. As we came to the curve of Big Salt Water, I could see the remains of Patuxet. Several seasons had passed since the entire village had died from the Strangers' bad spirits, including Uncle Seekonk's first wife and child. The cleared fields were empty and the houses gone.

White Flower and I quietly chanted a prayer until he told us to stop. Thoughts of family weighed so heavily it was nearly impossible to breathe. As Nippa'uus rose high, then began to descend, my legs were limp knowing that every step took us farther away from home.

Elisabeth

Now that the wind was fair again, Captain Jones gave orders to sail. We rushed to the deck. Everyone was eager to watch the sails fill and the Mayflower head westerly. The boys puffed up their chests and parroted the officers, "All hands ready to sail! Courses in their gear! Heave on the mizzen halyard!"

Truth be told, we'd been lost at sea so long that no one ventured to say where we would eventually land.

When I returned to the 'tweendecks, Mother was not happy with where we had been. She reviewed the terrors that awaited topside, including being blown into the sea. Her fiercest warning, however, concerned the crew. In particular, a seaman who often threatened our people with profane descriptions of how he'd cheer when we all perished.

"Ye can't imagine what these foul seamen would do," Mother said.

I did not need to. Only days before, Constance Hopkins had furiously described how, when she followed her brother topside for fresh air, this very seaman, whom we maids now called "The Cur," made disgustingly clear what he wanted. Mother would have tied me to the bed if she had known how he leered at Constance. "The Cur grabbed himself through his breeches as though he were about to relieve himself, like a horse," Constance told me, her hands trembling with rage. "His oaths, threatening that he would know me, burned my ears. My face flamed, I stomped on his foot and ran down the ladder." His threats confined us maids in ways our mothers could not. I raged at God for allowing this.

Attitash

Our captor had removed the blindfolds, which allowed me to give White Flower looks of reassurance. We had walked since dawn and were sore weary, arms aflame from the rope's chafing. I marked in my mind our west direction whereupon the path split, ours veering around two big boulders. The anxious knot in my belly tightened as dark loomed. We were close to Narragansett territory.

Near the top of the hill, we finally stopped where a small circle of stones marked earlier fires. Our captor said nothing, but loosened the ropes so our arms were free, then tightened them around our waists. He held on while we drank from a stream that splashed onto nearby rocks along the path and then squatted to pee. I found some notched wolfbane flowers and, his eyes giving me silent permission, crushed the faded petals in water and used the mass to soothe the burns on our arms. The Narragansett tied our ropes to a tree and motioned us to sit in front of him while he made a fire. The cold evening chilled the sweat on my back and White Flower and I both shivered. Huddling by the low fire, we accepted the dried journey cake he offered. He took our ropes and tied them round his own torso.

"What do you want with us?" I asked, not knowing if he could or would answer.

Nippa'uus was a faint orange glimmer through the trees

at the crest of the hill. At least two stars were visible. His eyes were on the fading light for a long moment—perhaps repeating my words in his mind. He gestured over the hill. "To Canonicus," he said.

Would we be wife-slaves to Canonicus, or would the sachem "give" us to one of his followers? Our captor pulled his fur about him and lay down, the rope stretched tight between us, his weapons in the crook of his arm. White Flower and I snuggled together under our furs. The wind moaning in the trees carried voices.

Mama. Papa. Grandmother. Little Fish. If we never saw them again, if we became wives to our enemy, we would no longer be Attitash and White Flower. We would be Narragansett. We had to escape. I thought my fear, combined with the cold, would keep me awake as I waited for our abductor to sleep, but I dozed into fearful dreams myself.

I was startled awake by an owl. I listened carefully. The Narragansett breathed deep, shuddering breaths.

Putting my hand over White Flower's mouth, I whispered in her ear, "We need to get my knife back. This is our only chance." We started to crawl toward him. The owl hooted again. I froze. It was not an owl. I strained to open my eyes wide enough to see in the waning moon's light. Eventually, Uncle Seekonk came into view.

Holding my breath as he crept nearer, I thought my cramped lungs would explode. White Flower exhaled softly, but our captor did not stir. Uncle Seekonk held his club high, then with a hideous crunch, brought it down on our enemy's head. The Narragansett jerked and Uncle hit him again. I reached for my knife and snatched it off the twitching body. Black Whale appeared and added a blow. The body stopped moving.

I feverishly sawed our ropes. Once free, I grabbed White Flower's hand. Without another look, we ran.

I could hear our men behind us and we continued as

fast as we dared on the dark hill. Finally sinking down to catch our breath near the two boulders, we were joined by Uncle Seekonk and Black Whale. There was too much to say, and no time. We had to get away before dawn, when more Narragansett were sure to be looking for us. Uncle Seekonk examined our faces in the dim light, asking us if we were injured and needed help. I needed rest and food, but I assured Uncle I could walk. White Flower, however, could hardly speak. Uncle settled her on his back, holding her legs. I stroked her trembling shoulders.

"How could one Narragansett capture two strong girls?" Black Whale asked condescendingly.

I turned to look at him, but could not see his expression in the dim light. "He could not! There were two of them; they blindfolded us and tied us up together."

"Where's the other one?"

"I don't know. Once we were tied up, they talked for a minute, and then I could only hear one man's footsteps. When he took off our blindfolds, he was alone. "

Black Whale said nothing.

As we travelled home, fear of enemies kept me awake, though at times my legs went on their own and dreams took over my head. The strange young woman from the pool-vision seemed to walk behind me.

At last, Nippa'uus' faint glimmer on Big Salt Water chased away the chill and showed us Patuxet again. Uncle Seekonk set White Flower down and we ate journey cake and drank from their water casks. I pulled White Flower to me to keep her warm while she slept. Uncle sang a prayer for his lost first family.

"Have you seen Tisquantum?" I quietly asked.

"Our Massasowet's servant? No, why would we?" Uncle Seekonk took a long drink.

I quickly stood, reminding our little party that we must stay ahead of the Narragansetts. Black Whale chuckled.

Papa nodded proudly and stood up, urging us forward.
As we passed the burial place of Yellow Hair and
the boy, I sang my own prayer. If Tisquantum had betrayed us, I was released from my promise not to reveal
that we'd buried Yellow Hair with the boy. I would tell
Mama but I could not accuse him of betraying us until I
was sure. When I could listen to his voice, I would then
know if matched the voice I would never forget. Once
I was absolutely certain, Mama and I would tell Our
Massasowet.

Elisabeth
Mistress Hopkins' groans competed with the wind
throughout the day and well past sundown. Only women
who'd given birth would attend her childbed.

Mother opened her small trunk and lifted several items
out. "Here's my sheep's wool to rub away the pain, and
betony syrup to help thy mother heal after she is delivered," she said to Constance who held onto a post with
one hand and her little sister Damaris with the other.
When mother left, both climbed into my bedding. Mistress Hopkins continued to give voice to her pain. I'd
expected to satisfy some of my curiosity about birthing,
being in such close quarters as we were, but I'd now heard
what no maid should. I pulled the covers over my ears,
vowing that if ever a man did take me for a wife, I'd refuse
to go to bed with him.

Hours later a scream the likes of which I'd never heard
rose above the wind, followed by a tiny wail. We poked
our heads out from the bed curtains and met Mother's
tired smile. "It's a boy. He is very frail—no flesh on his
bones a'tall." She gathered up the clouts she'd sewn for
the new babe and gestured for us to come along.

Mistress Allerton, great with child herself, brought her
daughters, Remember and Mary. Damaris gave Mary a

smug look. Her new brother's tiny face looked wizened, but Damaris held him proudly.

"His father has given him a name," Mistress Hopkins said weakly.

"Already?" Mother touched the soft hair on the babe's head.

"Oceanus," she said. "Stephen says our new son is the first to be born on the sea, and Oceanus was the ancient name for this Atlantic Sea."

Mistress Allerton frowned, and when we left, she murmured, "Master Hopkins did not look in the Bible for a name as he should."

"Well, the name is certainly an oddity," said mother.

"My husband said Hopkins got it from his foreign book, *The Odyssey*," Mistress Allerton said as if divulging a secret.

Mother did not try to keep her voice low. "Stephen Hopkins is not devout, even for one in the King's Church. I pray God watches over the child and spares his life."

I succumbed to the temptation and whispered, "Oceanus." The pagan name slipped easily on my tongue. "Oceanus," I repeated.

That evening Constance found me by the goat pen.

"Come topside with Mary Chilton and me," she said. Steerage was not as crowded as the 'tweendecks, but we could not avoid brushing against officers as they parted way for us.

We opened the hatch to fading sunset, the wind gentle on our faces. There was little room on the main deck, and we knew not to crowd the helmsman, his dim lantern lighting his compass. We scuttled to the aft side, looking down on the topside deck. Most of the men stood watch there, their faces revealed as dim shadows. The lone seaman standing watch on the main deck was chatting with the helmsman.

Constance Hopkins held up a tankard with a small smile. "The remains of Father's aquavit," she said. "He brought out a few drams of his best brew to celebrate the babe."

Mary Chilton, cozying up to Constance as always, took the cup first. Mary and I were both cloth-makers' daughters who'd left older siblings to come alone with our parents. But Mary seldom engaged me in conversation. When she handed me the tankard, I sipped 'til the glow filled me. Taking off my shawl, I hiccupped and giggled.

Constance drained the tankard. "Warms ye up!"

Bells rang for the change in watch and the seaman on duty motioned to us to go down. As he opened the steerage hatch for us, I tucked my curls back into my coif.

"Hurry," Constance said as she started down the ladder. "We don't want the officers talking to us."

Back in 'tweendecks, Desire Minter opened her curtains. "Elisabeth, what were ye doing topside? It's almost dark."

"Constance and Mary made me go," I lied.

"As if ye have no mind of thine own," she laughed. "But are ye not chilled without a shawl?" She pulled me in with her and shut the curtains.

My shawl! I knew Mother would give me the rod for losing it. I hastily bade Desire to sleep well and went back to the ladder.

The startled faces of the officers in steerage almost stopped me. Mumbling, "Fetching my lost shawl," I pushed through them to the ladder, glad to find the hatch cracked open.

It was dark now; just a few stars peeked between the clouds. I could only see the helmsman's lantern; not the new watchman whom I hoped could neither hear nor see me as I crept on hands and knees along the rail to where I'd left my shawl.

Finally, my hand touched wool.

Then, hands touched me.

I was wrapping the shawl about me when I was grabbed from behind. Foul breath assailed me. His hands were muscled stones pulling me against him. I tried to cry out, but my voice was lost in the growling wind and creaking ship.

"Lookin fer me, Wench?" I recognized the hissing voice as The Cur's. My struggles only increased his wrath. "Cain't stomp me like yer friend did."

He twisted my arm behind my back, forcing my knees hard against the deck as I whimpered in pain. He yanked a strand of my hair from beneath my coif, jerking my neck back. I thought it would snap in two when he pushed it forward again and let go. His hand groped, ripping my shift and scratching my neck. Evil fingers pinched my nipple. I managed to bite his hand. He let go, only to twist my arm harder behind my back. The wind blew hard, my cries lost in its voice.

The pain was vivid orange. Rough fingernails scraped against my thighs as he twisted my petticoats. I tried to kick him, but my legs were pinned. Something hot pushed against my thighs. I did not know if he would despoil or kill me. Waves of nausea shook me as his grunts brought images of rutting. I clenched my teeth and jammed my elbow back trying to connect with his ribs. His strength was that of a boar but I would not be his sow! I willed every bone and drop of blood in my body to turn to stone and repel the Cur. But he gripped my hips til I felt like a crushed berry.

"Whoreson cat!" he cried suddenly and fell sideways. I heard the hiss of a cat nearby. He quickly stood and gave it a savage kick, sending it across the deck to where it landed with a sickening thud. "Claw me backside, will ye!" he shouted ferociously.

Rolling away, I desperately scrabbled toward the hatch. I reached it and stopped. Deep inside my body felt empty—as though I'd slipped through a crack from being one of God's precious creatures to a mere animal. I had to get off the deck but the ship's officers would know I'd been assaulted if I went through steerage with scratched bosom and tattered clothes. Behind me, The Cur was spewing blasphemy. My heart thrashed so loudly I feared he could hear me. The helmsman's shouts spun in the crash of waves and wind. The cat emerged limping from the shadows. Ah, this puss could be my deceit. Gathering it in my apron, I stepped down the ladder toward the officers.

"Look what this puss did to me," I said, trying to make my shaking voice strident, but it quavered. "When did your cat start attacking maids?"

The officers jumped up, offering apologies and sips of brandy. This was more attention than I could bear.

"Thank you kindly, Sirs. I'll have my mother tend me." I caught my breath and tied the strings of my coif. At least my head was still covered. No one need know The Cur had seen and felt my hair.

"Lucky all ye got was a cat scratch, going topside alone like that," an officer said.

I nearly tripped over my skirts trying to flee down the ladder. Safe in the 'tweendecks, I gulped ale from the cask, then began trying to wash the taste, smell and feel of The Cur from my breasts and legs. But I could not wash off Satan's curse.

Giving up at last, I crawled into my bedding and pulled the pillow over my head to muffle my convulsive sobs. When my heart no longer careened wildly, my weeping ebbed. Cold blew into my emptiness, drowning out the crashing sea, the creaking ship, and the breathing and rustling of the hundred souls around me. Sliding my fingers up my thighs, I reached my private cleft. Grateful it still belonged to me, I tried to bring the warmth that comforted when I stroked. It remained closed and dry. Putting my finger in my mouth, I pretended I was a babe sucking a tit, and drifted into a fitful dream of snakes spitting venom on my tender parts.

4

Elisabeth

In the morning, I lay in bed and considered whether I could seek sympathy. Every one of us hated The Cur, but the Captain had stood by him when the elders complained of his blasphemy. Why would he not do so again? The Cur would not be blamed, I knew. I had asked for trouble going topside alone. I *was* trouble—an afflicted left hand and now besmirched. My family, indeed everyone in the 'tweendecks, would blame me. There was no one to whom I dared tell the truth. Shame twisted behind my eyes and I feared it showed in my face. My nipples stung and the hollow place under my unclean breasts pulsed. Cold flowed through me. An angry cat would remain my explanation.

All day I lay in bed, telling Mother I must have a touch of scurvy and eating the onion broth she begged from Cook. Silently, I offered my desperate prayer, "Free me from Satan's snare." The Cur had been drawn to me because I was possessed. It seemed no use to promise God I'd not succumb to Satan. I'd not used my left hand, but I'd taken strong drink and I ignored Mother's warnings. My blood seethed with terror at the thought of being forever in the devil's clutches. I could not live on the Mayflower with The Cur. My frantic mind repeated the same prayer over and over. "Dear Lord, spare me. Take this evil man from our midst. Send him to the sea, or overcome him with the plague."

That night, the heathen maid came to my dreams. She ensnared The Cur in a strange noose of rough strands. He reached for me, but the noose tightened around his chest and he gasped for breath. The heathen maid looked at me in reassurance. I woke nauseated and confused. Heathens were Satan's people.

When Mother found me awake, she insisted I get up. "Work will make thee feel better. Come, I've mended thy torn garments." She grabbed my arm and held it 'til I looked her in the eye. "Do I need tell thee again to stay away from topside?"

"Nay, Mother." I wrapped my shawl tightly and fled to the stinking goat pen where no one would talk to me. I sought solace, but as I made my way, a voice coming down the forecastle ladder riveted me.

"Get up here, lazy-arsed 'Puritans." It was my assailant's voice!

Drawing my shawl over my head to cover my face, I crouched down. My back cramped from my rigid pose, but I could hear The Cur without being seen.

"Sniveling, self righteous snots! We need hands to repair the sails."

William Bradford appeared.

"Why isn't your crew doing their work?" he asked.

"God's teeth, man! We need muscles, not sermons." The evil man spat down the ladder, narrowly missing Mistress Bradford, seated by her husband.

Master Bradford shook his fist. "Get ye topdeck! Leave us in peace."

Master Bradford led his wife to their household and pulled the bed curtains.

"Where are ye hiding the wenches?" he called. "I've got unfinished business with one of your hellcats!"

The pain behind my eyes intensified. I ducked my head, my nails digging into my palms.

John Howland stepped forward to the ladder. "If ye want help with the sails, make way for me." I peeked out to see him follow The Cur up the forecastle ladder.

As I huddled by the calming impertinence of the goats, a coolness touched my hand. I thought it was Penelope's nose but when I opened my eyes to pet her, I found it was the hand of Priscilla Mullins.

"That foul seaman troubles us all," she said. Her face was open and kind. Her parents had such wealth I had not dared approach her; now she wiped the tear on my cheek. Though she knew nothing of my shameful suffering, it comforted me to sit quietly with her. We even smiled at the bossy demeanor of Penelope towards the rest of the herd. Priscilla stood and brushed off her apron when a terrible cry came through the open hatch.

"Man overboard!"

We jumped up and ran to the port-holes. A fall into the sea meant certain death. The ship would continue; there was no way to return to rescue anyone.

"John Howland went overboard!" young Billington yelled.

A cruel joke! I would have taken a switch to that wicked boy if I could. But then I looked at young Billington's face and my bowels seized. It was true! God in Heaven help us! John Howland lost to the sea and The Cur still on board!

We were jostled aside in the commotion.

"Someone get the small boat," a voice yelled.

"No time, get the hook!" another cried.

I hung my head out the open port-hole and looked upon the roiling water below. My prayer consumed my body—every bit of blood in my veins surged with my prayer John Howland be rescued.

Young Billington peered up through the hatch.

Priscilla grabbed my arm with such strength I thought she would break a bone. "What happened?"

"He was topside, checking the rigging, when he was blown off the deck like a sea bird."

I strained to see out the porthole.

"They say he grabbed something as he fell," young Billington added with excitement.

A huge hook swung past the porthole.

"Get the hook down," someone shouted. "Hold her, boys!"

"Father of us all, save him!" I cried. No one heard me above the tumult.

The cries and shouts died down as if the Mayflower itself held its breath.

I recalled the smell of John's ink-stained hands, heard his voice laughing with little Humility, felt his arms when he picked me up during the storm.

Then a great roar engulfed us. Leaving Priscilla, I rushed toward the ladder. Uncle Edward tumbled down, surrounded by men pressing him with questions.

"Howland disappeared under the water, but then we saw a top sail halyard dragging in the water go taut!" Uncle Edward was heaving. His hair bristled when he pulled off his cap. "Then we could see nothing and wondered if our ship had left him behind."

"Tell me if he lives!" This time I kept my screams to myself.

"The halyard stayed taut, as if it pulled something." He took a deep breath. "We could only pray it was our man. The crew hauled on the rope." Uncle's eyes were so wide he looked like a fish. "Then Howland's head and shoulders burst from the depths!"

"He's saved?" asked someone.

"Yea, the seamen dropped the ship's hook. Howland grabbed it and they brought him in. The waves lifted him up high, everyone pulled and he was hauled up to the deck, limp as a jellyfish."

A cheer went up. I was startled to feel laughter welling up in my throat. Never in my life had I prayed so hard and never had my prayer been answered so quickly.

Aunt Agnes came over and Uncle Edward took several deep draughts of the ale she gave him. "The crew was amazed at how lusty Howland is." He wiped his mouth. "They think they have all the muscle," he said laughing.

"Is he well enough, then?" Aunt Agnes asked.

"Well? He's puking all over the deck just now, but that's the sea emptying out of him."

A few minutes later a gray-faced, coughing John Howland appeared on the ladder. He was trying to come down by himself, but Master Carver and our surgeon supported him. His hair was plastered to his head, his dark locks even darker.

They laid him down by the anchor windlass and I lost sight of his face. His racking cough rose above the crowd's noise. My own ribs fought against my lungs. Blankets were pulled from beds to wrap him. A boy was sent up to the cook for grease and returned shortly with a pot. I elbowed and ducked to catch a glimpse of Master Carver ripping off the wet shirt. John Howland was stretched out like a big fish and nearly the same color. He trembled. Our surgeon began rubbing down his muscled body. My view was lost again as I had to make way for Mistress Carver, followed by the entire Carver household. I could only hear scrapes and banging and comments about the particular shade of red his face had become. My fingers were clenched so tight my knuckles cracked.

Mistress Carver called for hot nettle tea. A view opened up and I could see John sitting up, his face a calmer color of pink. During the tumult of the rescue, my shame had receded. Now over, it rose again and gave a bitter taste to my tongue.

"This young man's life has been spared from a watery grave," Elder Brewster called as his maidservant came with the tea. "We are in God's hands as surely as Jonah!"

The crowd eventually returned to their households. Pulling the moldy covers over my head, I felt as though I were in a whale as I fell asleep.

I'm under the sea...the heathen maid is swimming too. My skirts are dragging, but she flashes naked legs as she swims out of sight. Through the dark green I see John Howland, surrounded by fish. He's below me...not moving...just drifting. He cannot see the huge mouth of the whale, waiting for him to drift into it. I try to call to him, but something grabs my skirts and pulls me down. I swallow water.

I awoke suddenly. Crawling out of bed, I reached for the piss pot. It was cold, but my nipple still burned where The Cur had pinched me. Yet it was my soul damaged, not my body. My attack would not be undone as quickly as Howland's rescue gave him back his life. I was trapped on the Mayflower—snared in my assailant's clutches. My left hand was but an outward symbol of Satan's possession of me. It was only a matter of time before The Cur would reveal our shameful episode. Desperately thirsty, I wrapped in my shawl and went to the large ale jar. Behind the curtains of those sleeping, I could hear soft snoring, mattresses rustling. Feeling in the dark for the jar, I touched a shoulder and cried out.

"Who's there?" a man's voice asked.

I froze. Not again!

"Elisabeth? Is that you?" It was John Howland himself.

Shaking with relief, my words escaped quickly. "I just dreamed a whale was about to swallow you and I was..." I bit my lip.

He drew in a sharp breath. "I am afraid to sleep for what I might dream; when I close my eyes, all I see is green water. My bedding sways and I believe I am held by the waves again." He took a long drink from his cask. "I have a terrible thirst from the salt water I swallowed. But why do you worry about a whale, Elisabeth?"

"I...." A sound stopped me. At first I thought it someone crying. But then a low voice moaned, accompanied by rhythmic thudding. I'd heard and seen enough on our voyage to realize it was man and wife. It seemed to come from my aunt and uncle's bed.

Thank the Lord it was dark so John would not see my red face and shaking hands. I held my arms against my ribs to stop the trembling, praying he would never know I'd been molested.

"'Tis good to hear sounds of life," he chuckled. "Sleep peacefully, Elisabeth. There is no whale, and I am not in the sea."

Sounds of life? I'd not be fooled into thinking it a pleasant sound. Would I ever think of a man's use of my body as "life"?

Attitash

As I expected, Mama agreed we would not tell Papa my suspicions about Tisquantum until I was sure. She did vow to watch for him, but we'd not seen him since we returned. Her discreet inquiries were answered with vague information that Our Massasowet's servant was spending the cold months promoting an alliance with the nations to the north.

In response to our capture, the council of Pniese agreed women and girls would not go outside the village without a warrior to guard us. I tried to maintain the calm I'd felt when Grandmother burned sweet grass and sang to cleanse me of the Narragansett, but Tisquantum was still a nettle in my mind.

Aunt Blue Sky and I arranged the heavy baskets of dried weachimin kernels on our backs for my first trip beyond the village since I'd been rescued.

Black Whale spoke to my mother. "Since Uncle Seekonk needs to build the wedge for the deer drive, I could walk with the women and set the snare."

Mama adjusted the carrying ropes across our foreheads. "Come then, Black Whale."

I walked just behind Black Whale, enjoying the sight of his muscular back and thighs as he moved. When we reached the sandy soil near a pond where we stored our winter supply, Black Whale moved on down the path to set his snare. As soon as we started digging, Mama and Aunt Blue Sky began teasing.

"What were you watching, niece?" Aunt chirruped. "You never took your eyes off the man ahead of you."

Mama grinned at Aunt as she dug. "My daughter trusts Black Whale to keep her safe. Maybe she saw the way his breechcloth swung and forgot why he walked ahead to protect us."

I blushed and tried to keep my mouth straight, but it curled into a smile. "Do we have enough dried weachimin to last all winter?"

Mama stood in the hole to measure its depth, and we handed her the baskets. "We have five more at home, Attitash. That's enough to last until spring. These baskets will take us to next harvest."

We placed the woven mats carefully over the baskets so dirt, rain, snow, and animals could not ruin the food—just as we'd done to shelter the bodies of the little boy and Yellow Hair. Seeing Black Whale coming back, I swept aside my sad memories.

Aunt Blue Sky called to him. "Where is the snare looped to the sapling? I don't want to step into it and be the deer you catch!"

Black Whale took a breath as if to answer, but only pointed with his hand back up the path. When he turned toward me, his mouth was clenched with the need to hold his tongue until Aunt finished her questioning. He looked nervous.

"What have you seen, Black Whale?" I asked, "A Narragansett?" I dared not ask if he'd seen Tisquantum.

"Waut-a-co-nuoag." He spoke slowly so our word for Cloth-men became four words. "A Strangers' wind-canoe out in the deep Big Salt Water."

"You must be dreaming." Aunt laughed nervously. "They always go back before the white frost—the Pepe'warr moon."

"Ahhe, they do. But I saw them!" Black Whale respectfully kept his eyes down, but his voice was clear. "They are here. Strangers who could stay through all the cold moons."

5

Elisabeth

"Did you hear the news?" Master Carver's maidservant asked, as Constance and I arrived at the goat pen. Jane was flush with excitement. Any little change became news in such dull environs. We set our milk buckets and began to milk our nanny goats. "The blasphemous seaman...you know which one?" she continued.

I dropped Penelope's teat and clapped my hand over my mouth, affecting a cough.

"The Cur?" asked Constance.

"Yea, that's the one."

"What about him?" asked Constance without much interest. She'd no doubt heard all she cared to about a man she knew only as a vulgar pest.

"He's dead," she announced.

The message filled my body with a riveting surge of joy. A hope arose within me that Satan's snare had loosened and I was free of his possession. Relief coursed from me in nervous giggles. It must have been how John Howland felt when he was pulled from the water and took his first breath.

"You're laughing, Elisabeth?" Priscilla took my hand.

"I prayed God would turn this Cur's threats back upon himself. I have never before rejoiced to see a man sicken and die." I watched her face; it remained smooth. "It delighted me that God answered my prayer so swiftly," I said without shame.

She took my hand. "Come then, we deserve to witness the results of God's will."

Topside was crowded, but we could see the ship's surgeon. Weights were tied to The Cur's feet, the gray and purple corpse was wrapped in a shroud. Captain Jones insisted on a brief prayer. I did not join in. God would send the wretched Cur where he belonged.

William Bradford rose. His words were measured, but his face shone. "This man tormented us. When we gently reproved him, he cursed us—said we were damned to the bottom of the sea to await eternity in hell." Of course, Master Bradford did not know that The Cur's torment went beyond merely threat! "Our God is a just God," he said. "It pleases Him that this foul man's curses now light on his own head."

At last the horrible bundle was thrown over. As it hit the water, sharks dove after it.

Priscilla shuddered. "It does ease my heart, though it makes me sick to see it."

My pure relief was quickly tempered when I went below and took up my mending. My right hand still yielded to the demands of my left; my tender nipples still burned. My heart sank. Satan may have taken The Cur, but he kept me in his grip.

As I LAID OUT my bedding on the floor, Mother and Father were disagreeing about whether we had been on the ship more than sixty days. The conversation ended without agreement. She turned to me.

"Elisabeth, ye must sleep." She pulled her night cap over her gray hair.

"I'm trying to pray, but God does not answer." Now that we were rid of The Cur, I could not form a prayer for anything but food—apples, fresh cheese, fresh bread.

"His lack of answer could signify ye ask for something ye should not have. Remember: *Thy will not mine be done, Lord.* " Mother whispered. "*As the hart panteth after the water brooks, so panteth my soul after thy, O God."*

Brook water! Back home in England there was plenty to wash with, to brew into beer, and plenty for our sheep. At sea, what little rainwater we collected did not go far. I was never given as much to drink as I desired. My hands were rough from washing in salt water. My hair had not been washed for so long it felt like it had been greased onto my head, like the dirty yarn hair on Humility's cloth poppet. I lay on the pillow, pretending I had a dipper of cold water. My soul could find God if I found fresh water, I told myself.

When I finally slept, the maid of my dreams returned, wrapped in furs and drinking fresh water from a stream. When I woke, her face was still with me and I could still smell the grass and fragrant wood smoke in her furs. I dared not reveal my vision; no one else had even hinted that they dreamed of heathens.

Rising from my bed, I crept to the portal and opened it. The smell of the sea had changed. It now carried the scent of fields and forests. The realization brought such a lump to my throat I could not swallow.

"Land, ho!" came the call.

Aunt Agnes grabbed Humility, and we joined the rush topside. The tree-covered hills on shore were so beautiful I closed my eyes and opened them again to be certain they were real. We wept with relief and excitement.

The arguments began immediately and soon rose to a pitch over whether to land in this place called Cape Cod or sail south. "Tell the captain to put us ashore!" one cried. "My wife's time of travail is near," said another. "All of us are weary and filthy!" "We need fresh water!" "We'll become a ship of ghosts!"

Captain Jones called some of the loudest to his cabin, including two who were not quarreling—Master Carver and Elder Brewster.

The Billington boys pushed their way up the ladder to the main deck where they could hear. Young John, his lank blond hair dark with sweat, returned shortly. He leaned close to me, and I backed away. "Don't be so high and mighty, Elisabeth. I have news." His grubby hand on my arm reinforced his urgency. "Captain Jones swore he would shut us all in the 'tweendecks until the tempers and confounded opinions cease," he reported.

I wrenched free from his grip.

"What good does your 'news' do me?" I said with some anger. "We might remain on this ship until we starve, or drown in a storm."

Young Billington was about to respond when John Howland came down the ladder and greeted us.

"Captain Jones has not been convinced to continue south. He's wary; this time of year Tucker's Terror is dangerous. The ship could be dashed to bits."

"I don't think God would put us in peril," Priscilla said firmly.

"So that's how we get to Virginia?" I asked.

"Only if we can get through Tucker's Terror," he said. He began coughing hard and stopped to drink from his ale cask. "The storms have blown us far off course; we are now heading for the northern coast of New England."

He saw my confusion.

"The colony of Virginia is considered everything south of the Hudson River," he said. The name of the river meant nothing to me. Evidently, we were north of wherever this river ran.

"Governor Martin told my father he has decided to try crossing the shoals and go south to the Hudson River, where we have our patent from King James." Priscilla spoke with the authority of a rich maid who can read.

"It's in God's hands," Master Carver reported when they returned at last. "The north wind is so strong we can only sail south, 'round the tip of this peninsula, to find the Hudson River."

It took all morning for our ship to reach Tucker's Terror. If the Mayflower went too close to the shallow shore, we'd be dashed on rocks; too far out we'd be lost. John came down the hatch to warn us all to hang onto the children and keep near the pillars. "We've been on the sea since September sixth and crossed the entire Atlantic."

"Is it October?" I interrupted.

"Nay, 'tis, the 9th of November," he answered.

Two months were lost to me, leaving only the memories of tedium and trauma.

"We've endured many a storm," he continued. "This passage, however, is the most hazardous. It could all end suddenly in Tucker's Terror, or a new life begins if we make it through."

Priscilla and I exchanged frightened glances.

He leaned toward the men gathered on deck. "This is a time to show our mettle! These shoals are rough waters."

The sun had just passed its midpoint when Father noted the tide had begun to flow back in, pushing us toward shore. When the wind dropped as well, the ship began drifting helplessly toward the dangerous shoals. The Mayflower pitched high and then plunged low as waves came from every direction.

Mother reached out and pulled me close to her. "Pray, Elisabeth." She had not held me since I was a child. I leaned into her. She was whispering softly, "Spare Thy faithful servants, dear Lord." I held my breath, attempting to hear her words over the crashing of the ship.

Had God brought us over the sea, saved John Howland and rid us of The Cur only to let us die within sight of land?

"Dear Lord, save Elisabeth," she prayed, pulling me closer. There were no words for my prayer, but a thin whisper of hope filled my soul. My body felt a shift in the Mayflower. I saw John Howland run up the ladder. He returned shortly, shouting, "Wind's reversed! It's coming strong from the south! Captain's turning back!"

The fierce winds drove us back north, as if God refused to let us reach our destination. By late afternoon, the winter sun had set over the hills and the ship put down anchor near the shore. But there was no peaceful sleep for us in the 'tweendecks. The feuding had worsened.

Constance edged into our household, her eyes clouded. "Elisabeth, come! Father is telling Governor Martin that he wants us put to shore to start our own plantation." Taking her hand, I followed her to where a crowd had gathered. Her father was speaking.

"I prefer to die by the sword on land fighting savages than by freezing or drowning," Master Hopkins shouted. "Those of us loyal to the King owe you Puritan separatists nothing in allegiance."

Uncle Edward spoke up, addressing the crowd. "Hopkins must come to his senses! Captain Jones told our governor he'll take everyone back to England if there's no agreement. We cannot return to a tyrant who starves and imprisons us!"

"If we were to settle here without the dissenters," my father said, "we would not have enough men. We are too accustomed to defying or obeying a king. We must learn to govern ourselves." Father chose his next words carefully. "If Christopher Martin can't govern, we should choose a new governor.

"Would those who claim loyalty to the King have us become like our countrymen in Virginia—answering to the lords who financed this and having no will of our own?" Uncle Edward asked.

I'd heard whispers about gentry in Jamestown dying in great numbers.

John Howland drew me aside. "May I have a brief word alone with you, Elisabeth?" Flattered, I followed him to the windlass. He leaned near to speak over the din behind us. His green eyes looked almost black in the dim light. "Do you know if your father favors Governor Martin, or would he be willing to support my master?"

"Support your master for what?"

"Governor." His mouth almost touched my cheek; I could feel his warm breath. "We must have a wiser man than Christopher Martin."

"Father and Uncle Edward both speak of Master John Carver with admiration." I raised my face to catch his ear. "They complain Master Martin pays no attention to what the Lord wants for our people."

"I might persuade your father and uncle that John Carver would govern wisely." He stepped away, his eyes moving over the groups of arguing men. He went to Master Carver; spoke a few words, then left in the direction of my father.

WINDS BLEW CHILL THROUGH our porthole as we progressed up the coast. A few men gathered at Carver's household. John Howland sat with his master, using a small lap desk with a hole for his inkpot. He sharpened his quill pen with his knife and began writing as the others spoke. Phrases such as "common good" and "obedience" floated up. I wished I could see John's writing, though of course I could not read anyway. "Any woman worth her salt has a man to read to her," Mother had told me many a time. "Our hands are always filled with work."

Many grew tired of waiting, but not I. The men not involved in writing the document cleaned their muskets; trying to get their powder dry after months of damp conditions. Father and Uncle Edward conferred quietly as they worked. When their discussion turned to who would best serve as governor, I could not hold my tongue. Keeping my face blank—an art I had perfected living in close quarters—I addressed Father.

"Do you think Master John Carver would be able to promote the common good?"

Father lifted his face. "Where did a young maid like ye hear such?"

"In Reverend Robinson's letter."

Uncle Edward smiled in delight. "Thy daughter will do well in this new colony, Brother!" He put an arm around Aunt Agnes, who smiled at me. "The Hollanders allow their young boys and girls to listen and learn. Elisabeth is going to need to do both if our small colony will govern without a king on our necks."

I told them how, wanting to know more, I had earlier gone to the Carver household and found Mistress Carver with Desire.

"Come listen, Elisabeth," she said. "I'm reading a letter from Reverend John Robinson." Her hands, holding the well-worn letter, had fine pale skin with light blue veins. "He gave us this letter in farewell."

I settled in beside Desire as Mistress Carver read aloud.

Lastly, whereas you are to become a Body Politic ... let your wisdom and godliness appear ... in choosing such persons as do entirely love the common good, and will diligently promote it."

I had let the words move back and forth in my mind until I understood them. A tiny spark of warmth had touched the chill of my cursed soul.

When I finished this recollection, Father leaned in close, speaking just above the constant noise of ship and shipmates. "If ye can keep this to thyself, Elisabeth, I will tell ye. I am prayerfully considering which man would indeed serve God's will by voting up a compact."

"Would Master Hopkins?" I asked.

"God only knows." Father lit his clay pipe and drew in sharply.

FINALLY, THE COMPACT was ready and Master Carver called the men together. When he began reading, my curiosity drew me out to where Aunt Agnes stood behind Uncle Edward.

> *"Ye Compacted Signed in Ye Cabin of Ye Mayflower,*
> *Ye eleventh of November anno domini sixteen twenty, In*
> *ye name of God, Amen. We whose names are underwrit-*
> *ten, the loyall subjects of our dread and soveraigne Lord,*
> *King James..."*

Why would Master Carver describe our men as loyal to King James when all of us were fleeing his dreadful rule? The king had put many of our men in prison and even hanged four of them.

> *"...a voyage to plant ye first colonie in ye Northerne*
> *parts of Virginia ... mutually in ye presence of God and*
> *one of another, covenant, and combine ourselves together*
> *into a civil body politick,"*

He paused as the ship's bell rang out to mark the time of the watch

> *"...enact, constitute, and frame such just and equal*
> *laws... for ye general goode of the colonie, unto which we*
> *promise all due submission and obedience.*

"Every free man among us must sign," said Master Carver. He looked around, satisfaction evident in his calm face.

Edward Winslow clapped Master Carver on the shoulder. "'Tis born of fear," he said. "But many wise men were born in fearful travail." Then with great conviction, he announced, "Before we settle, our compact will be signed and a governor chosen!"

The scene I'd just witnessed was one I could never have imagined. While my neck tingled with exhilaration, my chest clenched with anxiety. Nothing felt familiar anymore. The Cur's knot twisted tighter in my throat. In an effort to breathe again, I went to the porthole. The sun was setting over the forest. Dark obscured the oaks. Juniper bushes closer to shore screened what lay behind.

Attitash

"The council of Pniese must know the Strangers are here," Black Whale said. His bow was taut, the arrow notched. "I will tell them," he said and left.

Mama rushed to Little Fish in his cradleboard, lifting him out and putting him to her breast. I put my finger out and he grasped it. He let go of Mama's nipple long enough to smile at me, milk dribbling down his chin. Little Fish came into our world when the streams were full of melting snow and flashing fish. Now he stayed warm, greased and bundled in skins. The cold would not harm him, but the Strangers might throw their bad spirit sickness.

That night I curled up on our sleeping bench with White Flower. *Hot fire...Tisquantum dancing by the fire with Strangers. Black Whale throws water on the Strangers' fire and Strangers begin to disappear... the vision-girl stays with Tisquantum, then she goes too. Cold...cold...cold*

I woke whimpering. Mama held me as though I were White Flower. "We are strong People," Mama said softly. "Our Massasowet has all the Pniese—your father, your uncles—ready to defend us against enemies." She stroked my cheek. "Let the dream go, Attitash. Send it out to our Pepe'warr moon. She will take your dream when she shrinks again."

Looking up through the smoke hole, I could see the Pepe'warr moon's bright light. I let my dream go up with the smoke. Fearing sleep might bring the dream back, I resisted closing my eyes. Mama began to sing softly. I lay back next to White Flower and sang with Mama. "Rock-a-bye, Baby, on the tree top. When the wind blows, your cradleboard will rock." Our old song lulled me. But just as my eyes closed, Mama sang the next verse. "When the bough breaks, the cradleboard will fall, and down will come baby, cradleboard and all." I saw my little brother's cradleboard falling and opened my eyes in dread. Little Fish was sound asleep.

Elisabeth

"Why won't some men sign?" I asked Aunt Agnes, sitting down beside her.

"Some men only look out for themselves." Aunt plopped a squirming Humility on my lap, and handed me the wooden comb. "Men with selfish ambitions look to see if either Christopher Martin or John Carver would aid that ambition."

"But what supports only one man would work against the common people! We would end up on the bottom of the heap again, just like under King James." I held Humility firmly between my legs as I worked on her snaggled hair. "Anyway," I said, "Master Carver is too wise to do that."

Mother's brows arched. "And what do ye know about Master Carver?"

Truth be told, I had watched both men. Master Martin only listened to himself. John Carver listened before he acted.

"Father said Master Carver is wise."

"Yea, thy father understands what makes a good governor." Mother smiled as she looked at Father, deep in conversation with Master Winslow.

"But who would vote for Master Martin?" I persisted, pulling the comb very slowly so it would catch the lice as well.

"How would we know anything about other men? We know our men support John Carver." Aunt tried to wipe Humility's soiled smock. The child wiggled so much in protest that the comb jerked her hair. Conversation ceased while Aunt tended to Humility's wails. I dropped the lice in the sand candle to sizzle.

When Humility had quieted down, I tried again. "Will we really have our own law and governor?"

"Stop troubling thyself, Elisabeth." Mother waved her hand in dismissal.

"Desire says that—"

"—Trust the men to take care of this." Mother interrupted. "Keep thy mind and spirit gentle, daughter! Too much inquiring will turn thee rough."

Reaching for Humility, Aunt Agnes murmured, "We are not influential gentlewomen like Desire Minter and Mistress Carver. If ye do not accept thy lot, Elisabeth, it will drive ye mad."

I scooped up the meal's leavings of moldy cheese and fled to the goats.

Penelope bleated when I arrived and shoved aside the others, hoarding the cheese for herself. "Ye are a rough goat," I admonished. Constance Hopkins too arrived with her family's remains of dried biscuit crumbs.

"Is thy father signing the compact?" I asked.

"Not yet." Constance flicked her eyes about, looking for busybodies with alert ears. "Mother says Father will sign, but only when they sign." She pointed with her elbow toward a group that included at least ten men.

"Which ones?" I whispered, leaning close to her ear.

"Captain Standish and Master Allerton." Constance put her finger to her mouth as Edward Doty, her family's servant, came to take a turn mucking the goat pen. He nodded to both of us and began shoveling. One of his eyes always looked in a different direction from the other and I could not tell if he looked to Constance or me.

Constance took her leave, and I was about to follow, when Doty caught my arm.

"Elisabeth, did Constance tell you what her father demands?"

I shook my head and pulled free. Stephen Hopkins was nearby, deep in conversation with Captain Standish. Edward Doty put down his shovel and put his hands by his mouth to keep his voice close. "Hopkins insists the words *Having undertaken for the glory of God and advancement of the Christian faith*, be removed."

"You should not be telling me this falsehood," I gasped.

"Nay, Elisabeth! 'Tis true," he protested as one of his cocked eyes held mine. I recalled how Mother had said Satan had possession of an eye that wandered from its mate. Mayhap Doty saw only evil. "But he only asks this to torment Masters Martin and Carver," he said. "Both want his vote."

"How could such a dreadful proposal be made?" I tried to absorb this heretical request. "Why would they leave God out of it, but keep the king? Does it not say, '*and advancement of ye Christian faith, and honour of our king and countrie*'?"

Edward Doty let out of a soft whistle. "Well, since you know so much, you should know that King James"—Edward Doty's mouth made a derisive sound which Penelope imitated—"must be included. If not, he would never grant us land when he gets the new patent."

"What does Captain Standish say? Didn't he hire your master?"

"Yea. Captain Standish agrees the law should not direct what any man believes. The Captain and Master Hopkins are not like the King, who imprisons and kills those who refuse to belong to his church." Edward Doty made a mock bow to me. "Nor are they like you 'puritans'—separatists who would try to drain all pleasure from a poor man."

The insult stung, and I wanted to dispute Doty's false ideas, but I persisted in trying to understand Master Hopkins' alleged demand. "But Myles Standish and Stephen Hopkins would both be sent back to England for proposing this!"

"That strikes no fear in them," he replied. "They didn't get what they bargained for when they hired on, did they? Stuck up here away from the known world." Doty pushed the goats away with his shovel. "We would leave gladly and go home with the Mayflower crew."

I pondered the possibility that all those who were not of the Lord's church might leave us and return to England. It would be trouble for all, I was sure. "Isaac Allerton is one of us 'puritans,' as you call us. Why won't he sign?"

Edward Doty grinned broadly. "You are a forward young maid! Ask Carver's clerk. John Howland's keeping tally for John Carver." He pointed toward the windlass where John Howland was sitting, studying a list. I went to him, feeling confused. He spoke before I had my mind collected.

"Well met, Elisabeth! Your father signed the Compact, but did not tell me how he'll cast his vote for governor."

"Don't tell him I said so, but surely Father would vote for your master." Seating myself by the coils of the windlass, I asked, "Do you know why Master Allerton won't sign? I am only curious and not inclined to gossip." John Howland's brow creased and I thought I should have followed Mother's warning.

"I would tell you about Isaac Allerton if I could, Elisabeth," he answered stonily. "But this business is only for the men who vote. I do my master's work, but I can't repeat it."

"Because I'm a maid." I whispered, ducking my head.

"Why would a maid want to know?" he asked, but did not wait for an answer. "I have many more men to talk to now and must join Master Carver," he said and left.

My head pounded with his words. Was I only good for pinching, cooking, cleaning up piss pots? He had asked me about my father when he needed information. But now I was just a maid!

Everything was new, yet still the same.

AWAKENING LATER IN the cold dark, my fierce determination to understand returned. Everyone in my household still slept; John Howland sat reading his list by candle lantern. I crept near him and observed, prepared to be rebuffed again. He looked up at me, however, and smiled. "I am just about to make a copy for William Bradford's record of the compact…with all free men's signatures! The rebels signed!" His whispers carried excitement.

"Praise God." I whispered back.

"And when we vote, I believe Master Carver will be our new governor!"

"When will the vote be taken?" I asked.

"Today," he said with some solemnity.

"John, will you read to me the compact and names of the signers?"

"Aye, Elisabeth."

The words *just and equal laws* and *the general good of the colony* stirred me. When he finished, he pointed to the first name.

"John Carver—his signature is first—John Turner, William Bradford." He continued down the list, pausing with a smile as he read, "Isaac Allerton." He continued, "John Billington—he would not sign until Allerton signed. Myles Standish." He read several more, then paused again. "Christopher Martin."

"How did you get his signature?" I asked in surprise.

"Once we had the votes, Master Martin had no choice, if he would remain with us." He continued reading more names, then, swallowing hard, he said, "John Howland." I did not hear the next few names, as I kept hearing his voice saying his own name.

When he read Stephen Hopkins's name, I gasped in relief. I did not recognize all the names. Although I had been crowded in the 'tweendecks with these men for more than two months, I did not know most who had no family with them. Some of these nameless men leered at me as though they could see beneath my clothes. Others looked through me as though I were not there.

"Edward Tilley." Uncle Edward. I held my breath. I had never heard our name read out.

He then looked up and read directly to me. "John Tilley." Father!

"I want to learn to read!" I blurted without thinking, then hid my face in shame.

John gently took my hands away from my eyes. "Then I will teach you," he replied as if he were telling me I could learn to milk goats.

"You tease me!"

"I do not. You are a very inquisitive maid. Learning to read would satisfy such curiosity."

I clapped my hand to my mouth. "If my father agrees, I would try to be worthy of your efforts."

"Master Carver says all must know how to read. He'll speak to your father when this is all accomplished." John Howland finished reading the remaining names, but I scarcely heard him.

By early afternoon, Master Brewster called everyone together. We women and maids crowded close to the men. He quieted the remaining murmurs.

"The vote has been taken and tallied. All agree that John Carver loves and will diligently promote the common good. He will serve as our governor according to the compact." Elder Brewster's strong voice proclaimed. Master Carver nodded with humble grace when we applauded; John's eyes shown with pride. Master Martin turned his head, not joining in the applause. I knew I should not feel happy at a man's bitterness, but Christopher Martin had brought it upon himself, being so high and mighty with us all.

"No woman could sign, not even Mistress," Desire whispered.

"What would it feel like to be a man and sign a compact?" I whispered back.

Desire laughed. "We'll never be men, and I'm glad of that! She then whispered, "but some widows in Holland have legal rights."

Aunt Agnes had told me that widows in Holland could own the land, and not depend on their sons. But I could not believe they could sign a compact.

When we gathered back in our household, I told Father and Uncle Edward, "I heard your names."

They both looked at me as if I'd begun to speak in an upcountry accent.

"John Howland read the names of the signers to me," I explained.

Father lit his pipe. "Where's thy mother? Are ye gawking at men's work when she needs thy help?"

"Mother and Aunt are getting porridge from cook's pot now." I began handing out trenchers. "I saw your signature, Father. And yours, Uncle Edward."

Uncle Edward was smiling so wide his beard was

bristling. "Brother John, the document is like none ever seen while we lived under the king's thumb."

"Or the king's sword," Father added.

When Mother and Aunt Agnes returned with porridge, we all sat on the bed and stools, waiting for Father to bless the food. He seemed to have trouble speaking—swallowing several times and blinking his eyes. He cleared his throat.

"Bless this food to our use, God our Father. We thank Thee that Thou hast brought us safely here today. We live the words of Psalm 69: *Save me, O God; for the waters are come into my soul. I sink in deep mire, where there is no standing: I am come into deep waters, where the floods overflow me.*"

I could hear the emotion in his voice, but could not see tears.

"Thou hast brought us from the perils of storm and treacherous water, the perils of tyranny and anarchy. We will not perish alone in a wilderness, but settle this new land as planters. We thank Thee for Thy servant, Governor John Carver. He will work for the common good of all." When he'd said the final "amen," Father's brow no longer furrowed.

The upgrowns began to eat. Uncle Edward finished his porridge, wiping his mouth on his sleeve. "Tomorrow Captain Standish is taking the longboats to shore. We will begin to explore."

Aunt Agnes covered her mouth. "Must ye be in the first boat, Edward? Will there not be lions and other dangerous beasts?"

His eyes twinkled, "Who knows what we'll find?"

6

Attitash

Paddling away from the big wind-canoe were two small canoes filled with Strangers. Our little party hid in the trees that ringed the shore of Big Salt Water.

Uncle Seekonk drew in a deep breath and spoke slowly. "We followed the cloth-men this morning as they came to the pond where our dried corn is buried. They found our hard-stone kettle full, the one we bartered for some seasons back, and stole it."

"They took our weachimin?" I asked. "That we grew, picked, and dried?" I'd heard of our food being stolen before, but it had not happened to crops I'd harvested.

"Ahhe," Uncle said. I knew he carried terrible memories of Strangers' invading his first wife's village of Patuxet. He had returned home to find everyone dead, including his wife and child. Strangers had taken captives but used their bad spirits to suck the life from everyone else.

Black Whale motioned up the trail. "I saw a strange sight when I checked my snare this morning." I pictured the loop on the ground with a deer stepping into it and then pulled up by the rope fixed to the tree.

"What did you catch?" I asked.

"A Cloth-man."

"Did it see you?" I gasped.

"No. Before I got there, I heard cloth-men walking with their weapons clanking. I climbed a tree and watched. Most of the men stopped to look at our snare. They looked at the sapling, followed it with their hands where it bowed down over the earth, then continued on past."

"But you said you caught one."

He smiled. "One man was slower. When he came up he…" Black Whale lowered his voice to a whisper. "…he stepped in the snare and it caught his leg. He was jerked up, firestick, spear, heavy clothes and all!"

I clapped my hand over my mouth to keep from laughing. "What did he do?"

"He shrieked and kicked. His face was red, his hat lay on the ground and his stringy hair hung down. The other cloth-men came back. They laughed at him before they cut him down and took my rope."

White Flower let out a giggle. Black Whale hushed us both.

We crawled to a screen of juniper bushes with a view of the landing. Strangers were gathered around a fire, waving to those paddling in. As the canoes landed, I could see that some of the new Strangers were smaller and had long cloth ponchos that billowed out in the wind. Women and girls! As they sloshed through the shallow ice water toward us, my mind would not accept the pictures my eyes seeing. The Strangers had brought women to our land!

"What do you see, Attitash?"

White Flower was too short to see past the bushes, but I ignored her question as I watched the Strangers' wind-canoe filled with women. My mind whirled. Why had these cloth-men brought women? Could the vision girl I'd seen in the pool be real? I closed my eyes to see if this were a dream, but when I opened them again the women were all out of the wind-canoe, lifting big bundles of their cloth. They laughed and chattered in their sharp tongue as they came ashore, swaying and picking up their feet slowly. Their men carried heavy stone kettles from the boat and set them on the fire. The women filled them with water from the brook, then their bundles.

One of the young women turned and looked directly at

me. The sight made me gasp out loud and I bit my lip to prevent crying out. It was the girl I'd seen reflected in the pool! The strange girl's eyes were the color of quiet water. Curls like wood shavings peeked out beneath her hood. When she looked into my eyes, her mouth dropped open and her hands flew to cover it.

Elisabeth

I was giddy—all we maids were. After more than sixty days on a stinking, heaving ship, everyone was desperate to go ashore.

The first day we anchored, only armed men had gone to explore the temporary landing. Father, Uncle Edward, John Howland and the others had climbed down to the longboat, weapons clanking. We'd heard shots, but they brought no game when they returned safely the next day. They did bring boughs of juniper, though, and its sweet smoke diminished the reek of the ship and made our Sabbath confinement in stormy weather almost bearable.

Monday morning was fair, and the same group of men rowed ashore. The longboats returned later to fetch us. Desire, done in with a bad cough, was the only one of us six young maids who did not go. We piled in with laundry, kettles, casks and our damp bedding. Mother called out admonitions and I acknowledged them with a wave, concealing my joy at leaving the foul, cursed ship. I could hear Rogue's furious barking from the 'tweendecks. "Ye'll be next," I shouted to the dog, "when we find a place to settle."

When the longboat hit bottom in the shallows, I looked back across the water at the tiny Mayflower. Making a circle with my thumb and first finger, the Mayflower fit inside it. How could all those people, animals, and provisions be on that little ship?

"Ooo…aah," we squealed, wading to shore as our

shoes filled with the freezing sea. The trees beyond the wide sandy beach seemed to sway like my legs; the waves pushed us back and forth. I lost my balance. Before I was completely down, Uncle Edward waded in to rescue me, his boots full of water. Even when we reached the shore, the uncivilized manner in which we walked—our feet stepping high across the sand as though still accommodating the motion of the ship—made us giggle. Constance said she felt like she'd taken too much aquavit. Mary Chilton lost her balance and sat down abruptly in the sand.

Eventually, we arrived at the men's fire by the spring. Father assured me the spring water would not make me sick like the water in England. I drank. The clear, sweet water filled my mouth and slowly trickled down my chin. We filled casks to take back to the ship.

The men were all clanking around in their armored corselets. Father's and Uncle Edward's were as baggy as nightshirts. John Howland's corselet fit snugly over his broad shoulders. Patting my ribs, I remembered the odd feeling when I'd once tried on Father's corselet. Hiding in our bed curtains, I'd examined the corselet's cloth with metal plates sewn inside, like pieces of pot lid inside a quilt.

"Stay back from the trees. There might be savages in there," John Howland said. He then held out a rough looking rope. "Look!"

I felt the twisted fibers. The touch of the heathen rope gave me shivers. If there were savages about, we all needed corselets. "Where did you find this?" I asked.

"Master Bradford found it—or rather, it found him!" John laughed with great amusement. Bradford smiled with chagrin, but in good sport.

Carver's maidservant directed the men as they added wood to the fires and lugged water to fill the big kettles. I rubbed wet soap over the filthy shifts and shirts in my pile of laundry, then put them in the hot water to soak. The black rims under my broken nails were gone.

"My hands are nearly clean!" I called to the other girls.

"Yea, mine are clean too, but wrinkled and red." Constance put her bony hands next to mine.

I looked at Priscilla Mullins' pink hands. She passed her bar of soap so lightly over a dirty shift that she might have been anointing it.

While the clothes soaked, we draped damp moldy quilts on bushes where the sweet smoke blew the reek of the ship out of them. I looked toward the woods and froze, dropping the quilt I held. It was the heathen in my dreams!

Her face was rounder and her furs covered her shoulders, but the black eyes matched my dream heathen maid's. Feeling as though I'd fallen off the ship into the darkest depths, I shut my eyes, hoping to destroy the frightening apparition. "Get thee behind me, Satan," I whispered desperately. When I cracked my eyes open, the heathen maid was gone. I drew a breath raggedly, like pulling a stitch out of mending.

The other maids continued their scrubbing, unaware of my sighting. I plunged my hand deep in the hot water to retrieve the soap I'd dropped when the face appeared. The frigid air cooled my wet arm when I brought it out, but my mind was filled with seething stones. The Mayflower, its stinking 'tweendecks crammed with people, was like a safe haven now. I filled my lungs with the clean air, determined to hide my tortured soul.

When we finished the laundry, I walked with stronger legs to the longboat. As we climbed in, I looked to the woods one last time. Nothing was visible but green juniper and bare brown trees.

Safely back on ship, Mother met me with a fierce hug. I offered her the cask of fresh water. She hesitated, but after learning Father and Uncle Edward drank it, she finally took a small sip, then a bigger one. At last, Mother drank deeply and handed it to Aunt Agnes. "Thank ye, Elisabeth. Even if this fresh water kills me, I've not had my thirst satisfied so sweetly."

We maids set about draping the wet clothes around topside to dry. I kept my eyes away from shore and betrayed no reason for anyone to inquire about my state of mind. Thankfully, I would not be sent to shore again, as the longboats would only carry the builders and explorers.

Attitash
I didn't tell Mama I'd seen my vision girl, but White Flower and I whispered about it at night. A few sleep-circles later White Flower and I were walking ahead of Mama when we heard the Strangers' clank-clank. Parting the now snow-covered bushes, I saw the men approach the burial site where Yellow Hair and the little boy lay. *Keep walking,* I willed. But the Strangers stopped and began poking into the snow on top of the sacred site. White Flower's little hand felt sharp in mine. Mama came up behind us, carrying a basket of weachimin.

"Don't get so far ahead of me!" Mama could sound like she was shouting even when she whispered. We crouched in the bushes, quiet as a fox watching a rabbit. The Strangers stomped the light snow on the graves and shouted to each other in their stepping-on-shells words.

"Go! Leave," Mama's whisper was a command even Strangers would have obeyed if they had heard and could understand. But no one left. "Get out! Go back!"

One of the Strangers cocked his head in our direction. My rigid body held my breath outside. But he turned back to the grave and joined the others kicking at it with their hard moccasins.

"I never want to see *her* again," my whisper escaped.

"See who?" White Flower waited for an answer I was

not ready to give.

When the strange young woman with eyes-like-quiet-water came to our shore I had been shocked, but my vision had made me hope she would be different from the other Strangers. Now I knew that was a stupid, dangerous expectation. Maybe Yellow Hair's bad spirits had twisted my mind. Never again would I be fooled.

Their kicking knocked aside the earth. They began to dig at the grave, first with their long knives, then with their foul hands—like dogs. They dug down to the soft mats. When they pulled off the mats, exposing the bodies, White Flower covered her eyes, whimpering like Little Fish when smoke blew in his face. But we could not wave away their sacrilege like smoke.

Mama pulled White Flower against her. Only a trickle of blood from her bottom lip betrayed the force of her teeth holding back her howl. I had become a boulder, watching as a Stranger reached over Yellow Hair's body. The sacred red powder spilled onto the Stranger's clothes. He took the little bow Black Whale had made for the little boy. Another Stranger took bowls holding food for his journey to the Spirit World.

"They are violating our graves!" Mama's face contorted with anger. "Our Massasowet must gather the Pniese council. We will avenge this desecration!" Holding her arm tightly around White Flower, Mama motioned to me.

There was not room in my belly for both my horror and my last meal. The rabbit stew spewed out into a steaming heap on the snow. I pushed snow over the mess with my moccasin toe and followed Mama.

Elisabeth

New snow obscured our view of the shore one day. When the longboats finally appeared near the Mayflower, the explorers clamored back up topside. Master Carpenter Francis

Eaton came first, announcing excitedly, "Shallop's ready!" Master Winslow followed holding out a rucksack, "Come see the heathen curios we've dug up. We found another heathen grave." He emptied the contents of the rucksack onto Carver's table. "Look at the bowls, and a little bow and arrow for the child in the grave." As we crowded around trying to see, Edward Winslow answered questions. "The little heathen body was the size of...this boy," he said pointing to five year old Jasper More. "'Twas a rather fresh grave; his flesh was not much rotted and his hair was still there."

Mary Chilton looked a bit green at the description, and I clenched my stomach so my own queasy feeling would not be revealed.

"Most of the flesh and yellow hair of the other body remained too." Captain Standish said, as though he were describing a dog or a horse.

"Yellow hair?" I blurted out. "Did you disturb a Christian's grave?" I shrank back as Mother's hand grabbed mine and squeezed hard.

"Think before ye speak, Elisabeth!" she whispered in my ear forcefully. "'Twill bring the wrath of God upon ye with such forward questions."

"Beg pardon for my rudeness, Captain," I said in a low voice.

"Was it a Christian's grave?" Governor Carver asked, as though I'd not spoken.

"Nay, 'Twas a heathen grave," Myles Standish responded. "Made by heathens and filled with heathen goods."

"However, one of the bodies may have been a Christian," Master Winslow said. "No one has ever seen an Indian with yellow hair, dressed in sailor's cloth."

"Could it have been an Englishman?" Governor Carver asked.

"English, French, Spanish—all have left men behind

for the savages to murder," Stephen Hopkins said, waving his hand toward the shore as if it were filled with lost Christians.

"The yellow hair's body was too rotted to identify him," John Howland said, "but his clothes were those of a Christian." He picked up the little bow and arrow, plucking at the loose string on the bow. "'Tis rough made, but still works." I could not ask John Howland in front of others—especially his master—why they'd opened the grave.

Captain Standish took the bow and arrow and put it back in the rucksack. "Whoever he was, he was buried with another heathen, in a heathen grave. We did nothing to offend any church's commands."

Governor Carver's mouth was a straight line and his cheek muscles clenched. I wondered if he wanted to dispute the captain. "No more grave digging. Tomorrow we go out again. Winter is upon us. We must find a place where the ship can anchor and we can plant."

Attitash

When Mama informed the Grandmothers' Council of the robbery, they prayed fervently for the life of our people. They all agreed that our men must consider how to drive out these invaders. Our Massasowet called the Pniese into council. Uncle Seekonk accepted the talking stick. "Only five moons ago, when the weachimin plants were just sprouting, the cloth-men tricked many of our men to go with them to a big wind-canoe. They were killed without provocation; killed in cold blood; killed by firesticks as they stood with the cloth-men on their big wind-canoe." Uncle paused to honor those lost. "But we can defeat them! Just as Epenow defeated the cloth-men at Capawack!" The stir of hope I felt was mirrored in some faces.

Many times I'd been told the story of how Sachem

Epenow was captured and taken away by Strangers. He convinced them to bring him home to Capawack by telling them that they would find yellow rock there. He then jumped off their canoe and escaped. Years later, he led a surprise attack on another big wind-canoe. He wounded the captain, To-mas Dermer, who fled down the coast, but soon died of his injuries.

"To-mas Dermer was Tisquantum's last enslaver across the Big Salt Water," Grandmother whispered to me. "Dermer brought Tisquantum back to our land to speak for him while trading with us in beaver," she said. "But Sachem Epenow did not trust Tisquantum. And after he defeated Dermer, he delivered Tisquantum to our Massasowet." Grandmother cast a quick look at our Massasowet. "He knows that a man with two hearts must be watched."

"I wish he'd been watched more closely," I whispered to myself.

Papa took the talking stick. "You remind us of truth, Seekonk. These cloth-men will not stop with stealing food and violating graves. They will capture and kill again. Sachem Epenow showed us how to kill *them* instead."

The other Pniese nodded and murmured.

My father turned to our leader. "You are wise and brave, Massasowet. You know what will happen if we do not attack now. We can ask our People at Nauset to join us. Together, we can surprise the cloth-men as soon as they come again to sleep on our shores!"

I could not forget the sight of the little boy's body exposed. The desire for revenge seized me.

Mama's voice was a buzzing fly; she took hold of my arm. "Release your anger, Attitash, before it makes you careless. You must be calm, watching for danger. Leave it to our warriors to attack the grave-desecrators and drive them away." Her grip on my arm eased. "Pour some warm water for your brother's bath. Your anger will wash away with his dirt."

My anger was still a cold pit in my chest when I returned home. But Little Fish's hair was thick and soft. I breathed in the balm of his baby smell. The warmed water dribbled from his head down his back and caught in his round little bottom. Little Fish laughed and gurgled. I rubbed his hair dry by the fire and then gave him to Mama. While she was feeding him, I removed the soiled sphagnum moss from the cradleboard and put in fresh. When all was ready, Mama tucked Little Fish into his clean cradleboard. His eyes closed in blissful sleep, his belly bulging with milk.

My heart was no longer smothered. I would use my anger to be strong.

7

Attitash

Suki lifted her nose and began to whine at the sound of moccasins crunching on the snow. Black Whale entered our home, puffing hard and blowing snow. He greeted Mama and sat down by me.

"When the Strangers came ashore, I followed them easily. They move slowly—without any women carrying their packs." Black Whale's mouth curled in a small smile at me. "After sleeping all night in a shelter made of tree boughs, they set out again along the coast toward Nauset. Now is the time to attack."

"Eat well now," Mama told Black Whale, "then take food and go with Seekonk to Nauset and tell them to prepare."

Black Whale put journey cake and some dried venison in his belt pouch. He added layers of dry moss in his moccasins and an extra fur to keep out the snow. Fear circled my ribs and held my shoulder blades taut, pushing them into my back. When Black Whale went outside, I followed. He was looking at Nippa'uus already low over the forest, but when I whispered his name he turned to me.

"When do you leave?" I asked.

"As soon as Uncle Seekonk is ready."

"Be careful," I cautioned.

"Careful!" he barked. "Is that all you think of? You sound like my mother. Her eyes follow me wherever I go, like I was still a little boy." He stomped off toward our Massasowet's home.

My face prickled with hot anger. How could Black Whale think I was like Green Feather? I was not yet an old woman—I was still a girl!

I saw 'Rushes and hurried to catch up to her. "'Rushes!" I called.

She turned and started to smile, then stopped. "Attitash, what's the matter? Do you want to come and sit by my fire?"

"Ahhe. I mean—matta—no."

She raised her eyebrows and waited for me to make sense.

"I do want to talk to you; but not now, not with your mother, Green Feather."

"Do you want to go outside? It's cold, but—"

I did not let 'Rushes finish. "No, we might see your brother."

"My brother? Well, come to the women's relief place!"

When we arrived at the yellow snow near the woods, I spoke. "I worry about Black Whale being near the battle."

She held my eyes. "That's not all."

I looked away. "My concern is foolish." I pulled up my skirt and furs and squatted. The cold air bit at my bare bottom and the snow steamed in the dim afterglow. "When I told Black Whale to be careful, he snapped at me like he was the frog and I was the fly."

'Rushes laughed. "Oh, he does get tired of our mother watching him so carefully. He thinks he's a warrior, even though he's not been on his vision quest yet."

"But he and Uncle Seekonk must be careful. Strangers have firesticks! Can our arrows kill them before they kill us?"

"Epenow did." 'Rushes did not look as sure as her words.

Uncle Seekonk returned alone from Nauset next morning. He had run until the stars shone and then slept only until Nippa'uus dimmed its light. After he ate, he spoke to Grandmamma. "Your son, Red Hawk, and others at Nauset are sharpening their arrows and will join us attacking the Cloth-men." Uncle took another piece of bread from the pan. "Black Whale is enjoying the Fox Clan cousins. Their daughter, Seafoam's hair is cut to her ears. Black Whale could be back there next spring playing his flute for Seafoam."

Mama said something low to Uncle Seekonk as I pressed my hand hard against my mouth. Seafoam! My clan uncle's daughter.

All day I pounded weachimin and thought about pounding Black Whale. "You and your wandering eyes! Take that! Just because I don't have my woman-power yet and Seafoam does." I pounded harder, the yellow pulp covering my hands.

"Does that feel good?" Aunt Blue Sky's question did not need an answer. She laughed softly as she settled her belly, big with new life, on the sleeping bench furs. "You can stop pounding now, Attitash. It's getting dark."

White Flower crept under my sleeping furs beside me, but I kept my back stiff to her. I prayed Papa, Uncle Seekonk, and Uncle Red Hawk would be safe. Even Black Whale.

When I woke and looked up through the smoke flap, I could still see the cold moon we call Quinee Keeswush. All my family still slept. If I ran to where I could see the brook emptying into the Big Salt Water, I could watch. I had to arrive before Nippa'uus arose. Silently, I packed my moccasins with extra fur, and took some journey cake from the pot and then crept out.

The stars were moved into position to welcome Nippa'uus. I was cold, but knew I'd get warm as I ran. Nippa'uus was just peeking up, the sky over the Big Salt Water all light red and yellow. I could see the big wind-canoe, shifting gently on the waves. If only a storm would sink it, taking all the Strangers, including the girl with Eyes-Like-Quiet-Water. Stooping, I broke the thin hard surface of the creek with my elbow; then dipped my fingers in the freezing water. I drank the water; my fingers and throat thrummed with the cold. It hit my belly with a jangle. I heard a slapping sound and looked up. It was the sound of waves against the Strangers' small wind-canoe approaching the shore. I crouched down by the creek, straining with all my senses to find out what was happening. As it came closer in the early light, I could see Strangers—at least eight of them. Shrill voices bounced across the water as the Strangers pointed their firesticks toward shore.

Elisabeth

Dorothy Bradford watched through the porthole as the shallop carried Master Bradford's expedition away. She turned back toward us, picking up the little bow and arrow, holding it gently in her hand. "My little boy would delight in this," she said with a sad smile. "See how the barbarians work the wood with their crude tools?"

Mary Brewster picked up one of the clay bowls in the basket of objects brought from the heathen grave. "See the picture of the dog in their design. They must worship the dog."

I caught its faint odor. "It's foul! Do they eat out of these?"

"It's been in the grave. Of course it smells." Mistress Brewster replied.

"Why would the heathens put bowls and weapons in a grave?" I asked.

Mistress Bradford shrugged, plucking the string of the bow listlessly. "I was told the barbarians believe the soul makes a journey to their heaven, so they put food and tools in the grave for their use." Her voice quavered as she continued. "Mayhap it's just as well my husband insisted our boy stay back in Holland. "Twould be hard to bring him here where such savagery prevails."

The faint smell emanating from the objects and the notion of the Indian boy's soul needing food disturbed me. Did the heathen maid I saw know the little boy who was buried with the Christian man? Feeling the need for more familiar thoughts and smells, I wrapped Aunt Agnes' green shawl about me. It was dark green and unembroidered, except a row of straight ribbon stitch around the edge. Mother caught me sitting still and asked me to deliver the gifts she'd sewn for Mistress White's new babe.

Nodding politely to Mistress White, I gave her the embroidered belly bands and clouts. "Has Master White chosen a name for the babe?" I touched the tiny, fat fingers.

"Yea," she kissed him as he sought her breast. "My husband named him Peregrine. It's Latin." She saw my questioning eyes and laughed softly. "Of course it's in the Bible, Elisabeth. In English it means 'pilgrim'."

"What's a pilgrim?" I knew it was forward to ask a gentle lady so many questions.

Mistress White gently stroked the infant's forehead beneath his bonnet. "A pilgrim is someone making a journey to follow God's holy will."

8

Attitash

The sharp sound of firesticks had stopped, but the disturbance in my spirit had not. The Strangers' small wind-canoe continued west on the Big Salt Water's bay. I ran until it was out of sight and I was out of breath. When I came to the violated grave, I stopped. Fresh snow was on the grave, so I drew a calmer breath. There was a pain in my belly and in my back, however, which would not go away. If I ran far enough to see where the small wind-canoe landed, it might ease my fury. Running with no pack on my back was easy, but the pain did not stop. My back and belly felt like rocks pressed against them. I stepped off the path into deeper snow and relieved myself. My steaming hole in the snow showed brownish-red mixed with yellow. I put a finger to my woman-place and brought it out. Blood! Little black blobs smeared my finger. My heart surged. I was a woman!

Our grandmothers had been preparing me for this ever since I turned seven. They taught us little girls in the Moon-Lodge that our bodies were made of the flow of life—many kinds of liquids. They taught us that the power-flow I now saw in the snow was the blood that prepared me to become a mother. When I returned home, I would have my cleansing and new-woman ceremony. They would cut my long hair up to my ears. Once it grew back to my shoulders, I would be ready to marry.

I ran again until I reached the tall oak tree whose trunk showed a grandfather's face. I hoped to get home before

my skirt and leggings were stained with blood. The snow
was slippery, however, and my foot caught on a rock beneath the snow. I went down hard. When I tried to stand,
my ankle would not hold me. It was very tender and
seemed to swell beneath my fingers. Biting my lip to keep
from crying, I took a few limping steps forward. A sob
burst from my throat. I broke a lower branch from a tree to
lean upon. I was in no condition to defend myself against
a Narragansett or Tisquantum. I would as soon avoid my
pretty cousin Seafoam at Nauset but it was close by and I
needed help. I took two steps before the pain brought me
down again. When I tried to stand, I could not. Blue Jay
screamed, and Crow answered. The cold gripped the toes
on my hurt foot and crept up my leg. Praying to open my
heart to guidance, I noticed a tiny wisp of steam coming
from a large mound of snow a few paces into the woods.
Dragging myself backward on my bottom, I reached the
hole and leaned my face over it. A rich, rank smell filled
my nose, and the warm mist of the bear's escaping breath
eased my frozen mouth. I could just make out the dark fur
at the bottom of the hole. Above me, the pine branches
hung fat with snow. Breaking off a few of the boughs, I
put some beneath me, checked for landmarks and saw the
grandfather-faced tree. My mind seemed as numb as my
feet. I slipped into a dream of black bear and berries.

Before I heard snow crunching, I felt someone near
and awoke. Tisquantum? A Narragansett? I was too cold
to move; a moan of fear escaped me as a hand brushed
snow from my head.

"Attitash! What are you doing here?"

My relief was followed by rage that Black Whale should
find me so vulnerable. "Why do you care? I'm not following you and I'm not an old woman!" Pain and frustration
silenced me.

"What are you talking about? An old woman? You're

not even a woman yet."

Stifling my sobs to hide my weakness, I put my head down. "Go back to Nauset, go back to Seafoam. But tell Uncle Red Hawk I need help."

"Have you been hit in the head, Attitash?"

"My head is fine! It's my ankle." I tried to stand, and managed to get up, leaning on my right leg. "Why are you here, Black Whale?" The effort to stand and talk cost me. I had to squeeze my eyes shut to keep from crying out.

"The Strangers have come to shore again. I'm running with the message to attack them now. As soon as I have you safe at Nauset, I'll come back." Black Whale offered his hand to me.

I ignored it. "Go. Don't wait for me."

"You cannot walk! You stubborn girl!" He dropped his hand. "You can't sit here in the snow and heal yourself. Do you want to be captured again?"

Frustration and helplessness were not familiar to me. But there was no disputing his words—which made me even angrier. "You can't carry me!"

Black Whale put his shoulder under my left arm. I had no strength to get away from his grasp. He began taking steps, but my leg couldn't work in the snow. He was forced to stop. "Why won't you let me carry you?"

My only answer was sobs. Once my hair was cut to mark my womanhood, Black Whale and all the men would know what happened to me. At last I blurted out. "I'm a woman now! My power is strong and will suck away your power."

Black Whale turned his back on me and stomped the snow in frustration. He crouched in front of me. "Attitash, I can't leave you here. Uncle Seekonk has taught me the ways of women. It is true, when your power is strong, it can disrupt our decisions, and we can't touch you in love. But that doesn't mean I can't carry you."

I was silent and could not look at him—afraid that if he picked me up my blood might stain him even if it did not drain his power. "Take me on your back," I finally said. Black Whale bent over, and I leaned onto his back. Picking up my thighs with his arms, he pulled me against him. It jostled my ankle, and I gasped in pain; but I bit my lip and did not cry out. Putting my arms around his shoulders, my head rested against his furs. For so many moons I had dreamed of touching Black Whale; for so many moons I had dreamed of becoming a woman. Now all I felt was fear and misery. He began the slow walk to Nauset.

We stopped many times to rest, but at last we saw the smoke and then the woven mats of Aunt First Star's wetu. Black Whale's whistle brought out Uncle Red Hawk and Aunt First Star. They took me in, Black Whale silently turned to run back

They sat me on the bench, covered me with furs and propped up my ankle. The pain that gripped my leg up to my thighs receded to a dull ache in my ankle. Seafoam brought me a hot brew made from willow bark, and I breathed the woody scent of the steam. I was too weary to let my envy of Seafoam rise up, though I did hear an edge to her voice when she asked her mother if Black Whale had carried me.

The heat felt good, but I feared my life-flow was getting stronger. I whispered to Aunt First Star that I needed to go to the moon-lodge for cleansing.

Aunt's eyebrows went up. "When did you become a woman?"

"This morning; before I hurt my ankle."

"Oh, Attitash! I'm sorry your first power-flows came so far away from your mother!"

After we arrived in the moon-lodge, Aunt heated water for my cleansing and sang the new-woman song. Aunt First Star poured warm water over me and it washed into the pit. My woman-place felt clean and the sphagnum moss soft. I lay back on the bench and slept.

When I awoke, Nippa'uus was settling behind the trees. Aunt First Star brought bread and hot tea. "Willow-bark for your ankle," she said, "snakeroot for your life-flow pain." She gave me the bitter tasting black tea. "The warriors have arrived at my fire. They are preparing for their attack on the cloth-men. The power of your life-flow would interfere with their decisions, so you must stay here."

This was the first time I had been excluded from a council. I felt proud of my strong spirit, but I wanted to see Papa and Uncle Seekonk.

"Shall I send Seafoam to stay with you?" she asked.

I shook my head. Even though Seafoam and I used to have long talks when troubled and laugh together when happy, I did not want to hear that Black Whale was making eyes at her.

"Has Black Whale returned?" I asked. My face flushed hot; Aunt might realize my interest.

She brushed my hair back from my eyes. "He and the other young men are camped where they can watch the cloth-men."

"So where are the Strangers now?"

"Their small wind-canoe is still there and Hopamoch thinks some are camping on the beach tonight. Before Nippa'uus rises tomorrow, our men will attack and drive them away!"

Papa and Black Whale would be facing the Stranger's firesticks. Through the smoke hole I could see the stars fading. I opened the flap to look outside. Quinne Keeswush—the long moon of early winter—was low in the sky where Nippa'uus had gone. Footsteps crunched in the snow, and I could see our men running down toward the Big Salt Water. The tall bows they carried made frightening shadows on the snow. Looking around the moon-lodge, I found a pile of soft leather strips, used to make a pouch to catch life-flow. Filling one with sphagnum moss, I arranged it against my woman-place. Grandmother would make a new pouch just for me. This one chafed my thighs, but would work.

Then I remembered how our woman-healer had fixed an ankle. Taking two more strips, I put moss against the tender part of my ankle and wound the strips around my ankle and foot. Holding my branch as a crutch, I tried stepping. It was bearable. Wrapping myself in my warm furs, I banked the fire, and quietly hobbled along the men's trail in the snow in the dim light of stars and the fading moon.

A short time later, I heard the shuu-ush of the Big Salt Water as the incoming tide arrived on the snowy shore. A fire cast a circle of light, making shadows of the Strangers as they moved slowly about. They had made a barricade of tree branches and brought their pots and weapons out, laying them on the sand. Their little wind-canoe was in shallow water, bobbing about as the tide brought it closer.

I stopped well behind where our men were hidden behind low bushes. Their battle song—high pitched and loud—broke the silence. Our men rushed down, singing the words of attack and shooting their arrows at the Strangers. The fire revealed most of the Strangers running into the barricade, arrows whistling around them. Then they called out to others behind the pile on the sand. These Strangers ran into the shallow water, taking cover in the little wind-canoe.

My heart rattled like a woodpecker drilling. The Strangers were separated from most of their firesticks. A few of their cloth coats hung on the barricade, full of arrows. The thunderclap from a firestick tore through the air. I struggled to see all our warriors. It was impossible without the light of Nippa'uus to know which shadow belonged to whom. The Strangers in the wind-canoe yelled at the ones on shore. A rough tumble of words came back from the Strangers in the barricade. More shouting songs burst from our men, bows twanging and arrows flying, as the tide slowly brought the little wind-canoe into shore. Firesticks were cracking and some of our men began to move back into the safety of the forest, but Uncle Seekonk stayed behind a tree—pulling his bow and continuing to shoot arrows. A loud burst hit the tree he hid behind. Bark and splinters flew. Then he sang the war song, letting us—and the Strangers!—know he was well. All our warriors came back into the woods, and with an ease to my heart, I saw Black Whale meet them. Reluctantly, I turned to go before I was discovered. When I looked back, the Strangers were fleeing in the small wind-canoe, turning northwest towards Patuxet. I hobbled back to the moon-lodge.

Aunt First Star was standing outside when I arrived. "Attitash! What are you doing out here?"

"Just looking at Quinne Keeswush moon going down," I said innocently.

"Come inside!" she ordered. Then softer, "How is your ankle?"

I showed her my wrap, and she felt it approvingly. "If you can heal yourself, you can learn to heal others. Tell Seafoam I am going to see if I can help the men." Her voice trailed off, and I knew she was worried. I wanted to assure her the men were unharmed, but I dared not reveal I'd been out alone.

When the men entered later, we pummeled them with questions.

My little cousin Silver Fish was listening to his father intently. He finally asked excitedly, "Papa, did you kill any Strangers?"

9

"

Elisabeth

While we wait for the men to return, we may as well begin thy reading lesson." Desire picked up the Bible from the top of a trunk. "Do ye know the alphabet?"

My hands fluttered with excitement. I would hold a book—I would learn to read! "I can say the ABCs. I learned them when my brothers did."

"Look then," she pointed. "See the 'A' in Adam? Like a church steeple." Desire took her first fingers on both hands and put them together with her other fingers bent. I did the same.

"Good. Now 'B'." She turned the page. "Here, 'Behold'."

I traced the 'B' with my finger. "Looks like a honey bee."

Desire flicked the pages. "Here's 'C', for Cain." She studied the sign. "C used to be a circle, but Abel murdered Cain and the circle got cut open."

Sinister C. Easy to remember.

"And now E. See it here? E in "Eve" and thy name begins with E."

I traced the tiny sign. "B with the side removed?"

Desire smiled. "Listen to this." She held the Bible closer and read slowly, "*And Adam knew Eve, his wife; and she conceived and bore Cain.* Ye understand about men 'knowing' their wives?"

I giggled in assent; then protested as Desire closed the Bible.

"More please," I begged. "Father is away and Mother is distracted."

Desire's blue eyes searched my pleading face.

"Remember A, B, C, and D? Here, in Psalm 55, *Attend unto me, and hear me,*" Desire read. "See A?"

"Yea, I see A, but where's the passage about Satan tempting Jesus?"

"It must be in one of the Gospels." Desire began leafing through the New Testament. I was trying to look over her shoulder when I heard my name. Whirling around I found my mother, stony faced.

"What are ye doing?" I could not answer. Deceit was one thing; I could not lie or surely my soul would be in peril.

I followed Mother back to our household where she began groping beneath our mattress. I knew from experience to hold my hands out to her. She pulled out the rod. Whack! I squeezed my eyes shut to hold my tears and protests inside. Mayhap the rod would cleanse my soul. Struggling to compose my face, I opened my eyes.

Aunt Agnes held Humility close to her breast, her hand around the child's ears.

"She breaks the Fifth commandment to honor her father and me." Mother said to Aunt Agnes, and then turned back to me. "Elisabeth, I must mold thee to be obedient! Ye would displease thy husband, if ye could find a husband!"

My tongue was silent, but my mind was shouting. *I don't want a husband if he would not want me to read.*

Mother put the rod back under the bed. "Tell me why ye used Mistress Carver's ward to teach thee to read."

"Desire offered to." I put my hands under my apron. I would not let Mother know how much they hurt. "What is the harm, Mother?"

"Stop questioning me!" Mother sputtered, then commenced to cough harshly. "Who do ye think ye are? Ye are Elisabeth Tilley; we are none but common folk. Desire Minter must be laughing at thee with thy high minded ideas. Just because ye are no longer in England, ye are not transformed into a lady." Mother looked over at the Carver household. "Does Mistress Carver know ye involved Desire in thy scheme?"

No answer would satisfy Mother. I wanted to say, "We are not in England anymore. I will be transformed. Reading God's Word is a godly act. I will break Satan's power over me!" But instead, I meekly offered, "I beg your forgiveness for not seeking your permission, Mother," and turned away, afraid she would see me cry.

"Elisabeth, here is the mending." Mother grabbed my arm. "Ye have work to do." She let go and I picked up the basket. "Do not let thy left hand take over!" She coughed again, sounding too much like father since he caught chill.

I took up the needle in my right hand and painstakingly began stitching. At home I would have found an excuse to run to the meadow and vent my feelings where only sheep would hear.

Aunt Agnes spoke up quietly, as though she expected only Mother to be listening. "I intend for Humility to read."

Mother put down her mending and looked at Aunt Agnes. "Humility would not know who she is, or what she is."

"Well, none of us knows that. We are not at home. We will never see home again! We don't even have a home yet, except this foul ship. There is no hearth fire, not enough food, no way to properly bake bread, nor properly do anything. We sleep listening to almost a hundred other people snore. " Aunt Agnes paused and drew a long breath. "Our husbands were cloth workers, now they will be planters,

Joan. We may have servants ourselves! Humility may need to know how to read. Perhaps Elisabeth and Humility could rise to become gentry—mistresses instead of good-wives like us!"

Mother looked about her to see who might be listening. "Agnes, ye have been too long confined on this ship."

WE WORKED IN tense silence amidst the hum of people around us. Outside the wind blew and the Mayflower rocked. Finally, a call came down the hatch that the shallop was sighted. Mary, Constance and Priscilla hailed me and I followed them through steerage to the Main Deck. The men waved and shouted as they clambered out, dragging their weapons and a few geese.

"We found a place to make our home," Governor Carver announced. "A veritable plantation—fields already cleared, praise God!"

"And it has sufficient depth of water for our ship to anchor through the winter," Master Winslow added. He drew a great arc in the air. "We sailed along the circle of this cape—Cape Cod—'til we sailed north instead of west. There we found a harbor with plenteous fields before the hills rise up filled with tall trees."

How could this wild land already be tamed into fields? Humility began demanding attention so I took her to see the goats. We passed through the crowd of men shaking snow off their wet corselets. They gathered around Captain Standish, drinking ale, loudly talking about their first encounter with the savages.

I was edging toward the goats, when John called out to me, "Here's some corn. I know the little one likes to feed them." The goats bleated in anticipation. Humility laughed in delight as I let Penelope eat from my flat palm. When the goat tried to lick Humility's hand, however, she reached for me to pick her up, while Penelope bleated for more.

"This is the last, ye greedy goat," John Howland brought over one more handful.

"Where did you find corn? Is it growing in the fields?"

"Nay, all harvested. The savages had hidden a kettle. God was with us indeed." He tossed the remains of the corn back into the basket. "Master Carver says we must return like amount to them next year when we harvest the seed. Did you get the storm here?"

"Yea, it felt like we were back in the middle of the sea again." The muscles in my legs clenched in memory. "What was it like in the shallop?"

"Like a rock tumbling down a hillside! We had to pull the sails down, and then our rudder broke." He made a rowing motion, muscles bulging through his sleeves. "Only way to save ourselves and get to land was to row. But I knew we would not perish because—"

I interrupted, "Because you've already been in the sea and God saved you. Your father should have named you Jonah!"

John laughed heartily and it pleased me.

"Captain Standish was talking about a 'first encounter'" I said, "What kind of encounter?"

"Why, a battle!" John Howland held out his corselet which he'd slung over his shoulder. "See this hole in the quilting? 'Twas an arrow."

"A real arrow?" He did not look injured. "Are you hurt?"

"God's truth. A real arrow." He grinned broadly. "Nay, none of us was hurt. We all were behind the barricade or hiding in the shallop. I'd hung my corselet on the barricade before bedding down on boughs. The barricade saved us, but our corselets carry the tale of the battle."

"When? How?"

"The second day out, it was still dark as we were prepared to load our weapons into the shallop. They lay in a pile on the beach when there came a strange cry." He closed his eyes and made a most hideous noise: "Woach woach ha ha hach woach."

Humility set up a wail that almost matched his and struggled in my arms. "You frightened her!" I put my hands over her mouth and her screams subsided into sobbing.

"Hush, hush. I'm sorry!" John attempted to pat her shoulder. She wiggled out of his reach, but stopped wailing. "One of our company by the fire came running into the barricade and cried, 'They are men! Indians! Indians!' Then their arrows came flying amongst us."

"Did you shoot them?"

"How? We were in the barricade, and our arms were on the beach. Captain Standish, having his snaphance ready, made a shot."

"What's a snaphance?"

"Why, it's a flintlock musket. Standish is the only man to own one. It strikes the powder, so you do not have to light the slow burning matches and can shoot quickly." John gestured to where Captain Standish was shouting and waving his arms about to all who would listen. "We did bring back eighteen arrows, this long." He held his hands as wide as his shoulders. "with brass, hart's horn and eagle claw points," he said.

"Did you see any heathens? Were any killed?"

"We could not see much—they stayed in the trees, and it was not light. We don't know if any were hit, but one stepped out from a tree to shoot. His bow was almost as tall as you." John pointed to my cheek. "I made a run—dodging arrows—to bring our arms back from the beach. That's when I saw him."

I tried to imagine running through arrows with eagle claw points. "Were you not afraid?"

John laughed. "I took a shot at him, hitting the tree so the bark flew. He ran from the tree, but he may be wounded."

As he spoke, I looked to see Master Bradford in close conversation with his foster father, Elder Brewster. None of the men gathered with Standish seemed to notice, but I saw William Bradford cover his face with his hands.

"Hush, John," I whispered back to him with my finger over my mouth, casting my eyes toward the sad tableau. He followed my glance with questioning eyes. I leaned toward him to keep my voice low. "Master Bradford's wife died."

John Howland quickly silenced the others. Even Captain Standish was quiet. At last Master Bradford put his hands down and asked in a barely audible voice, "Did none search for her?"

Elder Brewster's face gave the reply. Master Bradford gave an anguished cry. Elder Brewster helped him to his feet and led him to his empty bed. When Elder Brewster returned to the other explorers, they learned the awful truth. Dorothy Bradford had fallen into the sea and drowned.

Nearly a week earlier, we had awakened to a wet snow on the topside. The furled sails were glazed with heavy ice. I'd found Mistress Bradford standing near the porthole, again caressing the smooth wood on the little bow our men had taken from the heathen grave. As I do too often, I abandoned gentle behavior and forwardly asked the mistress if I could see the toy. She kindly showed it to me, and I stroked the smooth wood. The feel made me close my eyes, and when I did my mind showed me the heathen maid—as clearly as in my dream. Her face was flushed with anger and her mouth saying words I could not understand. It seemed she was pulling the bow away from me, but when I opened my eyes, it was Mistress Bradford holding the bow firm. Tears filled her eyes as she wrapped it in cloth. My apology sounded empty to my own ears and I'm sure worse to hers. Mistress Bradford abruptly turned and walked away. I was left to pray for my redemption, but 'twas not til she drowned, that I wondered if my curse had passed to Dorothy Bradford. I could not rub from my mind the sight of her ballooned skirts disappearing into the water.

John now joined the other men who were gathered around Stephen Hopkins, sharing a bottle. Constance and Desire approached me. "Father let me have the small bottle to distract us from sorrow," Constance whispered. "Or celebrate that the heathen did not kill us."

I had not tasted aquavit since The Cur died.

"There's nay wrong with strong drink when ye are grieving," Desire announced as she took a sip. "It helps bring the tears along with prayers."

"How do ye know so much about strong drink, Desire? I have never seen anyone drinking aquavit before boarding the Mayflower," I murmured.

"My mother's husband indulges too much," she answered abruptly.

Though I slept a dreamless sleep that night, next morning I woke with a headache. Two lives lost. Master Fuller's servant Goodman Button had died of scurvy, and now Mistress Bradford. As I lay there, I could hear the tiny cries of Oceanus and Peregrine and was reminded of the regenerative power of God for His Chosen People.

10

Attitash

I listened to the scraping sound of Mama's wet stone sharpening her quahog shell. The dark purple streaks around a white center could make beautiful wampum and adornment, but this one was a tool. Once sharp, Mama carefully cut my hair. My ears felt cold and exposed. Everyone would know I was a woman now. I held myself erect and breathed the sage smoke Grandmother offered me, singing with her the prayer I'd learned as a little girl.

"You are no longer a little girl with her hair flying," Mama said softly. "When your hair grows back, you will be ready to have your own daughter or son."

I was almost ready—and our People counted on me— to bring new life. But now I no longer felt assured that the man I loved would plant his seed in me. If Black Whale no longer wanted me, I would be expected to settle for someone else—but I could not. Shimmering Fish had been stopping by our fire but despite his tall, muscled body and quick tongue, I only thought of Black Whale.

Taking Little Fish in his cradleboard, I hung it on a branch while I chopped wood. When my work was done, I molded balls out of snow and threw them. Little Fish laughed as Suki jumped about, trying to grasp a ball of snow with her teeth. I tossed a high one and Black Whale's dog appeared—jostling with Suki to catch it. Forgetting to hide the relief in my face, I welcomed Mowi—then Black Whale.

He gave back my smile. "I'll show you how to throw a

long way, Attitash!"

"Kwe, welcome back!"

"And good to be here when you're smiling! I haven't seen you smile since before I found you covered in snow with a bad ankle." Black Whale moved closer and his eyes went to my newly exposed neck. "How long will it take to grow back?"

I stepped back to hide from him my wish to have him touch my neck. "Why do you care?"

Instead of answering, Black Whale boldly reached down to test my ankle, and I felt the heat of my face would melt all the ice crusted on my fur hood.

I wanted to ask if he'd gone back to see Seafoam, but instead pretended to kick him with my good foot. "Don't think I have no strength, Black Whale. I am a strong woman now."

Little Fish crowed and Black Whale took the cradle-board off the tree. "What are these women doing to you, Little Fish? You're ready to leave the board!" He unlaced the leather as Little Fish wiggled in his eagerness to escape, shrieking with delight when Black Whale lifted him up.

"So what did you and Uncle Seekonk find?" I asked over the laughter as he swung Little Fish back and forth. A shadow crossed his face.

"We found them," he said. But before he could say more, Uncle Seekonk arrived. "You know my whistle," Black Whale whispered and left for his mother's fire.

After greeting the families, Uncle Seekonk reached out to stroke Ice Feathers' soft cheek. Black Whale's intentions pricked at my mind like pine needles as Uncle Seekonk wiped his mouth and settled into his tale.

"The big wind-canoe is at Patuxet," he began.

Papa shook his head in disbelief. "How did it get there? The storms have blown so hard, we thought it would be at the bottom of the sea."

"The spirits allowed them to survive. The cloth-men came ashore in their small canoe. They walked about and now are cutting trees. It looks like they are building a neeshwetu."

His words hit like icy rain. We thought our warriors had driven the Strangers away, but they remained in our land—building homes.

"The cloth-men never build!" Grandmother cried. "Never. They have always stayed on their big wind-canoes, and they have always gone back across the Big Salt Water!"

"These are different men, wife's mother; different from all the cloth-men you have seen. They dress the same, they talk the same, they even act the same, but they brought women and children. They do not run away. And they are building." Uncle Seekonk lowered his eyes from Grandmamma; respectful, but also as if he would close the flap on his words.

I heard Black Whale's whistle and slipped out, Quinne Keeswush moon floated in her almost-full ball between clouds. I saw Black Whale just inside the trees and walked slowly towards him. We met and he took one of my hands in his as we walked into the woods.

"How did you find me when I was injured?" I asked.

"When I came to the tall oak—the one with a face like an old man—I saw the furrow in the snow. I thought it was some injured animal." He laughed. "I had not tracked anyone who used her bottom to move! Then I saw the breath hole of the bear. I looked down and could see the bear's fur inside!" Black Whale's hand was warm on mine. "When I stepped back from the bear's hole, I heard breathing behind me. Your furs were so covered with snow that I did not know it was you."

"Were you frightened?"

"Not for myself, only that you were badly hurt. You are stubborn and might not tell me if you were." Black Whale walked a bit faster, and his words kept pace with his feet. "I was not waiting for gratitude, but you acted as though you wished I'd go away!"

"I do thank you, Black Whale." I stopped walking and put my hands outside his, holding his big hands in my smaller ones. "I wanted no one else. I know I'm stubborn; if I were not, I might be a weak, whimpering girl."

"If I ever have to rescue you again, you'd better be more willing." He smiled; then his face grew solemn. "Attitash, we are caught in a strange season. I will leave on my vision quest soon. If the Storm Spirits allow me to return, we shall see what our new neighbors are up to."

"Neighbors?" I tried to think of another tribe or clan that had arrived.

"Ahhe, the Cloth-men—the Strangers." He let go of my hand and knocked a snow-laden branch from a tree. "Uncle Seekonk and I watched them go back and forth in their little canoe. Some men are sleeping on shore; some spend the night in the big wind-canoe. We saw their women, Attitash. They don't have dog hair on their faces like their men. Their faces look almost red, like they've been too close to the fire. They even have little babies."

"Babies?" I tried to picture a Stranger's newborn. "What do they look like?"

"Like Ice Feathers, like Little Fish. But covered up in their cloth. Even their heads."

"Did you see a girl or maybe a woman …" My heart had begun to flutter like the three-note-bird. "…with eyes like quiet water?"

Black Whale stared at me. "We couldn't see their eyes. Why do you ask?"

I dug into the snow with my fur-lined moccasin. Black Whale might think I wanted the Strangers to stay if I described how the girl had appeared.

He waited. If Black Whale had been impatient, I would

have kept all my secret. But his quiet face and silent tongue led me to reveal it. "I saw a strange girl...in the surface of the pond."

"A vision?" His voice was edged with disbelief.

"Ahhe. A vision. She did not seem to cause trouble; she seemed troubled." How could I explain to Black Whale the look in the strange girl's eyes-like-quiet-water? "The vision gazed into my eyes—not with rudeness, but as if she were my friend."

"A friend?" Black Whale grimaced as if I had described spoiled food. "Did you take your vision to your grandmother?"

"I'm waiting to learn more." My story seemed like a fantastic tale told at night-fire to amuse. Wishing to distract him, I spoke without thinking. "Has Seafoam ever had a vision?"

"Seafoam?" Black Whale's brows drew together. "How would I know? Everyone has visions. Ask her, not me."

"Uncle Seekonk said you found her pretty now." My voice was so small I wondered if he could hear me.

Black Whale astonished me by laughing. "Of course she's pretty now that she's reached her full woman-power! Don't you think she's pretty, even with her hair cut?"

I did not answer. Black Whale took my hands again. "Seafoam is pretty. You are pretty. Seafoam is bright. You are bright. Seafoam is strong. You are strong. But you are stubborn and have visions I don't understand." Black Whale squeezed my hands and brought them to his lips. "I can't tell you or anyone else why I dream about you and not about Seafoam." He grazed my fingers with his lips. "You have a glint in your eyes, a bright spirit. When I get back from my vision quest, I'll play the flute I've been making for you. I'll dance the rabbit dance with you...if you want me to."

I leaned into him again; wishing I had resisted my need

to have Black Whale put the lid on my pot of jealousy. If he played his flute for me, my family would know that he wanted to be my husband. "Ahhe. I do want you." I reached my arms up around his waist, feeling his warm greased skin under his furs.

Black Whale cupped my face in his hands. I could not see much of him in the moonlight, but I did not need to. I breathed in his face, holding his smell of wood smoke, goose grease and a peculiar sharpness—his own male scent. Black Whale leaned over and touched my forehead with his lips. Then he reached inside the fur hood, took my hair in his hands and gently tilted my head back, bringing my mouth to his. The warmth spread from my mouth down to my breasts and then through my belly as he kissed me again. He pulled me hard against him, and I buried my face in his neck.

"Black Whale," I whispered.

"Attitash, my sweet, strong girl," he whispered back.

"Not a girl, a woman!" I protested, giggling. For a moment we stood, smiling at each other until he pulled me to him again and kissed my mouth. Sliding his finger inside my furs, he touched bare skin at my waist. Slowly his thumb moved over my ribs, and I felt my breathing bump against his hand. Our mouths had found each other again, my tongue rising to his until Mowi woofed and bumped me.

I pushed Black Whale away, laughing. "Mowi thinks I must go back inside."

"My dog is too jealous," he said and gave me another kiss before parting. It was not a brief kiss.

When I crawled into my sleeping furs, White Flower was awake.

"Where have you been for so long," she demanded.

"Out."

"Out where? Didn't you get cold? Was Black Whale with you?"

"White Flower, go to sleep. I'm tired. I did not get cold. No more questions."

She kept asking, but I pulled the furs over my ears. I licked my lips again, tasting Black Whale on my mouth. When White Flower finally breathed evenly, I moved my fingers over my body, retracing where his fingers had been, and beyond to where they someday would go. If he survived his vision quest alone in the snow and the cold Papsaquoho Moon.

11

Elisabeth

The red and yellow curtains hanging around the bed moved toward me. I tried to crawl away under the covers, but the curtains followed me, fastening like snakes about my neck. Trying to cry out, I tugged at the curtains, but they grew tighter until I had no breath left.

"Drink, Elisabeth, we must break the fever!"

Ice in my bones...Ice in my heart...Could not drink...lips sore and cracked...throat on fire...head so hot...eyes coals burning my frozen cheeks...hands frozen with cold. It had been winter forever... Had I survived?

"Elisabeth! Sit up, drink some hot tea!"

I struggled up...sipped a little hot tea...bitter...I could scarce swallow it...I lay back...felt someone on the pillow beside me...It hurt to turn my head...My neck felt the size of a horse's.

The curtains turned into a huge lump, gathering on my chest. Someone was wrapping them tight about me. "No, no, no" I screamed, but no one heard me. I turned my head enough to see Desire. She looked like a withered old woman. Like my grandmother had when I was a little girl. Bed curtains had wrapped themselves about her neck too and she was struggling to break free.

"No, no, no." Desire was not heard either.

I looked back and little Jasper More was leaning

against the bed; then Mother leaned over me. Father was just behind her. I knew who they were, even though the bed curtains were wrapped around their faces.

"What do you want, Mother?"

"Nothing, I want nothing. We have all we want."

"Elisabeth! Mistress wants me to change your shift... You're wringing wet!" Who was talking? I could not open my eyes. It sounded like Carver's servant, Jane .

Don't touch me...It hurts when you touch me...She could not hear my croaking whisper...or didn't care...I resisted...but my body was too weak...She pulled my shift off...wiped my body with a cloth.

The sea washed over me. It felt cool and lovely. I hung onto a halyard and looked about. There were dolphins swimming, and whales. A whale bumped me and threw me back on the Mayflower. I looked down in the water and saw John Howland swimming with the whale. The salt water filled my throat and stung.

"Elisabeth, we're going to the boat...to Master's new house."

I must have still been dreaming...It sounded like John Howland...It felt like John Howland...smelled like John Howland...I did not want to wake up.

"Don't cry. Desire is coming too. Master is carrying her to the boat. Our new house is ready. Easy, now."

The sun hurt my eyes...even while closed...as we bumped across gently moving floors...He wrapped my cloak closer about me.

"Hang on, we're at the ladder. We're going down to the long boat." Even in a dream, it was difficult to cling to him. My arms dangled like a poppet's.

We thumped into a boat...I opened my eyes...This

dream didn't end with eyes opening...He was still here...I closed them again...drank in John Howland's warmth and the sun on my face.

"We'll be there soon, little Elisabeth...Hang on."

Did I feel his lips on my cheek...ever so briefly?

Mother, Father, Uncle Edward, Aunt Agnes, even Dorothy Bradford were all gathered on shore. Where was Jasper now? Always running off! But here were his sisters Ellen and Mary More! Jumping about, jumping so high they did not touch the ground again. Laughing as I'd never seen them. Oh, there was Jasper. Grabbing his hands, they formed a circle and began playing ring around the rosy. But instead of all falling down, they all fell up. And kept going up. Mother, Father and the others fell up too. Mother reached down to me, "Elisabeth! Dear Heart, come with me." I tried to reach up to her, but my body sank back and my arms fell down. "Don't leave me! Don't leave me!" But they didn't hear my cry. The snakes were at my throat again.

Attitash

"Cloth-men are sick. Canoe after canoe brought sick to land who cannot even walk." Quadequina, our Massasowet's brother, had just returned from watching Strangers at Patuxet. "Many have gone to their spirit world."

"How many have they buried?" Papa asked.

"We don't know for certain, but at least twenty five or more." Quadequina accepted a small bowl of stew from Mama.

"Evil spirits killed all our People at Patuxet. Of course they would kill Cloth-men," Mama murmured. "Do these grave desecrators give their own people a sacred burial?"

"They have very strange Gods." Quadequina breathed in the fragrant stew and took a piece of meat. "Instead of burying in daylight and thanking Kiehtan for creating life, they bury at night. The bodies are wrapped in their cloth; they don't cover the body with sacred red ochre."

Hearing about the Strangers burying at night raised bumps on my arms. The picture of their violation of the little boy's grave burned in my mind. No wonder the girl with eyes-like-quiet-water looked troubled in my vision, living with such people. I had not told Black Whale that I saw her on land and the vision was real. Even when—if— he returned, I might never tell. All the Strangers might be dead. I felt a small sadness for the strange girl. But the evil spirits might be attacking Black Whale, and I must use all my heart's feelings to send protective prayers.

"Attitash, watch what your hands are doing! Now you'll have to re-weave that row." Mama put out her hand, took my basket and pulled out the row. When I brushed my eyes but did not answer, she put the basket down and looked at me. "Are you worried about Black Whale?" The smoke from the fire pushed through the hole above and hissed against the spitting sleet as Mama waited for my reply.

"Ahhe, I am worried he won't return." I took back the basket and began weaving carefully. "I prayed to Nippa'uus every morning since he left." I kept my eyes on the strips of bark this time.

"And now?"

"This morning Nippa'uus sent us little light." I looked up the smoke hole where sleet turning to snow whirled. "Without Nippa'uus, I could not pray to make him safe."

"It is easy to be brave when all is well, but strong women don't wait for Nippa'uus to shine." Mama's fingers flew as she wove.

"Mama, does his mother talk to her Spirit?"

"What makes you ask if Green Feather prays?"

"Well, if she does, her Spirit must not listen." I finished

my row, checking that it was tight. "Green Feather must be praying for his return, but she told 'Rushes they should accept that he might not come back."

"You cannot solve his mother's problems." Mama jerked at her basket as if it were a problem woman and put it down. "It is too soon to worry, but Green Feather worries anyway." Little Fish was playing with sticks too close to the fire. Mama held her arms out, and he dropped into her lap.

"And what's his sister supposed to do?" My voice sounded like White Flower's, it was so high. "Brown Beaver is making a flute for her, but Green Feather won't let her talk to him about..."

Mama shushed me with a look as the flap stirred.

"The wind spirits are angry today..." The rest of Green Feather's words were lost to us as she stepped in, the wind spirits blowing behind her.

"Green Feather," Mama's voice changed to a soft trill. "Come in. I am just brewing some tea."

"Close the flap and sit down, Sister," Uncle Seekonk invited as he came forward from Aunt Blue Sky's fire. "The wind spirits will knock you down out there."

"Better me than my son!" Green Feather closed the flap but remained standing. "Where did you leave him for his vision quest, Seekonk? Do the Narragansett have him?"

"Sit with me, husband's sister." Aunt Blue Sky moved over and patted the bench.

Green Feather hesitated, but finally sat and drank the tea Mama served. "What would you have me do, brother?" she asked Uncle Seekonk.

"Be calm, Sister. Tonight we sing the prayers for safety." He spoke to her softly. "Black Whale is well prepared. You know I have done everything for my clan nephew that can be done. He would build a strong shelter-lodge for himself. He knows what to do when the storm spirits are angry. He listens to the earth and to our brothers and sisters in the woods and water. If the Narragansett come, he is strong and young."

Uncle Seekonk turned to me. "Attitash, is your heart following Black Whale?" I nodded and tried to make my face calm to reassure Green Feather. "You will help us sing, then" he said.

I trembled and put my hands to the fire. If my heart was not strong, then my song might not be heard. But I needed to help Green Feather regain hope. She had given life to Black Whale, and he needed her courage to bring him back safely.

"I will sing," I said.

Wrapping my furs around me, I ventured through the snow to the edge of the woods. I waited beneath the trees, my eyes closed. Snow blew around me. At first I could see nothing but snow behind my eyelids, then I felt as though I were going into a lake in springtime. Instead of being surrounded by water, however, I was surrounded by singing spirits whirling in the air. Slowly the snow swirled into a shape, a two legged shape, white except for black hair gathered in a topknot. He was sitting in his snow covered shelter, rubbing his sticks together. A flame caught and he blew on it until the branches glowed. Relief filled me, settling in my chest and belly. The wind spirits took away the sight, and I opened my eyes to more snow.

Blowing on my lips and nose to warm them, I went to our Massasowet's fire where all were gathering to pray.

"Before we pray," our Massasowet announced as we settled down, "We will hear from my brother Quadequina and the other watchers at Patuxet."

"Thank you, brother Ousamequin," Quadequina said. "We have had watchers at night as well as during the day. We saw many of the cloth-men living in a longhouse. A few smaller houses are built of sticks, with grass on top."

Quadequina's hands made an angled shape, not round like our homes. "Twice the grasses on the roofs have caught fire and might have burned if the snow and rain had not come to put out the fire." We laughed grimly at the idea of putting grass on the roofs instead of woven reed mats.

"We have seen many adults and some small bodies buried at night. A few boys and girls are yet alive. Most of the cloth-men must be sick as we see only a handful of them walking about." Quadequina held up a few fingers. "Six men and one woman is all we see gathering firewood and hauling water. The warrior who walks like a strutting turkey and always carries his firestick has not gotten sick."

"The one that fired at us?" our Massasowet asked.

"Yes, the one with the quick firestick. He walks about with it, will not put it down. The others call him 'capan.'" He paused and listened to the wind spirits. "The spirits are angry that the cloth-men have come to Patuxet. The spirits have killed many."

"Ahhe, the Cloth-men are weakening." Our Massasowet spoke to us with a voice stronger than the wind outside. "We had hoped the spirits would drive them away or take them all to the spirit world. But they stay here; the storm spirits won't let their big wind-canoe go back." Our Massasowet's mouth was a firm line. "But we count only thirty men including some young. The spirits may be giving us a gift."

Grandmother's hands swept the air in frustration. "A gift? What kind of gift is this to receive? Strange creatures that steal even from our buried ones! They try to kill us and you call this a gift?"

"Hear me out, wise elder," our Massasowet responded, keeping his voice soothing. "We no longer have enough warriors to fight the Narragansett, and they will continue to rule us for many seasons. Already Canonicus—the Narragansett's Sachem—demands some of our hunt. Our young men are forced to paddle the Narragansett canoes for them. They tried to take your granddaughters—Attitash and White Flower!" His fury was barely contained in the tight set of his jaw. I wondered where our Massasowet's fury would have led had White Flower and I not been rescued! "There are even reports," he continued, "that the Narragansett are plotting to take me prisoner. We have only sixty warriors left here at Paomet, and the Narragansett have double that." He handed the pipe to his brother Quadequina who drew a breath and passed it on. "If the Cloth-men die from sickness, their firesticks would remain and could be used against the Narragansett."

A voice cried out. "If we could end the Narragansett' rule, we would be free forever!"

It was the voice of my captor! It was *Tisquantum's.* And still speaking false words, as if he were not using both us and the Narragansett for his own purpose. I willed my mouth to be quiet, but I could not control my banging heart. I looked around, but could not see him.

Papa took his own puff of pipe, keeping his eyes down as he asked, "How do we make the firesticks work?"

"Tisquantum knows how to fire them, Hopamoch." Our Massasowet nodded toward the back and then I saw Tisquantum, seated with other servants. My hands wanted to smother his breath; I clasped them together under my bent knees.

Papa did not respond, and I knew from the line of his mouth that he also did not trust Tisquantum. Would he listen to me when I told him of Tisquantum's betrayal? If only Black Whale would return safely—and soon.

"Lead us in the prayer of protection for young Black Whale," our Massasowet said to the Shaman. "And then we will pray for wisdom. We need a plan to use to our advantage the weakness the Spirits have brought to the Cloth-men."

As the Shaman placed his medicine pots carefully around him, the song leaders picked up their singing sticks. Grandmamma, Green Feathers and other women lifted their voices. Click, click, click, the sticks thrummed, and my whole body filled with the rhythm. When my breath filled my chest until my bones hurt, my voice soared with the song. It was as if it flew on its own wings and I merely listened. Beneath the words of the prayer were my own, not sung, but filling my song, "Black Whale, Black Whale, oh, Black Whale. Come home to me."

Elisabeth

"This is thy home, Elisabeth." Mistress Carver gently stroked my face. "With thy family gone," she said, using her fine white cloth to blot my forehead, "ye are as much a daughter to me as Desire has become."

Gone! A cavern opened up as I tried to comprehend that word, and pain filled the void. With deliberate will, I pushed the word away. My eyes followed Catherine Carver as she moved from my bedside, squeezing past a table and another bed to sit in her hearth chair. The entire wall on that end was taken up with the chimney and hearth where the maidservant, Jane, was adding wood to the fire with one hand, wiping tears from her cheeks with the other.

I looked for Desire and realized she was sleeping next to me, her breath shallow and her face white. The hollow place in my soul had grown. Everyone gone. If any yet lived, Mistress Carver would not be calling this my *home*.

The fire popped; something bubbled in a pot and the wind's shrill sighing came down the chimney. The smoke smelled sweet—wood smoke! I sat up in the bed but immediately lay back on the pillow as the room swam around me. I buried my head in the pillow to shut out the homely sounds and smells; there was no joy in the comforts of *home*.

A bit later, curiosity took hold and my hand crept out from the covers. A cold chill slithered through the clapboard wall. Something warm touched me and I drew back. "Liv-buss!" There was no mistaking the little voice. Was this her spirit? Was her spirit saying my name when the child had not spoken a word yet while alive? "Liv-buss!" the voice again entreated. The touch on my hand was light as a fly landing. I opened my eyes to see Humility standing beside me; one thumb in her mouth, the other tracing my fingers. Humility burst into a smile that brought sunshine into the little room and tears welling from my eyes.

"Humility!" Jane called and came to pick her up. "Don't wake Elisabeth up."

My fingers grabbed Humility's hand, and I let a small sigh of relief escape. "Leave her with me."

By late afternoon Mistress had helped me sit long enough to overcome the dizzies. I drank tea, Desire next to me. Mistress had just helped me back to bed when Master Carver and the young servant William Latham came in. John Howland followed and gave me a cautious smile. So, eight of us still lived.

"Has Elisabeth come to her senses yet?" Master asked his wife.

She laid a hand on his arm and nodded toward me. "She is herself again."

How could I be myself? I was an orphan—no mother, father, aunt, or uncle--and my sisters and brothers in England lost to me. I attempted to nod at Master Carver, but my neck did not seem connected to my head. I closed my eyes again.

Footsteps came toward the bed. "You're young and strong, Elisabeth. God won't let you be kept down."

I recognized John Howland's voice. If I had the strength, I would have asked him how he knew such a preposterous thing. God had let everybody else die. The bench creaked as he sat down.

"Up!" Humility's tiny voice forced me to open my eyes just enough to see through my lashes. Her arms closed around John Howland's as he picked her up.

"When did she…?" I could not finish.

"Start to talk?" John Howland tweaked Humility's nose. "After we all moved in here." He saw me glance at the small crowded house and pointed up the ladder. "William Latham and I sleep up in the loft since we moved from the Commonhouse."

"Is winter over yet?" I had so many questions on my mind that I had trouble sorting out which to ask.

"Just turned March." John gave me a searching look as if he had just met me at a market day. "You have a bit of pink in your cheeks." He reached out a finger as if to touch my cheek, then stroked Humility's instead. "They were almost gray when I carried you from the boat."

My body remembered his warmth as he carried me off the ship. My mind felt like a creaky old trunk lid being lifted. I could now recall Father and Uncle Edward dying… Mother coughing…Aunt Agnes wrapping her green shawl around me…Priscilla bringing me her mother's remedy for sore throat.

"Who lives?" My question hung. The noises of kettles, fire, Master and Mistress talking, all stopped.

The look of defiance I'd become accustomed to on Desire's face was still there, but now she seemed to struggle to maintain it. She set her tea cup down.

John gestured around the little room. "From this household, only Roger, the other servant, died. And little Jasper More."

So the dream of Jasper and his sisters was real. Just like the dream of my parents. I remembered Jasper coughing and feverish long ago. I attempted to look outside, but the shutters and door were closed against the cold. "Where is everyone else?"

John glanced toward door. "We have just three houses built so far. Most of the men live in the big Commonhouse. The families waiting for a house remain on the Mayflower—you remember living there all winter?"

It would take time to sort out dreams and reality, but I did remember there was more room on the ship after some of the men moved to shore after the Commonhouse was built. "Priscilla...?"

Setting Humility on the edge of my bed, John held her so she would not fall. "Priscilla lives at Brewsters' since all her family died."

"Even her little brother?"

He nodded, "She's the only one left."

"The others?" I took Humility's hands and clung.

John lifted his hands in a helpless gesture and looked to Mistress Carver. She answered, "Constance Hopkins lost no one." She tried to smile but it did not fit her face. "Mary Chilton lives, though she lost her parents. Brewsters are all well, like us, praise God." She took the pot from the fire and set it on the table.

My mind could not comprehend what they were telling me. Jane began setting trenchers on the table and brought one to me with a bit of cornbread. "Mistress Allerton and her babe died; Master Allerton and the other children survive." She bit her lip and abruptly asked, "Do you think you can eat?"

Humility scrambled off the bed, and John Howland turned around on the bench so he was at the table. I moved closer to the bench, my legs slightly forward so my knee touched his back. Even through my shift and two petticoats, I could feel the heat of him. The bit of corn bread I sopped seemed to be an alien plant in my belly. I determined that by the morrow I would be up.

Sleep came quickly in a smothering fog, but I did make it to the table next morning. After breakfast, John Howland took my hand and opened the door. The bright sun blinded my eyes and I closed them for a moment. "I thought..." I pulled air into my lungs until they hurt, so I could speak. "I did not know if....if you were alive."

"Of course I live. God saved me from the sea; nothing will take me." John squeezed my arm and I opened my eyes to see his smile. "Ye will get stronger every day if you walk and eat."

The ground was muddy and felt slippery under my stumbling feet. I sat down on the bench near the door and squinted into the sun. There were two other little houses, steep roofs covered with thatch, near ours. The large Commonhouse, where Mistress told me the men slept, was closer to the open fields. Men were at work there, cutting logs into the clapboard planks like the ones which formed the walls of Governor Carver's house. John Howland bid me stay in the warm sun with Desire and Mistress, and left to join the other men at work. He walked toward the cleared area surrounded by forest. Between the fields, a brook tumbled toward the sea.

"That's Brewsters." Mistress pointed to the house nearest ours. "Priscilla may be well enough to come out soon, God willing."

She held my arm and we walked a bit on the path from our houses down to the shore. I was chilled and fatigued in the short distance to where the muddy path gave way to sand sloping down to the sea. I leaned against Mistress, trying to take it all in. A wide stretch of beach was beaded here and there with large and small rocks. Some paces down the beach, a pile of rocks reached across the sand into the water. It resembled the stone fences at home but was too tumbled to have been built by human hands. Only fingers of the sea reaching up with high tide could form such a barrier. The Mayflower was barely visible out in the bay. It rose and sank with the swell of the waves, like a little toy.

"Are there any women and children still on the ship? Is Mary Chilton...?"

"Yea, Mary Chilton is with Mistress White." Desire coughed. "The babe Peregrine is well, and Resolved, too."

"Mary still has her sister and brothers back in England—like ye do." Mistress Carver touched her eyes with her handkerchief as she rose to go back inside. Desire, whose persistent cough grew worse, followed.

Mayhap Mary Chilton and I could go home on the Mayflower next spring, if others went back. I stayed on the bench with the sun on my face and was still there when the men arrived home for noon dinner.

"The Allerton house is almost done." John Howland sat down by me. "Did Mistress tell you we buried everyone up the hill? Nearly forty graves and still many sick."

"Could I go up to pay my respects when I'm stronger?"

"When you are strong enough to go about at night. We do not bury during daylight—we know the Indians watch us though we don't see them."

I struggled to make sense of his words. "But why not go to tend our graves?"

"There is little to tend. No markers. We don't want the Indians to know how weak we are now. If they see us burying so many—or see us mourning up there and then discover how many graves there are—they would believe we do not have the manpower to withstand an attack." John stood up from the bench. "Do not fret, Elisabeth. Those of us who live are the ones God chose to save." Or curse, I thought.

John pointed toward the edge of the forest, just beyond the clearing where they now worked on the logs. "We will make this a fruitful Promised Land. See back there at the edge of the wood? Plum trees!"

"Plum trees?" I squinted in the bright sun, seeing nothing but dark woods and bare branches of small bushes.

"Yea, look by the fields where the Indians grew their corn."

I looked, half expecting to see heathen tending a field, and saw some scrubby looking little trees. "How do you know they're plum? There are no leaves yet."

"We had some at home in Huntingdonshire, so I know the tree. My mother used to pick them." He had a distant look in his eye. "Huntingdonshire is not s' far from Bedford. Do you know it?"

I watched the white capped waves in the bay. "I never left Bedfordshire 'til we came on the Mayflower. But I've heard Father talk of Huntingdonshire. Did you have land?"

"Howlands don't have land." He looked along the horizon to the fields and woods again. "But here there is land aplenty!"

I tried to look at the frozen land through his eyes. The Commonhouse and four tiny houses were in a clearing which looked out on the sea; dense forests surrounded us beyond a snowfield. Under the snow and ice would there be green fields? I wondered why the Indians left this place if their crops were good. "Are the Indians near us now?"

"We've not seen any since we came to Plimoth but we've heard them and even seen their fires, so we know they watch us." He looked back at the Mayflower. "With little food and so much sickness all winter, we've had more to fear than arrows." As he spoke the wind grew worse, and his words flew back up the hill where everyone was buried.

"To be truthful, I never thought that God would take my…" I could not go on. My throat was seized. I wished I could have leaned into John as I used to lean into my father or Uncle Edward when I was a little girl. But John was neither father nor uncle.

A movement just inside the woods caught my eye. A heathen's face looked at me from between two branches. A streak of red paint went from his brow down over his eye. His hair, black as tar, was tied up in a topknot with string and a black and white feather. I started to point him out to John but he vanished before I could slow my heart enough to speak.

That night I tried to think of Bedfordshire to ease my mind; its sheep, wool, hot coal fires; its safety. Our houses here were so little; so defenseless. Sleep came at last, but in the middle of the night a dream interrupted. *The fur-covered boy holds Humility up, showing her the crescent moon in the sky. Humility laughs. Then wolf howls come from the woods. Humility opens her mouth and joins in the call.* I sat up to see Mistress Carver shushing Humility's cries.

12

Attitash

One wolf howling in the distant black night stirred my sleep. Black Whale's hand rested on my shoulder, and I snuggled against it. As sleep cleared from my head, I realized the hand was White Flower's. I slid away quickly and shook my little sister's arm. "White Flower! Move over; you're taking all the room."

White Flower gave me an angry look through the slits of her eyes. I shifted away slightly.

"What's wrong with you?" Her hurt look squeezed my breath.

"Nothing," I said.

I regretted pushing her out of my heart to make room for Black Whale. Putting my arm around White Flower as I had done every night of her life until this one, we snuggled until she fell back to sleep.

Again my thoughts drifted back to Black Whale. He'd left on his vision quest when the long-winter moon was a new crescent and now the waning moon had left us. Where was he sleeping, I wondered. Before we'd settled down to sleep that night, I'd asked Papa,' "Didn't the spirits like our singing? Black Whale has not come back."

"You sing like a wild bird, Attitash, like your mother does. She drew me in with her singing before you were born!" His face grew soft. "Remember how strong Black Whale is. When he was only twelve circles of the seasons, he could already fast from first light to early dark. He is well prepared to fast until his animal spirit finds him."

Papa pointed up through the smoke hole. "The clouds and snow have left us. Wapicummilcum—the river-ice-melting moon—will be here soon and bring Black Whale."

I heard the sister wolf howling again and gave up trying to get back to sleep. The first ray from Nippa'uus shone through the smoke hole. Perhaps the wolf was warning her pack that someone was approaching.

Papa must have heard the howls; he rose and went outside. I followed but stopped at the door flap and peeked through. When I saw Uncle Red Hawk and Papa together, I went to them.

"Black Whale was with us in Nauset, when Keeswush moon was full," Uncle Red Hawk told me before I could ask. "He had finished his vision quest and stopped to visit, but left us when the strange dog came."

Strange? Dogs were everywhere that our People were, but none of them was strange.

"Ahhe," said Uncle. "Seafoam called it "ghost dog.'" He took the jug of water I brought out and drank. I tried to remember the loving reassurances Black Whale had given me, but Seafoam's pretty face blotted out my memory.

"Where did the dog come from?" Papa asked.

"It must have belonged to the Cloth-men. We heard a firestick bang and the dog ran away. I sent Black Whale to track them and make sure the cloth-men and their dog went back to Patuxet." Uncle Red Hawk took another drink of water. "The dog had funny big ears that flopped down." Uncle flapped his hands under his ears. "Wouldn't that make a strange creature if she mated with Black Whale's Mowi?"

I laughed uneasily, "And Black Whale?"

"Black Whale's as eager to mate as—" Uncle Red Hawk began.

"—as a crazy dog," Papa finished.

Both whooped with laughter. I opened the flap and let their ignorant noise wake Mama. I did not see the men the rest of the day.

THE RIVER ICE WAS melting and it was time to make syrup. We women and girls were busy preparing the hollowed-out sticks to be used as spouts for catching sap.

That night at our fire, Grandmother announced it was time to hear again the story of the Great Celestial Bear in the night sky. I loved hearing of the stain from the slain Great Bear turning into the sweet sap of the trees.

When the story ended, I crawled under my furs where White Flower was already asleep. When I woke up later, there was no light, and the stars called me to go outside. Uncle Seekonk was standing out looking at the stars when I lifted the flap

"Look, Attitash! There's the Great Bear in the sky. He's just waking up! He's moving toward the Big Salt Water."

"I see it! What does it tell us, Uncle?"

He looked towards the woods. "I think it means Black Whale is moving home, ready to mate."

I watched the Great Bear and saw no movement, but wanted to believe there was hope. "Did Black Whale go to Patuxet?"

"Red Hawk said our watchers at Patuxet saw the Cloth-man's dog come back; the cloth-men were still lost, but Black Whale may have found them."

"Would Black Whale have killed the Strangers? Or—."

Uncle put his hand on my shoulder, and I knew I should not ask what he would not know. I'd just lifted the flap to go back in when I heard a soft wolf whoop and turned back. A silhouette was visible against the light of the moon. My eyes strained to make out a two-legged creature, carrying a bow and a pack on his back! It cleared the woods and came toward us, moving fast despite its burdens.

"Uncle! Attitash!"

Uncle ran to meet Black Whale, hugging him so hard they fell down in the soft snow like wolf cubs. I waited, warm with the sight. They stood up and brushed off the snow.

"You caught enough game for yourself and still brought meat back!" Uncle Seekonk picked up the heavy pack.

I started to follow Uncle back to our wetu, but Black Whale took my hand. "Wait."

Immediately, I was wrapped in Black Whale's arms, tasting his mouth, smelling his skin, feeling the strong muscles of his arms, Seafoam forgotten.

He held me out to gaze at me in the first rays of Nippa'uus. "My animal spirit came to me. The biggest deer, with a great rack of antlers." He brushed his hand through my hair, which nearly reached my shoulders. "Now I can have a wife."

"Ahhe, you are ready to be a father."

A frenzied barking rolled toward us and Mowi was all over Black Whale, licking, yapping, spinning, and licking again. Black Whale laughed and fell on Mowi rolling in the snow.

Such a flurry of hugging and talking when all our clans came to welcome Black Whale at his mother's fire! Black Whale pulled me to sit with him on the bench while he greeted them. While he talked, using his right hand to gesture, he kept his left hand around my shoulder. He did not mention dogs or Strangers' firesticks. His mother asked how he survived the blizzard; he let out a big breath and rubbed his eyes. "Let me tell you tonight. I'm too tired now!"

Green Feather shooed everyone out, including me. While Black Whale slept, I worked with his sister. We slashed a mark on the maple trees in the shape of flying geese. By late afternoon, Wind in the Rushes and I had placed most of the spouts to catch the liquid sweet. At the sound of Black Whale's soft whistle, 'Rushes smiled and waved me away.

I found him near the stream overflowing with melted snow. We moved beyond its noisy gurgling to where two trees grew entwined around each other—Trees-in-Love. Our kisses were interrupted by our words, and our words interrupted by more kisses.

"Attitash, you taste just like I remembered."

"Black Whale, you smell just like I remembered. I thought you were lost in the snowstorm!" I kissed him hard and long.

"I was; I heard you singing!"

He lifted me up, putting my legs around his waist, while he held my bottom. I leaned into his forehead, gazing into his eyes so that we looked at each other with owl eyes as little children do. He slid his hands inside my furs; his long strong fingers gently stroked the plumpness of my bottom. "I thought the Strangers might have killed you." I filled my chest with air so my breasts lifted up. He responded by tasting a nipple. I could not contain my sigh of pleasure. "You know I love you, Black Whale?"

"Ahhe, and you let me show you my love." He gently tweaked my nipple. "Does that feel good?"

"Hmm…mm." I swung my breasts so the other one bumped against his hand and he answered my need to feel both nipples tingle.

The air was cold where my furs and poncho were lifted up, but I felt very warm. I smelled the strong pine pitch of the Trees-in-Love he leaned against and felt the prickle of pine bark against my legs. "Black Whale."

"Mmmm" He pulled me to him, bent his head and flicked his tongue on my nipples. I arched my back in pleasure, and then sank back against him, my hands in his hair and my legs tight around him.

"Black Whale, your sister is waiting for me to hang the rest of our sap buckets."

"So, let her wait." He kissed me again. "'Rushes knows I just got home, and you'll be with me now."

"Mama will mind. My work isn't finished. Anyway, you haven't played the flute for me yet. Mama waits for you to signal your love. She waits for us to dance the rabbit dance."

"Soon." He kissed me again and took a strand of my hair, wrapping it around his finger, a wide smile filling his face.

I slid my legs to the ground and ran to help 'Rushes.

After a long day's work we settled at last by the big outdoor fire. Black Whale told how he was lost in the blizzard and heard my singing. He described following the Strangers' dogs almost to Patuxet. "On my way back, I tracked the Cloth-men. They seemed lost, and I could see their feet were badly damaged by the cold. I don't know if they found their way back to Patuxet."

That was all we needed to know. Black Whale was back with us, and the Strangers were so sick and helpless they would not be a threat. Now we could enjoy a tale.

Grandmother began her story. "*The wildcat is mean and ferocious. He has a short tail and big, long, sharp fangs, and his favorite food is rabbit.*" Grandmother's hands painted pictures as she talked.

"*One day when Wildcat was hungry, he said to himself, 'I'm going to catch and eat Mahtigwess, Great Rabbit, himself.'*"

We loved hearing the story many times. It was warm by the big fire; my soft deerskin poncho draped over my shoulders and lap. Black Whale's thigh moved closer to mine.

"*Great Rabbit made up his mind that he would use his magic power against Wildcat's strength.*"

As Grandmother built the story of Great Rabbit's clever tricks, Black Whale reached under my poncho and took my hand. As the story continued, he let go of my hand and slid his around my waist. He softly touched my ribs again, and I no longer heard anything Grandmother said. I did not dare to look at him or we would be teased.

When the story ended, he whispered to me to again meet him in the woods. He was at our Trees-in-Love near the running stream. Putting my hands inside the fur over his head, I felt the thick hair gathered in his topknot. Without asking, I pulled the thong from his topknot and ran my fingers through his hair, picking out pine needles and bits of leaves. Holding me close, he drew his fingers through my cropped hair. My thoughts had flown—I was all melting heat.

He took my hands again, but stepped back to look at me in the faint moonlight. "You are so pretty! I can't think when I'm with you!" He pulled me to him again and slid his hands down my hips toward the swelling of my woman place, but stopped. "Tomorrow, your family will hear my flute song and know I'm yours."

Elisabeth
"I am my beloved's and his desire is toward me."

As Desire read, I closed my eyes, and remembered my sister, Rose, listening to her husband read to her. Asking Desire where her name was in the Bible had led to this reading lesson.

"My parents chose my name from Isaiah," Desire answered. "But Father used to read this verse of King Solomon's to Mother. This one comes right after describing the woman's breasts as a cluster of grapes." We both giggled and Jane, stirring the pots, broke into a loud guffaw. Desire took a sip of tea to settle her laughter and continued. "Surely it influenced their search for the word 'desire' elsewhere." She smiled broadly, and picking up the Bible again, and flicked the pages. "Here 'tis the verse from Isaiah: *the desire of our soul is to thy name...with my soul have I desired thee in the night.*"

"I like the part about desiring the Lord in the night. It seems the Lord leaves me to Satan's wishes in my dreams."

"'Tis the same for me, Elisabeth." Desire took my hand. "I dream of a friend of mine from home. I have not seen her since she left Holland and went back to England a year ago. She..." Desire stopped, tears filled her eyes, and she let go of my hand. "In my dream, I hear the verse Solomon wrote." Desire paused and put her hands over her eyes. "I know not why it seems a temptation."

"Can you find the passage about Satan tempting Jesus?" I had been repeating, "Get thee behind me, Satan," to myself.

"I'll have to ask Mistress. Here, look at this." Desire leaned over the Bible, her hair swaying against it. "This tells about thy hair is as a flock of goats that appear from Gilead."

"Well, my hair smells just like the goats," I said.

Desire laughed. "Mayhap the goats smell better than we do, now that they're off the Mayflower and outside again!"

The door opened and William Latham arrived, struggling under the yoke which held two buckets brimming with water. John Howland came behind him, easily carrying another yoke and buckets. "The spring ice has melted and we didn't have to cut a hole to get water," John said, setting the buckets down by the hearth. He raised his eyebrows at me and I handed the Bible back to Desire.

When we'd finished eating, I took the trenchers out to scrape into the goats' pail. Penelope bleated at me from across the rail bordering our garden.

"Were you reading the Bible?" John Howland brought a bucket of scraps.

"Desire is teaching me."

He made a wry face "And I'd promised to teach you. Months ago!"

"Mother gave me the rod when she found out, just before she—" I gulped, my words clogging my throat. John waited for me to wipe my tears. "Mother, God rest her soul, said I'd never please a husband if I were too forward and learned to read."

John picked up the bucket, a teasing smile on his face. "Surely, here in the new world a bright pretty maid can find a husband," he said, adding with a teasing look, "even if she can read."

Governor Carver loudly announced to all as we gathered for dinner, "All the able-bodied men are to meet with Captain Standish before sunset. Some tools Francis Eaton left in the woods were gone when the crew returned after lunch yesterday." He took a slurping taste of the stew.

We children and servants were waiting for the upgrowns to finish eating and the smell of cornbread and goose stew tortured my hungry stomach.

"How could tools disappear?" Mistress Carver asked.

"We think the heathen took them," Governor replied. "Standish will drill us to be prepared if they steal from us again."

Next morning Jane lugged hot water to the big tubs outside, then put the laundry to soak. I stirred the clothes with a washing stick, then helped Jane wring out 'til my hands ached. We draped the sheets over bushes; then put the pillowbeers and clothing on the fence. Though the March sun gave little warmth, my neck grew hot from fatigue and I sat down to rest. I looked out to where the Mayflower bobbed on its anchor in the bay. Captain Jones planned to sail home in April—just a month away.

When the men came back, Governor Carver poured warm water into a bowl. "Come, young John. We must look civilized."

"As you wish, Sir," he replied. John took his knife, sharpened it on the leather strop 'til it had a razor edge and wet it. With his eyes closed, he slowly drew it along his jaw, leaving just a line of dark beard defining his face. Going slowly around his mustache and leaving the beard full on his chin, he put down the knife and opened his eyes to my watching him.

I put both my hands under my apron to make them behave. "How do you do that with your eyes closed?"

"Practice. Should have seen me when I first tried." He turned to William Latham, who watched intently. "One of these days ye must practice too, m' boy."

"Come now, John," said the Governor. "Put on thy corselet and sword." Fully adorned, Governor Carver picked up his gun and bandoliers and led John out.

After they left, I took the dry laundry down. It smelled of green grass, the salt air, and a hint of the juniper bushes. I put the sheets to my nose, wondering which one would cover John Howland.

I had everything in the basket when Rogue appeared, growling softly. I looked toward the woods and froze. What I saw could only be a dream. I closed my eyes to shut out the vision of a heathen man walking towards our village. When I opened them again, the savage was closer. He was very tall, with a feather in his hair where it was pulled back on top. A yellow stripe covered one side of his face and he wore a necklace of shells.

My mind felt like a shattered dish. The heathen walked slowly but smoothly, as though he were walking on air instead of our rocky road. He held his bow steady—no trembling or bouncing. A fur was slung over his shoulders, but his arms were exposed to the cold. I wanted to run and tell someone he was here, but my legs and feet would not move. My throat was as stiff as my legs. Our men were still marching about. No one was aware the alarm needed to be sounded.

I finally forced a step, then another, and stumbled into the house, slamming the door.

"What's wrong? Are ye ill?" Mistress caught my arms.

"'Tis a barbarian! Coming into our village!"

Mistress Carver peered out the door, and then stood back. "Father in Heaven, he's coming right toward us!"

I peaked over her shoulder.

The savage kept coming. He held both arms out; in his right hand he held a big bow and in his left he held two arrows. His skin was the color of a gypsy's and his hair black as a horse's mane. When he came to a stop, his face remained impassive. He was so close I could smell his strange, bitter scent. He wore only leggings that exposed his greasy upper thighs, a piece of leather hanging between his legs. The view of his bare body made my belly roil, and I looked away feeling faint.

Our men were at the end of our short road, standing in their marching rows and holding up their guns and sword as if waiting for the command to fire at our visitor. I was calmed by the sight of them—properly attired with their cloaks fastened back over their coats.

Then Standish fired a warning shot that brought people pouring out and hurrying toward the Commonhouse. Jane came out with Mistress by the hand. Desire and Humility came behind. My heart banged against my ribs as I held Humility in my arms and waited for Desire to stop coughing.

A motion from the Indian brought my eyes back to his frightening visage. He put the bow in his left hand with his arrows and held his right hand out as if he expected someone to shake it. It was quiet; even the birds had stopped swooping over the sea.

Sounds came out of his mouth. "Weh cum."

Captain Standish took a short step forward. Stephen Hopkins and Governor Carver whispered together.

"Weh-cum." The man said again. "Wehcum, wehcum."

"Good day. You are well-come too. Welcome!" Governor Carver spoke very loudly. He put his hand out and began walking slowly toward him. Captain Standish put down his gun and motioned to the rest of the men to lay down their arms.

I tried to hold it in, but a giggle of nervous excitement escaped my mouth. Governor Carver and Master Hopkins walked slowly toward us, followed by Captain Standish and our men. They met the barbarian in front of our door. Governor Carver offered his hand and the savage took it.

"My name is John Carver. Car-ver."

"Cah-weh," the heathen responded, and they shook hands again.

"Your name?" Governor Carver asked.

"Samoset." The Indian man kept his arms down and stood tall.

"Samuel? Welcome, Samuel." Governor Carver shifted his feet; he kept his hands held out from his side, palms up.

"Sam-o-set. Sam-o-set" the man spoke quietly, but with force.

"Sam-o-set." Carver repeated.

I whispered it to myself, "Sam-o-set."

Governor Carver introduced Master Hopkins, who in turn gestured to my Master. "Governor Carver is our sachem."

"Sachem! Ahhe, sachem—king!"

Governor Carver smiled, "Not king, governor."

"Might as well let them call you king. It's all the same to them," Master Hopkins said.

Myles Standish was shifting his feet in impatience and

stepped between Stephen Hopkins and our governor. "Captain Standish. Stan-dish."

Samoset nodded briefly at our captain and put his bow down on the ground, right at Governor Carver's feet. He held out two arrows, one in each hand. The arrow in his left hand had a sharp point, like the ones our men had brought back from the first attack. His right hand held a long shaft with no arrowhead.

Humility buried her head in my chest. I patted her shoulder, but could not find comfort myself.

Samoset held up the arrow with the point in his left hand and said, "War." Then he held out the empty arrow shaft in his right. "Aquene—peace."

Was this a trick? The heathen might be signaling for hidden warriors to attack. All our eyes were on Governor Carver.

"He's giving you a choice." Master Hopkins kept his eyes on Samoset as he spoke to Governor Carver. "Put your hand out to take the empty shaft."

My own hands twisted my apron into a tight knot. Governor put his right hand across his body to reach for the arrow in Samoset's right hand, "Peace."

I caught sight of Captain Standish's face; for a second, I feared he might grab Samoset's bow and arrow. Samoset handed the empty arrow shaft to Governor Carver and then put his real arrow on the ground.

"The sun is setting." Governor Carver looked inquiringly at Master Hopkins. "Should we offer him a bed for the night?"

Stephen Hopkins motioned toward his door. "Come into my house." Samoset did not move. "Welcome to my house," Master Hopkins gestured again to the door. Samoset hesitated and peered inside. Master Hopkins went ahead of him and held the door open wide. Samoset stepped to the door and went in. Master Hopkins, Captain Standish,

Master Winslow and John Howland followed and the door was shut. Slowly, women brought the children from the Commonhouse, chattering and laughing nervously.

Constance Hopkins called to me from her door; her apron was as twisted as mine and her white coif askew on her hair. "Mother took the little ones to Brewsters." She bit her lip and grabbed my hand. "Father says we must feed the heathen. Can thy mistress spare some food?"

Mistress Carver ladled some of the stew she had prepared for supper and instructed Jane to bake more cornbread. Some of the stew slopped over as I walked to Hopkins' house with trembling hands. Constance pulled me in, gripping my hand so hard I nearly tipped the entire pot. My nose filled with the powerful smell of the heathen, who was standing by the big fire, gesturing and speaking in low voice. Master Hopkins was listening with his head bent to him. Captain Standish, Edward Winslow and John Howland stood back. Carrying my pot to the low fire, I edged past the men.

"He knows a little English; Hopkins understands some of his gestures," John Howland whispered. "This man is not from the local tribe. He's from up north where he's the king."

My mind tried to fit together the new pieces of information. Constance reached into their corner cupboard and took down wooden trenchers for the five men. I stirred the fire up and hooked our pot so it would warm, furtively looking back at the savage.

Samoset pointed to his tongue and then made a motion like waves while he continued to speak in a low voice.

Master Hopkins said, "You learned our tongue from a captain in a big boat?"

Samoset nodded. "Capan Deh-meh."

Stephen Hopkins turned to other men. "Thomas Dermer was at Martha's Vineyard—they call it Capawack—

and there was a fight which Dermer fled."

"Would you like to eat?" Master Hopkins patted his belly and made an eating motion.

Samoset made the same motion back. "Ahhe. Eat."

Constance's teeth chattered as though a cold wind was in her mouth. I picked up a trencher and began ladling as Jane came through the door with more cornbread.

"Come, maids! Give us food," Captain Standish demanded.

I looked down at the trencher in my hands and moved a foot forward. Nothing spilled, and I took more steps. Keeping my eyes on the dish and the floor below, I was almost to the table, but Samoset was standing in the way. His fancy shoes were so soft they were like slippers. Raising my eyes, I met Samoset's. He was looking at me with a calm face, as if getting a trencher full of food from a maid like me was what he'd expected his whole life. I lowered my eyes and watched my hands so I would not spill, put the trencher in his, and glanced up at his face again. He nodded slightly and almost smiled. I realized I had not brought him a spoon or knife, but he was already picking the meat out of the stew with his fingers as he moved to the table. My breath came out in a sigh as I backed up two steps and bumped into John Howland. His hand went to the small of my back, and I caught my balance.

John patted my back lightly and whispered, "Elisabeth, the strong lass!"

I could not help smiling. The other men were all looking at me, and I bit my cheeks to hide my smile.

Jane laughed softly, "Now you have a heathen eating from your hand. Next it will be a wolf."

Samoset awkwardly sat on a bench to eat. When he finished, he wiped his mouth with his hand and stood. He pointed to Master Hopkins. "A Wampanoag come, talk your talk."

Captain Standish jumped up so quickly the table tilted. Constance and I looked out the window, but saw no other savages.

Master Winslow grabbed Stephen Hopkins' arm. "Find out where this man is!"

"Could you bring the man here?" Master Hopkins motioned as he spoke.

Samoset nodded, "Ahhe, Tisquantum come."

"What's his name?" Master Winslow asked.

"Tisquantum."

"His name 'tis Squanto? 'Tis Squanto," our men said together.

"I go, bring Tisquantum." Samoset moved toward the door.

"No! Stop him." Captain Standish moved toward the door. "We can't let him out in the dark. There might be others waiting for a signal!"

Stephen Hopkins stood up slowly and opened his hands to Samoset. "Sleep here. 'Til morning."

"Take Constance to stay with Carvers tonight, Elisabeth," Master Hopkins turned to me. "My wife and little children are with the Brewsters; my son Giles and the menservants here in my loft."

Before Constance could take off her apron, Jane and I had her out the door. 'Twas dark, but there were still people gathered outside.

"Can't you see these maids are weary," Jane shouted. She pushed aside young John Billington and William Latham, then took Constance by one hand and me by the other.

William Latham stepped forward and walked behind us to the Carver house. "What's happening in there, Elisabeth? What's the savage like?"

Others swirled around me, listening for my reply. My head seemed to be swelling within my cap. "He's not from here. And he's going to bring another heathen who speaks better English."

Young John Billington touched my shoulder. "Elisabeth, did you get near to him?"

I whirled around. "Of course I did! I gave him his supper!" John and the other boys stopped in their tracks, their mouths open. I put my hand out. "See, I'm not even shaking. Do you think you could do that?" I laughed at their faces. Each of them would want a gun or knife in his belt before he'd get as close as I had been.

"Did you keep your cutting knife close by or depend on Captain Standish and John Howland to protect you?" William Latham grinned at me and put his hand on the dirk in his belt.

"Nobody needed any protection, William. Samoset just talked."

Constance and I used the last of the hot water to bathe our hair, and were rubbing it dry when Humility woke up fretting.

I took her out to the stars to comfort her and heard John Howland coming from Hopkins' house. "Do Samoset and Master Hopkins understand each other?" I asked him.

"Yea, somewhat." He touched Humility's cheek. "Ye look near to sleep, sweet lassie," he cooed. She gave him a shy smile and snuggled closer to me.

I held my coif in my hand, shaking my head so my hair would dry. Too late I realized I was exposing my curls in the presence of a man. It was impossible to put on my cap and tie the strings while holding Humility.

John did not hide his delighted grin as he took the babe from me. Truth be told, his pleasure warmed my face. I covered my hair and changed the subject. "Why does our governor want to talk with this savage?"

"We are so few in number now, the heathen could

destroy us." John Howland held Humility awkwardly with both hands. "Governor Carver wants to make friends with the heathen but can't approach them without a translator."

Humility whimpered and I took her back, swaying back and forth, my motion like that of our anchored ship. "See, she's asleep already."

"You are good with this little one. You're the youngest in your family, no? What child did you practice on?"

"I was five when my oldest sister gave birth—she's Mother's daughter by her first husband." I was chattering too long. "Do you have children in England?"

"Children? My brothers are all grown, but none have babes yet." He gave me a long look and grinned. "Do you mean of my own? Nay, I can't afford a wife."

Was there a woman to whom he read the Bible back home—perhaps Song of Solomon? His warm hand stroked Humility's hair and brushed my shoulder. The smell of musket powder was on his hands.

"Best take the little one to bed, Elisabeth. Good night to thee."

The intimate, "thee"—instead of "you." After he left, I tried it out in a whisper. "Goodnight to thee, John."

That night John Howland's low voice mingled in my dreams with the wild sound of Samoset's.

Attitash

It had been only a few sleep-circles ago that my spirits were as high as flying hawks. Black Whale had played his flute, declaring his love with song. I'd gone out to him, all my family witnessing his declaration to all our people. My smile came from the center of my heart, and the light in his eyes answered mine. He stopped an arm's length from me and continued to play his own special tune. Then he began a different song, the rabbit mating dance. I sang the song to his flute, and in front of all our Otter Clan held out my hands to let everyone know I was willing. The sticks clacked as he and I moved toward each other, then away.

He'd put the flute at his side and taken my hands. "Attitash, I promise all my hunt to your mother's fire until our first baby is born. May I bring my half of the circle to yours, that we will make a whole circle?"

"Ahhe." My hands gripped his. "I will make a gift to your mother. If she accepts my offer and my mother accepts yours, we will join our halves to make a circle."

We'd only had time to ask our families for their blessing before our Massasowet sent Black Whale to Patuxet with Samoset.

I set to work making the gift. Grandmother examined my leather. "You found a nice piece for Black Whale's mother. It will be pretty if you ever finish softening it, but won't make an acceptable marriage offering like this."

"My hands are tired. It takes so much leather to make a poncho." I took it from her. "What if Black Whale doesn't return safely from Patuxet?"

"Hush, are you trying to tempt the bad spirits, Attitash?

"Can Samoset be trusted?" I asked.

"Samoset? Do you trust the cloth-men, more than Samoset?" Grandmother smiled grimly and kept her eyes on the syrup kettle.

"No." I fingered the rough hide on my lap. "But he might betray our men so the Strangers won't kill him."

"The cloth-men's bad spirits threaten us all, not just Samoset." Grandmother blew on the fire under the syrup kettle. "Massasowet sent him first to face their bad spirits."

My mind felt as heavy as the buckets of sap I'd carried, and my spirits were as sore as my hands.

Start working or the spirits will think you don't want him back!" warned grandmother.

My face flushed hot. The bad spirits could not always be listening! I sat in silence working the hide between my hands until it began to feel more like skin.

Grandmother reached over and felt it. "Keep scraping and working. It's coming, but it's not soft enough yet."

I sighed and shook my hands to get the kinks out.

"Once you've given this to Green Feather, you can't ask to take it back to finish. It must be so soft it wraps her shoulders. This would just sit on her bones."

By the time Nippa'uus was high overhead, the hide felt more like leather. "Could I have one more taste of syrup, Grandmamma?"

"So much work and you want to eat it all at once." Grandmother stirred the kettle, then took her spoon and put a tiny drop on her flint knife. She blew on the drop to cool it and handed the knife to me. Holding the drop on my tongue to savor the sweetness, I picked up the hide again. If Black Whale returned and if his mother accepted my gift, we would begin making a papoose. My woman-place felt slippery. My eyes and ears were fixed on the path from the woods instead of the piece on my lap. "Will it hurt when Black Whale plants his seed in me?"

Grandmother lifted the spoon and drizzled a lick on her knife. "Let him kiss you wherever he wants to." She gave me the drop of syrup. "You'll be ready."

"Wind in the Rushes said it hurts."

"A little pain now prepares you for more pain when your baby comes." Grandmother stroked my belly lightly. "If you give pleasure, you'll receive it back."

A whistle pierced through the woods. Black Whale! I ran down the path and into his arms, laughing and crying at the same time. We went to our Trees-in-Love and Black Whale pulled me tight to kiss me, then released me and took my hands.

"What happened in Patuxet?" I asked. "Is Samoset safe?"

"Ahhe. The cloth-men chose the Aquene Arrow."

"Do the Strangers know the Aquene Arrow means they will not fight us again?"

"They do. The Strangers are desperate. The bad spirits have taken so many of them they have few warriors left." Black Whale held my waist under my furs. "Our Massasowet will bring your father and other Pniese with him to negotiate."

I feared my father would be harmed, but Black Whale assured me sixty men would go with our Massasowet. "Tisquantum will speak the Cloth-man tongue." Black Whale pinched my hip lightly, but I flinched as if he'd hurt me and wrenched away.

"Tisquantum is trusted to speak for our Massasowet?" I spit the words out like nettles on my tongue. "He can't!"

His eyes showed his anger. "Now what? You suddenly know more about Tisquantum than our Massasowet? Do you think you're a Sachem?"

"I have not told you before why I did not trust him; I only learned without a doubt while you were on your vision quest."

I feared he might not listen—that his pride would take him away from my words. But I carefully told him the disturbing details of hearing Tisquantum's voice during my capture. He listened and did not interrupt until I described Tisquantum speaking to the Pniese.

"Have you told anyone else," he asked.

"Only my mother; I wanted to be sure it was Tisquantum's voice I heard; then I wanted you to be the first to know." I touched his cheek tentatively, but quickly withdrew my hand. "But we must plot carefully how to warn our Massasowet."

"Tisquantum speaks the Strangers' tongue best, so our Massasowet must know how to use him but still have protection against betrayal." He took me back in his arms. "You'll be one of the women to carry and cook for us."

My feet were ready, but my spirit hesitated. "I will never be alone with Tisquantum!"

"Never," he promised. But you'll get to see how the cloth-men live."

"What are they like?"

"You'll see. Their houses are smaller than our wetu—summer homes. They're made from trees instead of reeds and no weaving to keep out the cold wind. Samoset slept in one—or tried to sleep. He gagged on the foul smell of the Strangers."

"Did anyone see you watching the Strangers?"

"Only a girl."

I clung tightly to his hands. "What did she look like?"

"Her face looked like she'd been under water for too long; all color gone. Her hair was covered by a white cloth, but some peeped out like curly wood shavings the color of deer." Black Whale took a long strand of my hair and touched it to his cheek. But he did not look at me, his dark eyes turned to his memory. "Her eyes were like still water in a small pool."

Eyes like still water! My hands quivered. "Tell me more."

"She was short and very thin. I only saw her for a moment—I left before she could call out an alarm."

"Remember my vision? That's what she looked like!"

Black Whale searched my face. "Do you think it's the same girl?"

I leaned against him, feeling his heart beating strong and slow. "Maybe. Or perhaps they are all thin, with eyes-like-quiet-water and hair like wood shavings."

Her face stayed with me while I took my story to Grandmother.

OUR MASSASOWET LISTENED carefully to Grandmother. She repeated my tale exactly as I'd told her. Mama, Papa,

Uncle Seekonk, Black Whale and I watched our leader's face, but even his eyes showed no emotion. When Grandmother finished, Our Massasowet turned to me. "Attitash, never will you—or any other Wampanoag woman—suffer this again. I am sorry you have suffered. And I thank you for not spreading rumors until you were certain Tisquantum was present when you were captured. However, as you recognize, honored elder," he addressed Grandmother, "if our People are to be safe from the Narragansett, we need help from the Cloth-men. Unfortunately, only Tisquantum speaks their tongue well enough to negotiate for us."

"Ahhe, we are indeed between a storm at sea and a storm on land," Grandmother replied.

I looked at Black Whale. This was the first time he'd been included in an Otter Clan decision.

Papa spoke. "Our Otter Clan has an idea." He nodded at Black Whale, giving him silent credit. "When you and a few of us Pniese go to negotiate with the Cloth-men, we must first leave our weapons across the river. If you ask the cloth-men to send one of their valued men to wait with our armed People across the river to be our hostage in good faith—Tisquantum could not convince them to betray us."

I could not resist glancing up at our wise leader. He was nodding thoughtfully. Black Whale struggled to keep his face silent, but his eyes gleamed with pride.

"We will demand this. If they agree, their need for our help may be as desperate as our own." Our Massasowet stood. "We will speak of this to no one. Now, we must all sleep. Tomorrow we got to Patuxet."

Black Whale and I were not ready to sleep yet. We settled by the dwindling fire and he asked me to do his hair. I'd watched Mama work on Papa's, and my fingers tingled with the chance to do Black Whale's. He settled between my legs and I undid his topknot. His heavy hair fell below his shoulders as my fingers stroked the short hair between his crown and forehead. It had grown out during the winter and felt like Suki's fur.

Tomorrow we would leave for Patuxet—the cursed place filled with Strangers with whom Tisquantum had the power of words. I had hope now. I savored the solid resistance of Black Whale's small temple bones beneath my thumbs. Easing the tangles out with my fingers, I collected lice and dropped them in the fire. After I calmed his long hair with bear grease and redid his topknot, Black Whale handed me a black and white feather to place in his hair. I reached into the edge of the fire for a spent coal, and carefully spread a streak of black on his cheekbones. His deep breathing stirred my own and I savored the charcoal and bear grease smells mixed with Black Whale's own scent. "Whenever we're apart, I remember the feel and smell of you."

"And I know yours." He stood and adjusted his journey belt. "If the Strangers' bad spirits take one of us…"

"Matta—No! That can't happen." I pulled him against me and spoke into his bare shoulder. The salt of my tears mixed with his body grease.

13

Elisabeth

Everyone in our little settlement was abuzz over the impending visit of the heathen king. He and all his party were staying just across the tidal brook.

Prior to his visit, however, he had demanded that one of our men go to his camp as a hostage. This would help to ensure a peaceful negotiation. Edward Winslow volunteered, saying he had little to lose—his wife slept the terrible sleep of one whose soul would soon leave her body. After he crossed, we stood by our doors watching.

Massasoit's face was painted scarlet, he wore no hat, and his shaved head shone with some kind of fat rubbed into it. The men with him also painted their faces, but with different colors—white, yellow, black. Only King Massasoit wore a great necklace of purple and white shells. Stephen Hopkins beckoned them to an unfinished house, where they stopped at the door to await Governor Carver's entrance. The drummer and trumpeter provided flourishes for the procession. Captain Standish and other musketeers, including John Howland, led the way for Governor Carver, flanked by Lieutenant Governor Allerton.

King Massasoit grasped the hand Governor Carver offered and followed him into the house.

John Howland came home near dark and reported that negotiations would resume in the morning.

EARLY THE NEXT day, I stepped out the door to carry the piss pot to the muck heap, only to find an apparition.

When the moon's light is the same as the first pale rays of sunrise, dreams are real. A creature stood in the garden. She was tall, as tall as John Howland. Uncovered hair hung above her shoulders in tresses dark as night sky. She was covered in furs and looked like a bear with a maid's face. Knowing it might be a witch's familiar, I stopped. She took a step forward. She was the one I dreamed about.

She lifted empty, open hands to me and spoke with a maid's voice. "Win-sow. Woo-min." I could not understand her words, but this was no dream. This was a living heathen—the vision-maid.

Just behind me with another piss pot, Jane stepped up and yelled, "Stop or I'll throw this mess at thee!"

Attitash
Eyes-Like-Still-Water did not shout as Shrieking-Woman did, but held her ground as if she already knew me. It was now five moons since I'd seen her with the other Strangers washing their cloth. She was so thin that her flat breasts barely showed against the tight cloth. Her long skirt, the color of the sour red bog-berries, covered her legs and she wore no feathers or pretty stones. She held a pot, which I hoped was not their food; it smelled like the yellow-snow place in warm sun.

"Win-sow woo-min." I said again, but Eyes-Like-Quiet-Water did not seem to understand the sounds Win-sow told me to say.

When he'd arrived as our hostage, we'd given Win-sow food and furs to sleep on. He would not take off the small-stone clothes that covered his chest, and his face stayed worried. Only that night, after we sang and danced for him, did he finally use words and motions which Sagamore Samoset could understand.

"Many bad spirits sicken Win-sow's wife. He wants to

know if she is still in this world." Samoset told us. "He wants someone to cross the brook and find out how she does."

I knew that if one of our men went across the brook, Strangers' firesticks would point at him. "I will go. If a young woman crosses the brook, it would not raise an alarm."

After much discussion and advice, Mama agreed. She sent blackroot to make a healing tea for Win-sow's wife.

The time before Nippa'uus rose was chosen as safest. I prayed all night for courage and wisdom so I would not be attacked by their firesticks or bad spirits. I prayed Black Whale and Papa were unharmed.

The appearance of Eyes-Like-Quiet-Water might be a sign the Spirits were helping me. I tried to show with my hands and face—making sick looks and the shape of women—but she continued to look puzzled. I took another step forward, watching Shrieking-woman carefully, but she stood solidly next to Eyes-Like-Quiet-Water.

Elisabeth

Her face intent, the vision-maid pointed to other houses with arched, questioning brows. "Win-sow, woo-min." She cupped her hands over her round breasts, released them, and made motions I could not comprehend.

"What's it saying?" Jane put her pot down.

As I dumped my own pot on the muck heap, I repeated the vision-maid's words in my mind. Slowly, then fast. "Winslow?"

Shaking her dark tresses out of her eyes, she smiled. "Ahhe, Win-sow, Win-sow woo-min."

"Master Edward Winslow must have sent her." I whispered to Jane. "He may want to know if his wife lives. We'll take her to Winslow's house."

"Master Carver will be wanting his breakfast." Jane

stepped backwards to our door, her eyes riveted on the visitor.

"Wait here," I said loudly to the heathen. "I must fetch my cloak." But when I returned, she had vanished. My eyes searched the gardens and I called out "Halloo." The breeze brought a pungent whiff and I saw the bushes move. The vision-maid stood up slowly.

"Winslow's woman is there." I pointed up the road. "Come with me." Taking a few steps so she'd see what I intended, I looked back. The Indian waited, her eyes fixed on me.

"Come," I beckoned with my hands. "We go to Winslow's house." Pulling my shawl and cloak tight, I stepped toward the garden gate, scanning our little road for men with muskets.

The only one I could see was Goodman John Billington, leaning against the house where Squanto and the Indian governor waited to begin another day of talks with Governor Carver. Goodman Billington sagged against the house, his head slumped down, his red beard against his chest. Not wanting to risk his assumption that my companion was a bear, a witch's familiar, or hostile, I went behind the Brewster's house to reach Winslow's. Vision-maid followed several paces behind me.

Attitash
When Eyes-Like-Quiet-Water left, I hid. She might be going to get someone to attack me. She came back alone, though, wearing a cloth poncho; I revealed myself.

As I followed her, I saw a Stranger with hair like fire, but she avoided him. We came to another little wetu made from tree branches and mud. The smell of bad spirits at the entrance made me step back. Eyes-Like-Quiet-Water spoke, and a Stranger came out. This one looked like Yellow Hair would have looked if he'd been healthy—even fur on his face—though it was more the dog color of Win-sow's. His clothes were the Strangers' cloth, like Win-sow's, and Yellow Hair's. Wonderful plants must have been used to color the cloth bright green. The Stranger listened to Eyes-Like-Quiet-Water and then insulted me by looking straight into my eyes. Averting mine, I brought out the small carved rock Win-sow had given me. The Stranger gasped and called into the house, then took it from me. A girl came out, whose hair was the color of a beaver's, and her eyes were like the sky. She put her hand over her mouth, but did not shriek. Eyes-Like-Quiet-Water spoke with her and turned to me. "Winsow woo-min's very ill."

Win-sow had told me the funny word "ill." I pinched my nose to show her I could smell the bad spirits' presence. Eyes-Like-Quiet-Water nodded. I reached into my pouch and pulled out blackroot. Eyes-Like-Quiet-Water and the Stranger stepped back as if the bad spirit were in the blackroot instead of in Win-sow woo-min.

Elisabeth

"Why did ye let the heathen touch thee?" Mary Chilton stood at the door of her master's house.

I ignored her and turned to Gilbert Winslow. "Do you know why the heathen's here?"

Master Gilbert's face was drawn with worry and lack of sleep. "I don't. But she brought a button from my brother's coat."

Master Gilbert opened his hand and revealed the silver button. "Edward may have sent this heathen to discover how his wife fares. If so, I have only bad news for him. We've been up all night bathing her with cold cloths, but she continues to worsen." He drew his hand over his eyes, then looked at the plant in Vision-maid's hand. "She seems to offer some heathen remedy. But we can't let her near my brother's dear wife." He pocketed the button. "I must talk to the Indian king's translator. Squanto can tell us what she wants." Gilbert Winslow motioned to Vision-maid to follow him and started down the path. Mary Chilton hid behind the half-closed door. The look of terror in Vision-maid's eyes caught me.

Attitash

I could not move. My courage had stayed strong, but now I was beginning to feel I would rather be on the Big Salt Water with the Sky Fire Spirits crashing than here with these Strangers.

The Stranger had not even looked at my healing plants, but said, "Woo-min ill."

Eyes-Like-Quiet-Water spoke to the Stranger. He finally looked at my plant, but sniffed as if it were rotten and motioned again that I should follow. "Come to Massasowet."

Ahhe, so the Stranger would take me to our Massasowet! Papa and Black Whale would be with our leader. They could give me a message for Win-sow. Tucking the black-root into my pouch, I walked carefully behind Eyes-Like-Quiet-Water. She followed the green-coated Stranger to another house. I could not stop the small cry of joy when I saw Black Whale standing beside the entrance. Black Whale started to call to me, but the hair-like-fire Stranger raised up his firestick and pointed it first at me, then at Black Whale. With his bow and arrow back on our side of the river, Black Whale had only his cutting knife in his belt. Black Whale's eyes lost all their sparkle and the veins stood up on his arms. His hand still gripped the knife when Tisquantum and the Stranger with green-moss eyes came out.

Elisabeth

"Billington! Are ye besotted?" Gilbert Winslow yelled, as Squanto and John Howland came rushing out the door.

John Billington lowered his musket, muttering, and the Indian with the black and white feathers lowered his knife. John Howland, still holding his quills and paper, told Squanto to take the knife away from the Indian. There was much gesturing, with the Indian soldier pointing to Billington's musket. Captain Standish came out, adding his shrill voice to the shouting match.

Vision-maid left me and stood with the Indian soldier. I noticed she had her left hand on her knife, glinting under the edge of her fur. My own cutting knife I kept firmly in my own left hand, beneath the folds of my cloak.

Governor Carver and Massasoit came outside, followed by our other men. I was startled by the calm manner both leaders used with the quarreling soldiers. Something in a look that passed from Massasoit to my master gave me hope that our leaders seemed to understand each other beyond Squanto's translation of words. Their persuasion diffused the hostility at last. Weapons were allowed to remain in their owners' possession, with promises from both Standish and Squanto that they would not be used.

At that point, John Howland waved at me as if shooing sheep. "Elisabeth, get thee out of harm's way!"

I stood my ground. "We're here because this heathen maid brought a message from Master Edward Winslow."

Gilbert Winslow described to our men what had transpired. Vision-maid spoke to Squanto.

"She give medicine to Winslow's woman." Squanto told us. Vision-maid pulled dried plants from her pouch.

"What will this medicine do?" Governor Carver asked.

"Bring Satan to Mistress Winslow," Master Allerton warned.

"Will the medicine work?" Gilbert Winslow asked Squanto.

Squanto's face was impassive. "Yes, No. Many our people die, we so much ill, no many medicines."

"And some die when they do have this...medicine?" John Howland asked.

I wanted to speak. I wanted to say I trusted this Indian maid more than I could trust Squanto. That look in Squanto's eye was like the look in Master Allerton's eye—conniving. I could not speak, however. I had no evidence. John Howland would think I had not recovered my senses after my fever if, based on a look in someone's eyes, I wanted to use a heathen plant on Mistress Winslow.

Attitash

Tisquantum's face was stone when I held out the blackroot. "What is Tisquantum saying?" I asked Black Whale. Is he telling false stories about my medicine?" But he was too intent on making certain the warrior who had threatened us was keeping his firestick down.

Eyes-Like-Quiet-Water motioned to me to give her the plant. Thinking she wanted to smell the plant or taste it to determine its healing power, I started to give her one stalk. The man with eyes-like-green-moss spoke sharply to her, and she pulled her hand back. Eyes-Like-Quiet-Water turned away from me and leaned toward him. The trust I had begun to feel vanished.

Papa stood in the door of the Strangers' house. "Attitash, give the message to Win-sow that his wife is very sick, but has not yet gone to the Spirit World. This man," he pointed to the Stranger wearing green, "is Win-sow's brother. He and I will walk with you to the brook's edge so no alarm will be raised."

A low wailing cry floated from the house of bad spirits. I knew it might already be too late for my medicine. Black Whale's eyes said goodbye to me. His eyes told me I was right not to trust the strange girl with my medicine. How could our Massasowet believe we might never fight these Strangers?

When we reached the marsh and waded across the brook, Win-sow was waiting on the other side. I had thought to comfort him, but now my only message to him was downcast eyes. He knew the bad spirits would take his wife. I knew more of our People would also be taken.

Elisabeth

"Master Winslow trusted the Indian maid, or he would not have sent her," I told John.

"At-ti-tash," John answered.

"What?"

"The Indian maid's name is Attitash," John said.

I stumbled over it, "At-ti-tash."

"Squanto says she's the daughter of King Massasoit's trusted Lieutenant, Hobbamock."

This Hobbamock had surely expected me to receive his daughter's offering. I swallowed the bitter taste in my throat, but failed to keep the anger from my voice. "Why did ye not let me take the root medicine, John? Ye act like a protective old uncle."

He nodded at the Indian soldier and took my arm. I shook free, but followed him. When we reached the Carvers' garden, I turned and addressed him with frustration. "Do you really think Satan was in those roots the Indian maid brought?"

"Elisabeth, whether or not Satan dwells in the plant, there are those among us whose perverse souls wait to accuse a young maid of witchcraft."

"Witchcraft?" I reeled in horror. "Who would make such an accusation?"

"Master Allerton, for one," John replied.

So, I was not the only one who did not trust certain conniving looks! "Why should Master Allerton suspect me?" I demanded.

John lowered his gaze, as if from a shameful sight.

"Thy left hand."

I clasped my left hand in my right; it wanted to claw Isaac Allerton's wicked face. "How...?"

"Everyone on the Mayflower heard thy mother's demands that ye cease sewing with thy left hand." He raised his eyes to mine. "Some see evidence ye are possessed."

I felt a surge of rage. "Do ye think I am, John?"

"Nay." John made bold to take my left hand in his. "My mother used her left hand—only at home—but we children saw it."

"Did anyone think she was a witch?"

"No one formally accused her. Father tried to protect her, making certain she did not reveal it." His jaw set and a muscle twitched in his cheek. "My grandmother's neighbor was burned at the stake..." He broke off.

A well of dizziness made me sway.

John took both my hands and held my gaze. "Elisabeth, I want no harm to come to thee; but ye must be cautious! Even if false accusations are not brought, this Indian maid—Attitash—could be the innocent bearer of her people's attempt to attack us with poisonous plants. Remember, we have not yet signed an accord!" John put his finger lightly on my cheek. "Do ye believe I am acting in thy best interest?"

I could not resist his warm touch.

"I believe." I moved my cheek slightly, so his finger traced it.

HOURS LATER THE MEN emerged from their council and paraded to the river where Massasoit embraced Governor Carver. I could scarce believe my eyes—our governor embracing a barbarian!

The events of the day whirled through me, leaving me anxious. We could see across the river to where so many Indian men and women were gathered that they filled in the clearing between the river and the woods. But I could not see Attitash.

"Elisabeth, can ye imagine what these conditions of peace could mean?" John Howland moved next to me. "Everything is new."

His good humor grated against my own dilemma. Peace would not be mine to enjoy if I were suspected of witchcraft. I stopped my tongue and concentrated on his question. "I hope our lives are no longer in peril from the heathens."

"We'll still be vigilant, but our prospects are good, praise God!" He looked across the brook, shading his eyes with the helmet in his hand. "Now Winslow can return to his wife's watch."

I went home to build up the fire for supper.

THE MEN'S JUBILENCE preceded them through the door in the form of hearty laughter and shouts. John Howland was rubbing his hands and bouncing on the balls of his feet.

Governor Carver entered with a flourish. "We have a treaty, my dear!"

Mistress embraced her husband, then went about making certain Jane and I served the food quickly. It was impossible to set my face in a pleasant mood to match the household's.

"Now, tell us how ye brought the heathen to an agreement," Mistress instructed, once the trenchers were filled.

"We told King Massasoit that William Bradford and I had drawn up a list of what we need to ensure peace," Master Carver leaned back in his chair. "We informed him that if he could agree to these, we would come to their assistance if they were attacked." Master took a large mouthful of stew. "Massasoit replied—with words I hope were translated correctly if not fluently—'We two people should be allied in time of war.'" Governor Carver picked up his beaker of ale. "John, did you get all those words down?" "Yea, I did," he replied. "Massasoit said, 'No weapons will be brought into each other's community.' That's when Stephen Hopkins brought out his Aquavit and more cold water." John chuckled "Massasoit was sweating, whether it was the closeness of the room filled with so many people and so much smoke or the aquavit, I could not tell."

Governor Carver picked up the compact, telling us Squanto translated each item as it was read. "That neither he nor any of his should injure or do hurt to any of our people. And if any of his did hurt to any of ours, he should send the offender, that we might punish him."

I dared not ask if "offending" included giving each other medicines.

"And their king agreed to this?" Mistress inquired.

"He did." Governor went back to his list. "If any of our tools were taken away when our people were at work, he should cause them to be restored, and if ours did any harm to any of his, we would do the like to them."

"That's when King Massasoit and the other Indian men interrupted Squanto," John said. "They told us they did not take any tools. Perhaps a young man picked them up to examine them. But they complained we took a kettle of theirs which they had traded furs with other English to obtain. And they complained that we took their corn."

Governor Carver's face flushed, and he was silent for a minute. "I told them 'Yea, we did take the corn. We would have starved if we had not.'"

"Did ye tell the heathen we will repay them?" Mistress asked.

"I informed them the kettle would be returned, filled with corn, when we have harvested sufficient to feed our people through the winter and to plant next season."

"Did that satisfy them?"

"It must. They want peace. I told them we will leave this condition in the agreement; thus, if it should happen again, both will insist that such be returned." Governor Carver picked up the paper and read, "If any do unjustly war against..." My ears did not listen, however, as I pondered how Attitash's people would learn to trust my people if we insisted on keeping the kettle now as well as the corn until our harvest. Resolving to ask later, I listened again.

"Lastly, that doing thus, King James would esteem of him as his friend and ally." Master Carver handed the paper back to John Howland.

"Does that mean their king can expect friendship from King James?" I made bold to inquire. "The king we fled?"

Governor Carver did not reprimand my impudence. "King James will never come here, Elisabeth, so it means nothing." Governor gave me a wry look and handed me the heavy paper filled with marks. "Look at the compact, Elisabeth—thy reading lesson."

My breath quickened, but then I remembered the rod whacks Mother had given me and gave the paper to John Howland. "I am but a servant."

"We will not be servants forever; ye should prepare now." John said quietly.

"Now that my mother has gone to the Lord, do ye think it still breaks the commandment to disobey her?"

"We are thy father and mother now, Elisabeth," Governor Carver said. "My dear wife Catherine and I both read, as does Desire."

Mistress nodded. "Eve was made from Adam's rib, not his elbow. God gave both male and female a good mind, Elisabeth. He must want it used."

It seemed as though my soul and my mind were both cracking apart from the strain of these new admonitions. How could I comprehend all this in one day?

"See this mark, it's King Massasoit's." John pointed to a mark that was scarcely more than a smudge of ink. "And here's Master Carver's." John waited for me to find the C, but I felt as if a veil covered my eyes and I could not recognize any letters.

"Did not Desire teach thee a bit?" John looked at her and she nodded.

"But not enough," I answered too quickly.

He laughed. "Time now for a bit more."

I had just found the C, when Jane and Priscilla opened the door and came in with water pails. An anguished wail followed them.

Priscilla closed the door. "It's Master Winslow. He just learned his wife has gone to the Lord."

"God keep her soul." Governor said.

God had so many souls to keep, I thought. To go to the Lord without her husband at her side must have been sorrowful indeed.

"The Lord used her husband to His purpose," Master Carver said firmly. "Without Edward's brave willingness to do God's will and remain with heathen, we would not have a treaty!"

Heads nodded solemnly.

"A most remarkable day, John." Governor Carver's voice sounded exhilarated and exhausted.

"Astounding, Sir." John's reply held no trace of weariness.

I waited 'til I heard John climb the ladder to the loft, then whispered to Priscilla, "Are ye asleep?"

"Not yet." She slid her arm against mine and took my hand. "What keeps thee awake?"

"I saw a heathen maid up close today. She had bare legs, black dots painted on her chin and a peculiar odor."

"Mary Chilton saw her too."

If Mary Chilton had not told Priscilla that John

Howland made me refuse the heathen remedy, then I would keep that subject quiet. "I talked to the heathen maid."

"She can't speak English!"

"She tried to say 'Winslow's woman', but I could scarcely understand. We talked with our hands and our eyes."

Priscilla snuggled deeper into the covers. "Do pray for Divine guidance, dear friend. We'll soon see if we've made a pact with trustworthy Indians or the devil that controls them." Priscilla closed her eyes. "Pray God to keep us safe from the heathen."

Attitash

Black Whale folded me in his arms when he came back across the river for the ceremony. "If the grandmothers approve it, we have a treaty. Now we can leave this dreadful place." He remained silent when we sang to honor our leaders. The Strangers' sachem embraced our Massasoit. Loud noises came from a gold cup that one of the young Strangers blew through and I nearly stopped singing myself. I could see Eyes-Like-Quiet-Water on the other side of the river.

During our journey home, we stopped to look out through the trees to the Big Salt Water. Papa told us Strangers call the place Pli-mot instead of Patuxet.

"I don't care what they call it." Black Whale wiped the drying mud from his moccasins. "Let this be the last time I look on this place. Pray their bad spirits don't follow us home."

By the time we camped that night, we were all hungry, and the sky over the forest was many colors. When our fire was built and supper cooked, our Massasowet called all our people together to tell us about the treaty.

He recited the agreement slowly, so we could commit it

to memory ourselves. Papa and Black Whale's lips moved silently with our Massasowet's, having already learned it. I listened to see if there was anything in the agreement about not trusting each other with medicines. After words about not fighting each other, there was an agreement that we not take their tools again.

"We only took their tools to see how they were made, then gave them back! They took our kettle and weachimin, and they kept both!" Black Whale's voice rose as he spoke.

"We can let them have the weachimin. Their women and children must eat, and they need some to plant," our Massasowet said. "The Cloth-man sachem Ca-ver promised to pay back the weachimin, and give us our kettle after their harvest. It's in the agreement!"

"How do we know they will remember it correctly?" Mama asked. "Did they all repeat it twice?"

"They make marks—like designs—on their paper. The marks remind them." Tisquantum told her.

"I don't trust designs! Why can't they learn to recite it?" Black Whale's mother chimed in. "Who is going to watch them to make sure they abide by it?"

"I will send someone to Patuxet to watch them," our Massasowet responded. "Now, let me tell you the last points."

"If any make war against their people, we would help them; if any war against us, they should help us." Our Massasowet paused and took note of the hope in many faces around the fire. "This is how these aliens can save us from Narragansetts. All sachems friendly to Wampanoag will be included in the aquene treaty." He then recited the condition that both sides would leave weapons behind when visiting the other.

"They had one last assurance, for aquene," our Massasowet said. "Their sachem, called King James, would consider our people his friend. King James will not send more wind-canoes and firesticks against us." Our Massasowet lit his pipe, drew on it and passed it to all his Pniese.

Grandmother announced that her council had approved all that was negotiated, but asked about violating our graves.

Our Massasowet rubbed his forehead. "It's not in the treaty. I would need to speak to their sachem alone, which I cannot do without knowing their tongue. Tisquantum assures me Sachem Ca-ver and his man Bad-ford gave him their word that the cloth-men will never desecrate our graves again."

I dared not look at Tisquantum myself. I wanted his pledge on pain of death that this was the truth.

"We will be the guardians, Attitash," Mama whispered to me. "It would take more than words to assure us they will never do this again."

"Who will go to ensure that the Strangers do not break their word?" I asked Mama as we left our Massasowet's fire.

"I don't know if he has chosen." Mama answered. "I hope he sends a young warrior to Patuxet."

WHEN ALL WAS quiet, I heard Black Whale's low whistle, and gathering my fur, I went to him. He waited for me at the edge of our camp.

"Do you think our Massasowet would send you to guard the Strangers at Patuxet?" I said as he took my hand.

"Where did you get that idea?" Black Whale kissed my fingers. "Our Massasowet has said he needs a seasoned warrior who has the trust of the Cloth-men. I am the last one he'd choose."

Relieved, I leaned against him as we walked. "Where are we going?"

"I have a place prepared for us by a brook. I know you like the smell and sound of fresh water." He stroked my shoulder, feeling where my hair now fringed the skin.

"Will you prepare me, too?"

Black Whale moved his hand around my waist as we walked. "You women are not the only ones who know how to plant seeds." He stopped. I looked about me in the light of the half moon and stars. There were pine boughs on top of soft leaves under a big tree.

"Do you like it?" There was a catch in his voice, and I realized he felt shy now.

"Ahhe." The brook bubbled like a boiling pot as the spring melt tumbled over its stones.

Black Whale put his fur down over the pine boughs. "Come, sit."

"I am ready to give your mother my gift." I'd brought the finished poncho with me and showed it to him in the dim moonlight.

He felt the soft leather and smiled. "It's beautiful. She could not reject this gift. But—"

"What?"

"My mother worries much about bad spirits," he said. Then asked gravely, "Were you in the house where Winsow's woman died?"

"Matta—No!" I took the poncho back from him. "You were by their house with our Massasowet. If all of you were so close, why would she worry only about me?"

"If she does, Uncle Seekonk will convince her otherwise." Black Whale pulled me close. "At last, we're far away from the Strangers." He lifted my fur off my shoulders. "Our circles will be joined, and our mothers will be happy." His hands touched me everywhere. "I would give you a child."

I kissed his neck where it met his shoulders. "I want to sleep all night with you!"

The trees sighed in the wind, and I could faintly hear the Big Salt Water surge against the shore. All I knew was the sweet, strong taste of his mouth, the taste of salt on his shoulders and arms as my mouth explored him. When he stopped kissing my nipples, I could not bear it; my belly and navel trembled with anticipation. When he entered me, I closed around him, and bit the back of my hand to keep from crying out. Mother Earth may feel an ache when we first plant the seed. If she does, it is an ache mingled with joy. The Big Salt Water seemed to heave and surge, and then all was quiet.

"Did I hurt you?" He sagged against me, and I clung to his back.

I returned his soft kiss. "I belong to you now, Black Whale."

"And I to you, Attitash."

I snuggled against him and we slept.

The moon was low when I woke. I touched Black Whale lightly and he said my name. This time we were quick, his voice, soft and high when he cried out. We rested only a moment, knowing we must go back to our people's camp.

'Rushes was already curled in her furs by the fire when I crawled next to her. Black Whale rustled his way to the other side of the fire. I listened to the tide nibbling the shore, my tongue savoring the lingering taste of his kisses.

A gentle stroke on my cheek woke me in the early dim light before Nippa'uus. I reached to catch Black Whale's fingers with my own. My thighs were heavy, but when we started on the trail back home, my legs filled with strength.

As we passed the pool where I'd first seen Eyes-Like-Quiet-Water's face, I felt a chill. She'd given in to the Moss-Eyed man's demands and refused my medicine. I did not want to think of her. I was eager to get home. I wanted to forget her.

14

Elisabeth

'Twas the first Sabbath in April, as we marched to Sabbath morning service, when Widow White gave a small cry of alarm and pressed red-cheeked little Peregrine tight to her bosom. A tall Indian man was coming down the path leading from the woods. Attitash and a little girl were following him. Behind them came a woman with a young babe in a curious sack on her back.

The man raised his hand, so much like Squanto that I knew it was in greeting, but some of our women shrieked. Widow White cried out, "Are we being attacked?" Her babe raised his head from her clutch and wailed.

Isaac Allerton took her arm and pointed out the cannon, visible on the platform above the Commonhouse. "Do not be alarmed, my dear. Captain Standish is always ready to defend us."

I whispered to Desire. "Does Master Allerton expect our captain to fire a cannon on a mother and child?"

Allerton looked at Desire and me, his brow furrowed in warning. "I would hope none of our young maids encourage heathen women to become familiar." Desire rolled her eyes.

I had not seen Attitash since the new moon grew big and disappeared again. I wanted to smile at her, but could not in the presence of such a pompous would-be protector.

Governor Carver went to the man called Hobbamock and greeted him with a firm handshake, which soothed Susanna White and most of us. The Indian babe peeked over the lacings, his fat cheeks dimpling and dark eyes wide, his thick black hair sprouting from beneath the fur tucked around him. Attitash's face was turned away, looking to the sea. I could not tell if she was frightened of our cannon or simply shy.

Attitash

"Our Massasowet asks me to live at Patuxet," Papa said. His words hit hard, like sleet landing on fire. Black Whale's hand tightened around mine.

Mama's voice was an eagle claw. "Patuxet is filled with the tears of our lost people—killed by the cloth-men!"

I tried not to look at her directly, but her eyes pulled me in, showing the terrors of her life.

Papa lowered his eyes respectfully. "We will never forget them, wife. But this treaty could end the killing." His face was still closed, but I heard the same memory in his voice I'd seen in Mama's. "The cloth-men will know I'm watching them. This is our only chance."

"Their word is as useless as broken shells," Grandmother said and smoothed back Little Fish's hair as he slept in his cradleboard.

Mama dropped her eyes to look at her fingers. "I wish we didn't need the Cloth-men, but we do." She raised her eyes to Papa. "I will bring my fire with you, Hopamoch. I will plant our weachimin there and my daughters will help me." She did not have to ask if I would go with her, as I could not leave my mother's fire, wherever that may be, until I became a mother myself.

Black Whale whispered to me, "Hopamoch must know Massasowet is making a mistake." He had never used my father's name to me. The words hung in the air between us. He got up and left our fire. It took all my will not to follow him.

When we were ready to leave for Patuxet, I found him

standing by our Trees-in-Love. When I stepped closer, he turned to me. The light I so loved in his eyes now shot sparks. "I can't go there with you, Attitash."

"Why are you angry with me?" I stood tall and looked him in the eye.

"I'm not." He reached for me, but I stepped back.

"You look angry."

"I'm angry at the Strangers, angry at Our Massasowet." He rubbed the groove between his eyes, but it remained.

"Then why...?"

He held out his hand and I slowly accepted it. He pulled me to him, holding my head against his shoulder and stroking my hair as he spoke. "I can't be in Patuxet with you, wife. They keep our kettle, but want their tools, and say nothing about desecrating our graves. And I can't stand by and watch the empty cloth-men look at you as if you were wampum they'd won in a game. I would break the treaty myself!"

I felt the quick beat of his heart with my fingers. "I saw their looks, husband. But my strong woman power rejects their eyes."

"Your woman-power is too strong. It washed away my seed along with the Strangers' looks."

The bitter accusation made me dig my nails into my palms. I could not tell him that my woman-power flow had not come when the moon was full. To tell him too early—before two moons had come and gone—might bring my woman-power back.

"Soon my love will accept your seed." I gripped his back where the muscles tensed over his ribs. He took me fiercely, pulling me to the ground. I did not hold back— touch for touch, taste for taste.

My breath was still heaving when Black Whale stood and adjusted his leggings and breech-clout. "Tell your mother and father to keep you well."

I HAD CARRIED my anger with me to Patuxet. Now, the Strangers stared at us like we were the ones who'd come across Big Salt Water! When I saw Eyes-Like-Quiet-Water, I could see memory of death in her face, and turned away toward the sea.

Papa led us to the small sheltered cove which would become our summer home. While Mama unpacked our belongings, White Flower and I explored the woods on a path which branched two ways.

We took the path leading uphill to where the brook separated Patuxet's fields. We stopped where a view opened up from the woods. Beyond the fields, the path led to the Strangers' new village. A few small wetus and a neesh'wetu were on each side of a path. They were made from flimsy-looking sticks with dried grass on top. All were angular, not circular like ours. Chopped wood was stacked up shaped like our wetu, but no entry and it did not appear to be hollow. Even though it was a fine day, there were no fires outside the house. Smoke came out of the hole in their grass roofs as if it were cold winter. I took it in quickly, then led White Flower back and took the short path to the beach. There a wide swath of sand at low tide cradled many rocks. The shore curved out a few paces away, guarded by a tangle of larger rocks. We climbed up two boulders leaning against each other and could see some of the Strangers' women collecting mussels. Eyes-Like-Quiet-Water was not with them. A chilly rain from the sea soon sent us back to our new home.

Mama and Papa were already building our wetu. By the time Nippa'uus pushed away the rain and shone from the middle of the sky, we had the cedar saplings cut and were bowing them to make a frame. It would be like our old home, except I was once again sleeping with my little sister instead of my husband.

As Mama and I sorted woven reed mats, the sight of

the little boy and Yellow Hair in their desecrated grave was behind my eyes. I recalled the death-memory I'd seen in Eyes-Like-Quiet-Water and wondered whom she'd lost and how she mourned them.

"Do the Strangers honor their dead?" I asked Mama.

"You ask me too much about the cloth-men," she said.

"Ahhe, they do." Tisquantum startled me. I'd not seen him come down the path. "We have only their sachem's word that they won't defile ours again. But if we open the cloth-men's grave, this would make them fear us and respect ours."

"You must shake off the ways of the cloth-men! We respect the dead, even the dead who are not ours." Mama fixed her narrowed eyes on his face.

I wanted to grab his throat and ask him why he'd not respected *me*, but Mama commanded his attention with her powerful voice. "We cannot become like the Cloth-men. We would be disobeying our Massasowet and flouting the wisdom of all our People which keeps the bad spirits away."

"White Cloud, you cannot think I would not obey our Massasowet," Tisquantum said, sounding more as if he were taunting her than being sincere.

Our treaty was a web blowing in the wind.

Elisabeth

"Our governor has assured me the heathen must live here to keep the treaty," Elder Brewster said. "But no heathen will spoil our Sabbath." He began reading Psalm 8. *When I consider thy heavens, the work of thy fingers, the moon and the stars, which thou hast ordained; what is man, that thou art mindful of him?*

Only the heaving water in the bay was visible when I tried to see through the crack in the Commonhouse shutters. We were crushed against each other on the women's bench. Our meeting space was crowded with men's belongings and bedding piled against the wall leaving little room for our benches and the rude table wedged at the front for Elder Brewster.

The service was no longer than usual, but after two hours of prayer, singing and testifying, my back and shoulder ached.

When we began singing the Psalm, a high sweet tenor, singing not the melody but an accompaniment, disturbed the pure song. Master Hopkins must have known the Lord does not want harmonizing! Constance was standing next to me and put her hand over her mouth. "My father will be rebuked!" she whispered to me.

I had to admit Master Hopkins' harmony gave pleasure to my ear which distracted me from the meaning of the words. I felt as though I were out working in the fields singing harmony songs, like *Frog went a' wooing*, instead of singing in the House of the Lord.

When the service finally ended and we walked back, the drizzling rain chilled me, even with Aunt Agnes's woolen cape. I pulled it tight about me, catching the memory of her scent in its folds and wondered what she and Mother would think of savages living so close to us.

"Where will Hobbamock live? Will he plant?" I asked Master Carver during dinner.

"His homesite's just south of here, a short walk beyond the rocks that divide the shore." Governor said between mouthfuls. "And yea, we will give them land to plant, just next to our own fields."

I wondered if Hobbamock and his family had been the ones living here and clearing the land. "Are we giving them back their land?" My question hovered in the air. Governor Carver's brows knit together and he brushed his mustache as if to trap words.

"God gave us this land." Mistress's tone and face

admonished me.

I sought to divert their attention from my failure to appreciate God's divine intention. "Will we meet his family?"

"Hobbamock will keep his family at his homesite." Mistress took a large bite of the goose John Howland had shot. "This tastes almost like mutton!"

After supper John brought out his quills and ink-pots and announced he would finish his letters to send back with the Mayflower as Captain Jones was ready to sail back to England. John's eyes moved over the letter. I did not want to know how he phrased the terrible news to my brothers and sisters of our parents' deaths.

He put down his quill "Have ye read anything yet written by hand, Elisabeth?"

"No, I've only read the Bible."

His finger moved to the bottom of the page. "I've written 'Elisabeth', now make thy mark. Ye've done that?"

"Nay," I whispered.

"Then I can fashion one for ye." John took a discarded paper and made some marks on the back. It looked like all circles. He paused. "It takes some time to learn and we can't waste ink. I will make thy mark now. Later we'll practice in sand on the beach until ye've mastered it."

"Are ye assuming my agreement?"

John Howland caught my teasing tone and laughed. "Beg pardon, indeed." He made a flourish and in dramatic voice asked, "Doth the young mistress grant permission for the humble clerk to inscribe her mark?"

Mistress Carver looked up from her sewing. "Think twice before ye grant our clerk his wishes, Elisabeth. This fellow's charm is a force to be reckoned with."

Trying to keep my face straight, I bowed my head rather regally. "The young mistress grants the clerk permission." I became serious again. "One more letter must be written," I said, "to Humility's mother."

He dipped his quill. "What shall I tell Widow Cooper, beyond the deaths?"

Words would not come. Humility's mother had sent her babe across the sea with Aunt Agnes to give her child a new life. Desire pulled open the curtain of her bed. "Write that Humility is well and that Mistress Carver treats Humility like her own."

Taking Humility, I left John writing and went into the garden. The stars were just beginning to come out. I showed them to Humility, telling her that her mother was looking at the same stars in England. She knew not what I meant, but delighted in the lightning bugs that danced beside her.

John Howland came out and stood near us. Reaching up to the branch of a sapling he broke it off. "It's too dark to see, but feel the tiny bud on the end of the twig?" John put it in my hand. "Roll it, like this." He broke another twig and rolled it between his fingers.

I did the same with mine and felt the fragile softness.

"It's stronger than it looks. It has stayed all through the long winter. Even if we have another spring snow, it will bloom." John touched Humility's cheek, then let his hand brush mine. "I've watched thee, Elisabeth. I can tell ye are like the trees, strong and young."

"Not so young. I'll be fourteen come August."

He dropped his hand from mine and ran his fingers through his thick wavy hair. "Fourteen? Ye are not yet fourteen?"

"Soon!"

"Ye have much assurance." John smiled wryly. "Though perhaps too much courage and too little wisdom."

"I'm trying to be wiser. There is so much to learn."

"What are ye learning?"

"About the upgrowns." I laughed softly. "Well, I don't know much. But I am learning about Master Allerton's kind. My mother probably would have agreed with him that I should shun all the heathen." Humility was slumped against me, her breath soft on my neck. "Their babe isn't wild looking, but the men are."

John looked out to sea where the Mayflower was loaded and would be sailing in the morning. "God help us," he said. "We needs must accept these wild people if we are to survive. No one else is going to aid us."

Early next morning, the Mayflower sailed with our letters, but much lighter for the fifty dead and fifty of us who stayed behind. I watched her sails disappear with a lump in my throat. I did not want to be in the foul 'tweendecks again, but the ship was our only link to home. It felt as though a rope—not as strong as the halyard John Howland had grabbed to save himself—was breaking. And if the ship was lost on its return, no one would know where we were.

Priscilla and Constance linked arms with me, and we left the shore. "We cannot survive here without more supplies," Constance said.

"I've lost everyone," Priscilla murmured. "What else would God require of me?" She cast a glance at the cooper, John Alden. He was the only crew member who'd chosen to stay with us. Perhaps sealing our barrels interested the cooper more than those of the ship. But I guessed it was Priscilla herself who was his attraction, not his work.

"Mother fears our family will be next to sicken," Constance said.

I did not speak of my own loss. At least I had my sisters and brothers to write to. Leaving my friends at our field, I continued to our burying grounds. The graves were not marked, except for Mistress Winslow's freshly piled earth. John Howland had shown me where in the dark of night last winter they'd buried Father, Uncle, Mother, and Aunt. I sank down on the ground and did not hold the tears back. Rose and my brothers would be broken hearted when—if—they received the letter John wrote for me.

Edward Winslow arrived, and with a small nod at me, went to his wife's fresh grave. As I started back, Attitash was standing in her field, her rude hoe in her hands, watching me. I nodded, attempting a smile despite my mournful mood. She turned away and began chopping the ground.

"At-ti-tash!" I called, but she did not look. I could not tell if she did not hear me, or if I had not said her name so she could understand it.

When I returned to the field, I tried to devise a plan to talk to meet her without drawing attention from those who would accuse me of witchcraft.

We had emptied the water casks by mid- morning and I took them to the brook to fill. The morning sun was warm for early April. Climbing up the bank, I looked into Hobbamock's field where his wife and daughters worked. Their hair was plaited, their shoulders bare and their breasts slipping out from their leather ponchos. They showed no more concern about that than Rogue would of her teats. No wonder Master Allerton thought Satan controlled them.

Attitash

Planting in the violated ground of Patuxet was wrong! The cold rage that had settled in my belly when Eyes-Like-Quiet-Water refused my medicine now spread over my body. The only way I could lose the anger eating at me was to return to my husband and home. The air was so heavy it slowed my hoe as well as my breath.

Mama's hoe was so fast it created its own heat. "The Strangers are still here, we must plant. The herring are starting to run and the weir will be full of fish when the tide goes out so we'll have plenty to plant with the weach-imin kernels."

When I went for water, I watched Strangers in their field using hard-rock diggers to loosen the earth. Even Sachem Carver was working in the field. Eyes-Like-Quiet-Water and the other women wore so many clothes they were wet with sweat.

"How do their men catch enough fish if they have to work in the fields?" I asked Mama when she joined me to splash water on her face.

"Your father says they do not know much about fishing. And with so few women here, they need the men to help in the field."

Win-sow came near the brook and raised his hand to us in greeting, then went up where his wife was buried. Eyes-Like-Quiet-Water came soon after and called out to me. Tisquantum must have told her my name! I ignored her greeting.

The weight of my anger made my arms and back weak. When at last we finished the field, I did not feel the pride I usually did. I reached to take Little Fish, bundled in his cradleboard, but Mama refused.

"I know you miss your husband and long for a child." She kissed Little Fish and put his cradleboard on the tree. "That leaves a hole which your anger against Tisquantum and the Cloth-people fills. Before we plant, go to a quiet place and pray. Tomorrow the bad spirits will ruin the seeds if you do not rid yourself of anger." She picked up her hoe and beckoned White Flower to follow her. "After we've finished planting, you can go home to Black Whale."

Deep in the woods, where beavers had caught the brook and made a pool, I sat and closed my eyes. How could I release my anger without Black Whale in a place where our People's souls might still linger in pain?

The brook gurgled and a three-note bird sang. I hummed my prayer slowly. My voice grew tired, but still nothing. At last my Good Spirit came to me—not as a bear—but an old, old woman, older than Grandmother. Her long white hair streamed out behind her; the leather of her dress was in shreds. She smiled and the lines in her face twinkled like stars. My breath eased.

"Give me your anger, Attitash," she said kindly.

I felt my hot heavy anger in my belly and willed it to go to her.

She caught it in her arms and threw the lump in the air. It shattered into pieces, glittering like the points of light on water. My Good Spirit laughed out loud, and as she laughed, the glittering anger pieces fell into the brook and washed away. I laughed with her, laughing so hard I fell onto the ground and rolled. I stood again and danced the swim of the smallest fish and the flight of the three-note bird that sang above me.

When I stopped to catch my breath, I still did not know if Black Whale would come to me again, but I knew I could plant seeds and hold my little brother.

Elisabeth

When I went to the brook, I could see the Indian women again. Still no Indian men were working. Attitash looked to the brook and this time she smiled at me, though she did not approach.

By mid-afternoon, my damp shift clung to my stays, and I longed to unlace them and take a deep breath. Under my limp coif, my hair stuck to my head.

At last, we maids went home to help prepare supper. It was quiet and cool in the house. Desire had taken with a fierce cough at noon and had not returned to the field. She was reading in her bed, her dark hair spread out over her shoulders. With no men in the house, I was free to take off my coif and shake out my hair.

I took her hand. "Do ye feel better?"

"Yea, rest helps." Desire took a drink of the fresh water

I'd dipped. "Mistress Catherine took Humility with Jane to collect mussels. They'll be back soon." She picked up her open Bible. "I am reading from Proverbs. Master Carver read this to Mistress Catherine before their child died. *Her price is far above rubies.*" Desire took a deep breath and coughed. 'Tis about Bathsheba, King Solomon's mother."

Mistress Carver came in, Humility asleep on her shoulder. "This reminds me of you, Catherine," Desire said softly, and read, "*Her children arise up, and call her blessed; her husband also, and he praiseth her.*"

"The Lord took my only child; I have no children to call me blessed." Mistress Carver set the bucket of mussels down and put Humility in bed.

Desire was seized with coughing again, so I spoke. "Mistress, you have Desire and you are like a mother to Humility. Sometimes…sometimes I feel you are a mother to me."

Catherine Carver put both her hands over her eyes as tears slid down her face. Then she reached out her arms and embraced us. "God has given you all to me." She stood and wiped her eyes carefully with her handkerchief. Mistress waved at the flickering fire. "My husband and the other men will return. Put your coifs back on, both of ye. Elisabeth, build up a proper fire for tea."

The new wood was just catching fire when William Latham came running in. "Master Carver fell ill! They're carrying him here."

Our surgeon Samuel Fuller kept his voice even, unlike the stuttering of my heartbeat. "He was healthy this morning?"

"Yea." Catherine Carver's voice was frail and high pitched.

Several came in carrying Governor Carver and hurriedly placed him on the table. The Governor lifted his head, his eyes opened slightly and then rolled back.

"When did he fall?" asked Master Fuller.

"Just a half hour ago." John's voice matched Samuel Fuller's but I could tell from the way he clenched his hands that he felt anything but calm. "We were spading the field, and Master complained of a fierce headache. Next thing I knew, he was lying on the ground."

"Sunstroke," said Fuller. "I'll give him a physick. He's too young to die; he will come around." Master Fuller reached into the satchel of supplies he used when he acted as surgeon. "Where's the hot water to steep the medicinal herbs?"

I blew on the big fire's embers. "Stop lolling about, William. Get more wood," I ordered.

Desire, her face stark white, held Humility on her lap.

"The Lord keep thee, my beloved." Catherine Carver held her husband in her arms, her face close to his. She gave a little cry when Master Carver's eyes opened and found hers. He moved his lips silently; then his eyes closed again.

William dumped logs by my feet, then threw a terrified glance at Master and ran back out the door. As soon as the wood caught fire, I went to the rain barrel in the garden to wash soot and tears from my face. Widow White, whose late husband was Mistress Carver's brother, stopped by our fence, her babe under her arm. From the look on her face, I knew she'd heard. "Is John Carver still breathing?"

"I hope so." I reached for Peregrine. "Let me take your babe, Mistress Carver needs you."

Susanna White went in ahead of me. The fire burned brightly and the teapot was on the table, but no one was drinking tea. I looked to Master Carver. He was still, his face a faint blue. As Samuel Fuller pulled the blanket over John Carver's face, Catherine Carver turned with a wail to her sister-in-law. Widow White's babe in my arms began to cry too.

Mistress Carver stayed up all night sewing her husband's shroud. "Only one day since the Mayflower left and John was re-elected governor," she said. "And now God has taken him."

Attitash

"What will happen to the treaty now?" Mama asked, holding tight to Papa's hand. "Sachem Car-ver embraced our Massasowet. He was a Cloth-man I could trust." Papa's despair unsettled us all. Win-sow, Green-Moss-Eyes and other men were digging Sachem Carver's grave when we arrived to pay our respects. Sachem Carver's wife held herself tight. Eyes-Like-Quiet-Water stood close, the little girl clinging to her. Small sobs filled the morning air. When the grave was dug, the cloth-enclosed body was gently lowered. The men shoveled dirt over it. The woman sachem, her cries like the shriek of sea birds, threw clods of dirt into the grave.

Mama and I stole glances at each other. The Strangers had not put anything in the grave. No bowls of food, no hunting tools, no beads. How would Sachem Carver make a journey?

That night, Grandmother was in my dream. "There is danger all around us," she whispered. "Danger from the Narragansett, from Tisquantum, from Sachem Corbitant—he wants our Massasowet's power."

Fully awake, I tried to believe the dream had no meaning. Corbitant was sachem where my clan uncle Red Hawk lived. Surely there could be no danger there.

Elisabeth

Our weeping had not run its course, when Elder Brewster called us to the meetinghouse. John Howland's face was a mask. The effort it took to hold his emotions showed in the slow movement of his jaw muscles.

"If we are to avoid destruction from the savages, we must immediately elect a governor to enforce the Conditions of Peace," Elder Brewster announced. Someone called William Bradford's name. He rose and said his health was not completely restored yet, but he would be willing to stand for election to be governor if another man were to be his deputy governor. Isaac Allerton announced he'd be willing to serve in that capacity. William Bradford's face showed no expression as he thanked Master Allerton. I struggled to keep my own face calm. No one else spoke up or objected, and the election was accomplished with murmured "yeas."

After we returned home, Mistress Carver sank into her husband's chair and asked John Howland to sit on the bench next to her. "My husband always said, 'young Jack Howland is like a brother to me.'" She leaned over and touched his hand. "Now ye will take care of us."

When Mistress went to bed, John Howland paced up and down, then went outside. I could not bear the house without Master, and followed John into the garden.

"I'm sorry, John," I said and stood near him, not knowing whether he would break into pieces if I touched him.

"Did ye hear what Mistress said?" John did not wait for my answer. "John Carver called me 'Jack.' He did treat me more like a brother than his servant." He swallowed hard, but a sob escaped him. "I don't know what to say…I just…"

"Ye don't need to say anything now." I did touch him lightly on his arm.

"I thank thee for that." He put his cold hand on mine. A warm thump against my legs from Rogue's tail made me reach down to pet the dog, taking the comfort of a creature who knew not our loss. John Howland had planned on improving his lot through the good will of his master and my guardian. Now John Carver was gone.

And so was our security.

As I crawled into bed, I whispered to Desire, "With Master Carver dead, Mistress must find a husband to provide for all of us. William Bradford is a widower. Mistress Carver could be a governor's wife again." Desire did not answer and I continued to whisper. "Have ye thought of what Mistress will do now?"

"I think only of her grief. Her love for John Carver was rare, Elisabeth!" Desire's whisper was firm and she patted my arm as though I were Humility. "She is a wealthy widow. She needn't give herself to another man."

Desire gathered me in and we wept in each other's arms until both of us slept.

15

Attitash

The oak leaves were as big as squirrels' ears. It was time to plant weachimin. Mama and I began digging the holes to receive the seed. The dark red, brown and orange kernels went happily into the ground.

Papa left early to check his weir before the tide took fish back to the Big Salt Water. When he brought back a basket full of fish, we hacked them with our sharpened shell knives and put a piece in each hole before we put earth over the seeds. In seven sleep-circles the weachimin should be as tall as my smallest finger. Then we would plant the beans and squash. When those seeds came up, I could go to Paomet—if Black Whale wanted me.

As the day got warmer, I wiped the sweat on my face with my hair and tasted the salty strand. Walking to the brook, I splashed water on my face and neck and then climbed the bank to look at the Strangers' field. Men were walking down the field throwing seeds without placing them in the earth.

Morning and evening we prayed for rain and warmth from Nippa'uus. Rain came after four sleep circles, gently melting into the ground. Now Mother Earth would receive the weachimin seeds. Tiny green shoots pushed through the ground! We would not starve.

After the seventh sleep-circle, we found weachimin shoots as tall as our fingers. Mama, White Flower and I dug new holes close to the weachimin and planted the beans. Just beyond the beans, we planted squash. The beans would curl up the weachimin stalks as they grew, and the squash would grow between. As we worked in the warm sun, the redwing blackbirds trilled and clacked from the waving reeds, and a marsh hawk floated above us. If Kiehtan continued to watch over us, we would eat well all through the cold moons.

The anger no longer shouted in my ears as I went to the willow trees where the brook narrows. I heard someone try to say my name.

"At-ti-tash. I am E-lisa-beth."

I turned to see Eyes-Like-Quiet-Water standing there, holding a child.

"E-sa-pett." I tried to make the sounds. "Ahhe?"

"Yea, Elisabeth!" She smiled.

"Esapett." I tried again and her smile grew.

"Yea, At-ti-tash."

I opened my pouch filled with herring and weachimin cakes. The little child reached out her hand but a warning sound came from an older woman coming quickly down the path.

"Humility," Esapett spoke sharply to the child, but the child's fingers already held the weachimin cake. As she popped it in her little mouth, the woman coming toward us loudly called out Esapett's name. Esapett grabbed the child up, whacking her little bottom hard. Tears glinted in the child's eyes, but she did not cry out.

The older woman took hold of Esapett's hand and roughly led them away.

I went to our fields where Suki met me, barking and prancing between my legs.

"Stop pestering, Suki!" Mama cuffed the dog.

"Why do the Strangers hit little children?" I asked.

Mama shrugged. "Tisquantum says their gods tell them to teach their children by hitting them."

"Don't their gods love children?"

Mama laughed without smiling. "Love? The Strangers are made of cloth. They don't know love."

Maybe loveless people could not grow food. I did not look at their barren field, only at our own.

Elisabeth

I ran to our fields early, hoping to be the first to see bright green sprouts pushing through the earth. Green that would promise a harvest to replace our nearly empty food supplies. Bright spring sun could not force the horror of dark winter from my heart—a winter of long, frozen months with no food. None of us, not even the strongest men—not even John Howland, could survive without food.

The bleak sameness of the dark soil frayed my spirits. Next morning I dawdled, hoping to hear shouts of discovery. Only silence greeted me when I reached the barren field. Then, a loud clatter commenced in Hobbamock's field. Attitash and her sister were clapping sticks, accompanied by shrieking at the crows that circled above the bright green of their field.

"Why does God allow the heathen's seed to flourish?" Jane demanded.

"Yea, Hobbamock doesn't go near his field, only his women tend it, yet it thrives." John Howland tossed a stone at the crows.

Humility clung to me as always, and began whimpering for water.

"She needs to drink," I told John.

When we reached the spring above the brook, I saw Attitash put down her sticks and walk toward her side of the brook. Looking behind to be sure no one would see me talking to a heathen, I called her name softly. She turned.

Attitash

Esapett's face was drawn in, as if she'd be an old woman soon. She pointed toward our field. I ignored her and got my water quickly. But the child she called "Umil-ity" began speaking in a high voice and I could not keep my face turned away. She reached out her little hand, but I made no move to give her food. Esapett looked like she'd taken a long breath she needed to let go. She pointed again to our field, speaking quietly in her garbled words.

I took a kernel out of my pouch and offered it to Esapett. "Weachimin."

"Wee-chim? Corn?" Esapett looked back toward her field.

I did not understand her tongue, but pointed to my field with its little green shoots and then to her field with nothing. "Cone? Weachimin." Digging into the creek bank with my cutting shell, I put in three kernels of weachimin.

Esapett nodded, then frowned. She pointed up to the field where men worked with just a few women. "No wo-man plant." She tucked her long skirts between her legs and covered her small breasts. "No wo-man plant." Esapett shrugged her shoulders in frustration.

I shrugged back, nodded, and returned to my field. That night I took my confusion to my family.

"Only men plant." Papa laughed. "The young woman can't tell them what to do. They won't listen."

"But they will starve." Only a few sleep-circles ago I had hoped they *would* starve.

"If they don't have their own crops," Mama said, "they will want some of ours." She took a plate full of fish from the boiling pot and put it on our wooden platter.

"And if we don't give them some of ours," Papa replied, "they will not help us against our enemies." He took a handful of fish and smacked his lips. "Tisquantum could teach them how. Now that their planting has failed, they should be ready to listen."

"Tisquantum! How can we trust him to teach them?" The bitterness in my mouth made my words prickly.

"Who else? He's the one they trust to speak their tongue." Papa's words were prickly too. "I will be with him, so he won't dare try to betray us."

Papa brought Tisquantum over and laid out his plan. Mama and I waited silently.

"But it's women's work! I know nothing about that!" Tisquantum's arrogant face made me want to spit on him. I was tempted to accuse him then and there of conspiring with our kidnapper, but held my fire for when it was essential.

"Haven't you noticed their women don't plant?" Mama attempted to keep the derision out of her voice, but Tisquantum turned his back on her.

Papa ignored his rude behavior, reminding Tisquantum that the Grandmothers wanted the Strangers to survive and defend us. "That won't happen if they don't raise a crop, Tisquantum. They do everything wrong. They plant seeds without digging a hole. They bring no fish to feed Mother Earth."

They left together to tell Sachem Bradford they could help the Strangers plant. They returned later and Tisquantum, with eyes on the ground, asked Mama to show him how we plant weachimin. Papa came along to make sure Tisquantum would do what we told him.

"They won't plant the weachimin with squash and beans so they can grow together. Sachem Bradford said each seed must have its own place in the field. He had words from their 'book'—their way of telling stories with marks. Their Kiehtan wants each kind of plant in a separate field."

"You're trying to trick us," Mama scoffed. "What kind of Spirit doesn't want the weachimin to carry her sister bean vines up the stalk? Or doesn't want the squash stretching out to keep the rain in the soil and keep out wild plants?"

I assumed Mama was right about Tisquantum tricking us, but Papa laughed. "It's not believable, but the Strangers did plant a very small seed they call 'bar-ley' in one field and another one they call 'pea' in a separate field. The weachimin they threw on top of the earth, just like their other seeds, in another field."

"They use the barley for their strong drink and the peas to make a mushy stew," Tisquantum informed us, "Or would have if any of their seeds had come up."

Elisabeth

"Why not ask Squanto to teach you their way of planting?" I tried to keep my face blank. "The Indian corn thrives. If God gave us this Promised Land, He must want us to grow food." John Howland did not reply.

Mistress Carver looked up from her trencher. As usual, she was eating little. "My brother, Reverend Robinson, and my John used to discuss our Lord's command in Deuteronomy. *For the Lord your God is bringing you into a good land, a land of brooks of water, of fountains and springs, that flow out of valleys and hills.* They agreed this tells us we must use the land as God intended." She took a tiny bite of bread. "What you must discern is what God intends us to use in this new land and what must be shunned. In Holland, we prayed often to know which of the Dutch people's ways were God's ways."

John Howland chewed in silence, then wiped his mouth with his sleeve. "Tonight I will discuss this passage with William Bradford."

Evening shadows were long, and we had put the bedding down when John returned. He rubbed his face with weariness as he sipped his ale. "If we don't get any barley, we'll have to do without drink until a ship comes with supplies."

"If we don't have peas or corn," Desire reminded him, "we won't be here to miss the ale."

"Well, it's in God's hands now." John gave us a brief smile. "The barley and peas are our English seeds. They will grow or no, according to God's will. We also agreed to let Squanto show us how the heathen plant their corn."

Attitash

White Flower and I watched from across the brook as Tisquantum showed the Strangers how to dig the hole, cut the fish and plant the kernel. His hunks of fish were cut too large and he worked very slowly, telling long tales White Flower and I could not hear.

"Probably telling the Strangers how only he can properly give the fish's spirit to the weachimin," White Flower laughed. "The weachimin plant needs a woman."

Black Whale would be angry we were helping the Strangers survive. It had been almost two moons since I'd seen my husband, but no message had come. I no longer could be certain he would want me. My dreams brought him to me, but often he would not look at me. In other dreams he held me in his arms and the emptiness when I woke shivered my blood.

Leaving the planting to Tisquantum, my sister and I took our little brother to get fresh water and bathe. The brook ran fast between our fields, and bushes screened us from the Strangers. We walked along the bank 'til we rounded the bend. There the water sang loudly as it left the pool and tumbled down the dam of rocks and beaver-hewn sticks. I picked up Little Fish and carried him until we reached the quiet pool above.

"Keep Little Fish while I bathe, White Flower." I sat Little Fish on the bank and pulled off my wraps. The still water was dappled gold from the early morning rays, like Esapett's eyes. The water took my breath, but I lowered myself until everything below my neck was under water. My woman-place squeezed with the cold, but it warmed as I rubbed myself with a smooth stone.

"You can come in now, White Flower. I'll take Little Fish." I reached for my brother, and he tumbled into my arms. Little Fish kicked water so fast White Flower shrieked as she stepped into the pool.

Holding Little Fish against me, I sank into the water. Tonight the moon would be a full ball. My power-flow had not come to sweep away new life. Would Black Whale not be filled with delight to know this? Hearing a call downstream, I thought I saw Esapett on the bank. As I lifted my hand to shield the bright rays of Nippa'uus, Little Fish slipped away.

I lunged for him, but he disappeared. Ripples circled around bubbles, as White Flower shrieked. A ball of wet black hair bobbed toward the rocky spill on the side of the beaver wall. I dove down into the water, but my hands groped empty water. Coming up for air, I could see nothing but Esapett, climbing on the sticks and rocks. I dove again, my eyes straining and frantic hands reaching. Out of breath, I came up again and shook my hair out of my eyes. Esapett was standing on a rock in front of the water's spill. Her hair streamed water and her cloth clung to her body. She held Little Fish, patting his back. At first I was relieved he was not screaming. Then I realized he might not be breathing. My own breath snagged. As I swam toward them, I heard his choking cry. Weeping myself, I reached the rock. Little Fish saw me and screamed louder, flailing with his hands. Esapett gave me Little Fish and we struggled to the bank. I gathered him to my cold wet breast and hushed him with soft words. He grabbed my nipple with his teeth, and I let out a yelp.

White Flower came running to us, carrying our clothes. "I tried to reach him," she cried.

"I'm the one who lost him." My fury at my own failure mingled with anger at Black Whale. He'd abandoned me because he hated the Strangers. Now Esapett saved Little Fish, not him.

White Flower held Little Fish, singing to him while I found my dry dress. When she returned him to me, I covered his cheeks with kisses. My relief was not pure, however. I still wanted to drag Black Whale back to me by his topknot. Closing my eyes, I recalled my good spirit. Once again, I gave her the heavy ball of anger. She tossed it in the air 'til it broke into bright pieces and I laughed with her. With a light heart, I opened my eyes. Esapett was gone.

Elisabeth

My cold wet clothes clung to my body as I stumbled along the bank toward home. There was emptiness in my arms but my breasts stung. The ache in my hollow place had intensified when the Indian babe grabbed my breast. Tears for a child of my own fell on my wet shift. I could never bring a babe into this world to suckle from breasts the Cur had violated.

When I reached our burial ground, I sat down in a sunny sheltered spot to remove my stays so I could dry out my shift and petticoat. The laces were tight from the water, and I was struggling with them when Mistress Carver arrived. She began silently working on the knots without asking me what happened, which gave me time to consider the telling of my tale.

"I was getting water when an Indian babe fell in" Mistress made no comment and I continued. "He was carried with the current toward me. He was much heavier than Humility." My laces came free and I shed my stays.

"His little brown face was turning gray when I pulled him from the water. As soon as I slapped his back his breath came, and when he cried out his color returned." Though I waited, Mistress Carver still did not comment. She had not commented on much since Master Carver died. After she pulled my wet petticoats off and wrung them out, she finally spoke. "Ye must dry thy clothes before the men see ye." Then she went to her husband's grave for her daily visitation.

Priscilla found me drying my clothes and was helping me when Attitash appeared. Her mother and little sister were with her and all were smiling. I could not comprehend what they said to me, but I did understand their effort to say my name. It sounded rather like the way Humility pronounced it. The babe was asleep in the leather wrapped board which the mother carried on her back. He wakened, but was not crying as she unwrapped him from the board.

"Catabatash." Attitash patted her brother, then reached out and patted my hand.

"What does she mean?" Priscilla asked.

Attitash repeated her words, then said, "T'ank"

"Thanks?" I asked.

"Ahhe, t'ank—Catabatash."

Priscilla was staring dumbfounded at Attitash and then at me. I told her what had happened. Priscilla still looked bewildered as Attitash held her little brother out to me. He was as naked as when I rescued him from the water, but now he was dry and smiling. When I took him, he pulled a strand of my hair that escaped my coif. I did not try to hide my smile.

16

Elisabeth

When one week had passed with no new seeds sprouting, many of our company began echoing Isaac Allerton's admonition. "You used Satan's people to teach us how to plant! Did you expect God to reward your lack of faith?" Mistress Carver paid no attention. But then, she paid little attention to anything, spending the day praying over her husband's grave.

The ninth day after planting, rain fell all day. No storms, no wind; just rain all day. On the tenth, at sunrise, I went to the field with John Howland and William Latham. William ran ahead and was shouting before we could hear what he said. When we got near, we could see a glimmer of green. Priscilla and Constance Hopkins joined our whoops of laughter mixed with tears. Whether it was God's will or Satan's, we found bright green blades bursting through the soil in every corn row.

Attitash

Now that the cloth-men's crops as well as ours were growing, I had too much time to wonder if Black Whale wanted me to go to him. One night, Black Whale did not come to my dream at all; only a restless bear slept against me. Rolling away from White Flower, I went outside. Standing in the light of the nearly round moon, I looked at the stars. They were not bright, but I could see the bear stars, my own Good Spirit. A rustling on the other side of the fish-drying fire startled me. Straining my eyes, I could make out two lumpy shadows beneath the branches of a low hanging tree. The smaller lump gave a soft bark and the bigger lump reached an arm out to silence it.

I was there to catch Black Whale's hand as it touched Mowi. Pushing the dog aside, Black Whale pulled me to him. He picked up his furs and wordlessly led me toward the brook trail. Tears filled my eyes as I breathed in his scent and felt his warm skin against my waist.

"When did you come?" I whispered. "Why?"

"I must be with you, wife." Black Whale stopped then and kissed me deeply. "Even if it forces me to be near the cloth-men, I must be with you." He released me. "Yesterday I ran 'til Nippa'uus went down, then walked the rest of the way." He stopped and threw his furs down under the trees by the pool.

We were just below the falls where Esapett rescued Little Fish, but I did not tell Black Whale what happened. As soon as he kissed me on my mouth, I wanted him to kiss me everywhere.

When we woke, the moon was nearly gone; we lay wrapped in its faint light. Nippa'uus would soon rise.

"You are really here, not just a dream." I traced the hard muscles in his arm.

He laughed. "My mother had so many things she wanted done, I did not want Brown Beaver and 'Rushes to have to do it all. But I kept watching the moon grow fatter every night." He stroked my hip.

"I was going to come visit you," I said, then paused. "Hoping you'd want me."

"Want you? Attitash, I always wanted *you*; I just didn't want the Strangers!"

"We'll leave them when the crops are harvested," I kissed his wrist on the tender flesh beneath his calloused palm. "We'll be home in Paomet for the green weachimin celebration."

Black Whale playfully slapped my bottom. "We see eye to eye on that!" He leaned over and planted a quick kiss on my rounded hip.

"Stop!" I laughed and pulled him up to face me. "*Now* we see eye to eye." I leaned into his shoulder. "So much has changed with the cloth-men since you left."

"We heard Sachem Carver died. Is there still a treaty?"

We walked back to Mama's fire while I told him all I knew about Sachem Bradford and how we'd convinced Tisquantum to teach the Strangers how to plant. I would wait until the full moon passed to tell him my new life was growing. I did not tell him how I'd nearly lost my brother, that a Stranger saved him, and that even Mama was friendly with his rescuer.

Elisabeth

Priscilla took the cask of water I brought her, her hoe laid beside the four-inch high corn. "Elisabeth, how is Mistress Carver?"

"She grieves," I said.

She handed back the cask and picked up Humility who was hanging on my skirt. I was glad for the relief from her constant demands. She wanted Mistress Carver to cuddle her, but Mistress only turned her head aside and wept. Priscilla pinched Humility's cheek and she giggled. "Because Governor Carver was a young man, and died so suddenly, she was not prepared for the Lord to take him."

"How old was he?"

"Mistress Brewster said he was thirty-six."

"Really? I always thought of him closer to my father's age, not John Howland's."

Priscilla laughed, and gave me more gossip. When I got home, I repeated much of it to Mistress Carver. "Susanna White accepted Edward Winslow's marriage proposal, and they are already wed. Mary Chilton has moved back to

Winslow's with her Mistress."

"Susanna White is still grieving for her husband," Mistress said, surprising me by commenting. "But she must have a father for her sons. Resolved is just a little boy and Peregrine but a babe. Pray God Edward Winslow and Susanna White give each other comfort for their losses."

Mistress then turned her face to the wall and again refused food and drink.

"Please, Catherine! You must nourish your body." Desire sounded as though she were speaking to a little child instead of our Mistress.

AFTER WEEDING the sorrel and parsley in our garden beds, I prepared to sleep. There were no reading lessons, no conversation by the fire or in the garden. I was hot and tired, and wished someone in my house beside Humility would smile at me. I pulled the sheet over my head and drifted off to sleep.

> *When I looked out again the room was dark but I could still see. My father was sitting in Governor Carver's chair reading the Bible. No one sits there anymore. Not since our Master died. Father smiled at me and turned to his Bible to read. Then, instead of Father, it was John Howland sitting in Master's chair. His face was relaxed, as it used to be, and he held in his hand John Carver's Bible.*

I sat up. Jane was asleep beside me. Crawling out, I looked at John Carver's chair in the dim light. It was empty. I heard a shifting of feet by the door and saw John Howland standing there, the door open and the moon shining dimly on his face. He turned, but did not speak. I walked toward him slowly. Desire and Mistress had their bed curtains closed, and I could not tell if either might be awake. John stepped outside as I drew near, and I followed him.

"I just dreamed about thee."

He stopped and turned back to me. "I dreamed of thee too, Elisabeth! I dreamed ye were no longer a maid…" He stopped and rubbed his eyes as if waking up.

"I dreamed my father was sitting in our master's chair." I put my hand on his. "He was reading his Bible. He wants me to learn to read his Bible."

"And so ye shall." He took my hand in his. It was warm. The hard calluses below his fingers rubbed against my own, and he stroked the soft swelling at the base of my thumb.

"Then I dreamed that ye were sitting in Governor Carver's chair."

He dropped my hand and covered his face as sobs shook his body. Putting an arm around his waist, I patted him as though he were a babe. At last his sobs stopped. "He was such a loving and kind man! More like a friend or a brother than a master." John spoke so softly I could hardly hear him.

"And he was not very old." I felt rather bold speaking that way of someone more than twice my age.

"He was young. But to a young maid like thee, we all must be old." John wiped his eyes with the sleeve of the long shirt he slept in.

"Maybe I'm like your dream. Maybe I'm not a young maid anymore."

He gazed at me in the moonlight as if he had never seen me before. "Yea, these times bring young maidens into full bloom too fast."

I wondered if he referred to my tingling, aching breasts which seemed to be bursting out of my waistcoat lately.

"Mistress spoke to me this evening." His gaze left my face, and he looked toward the silent house. "After the rest of the household was asleep."

"She spoke to thee? She does not speak at all these days!"

"'Tis true, but when I came in she asked me to sit by her." John gestured to the fire. "I did sit in Master's chair, just as in thy dream."

"What did she speak about?"

"Master's will. Remember when he wrote it out?"

"And took it to Isaac Allerton to witness."

"Yea," John cleared his throat. "Mistress says she's not long for this world."

Tears slid into my throat. "She won't eat. She does not want to live!" I swallowed hard and blinked my eyes.

"Mistress told me again, 'My John loved you like a brother.'" His voice broke, and he stifled his cry. "She told me that our master's will gives all to me if she follows him in death."

"Ye...would..." My voice could not follow my tumbling thoughts. "Ye would... not be a servant?"

"Elisabeth, I don't want to profit from another man's tragedy!" He slowly regained his composure. "I cannot comprehend my fate." John lifted my chin to look at me. Tears welled in his eyes and one slid down each cheek. "I don't know what will happen, but God seems to be watching me. And I believe God is watching thee also, Elisabeth." John took my hands and spoke very softly. "Ye are almost a woman. If Mistress does not survive, Desire and ye must go live in another house."

"Why can't we live here?"

"Others would talk if ye remain in my house. Ye are no longer a child."

In three months I would be fourteen, but could anyone truly care about propriety in these terrible times? I lowered my head so he could not see my warm face.

Attitash

Mama faced up river when I swam 'round the bend to meet Black Whale. He held me at arm's length when I floated to him. His wide shoulders and strong arms rippled with the motion of the water, as my eye followed the line of his chest and waist. I reached out in the water and traced the smooth skin across his hip bone with my finger. Before I could go further, he moaned and pulled me to him, his heat making me gasp.

Our urgency relieved, Black Whale floated in the water and my mind became troubled. I was again remembering my little brother being carried away by the water. I had to tell him how I failed when my brother's precious life was in my hands.

"Maybe I'm too young to be a mother," I said, unsure how to begin.

"Too young?" He started to laugh but saw my serious face. "You have fifteen circles of the seasons. You're a woman now."

"But I acted like a young girl. I was lonesome for you and my mind stayed with you instead of my brother."

He smiled when I described thinking of his embrace while holding Little Fish in the water, but his mouth gathered deep furrows when I told how my brother slipped from my grasp. "Did you try to catch Little Fish?"

"Ahhe, but the current was so fast! I dove right into the water. If Esapett had not grabbed him and pulled him out, he would have drowned."

"Who grabbed him?"

"Esapett—the girl with Eyes-Like-Quiet-Water."

"No! How did she get there? What did she do with him?" He rubbed his face and climbed out the far bank. He kept his back to me, then turned suddenly. "Don't you see the danger she is to us?"

"Esapett saved him! She was coming to see us."

"See you? Why would she do that? She must have used her evil power to draw your brother into the water."

"She saved him and gave him back to me." Tears clotted my voice. "I was the one who almost lost him." I turned my back. "You stayed back safely in Paomet! You know nothing of what has happened here!" I spoke over my shoulder, not wanting to look at his face. "You should be grateful to Esapett. Mama is grateful to her."

I heard him splash back into the water and looked toward him. His face showed nothing. "Your mother is grateful?" he asked at last.

"Talk to Mama yourself."

"I will." He climbed out and walked away. I followed at a distance. Mama was back in the field, while White Flower and Little Fish ran about chasing away rabbits from the new plants. Seeing Black Whale stalking toward her, Mama put down her hoe and went to greet him. I moved close enough to listen without intruding.

"Attitash told me about Little Fish," he said, his face as heavy as his voice.

Little Fish heard his name spoken and came toddling over. Mama sat down with him and he reached for her breast.

"Attitash says the Strangers' girl saved Little Fish," he continued, then respectfully waited for Mama's response. She turned to him.

"We are all grateful to Esapett," She answered firmly.

Black Whale's shoulders stayed stiff. "Attitash says she's too reckless—too young—to take care of her own papoose."

Mama knew I was within earshot, but she looked only at Black Whale standing in front of her. "Attitash learned a most important lesson. Some women don't learn it until it's too late." She leaned down and kissed Little Fish's cheek. She gently squeezed his mouth until he let go of her nipple, then handed him to me to put in his cradleboard.

Black Whale's shoulders sagged. "Maybe I'm not ready to be a father," he said weakly. He bent his head and sat down beside Mama. "I abandoned my wife."

"You came back." Mama put her hand on his shoulder.

"I was lonesome for her."

A little fragment of resentment towards Black Whale broke free from my heart. I almost laughed, as I had when the spirit grandmother tossed away my heavy burden of anger.

"Her Good Spirit used a Stranger to save him," Mama said. She smiled. "Attitash is ready; Kiehtan will make new life in her."

When the new arc moon —a smile of delight—glowed, Black Whale understood, and each time we made love, he caressed my navel and kissed it.

THE FISH HAD FINISHED running up the stream, and all the leaves were full. Papa and Black Whale began work on a new canoe. They girdled a big tree trunk and burned a hole in it for days until the tree was ready to fall. As we made new pots with the river clay, the men chipped out the soft burned wood to hollow the new canoe. Tisquantum did not help, but gave advice on his own methods. When the canoe was nearly ready, he came not with advice, but with news.

"Sachem Carver's widow is dying."

Papa put down his stone ax and wiped his brow. "We will go say farewell."

Elisabeth

Even though we did not expect Mistress Carver to live long, her dying came suddenly. Early one morning Desire could not rouse Mistress to drink tea. By mid-afternoon the surgeon had closed her eyes. Desire and Jane wept as they washed her body. Jane had already taken out the soiled bedding, and I helped wrap Mistress's fragile remains in her shroud. Her body did not seem as if it had ever been Catherine Carver. Not the Catherine Carver who loved her husband; who delighted in taking care of Humility; who kept all of us busy making her household run. Her body was empty, cold.

When we finished I went to the field to tell the men. John Howland knew why I came. "Come home now," John called to William Latham. "Our Mistress is in the hands of the Lord." As we walked back to the house, John took my elbow to steady me. He stopped and looked up at the woods.

"Look," he pointed up the hill. "See the white?" I looked and could faintly see a blush of white against the green of the trees. "After we've finished with the preparations for burial, I will take thee to gather blossoms for our mistress."

The blossoms smelled as sweet as any I'd ever picked. I buried my nose in them and remembered Mistress Carver talking of the flowers in her gardens. She had buried two babes and spoke of them as *little flowers picked too soon*.

"Ye are a blossom now too, Elisabeth." He spoke very softly, but did not touch me. He broke off a small branch heavy with blossoms and gave it to me. "Our master told me he loved her for her mind and her soul, not just her beauty." He looked into my eyes. "Do ye know how rare are thy gray eyes flecked with gold?"

I shook my head, blushing.

"Ye have the look of a fully bloomed woman." He reached for the wayward strand of hair on my cheek but then withdrew his hand.

Attitash

Mama and I plaited our hair, rubbing fat on it to keep it smooth. Papa looked approvingly at Mama's tall firm figure.

"Wear your ponchos," he said.

"Why?" Mama replied. "It's too warm!"

"The cloth-women cover their bodies," he said.

I protested. "They cover their hair, their arms, and their legs, too! Do we have to become like them?"

"They do not respect a woman's body and think it should be covered," Papa answered. "We must do what they do as they send their dead to the Spirit World," he said firmly.

"Then just our breasts," Mama decided. "Not our hair or legs."

"Whatever you do, you carry dignity and beauty, Wife." He smiled.

He asked Black Whale if he would come with us.

"I didn't know the sachem's widow. I'll stay and work on the canoe, Hopamoch," he answered. Nor would you want to know her, I thought. He might be back with me, but he would not be back with the Strangers.

As we came near the edge of the woods where the plum bushes were heavy with blossoms, we heard voices. When we came around the corner, Humility was clinging to Esapett. The moss-eyes man Jon-owlan was with them. Esapett's eyes were a little swollen as if she had been crying, and I could see tear streaks on her cheeks. She was holding a branch of the plum bush with its white blossoms. I lifted one blossom from the bush and smelled its sweet fragrance.

Mama looked at me in surprise.

"Do they need blossoms for their spirit journey?" she asked.

Elisabeth

"At least we have flowers to cheer her grave," Mistress Brewster said as we laid them onto the fresh dirt. "Come now, Elisabeth. Ready thy things to bring to our house. Since it's so crowded, leave what ye don't need."

John roused himself from staring at the fire and offered to carry the trunk. I asked him who would be living with him now that Desire and I would live elsewhere.

"Governor Bradford along with others. That will give Brewsters space for thee."

"But what will Jane do?" William Latham asked.

"Master Eaton has asked her to be his wife. Governor Bradford will marry them tomorrow." John gestured to William to open the door.

Jane would be a master carpenter's wife instead of a servant! She had hinted at this, but had not told me it was settled. "She loves that motherless little Samuel," I said.

"Yea, but me thinks she loves the father too," John replied and smiled.

"Who will cook for us?" William asked.

"Jane will continue to do so. The Eaton's will be living with us."

After we'd made up our bedding, Mistress Brewster sat and lit her pipe. She would indeed be kind to us. How many more mistresses would I live with? How many more would die while I was with them?

I sat next to her. "Mistress Brewster, do you think my affliction is cursing us all?" I held my left hand under the folds of my skirt.

"Whatever do ye mean?"

"'Tis obvious, no? My mother died, my aunt died, my father, my uncle. The Carvers were well until I lived with them." My hollow-place ache was making my breasts hurt, but I could not tell Mistress the terrible truth of my curse.

"And so were the other forty some who came over

with us on the Mayflower and have since died. Stephen Hopkins told us only sixty survived of the five hundred at Jamestown—when ye were just a babe. How can ye believe ye are the afflicted one?" She put her arm around me. "Don't be foolish, thinking ye alone are the cause instead of what God ordains. No mere mortal can cause someone to be lost or saved."

I bit my lip. "None of us young maidens have died, but fourteen of the eighteen married women are gone now."

"In this land we have none of the God-given herbs for women." Mistress patted her almost empty betony bag. "God must show us a new way."

17

Attitash

"Attitash, drink more of that tea. Its raspberries and black berries make a woman's body strong." Mama lifted the kettle with a stick and held it out to pour into my cup. She had been treating me with special care since the third fat moon had passed without my power-flow. Mama put the kettle back and wiped her forehead. We were both warm, having spent the morning collecting clay from the riverbank for new bowls. She glanced at the slight roundness over my naval. "We must have children to follow in our footsteps."

My heart soared. "When will I know it's growing well?"

Mama smiled a broad smile. She dropped her voice to a soft whisper and leaned to my ear. "Listen to your womb; the new life will tell you."

"Listen?" I tried to put my ear near my belly, but could not.

Mama laughed. "Not with your ear, Attitash, with your heart—like you listen to dreams. New life will tell you when it needs you to rest, and when it needs you to eat. It will tell you when it is time for others to know." She held her hand over my belly. "You will feel it."

I tried to clear my heart so I could listen.

"Do you remember how you could feel Little Fish bumping before he was born?" she asked.

"That was a sign?"

"The first sign won't feel like a kick, more like a little tadpole fluttering." Mama poured herself a little tea. "You may not notice it until the weachimin is ripe."

The tea was good, though many things I once desired now tasted foul. Mama passed me a bowl with oysters simmering in broth.

My nose wrinkled at the strong smell. "These make me sick. Can't I just drink cold water and eat weachimin mush?"

"You want your new life to grow? You must eat what it needs."

Sipping a few mouthfuls, I pressed my hand against my belly. It felt hard. I remembered Esapett's flat body. "Mama, the Strangers are so thin. What are they eating?"

"Their weachimin won't have ears for another moon or two. Their other crops barely show." She scraped the bottom of the kettle and took a small bowl of stew for herself. "I don't know if they have any more of the weachimin they took from us."

I thought of Humility and the papoose, looking so thin. "Should we give them some?"

Mama looked at Little Fish's plump legs as he toddled around our field, helping White Flower chase crows. "Our food stores are all at Paomet. We would have to walk two circles of sleep to get more."

I kneaded my clay so my bowl would be as smooth as Mama's. "Why don't we give them some fish?"

Mama's bowl had already begun to be shapely. "We have only two men to fish. They have almost forty. How could we catch enough?"

"Do the Strangers offer food to Papa and the others when they visit them?" I lifted my pot and felt its solid weight. The shape was not pretty like Mama's.

"Of course, but small portions; and they offer no meat." Mama took her shell, which was scraped to a fine point, and began making an intricate design on the side of her bowl.

I held my bowl up. "What did I do wrong?" I asked in disappointment.

Mama set hers down and looked not at my pot, but at me. "Did you listen to your clay?"

"Listen to my clay?" Closing my eyes, I held the bowl in my hands and pressed it against my face. At first I heard nothing. Then I heard the ripple of water as it pours over the clay in the riverbank. The sound of a bird's shrill whistle came to my ears; the soft sound of birds' wings beating came through my hands and face from the bowl. I opened my eyes and began to work. The sound of stones tumbling against the clay as the water rushed over them came through my hands as I worked. At last my bowl took shape. The bowl showed what I'd heard.

Wishing my baby could take shape that easily, I tuned my heart to my womb. At first I heard nothing but Mama's shell knife scraping. Then I felt, more than I heard, a tiny sigh—like a baby going to sleep. I drew a deep breath and let it out slowly. New Life felt safe. I too slept well that night.

"WE WILL TAKE THEM some of the fish Hopamoch and Black Whale caught this morning," Mama announced. "We will give only to the cloth-women with little ones."

Carrying the fish in a basket, we went by the field and found many Strangers hoeing. The new weachimin leaves hung limply.

"These plants won't grow if they don't have rain soon!" Mama stepped over to one of the plants. "Our weachimin needs water, but the squash vines at least keep the soil from drying out."

"Do they pray for rain to their God like we do to Kiehtan every day?" White Flower asked.

Before Mama could answer, Esapett came out of the field. Her arms were very thin, almost like sticks, but she did have muscles. She stopped when she saw us and smiled, putting her hands out to Little Fish. He grinned at her, but clung tightly to Mama.

Esapett walked with us to their settlement and gestured toward a different house than the one where Sachem Carver had lived. Humility came running towards her. The older woman came out of the house and gave us a quick look. Mama and I stepped back, waiting to see if the older woman wanted us at her fire. Esapett spoke quietly to her in their garbled tongue. After a pause, the older woman beckoned to us to come in. We waited until Esapett joined her elder inviting us inside.

The room was very warm and smoky. It smelled like people had not cleansed properly. Sour sweat and the faint but sharp smell of blood assailed my nose. The house had three fires on the floor against a wall and many hooks for pots. Instead of a smoke hole in the center, there was a hole against the wall, but I could not see the sky. The house was crowded with sleeping benches and their cloth. The young coughing woman with dark hair lay on one of the sleeping benches.

Esapett called the older woman "Mis-tess." I was careful not to raise my eyes to Mis-Tess, but Esapett looked directly at her. Mama gave Mis-Tess a small bag of raspberry tea and one fish. She indicated it was for little Humility, clinging to Esapett.

"For Humility?" Esapett asked with a bright smile, showing the fish.

The foul smell and the coughing closed my throat. "There are bad spirits in this house," I whispered to Mama. "It smells like blood, and one of them is sick."

"Ahhe, we must think of your new life." Mama held her hand over her own nose.

I fanned my face as if I were too hot. Esapett nodded and fanned herself, then followed us outside. We all stood by the fence, watching the funny animals that looked like a dog had mated with a deer. Little Fish started squealing at the animals and they answered, "Maaa." Esapett made a little sucking sound with her mouth and called, "Cum cum goats." The animals trotted over to us.

"How do they get animals to stay in fences?" White Flower asked. The cum-cum goats bounced from their back hooves to their front hooves, and we all started laughing.

"More babies?" I asked Esapett. She held up three fingers, then took us to Hop-ken's house. Thankfully Consance and her little sister came outside and we did not have to enter. Her mother—who Esapett also called Mistess—came too, carrying a very small baby with sunken cheeks. I gave a small fish to the mother, who took it with a big smile.

"More babies?" I asked Esapett.

Esapett held up two fingers and took the last two fish. "Tank ye, cata-ba tahbah."

"Catabatash," I corrected with a smile. Then it was my turn. I tried the word Papa had taught me. "Fah-tee-waal."

"Fare thee well," Esapett answered.

We returned to our home where I found Papa and Black Whale about to go fishing with the new canoe. I asked Papa why the Strangers couldn't fish.

"Tisquantum says the cloth-men don't have nets, so they lose most of the fish they catch." Papa put his nets and sinew fish lines in the canoe. He pushed the canoe off the sand. He and Black Whale waded in the water until the canoe was launched, then jumped in.

I joined Mama and my brother and sister in our field, where the big yellow squash blossoms were thick. There was no further talk of Strangers. My husband would eat well tonight, and New Life would grow. But somehow I would find a way to help Esapett's people's young ones grow as fat as Little Fish.

18

Elisabeth

During the night, William Latham came to ask Mistress Brewster for help. John Howland was hot with fever. I followed Mistress to their house, filled with fear. His limbs were trembling and he coughed fiercely. Mistress said he'd convulsed earlier as if seized by Satan. "This will help his pains," Mistress said as she brewed tea from the rue herb. We'd brought cuttings from England and now grew rue in our garden. "But I need betony to cut the fever; we have used up our stores."

"I'll go look in the woods when it's light," I said. I did not tell her the remedy I would actually seek.

John was still burning with fever when I set out for Hobbamock's hut that evening. When it was in sight, I hid behind bushes, hoping to meet Attitash when she came to their field. Black Whale came out of the hut first and went down the path toward the shore. I watched his nearly bare body from the safety of the bushes. His back was muscled, and his ribs did not show.

"Esapett." I jumped. Attitash stood on the path. She had not made any sound walking on the path, but I heard her soft voice.

"John Howland is ill; bad illness." I shook as if I were possessed and rolled my eyes.

"Jon-owlan?" Attitash wiped her hand across her brow as though it were very hot.

"Yea! I need medicine—herbs." I pointed to the bag she had hung at her waist. "For ill?" I was beginning to speak like Humility.

Attitash put her hand out and held my wrist firmly. She was taller than I and her grip was as strong as John Howland's the time he made me refuse her offer of medicinal roots.

My mind struggled for a means to communicate. Attitash turned her back on me, and I thought she'd given up trying to understand. But she looked back over her shoulder and motioned for me to follow. If John had known what I was up to, he surely would have ordered me to bed until my mind recovered.

At her family's hut, Attitash gestured to a log by the outside fire. A clay pot bubbled with enticing smells. I waited while she went inside her home. Attitash's mother peeked through the flap they used for a door. The little boy clung to her, naked despite the early morning chill. Attitash came back out and handed me a basket with dried roots and bark. Taking the rude mortar and pestle made from rocks, she pounded some of the black root, red berries, and bark, and put it into a leather pouch. She gestured sprinkling a pinch of it into water seething over the fire and then drinking it. She then ladled some stew into a small clay pot.

"Give Jon-owlan," she said, handing me the pot.

The image of John wrapped in a shroud made my feet fly so fast some of the stew spilled and I had to slow down. When I arrived, the door to his house was propped open. Insects were hovering, but without a breeze in the house the hot weather would burn up a feverish man. John's face was pale and his breath labored.

"I have food," I announced to Mistress Brewster, and poured the stew into a bowl before she would notice it was in a heathen container. I put the root and bark poundings into a cup of hot water, and let it steep while I tried feeding him. Mistress propped John's head, and I held a cup of the stew broth while he drank. John opened his eyes but did not seem to see either of us. He swallowed painfully but got a little broth down. I repeated the process with the tea concoction.

"Where did ye find this?" Mistress whispered.

"Hobbamock's daughter."

Her eyebrows flew up. "Ye went to their homesite? Who was with thee?

"I went alone. I was desperate, Mistress. Their daughter—Attitash is her name—is good to me."

My mistress stood and went to look out the door. "Did anybody see ye?"

"Nay." I crossed my fingers, defying Satan's power with my sign. Surely I'd been careful, but one could never know for certain whose eyes were watching. "I am not about to let John Howland follow Master and Mistress Carver, my family...all the others."

Mistress closed the door and lifted her hands in prayer.

John's face had a little more color when I gave him the next cup of tea at noon, and he opened his eyes to eat some stew.

I prayed all day that Attitash's concoction would not bring Satan's power. I was loath to leave him that night, but Governor Bradford promised to sit up with him. My dreams were full of shrouds and Mistress and Master Carver praying. Waking before dawn, I hurried across the road and found all the men sleeping. I touched John's head and it felt cool. Raising my hands to heaven, I trembled with relief and fatigue as I thanked God for giving Attitash the remedy.

"I told thee God saved me when I fell into the sea and He wills that I live a long life." Startled, I opened my eyes to see John smiling faintly. I helped him to sit up so he could eat.

"What did ye put in this stew?"

My mouth quivered with emotion, and I replied softly, "rue from our garden."

"Hmm. Tastes almost like venison, but we've seen no deer lately." His voice was weak, but his eyes met mine.

I turned away, not trusting my face. "Truth be told, more of us will take sick if we don't ask the Indians for food. God persuaded the heathen to aid us again," I said.

"So ye got this from the Indians?" John asked calmly.

I gave a small nod of assent. "If we don't get rain soon, there will be no crop. Governor is proclaiming Thursday devoted to prayer for rain."

John closed his eyes briefly then sat up straight. "I've been too long in fevered dreams."

He spent some time writing before fatigue made him drop his quill.

That afternoon I was eager to leave hoeing the sparse weeds and run home to check on John. Mistress Brewster met me outside the door, her face so stricken that I feared he had taken a turn for the worse.

"It's not John," she said, relieving my fear, though it was short-lived. "It's Jane. I found her in the garden blood-soaked with Master Eaton's son wailing next to her lifeless body," she said, taking me in her arms and weeping. That night, she and I sewed Jane's shroud.

In the morning we gathered on the hill as Francis Eaton laid his second wife's body in the newly dug grave. Sobs wracked me and I hung onto Priscilla so as not to collapse.

Mistress Brewster took my arm as we walked back. "Ye've seen enough death to know the Lord calls us when He wants us. Jane may have been carrying a new babe—if so, God took it before it was formed."

That evening William Bradford came to Brewsters.

"I need help, Mother Brewster," our governor said. "Do you think that you could spare us Elisabeth during the day? We've no cook for us now, and you have Priscilla to help."

"Yea, we can manage." Mistress patted his arm. "Ask Elisabeth if she's willing."

William Bradford looked at my feet. "Well, what say you?"

"I would cook for your household, and do the washing. But I must say, Sir, where will the food come from?" Despair and anger pitched my voice high. "All of us are hungry. Jane might be with us still had she enough to eat."

"God will provide." His mouth twitched and made his mustache jump.

I tried to believe our governor, but if God was providing, little of it showed up on our table. The corn stores were so low we were only given a handful for each mouth. The men brought home a fish or two, but even the ducks seemed to have disappeared. Lack of rain left the corn plants limp. Our bodies were like the crops. We were all so bony that, in hot weather, we maids were not even wearing our stays and the men's ribs were visible beneath their sweat-soaked shirts.

Attitash

"Today we will give special prayers and dances to Kiehtan for rain." Mama stripped beans from their vines.

"The Strangers' weachimin does not grow." I looked across the brook to the dusty field. "Is that because they plant it without beans and squash?"

"Ahhe, the earth dries out fast under weachimin if nothing covers her." Mama laid the beans in her basket. "You gave Esapett dogwood bark for fever. But why did she need the partridge berry?"

"She shook all over and rolled her eyes, showing me that the man—Jon-owlan—was seized by bad spirits. Partridge Berry calms the seizing spirits, does it not?"

She nodded, then asked with concern, "You didn't go to their houses, did you?"

I kept my eyes down, hiding my irritation that Mama thought I was not using good judgment. "Of course I didn't, and I only gave her a little pinch. I know we can't dig more 'squa-root or find partridge berries until the leaves turn color."

Mama rewarded me with a smile. "You've learned well. If Jon-owlan needs food, the stew will help. If he is possessed by the seizing spirits, the 'squa-root will help. But if he has the Stranger's bad spirits, we have no medicine for it. That's why so many of our people die."

She called up to White Flower, who was chasing crows from the platform. "Come down!" she shouted. Then turned to me, "We'll sing prayers for rain."

Elisabeth
At first the day of prayer seemed tedious. I longed to gather mussels or tweak the little herbs in our garden. Anything to actually bring us something to eat rather than just sit in the Commonhouse. But the songs lifted my spirits in spite of our dire condition; something soft and cool filled my heart.

After a meager supper, mute with heat and exhaustion, I was drawn to the cooling seashore. I leaned into the wind, letting it tangle my skirts. Closing my eyes, I breathed in the smell of seaweed, fish and salt water, ignoring the cries of children and seabirds.

I opened my eyes to find John Howland holding a pointed stick. He led me to the wet sand and used the stick to make a large E, then added curlicues. "Do ye see what I wrote?" he asked.

"My mark?"

"Yea, Now do it thyself." John put the stick in my right hand.

I removed my shoes and the cool sea foam surged against my ankles as I attempted to write at the tide's edge. It took me several tries, letting the surf erase the failed attempts. Hoping the mark would look better, I glanced about to make certain no one watched and took the stick in my left hand.

"Not with thy left hand, Elisa!"

Glowering, I used my right instead. Finally my E looked like his. I tried to add curlicues, making more mess than mark. He showed me again. After the next tidal surge, I managed one that made him smile.

"Ye are ready for ink and paper."

I gave him back the stick. "Write my whole name, if ye please." I counted nine letters as he wrote them, but had only studied my name a moment when the surf obliterated it. John's stick moved faster and I read my name carefully four times before it dissolved under the water.

"Do ye know this?" John pointed to new writing.

"John," I read.

He laughed with pleasure, bowing elaborately. "I am indeed, John. And this?" He carved a large A.

"A for Adam."

"Yea, and Allerton." John grinned mischievously.

"Jack!" I grinned back.

A giggle behind us turned our heads. Little Mary Allerton and her big sister Remember were watching. John wrote their whole names while Remember informed me she knew the entire primer, "From Adam to the Fall of man."

It was oppressively warm in Brewsters' house, and I was too excited to sleep. In my mind I kept seeing "Elisabeth" in the sand. When I did sleep at last, I dreamed of brooks full of noisy water.

"Praise the Lord, He heard our prayers!" a voice cried.

We joined others outside, raising our arms to praise God. Rain! John Howland was leaping like King David dancing before the sacred Ark. Priscilla and I joined hands and swung each other until John Alden grabbed Priscilla away from me to lift her high. Mistress bade us to set out buckets to catch it as it soaked our caps, our hair, our clothes and our skin. It continued to rain all day and we went to the field late afternoon to find the drooping corn leaves standing proud once again.

"Still, we can't eat rain, and we can't eat crops that have no fruit yet," John Howland told Master Bradford at supper. "Mayhap King Massasoit has stores he would give us."

"Squanto says they have no more food." Governor Bradford said.

"What does Hobbamock say?" I asked. "His wife and daughter brought fish for our little babes. He might give you a different answer than Squanto did." The look on their faces told me I'd said enough.

"We could ask him, Sir," John Howland offered. "If he's willing, Hopkins and Winslow could go with him to ask Massasoit for food."

Governor Bradford considered this for a moment then told John it was worth trying.

"Take this back to Attitash," I whispered, handing him the small heathen bowl.

Attitash

Jon-owlan handed Mama the bowl I'd sent with his stew, looking not at Mama, but at me. "Catabatash."

He sat by our outside fire and accepted Papa's pipe. He struggled with our tongue, asking Papa to take Win-sow and Hop-kins to our Massasowet and beg for food.

"I need to pray and talk with my wife, before I decide," Papa told them. Jon-owlan thanked Papa and returned to his home while Win-sow and Hop-kins waited for Papa's decision.

"Does our Massasowet have enough weachimin?" Mama asked.

"If we don't get more weachimin for the Strangers, they won't survive. We'd lose their firesticks against our enemies." Papa lit his pipe, and shared it with Black Whale and Mama. We all began singing a prayer.

Mama stood and began packing food for the journey to our Massasowet. "Tisquantum must speak their tongue. But he must not be alone with Win-sow and Hop-kins. Black Whale will go with him. Attitash will carry the packs."

Papa nodded in agreement. "Black Whale can keep her safe."

Next morning we set out early to take the Strangers to our Massasowet. My new life was murmuring quietly in my belly to the rhythm of my pace. Win-sow and Hop-kins walked behind me. Their thin bodies were loaded down with heavy metal clothes and weighty fire sticks.

It was not yet dark when we reached the Titicut River. Our People there were collecting fish from the weir and gave us some of their catch. After we ate, we bedded down by the river. Black Whale loosened the string on his bow and placed his quiver of arrows where he could reach them, then crawled into our nest of summer deerskin. We began singing our night prayer, and I saw Win-sow raise his head from his sleeping spot several paces away. I hushed my voice to almost a whisper, and we finished quickly.

"Tisquantum said Sachem Bradford wants many kettles of food." Black Whale cupped his hands around my breasts as I snuggled into him. "They're bigger," he said.

"The kettles?" I said, giggling.

He tweaked my nipples.

I listened to see if New Life knew her father. I felt a

cool blowing, like the surface of still water when a breeze comes. "Do you think a cloth-woman talks to her baby before it's born?"

He was silent a moment. "I don't know if their women give birth. We can't see their legs or arms, much less their breasts. Maybe they don't make love like we do."

"They must, they have children."

"Their women don't seem real." He bent and kissed my hair.

"If they were not real, they would not be starving." I could not tell Black Whale how much it troubled me to see Esapett and her people starving.

Elisabeth

John returned that night and reported that Hobbamock left with Hopkins and Winslow. "They are our best hope," John said. "They understand the savage mind better than any." John paced the garden, looking to the southern hills, as if that would make them appear. "But even they may not be able to persuade Massasoit."

I did not answer, as he would not stand still long enough to listen. Never had I seen him so restless. Of course we were all worried that they would return empty handed—or not at all.

"John Alden and I will take the longboat and do some sea fishing," he finally said. "There's no great effort required, and the sea air will do me good."

I resolved to do some good myself while John was gone. It was time I applied myself to learning to read. Mistress Brewster needed no persuasion to assist me. That very evening she opened her Bible and we began. After I showed her what I knew, she took out her sons' primer and led me to more letters. At the end of our session she declared that I would have plenty to show John Howland if he returned safely from his fishing expedition.

19

Elisabeth

It was a calm sea when John Howland and John Alden took the longboat into the glimmering sea. By late afternoon black clouds appeared in the west as Priscilla and I hoed weeds. The wind grew ferocious, and we were running back when the storm caught us.

"Here! Into the Commonhouse!" Myles Standish yelled from the door as we came near.

Our clothes were wet and our coifs were plastered to our heads. There was nothing to do but take our coifs off and shake out our hair. We stood together, our stern faces defying any of the men to let their eyes linger on us. William Latham gave me a quick look, and then turned away; young John Billington rested his eyes on me. A brilliant flash of lightning lit the inside of the Commonhouse, accompanied by waves of thunder and wind shaking the building as if it were a ship out in a tempest.

I tried to picture the little boat bouncing up and down on a storm-struck sea. God had saved him once and he would not now die a young death, John had assured me. My heart wanted to believe it, but the image of him thrashing about in the depths of the waves would not leave me.

William Latham saw my distress and touched my arm. "Don't worry, Elisabeth, they would follow the coast and put to shore."

I put my other hand beneath my apron so the Billington

boy would not think I allowed him this familiarity. Young John seemed not to notice, but his fingers wiggled as if he knew not what to do with them.

When the storm had diminished and people were leaving the Commonhouse, I put on my damp coif without tying the wet strings and started walking with William Latham and young John Billington. Almost immediately, Giles Hopkins called to William and he went back to him.

I looked ahead for Priscilla, but could see no one in the gathering dusk. I began to walk faster. A sudden gust of wind blew off my coif. John Billington grabbed it, but instead of putting it in my outstretched hand, he reached to place it on my head. I snatched the cap and stepped back, but young Billington took my arms roughly, pulling me to him, his mouth pressed to mine. When I tried to squirm away from him, my feet slipped in the mud. His tongue pushed at my mouth, and though I attempted to bite down, he gripped my hair to pull my head back. With his other hand, he held my face, so that I could not move my jaw. Putting an elbow against his chest, I tried to make space for my breath. A sound escaped my clenched mouth, which I did not think I could make. Gathering my strength, I stomped on his foot and he jerked back from me. Taking advantage, I slapped his face hard. It hurt my hand, but I found much pleasure in the feel of his face recoiling from my hand and the shock in his eyes.

"Matta!" A tall figure ran toward us from the shadow of a rock by the shore. I realized it was Attitash's mother making a great noise. She was pointing her finger at young John with a derisive grin.

"Bloody savage," he shouted, which made her laugh wildly.

"Ahhe, Esappet," she called out and I took it as a compliment to my fortitude.

I looked around. Billington had disappeared. I ran on.

When I reached Brewsters' house, I looked back toward shore. Attitash's mother stood silhouetted by the sea.

Smoothing out my hair, I tied the strings of my cap and dried my eyes with my apron. My jaw hurt and my head ached where he had pulled my hair. I hesitated a moment more, loath to enter the house and face embarrassing questions.

Master and Mistress Brewster and Desire were deep in their Bible study. Priscilla sat reading to the Brewster boys and young William More. Only Desire looked up when I entered. I put my finger to my lips, and she swallowed her question.

"I'll wash if there's enough warm water," I said, as I turned my back to them and stood by the big pot on the fire.

"There's plenty warm water," Mistress Brewster said, looking me over. "The storm did drench thee, child."

I dipped the warm water into a bowl and splashed it over my face. Taking a cloth I began to scrub my mouth, but it did not feel clean. I climbed into Desire's bed, pulled shut the curtains and stripped off my damp clothes. With no dry shift to change into, I poked my face out of the curtains and motioned to Desire.

"Look at Elisabeth! Her hair's wet," young Wrastle Brewster crowed.

His father back-handed him without even bothering to put down his Bible.

I shut the curtains. Desire handed in a clean shift. Putting the pillow over my face, I shuddered with spent emotion. Satan continued to threaten me; even boys my age were drawn to do evil to me.

Next morning I hurried to cook breakfast at Governor Bradford's.

After I'd finished washing up, I went into the garden. Desire was there and demanded to know why I was so distressed the night before. My story spilled out.

"God was with thee if young Billington only got a kiss." Desire put her arm around me. "Don't ever be alone with him again."

"Well, I did not want to be alone with him last night!" I said hotly. "I tried to be civil to him, since he was with William Latham. But he took advantage of my kindness!"

"Thy kindness gave him leave to be familiar with thee." Desire's eyes brimmed with tears. "Boys want to be men, and a man will take the slightest kindness from a woman and use it to justify a base need on his own part. They will take more than just a kiss." Her mouth trembled and she put her hand over it.

"What happened, Desire?" I took her hand.

"It was so long ago," she clung to my hand as if she were younger than I. Her blue eyes glittered with tears. "Mother said it was my fault; that I'd been too forward." Sobs overwhelmed her, and she sank into my arms. "If Father knew how Mother's new husband betrayed her…and fouled my heart forever." Coughs followed the weeping, and I fetched some ale.

"I can never marry," she said flatly when she'd washed down the tea. "Elisabeth, save what ye have." I looked down. The Cur left me without a pure body to offer a husband. She put her hands on my shoulders. "If Billington bothers thee again, tell Elder Brewster he needs to speak to the boy. No use to speak to his father. Goodman Billington is an old goat who leers at all of us."

Pondering Desire's bitter memories, I spent the day in the field, avoiding the other maids' looks and questions.

William Latham came to the field carrying drinking water that afternoon. He also carried news. "John Howland is back and brought us a fish, Elisabeth. He let me carry it, and I set it out by the back door."

Wanting to see the fish, but even more wanting to see

John, I ran home. I found the big shad wrapped in a cloth. I lifted it to feel its weight.

"I caught it just this morn. It'll keep in the wet cloth 'til ye cook," said a voice behind me.

My heart raced as I spun to see John smiling. I wanted to throw my arms round him but Latham wandered back and saved me from myself. "I'll fix it for supper tonight," I said and stepped inside." I took a cup of tea for myself, but my hands shook so I had to put it down. "The storm came to thee at sea?"

"Yea, but God was with us." John ate the corn bread in one bite.

"What was it like out there?" William asked. "The storm was mighty awful here!"

"Oh, 'twas fierce all right! Have ye heard of a water-spout?" John asked. "The wind pulls the water upward until it becomes a funnel from the sea to the cloud! 'Twas an awesome thing to behold."

"Did it catch you?" William was bouncing on his feet with excitement.

"Nay, or we would have been thrown to the heavens. We made it to shore before it reached us and we stayed there in the shallows 'til morn."

"The storm cleared up here soon after sundown," I said. "We left the fields and ran to the Commonhouse when it began." I stopped, suddenly aware that my tale would get *me* into troubled waters.

"Young John Billington was right worried that you and Master Alden would perish," William told John. "But then he got distracted by Elisabeth."

My hand stopped with my teacup halfway to my mouth.

John Howland's eyebrows lifted. "Oh, Elisabeth is distracting." He smiled at me, and I thought perhaps we would get past this thorny discussion.

But William continued. "He's courting Elisabeth now."

"Stop these false rumors!" I hissed between clenched teeth.

"Oh, don't protest! I saw you kissing young Billington!" William stuffed the last of the bread into his prattling mouth.

John's face looked as if someone had taken his hair by the back of his neck and pulled it tight. Before I could speak, Governor Bradford came in the door. We all went silent.

I moved woodenly to bank the low burning fire. "I'll be back to cook the fish." I walked to the door, careful not to look at the men. "Tell me when you're ready, Governor."

Before I'd had time to cool my face with a wet cloth, John Howland came to Brewsters. "Shall I get thee more corn from the stores?" He did not look at me, so I murmured an assent and took the fish to his house to prepare. My hands were scratched from fish scales when John came through the garden gate, carrying a small sack of corn. He put the sack on the boards where I was scraping the shad, then sat down on a stump. I looked to see his expression, but he sat with his arms propped on his spread knees, his hands dangling, and his head down as if he were studying his hands. I wanted to stamp on his foot to make him acknowledge me.

At last he looked up at me, then at the sack of corn. "Is this sufficient for you?"

Even if his tone had not been cold, the "you" would have chilled me. I bit my lip and breathed through my nose so he would not hear my huffing.

"And when did I become 'you' instead of 'thee'?" I asked, controlling my anger.

John spoke as carefully as I had. "I am giving thee... you, the respect deserved by a maid old enough to kiss."

My mind scrambled for a dignified answer. Instead of finding a womanly response, however, I had to put my hand over my mouth to stifle my oath—bloody man!

"I am not in a position to say who you would welcome to court you." John continued to speak as though I were some stranger. "You are young, but surely ye—you have the sense not to choose a Billington."

"I am not a wayward girl, taking kisses from any boy who offers. Can I speak the truth to thee? I tried to stop young Billington... I did not want him near me. He..." I pushed up my sleeve past the blue and purple bruises on my arm.

"God in heaven!" John took my hands and kept hold of them. "Did he hurt thee elsewhere, Elisa?" He spoke with a soft fury.

"No....I mean...not much...I mean I slapped him back." He pulled me to him and I was silent, hearing his heart beat next to my ear.

"I told Desire," I said at last, raising my head away from his warmth. "She said to tell Elder Brewster, if young John doesn't leave me alone. But I can take care of myself."

"That stupid boy won't trouble thee again! Not when I'm done with him." John gripped my shoulders. "To think of thee, so young and fresh, having thy maidenhood threatened by that whelp!" He took my hand and traced my palm, moving his fingers to the mound of my thumb, which grew curiously warm. I doubted he'd be so ready to defend me had he known Billington was not the first to intrude on my person.

"Thy cheeks are warm." John traced one with his finger. "On such a hot day, thy coif does not shield thee from sun." He took the strings in one finger. "May I?"

"If my cap is to come off, I'll do it myself." I took back the strings and untied them.

John's brows lifted in question. "Do ye fear me?"

"Nay, but I must tell thee, Jack. I...we...took our coifs off after the storm. They were rain- soaked."

"Yea?" He waited, puzzled. When I did not respond, he added, "Is that not sensible?"

"But we maids were in the Commonhouse, and they... William Latham and...and young John...were there, too. So young Billington saw my hair."

"Seeing thy hair did not give him leave to touch thee." Then, gently, he said "I would touch thy curls, but only if ye gave me leave."

I removed my coif. It felt right to have John reach behind and loosen the twist holding my hair up. He pulled his fingers gently through my tumbling curls and leaned to kiss the top of my head.

Governor Bradford's voice intruded through the open window. I stood away and picked up the fish. "I believe the governor is waiting to eat thy fish."

We ate well that night. William Latham avoided my eyes at first, but after John Howland took him out to get more wood, he came back mumbling, "Beg your pardon for not seeing the truth in front of my eyes." Whatever John had said to him, it suited me.

After I cleaned up, I took a bucket to get more water from the rain barrels for our Saturday night bath. We had eaten late and the evening shadows were long on the fields between our garden and the woods. John joined me with another bucket and I spoke my mind without thought to whether I was being too forward. "Can I ask thee a question?" He seemed to want to tell me something first, but I persisted. "When ye kissed a maid for the first time, did ye ask her permission?"

"'Tis a good many years since I first kissed. I was but fourteen." He bit his lip. "She was older—sixteen." He ran a finger across my cheek. "Elisabeth," he said, unsure of how to proceed. "Did ye hear that young John Billington's gone missing?"

"How? When?"

"Governor just told me Goody Billington came to him before supper. Her son John never came home last night. She thought he'd show today, but no sign. His father went out with his whip. He'd have beaten the boy within an inch of his life if he'd found him. Governor Bradford says the wretch is either lost or the savages got him.'"

I felt no alarm. It was evident to me that young Billington felt too humiliated by my slap and Attitash's mother's taunting. He'd come home when he'd had enough time to lick his wounds.

Attitash

Mama told me how she saw the young man impose himself on Esapett and how she'd given him what he deserved. "They not only treat our girls and women rudely, they do not respect their own. He's a coward, running away when I taunted him. But Esapett is stronger than I thought." Cowards like to prey on children, she said, and anyone who pushed himself on his own kind would be an even greater danger to us. She warned White Flower to avoid this boy when he returned.

"Win-sow and Hop-kins are not like that boy," I said. It was true. During the journey to our Massasowet's, Black Whale was surprised that they showed us both respect. They tried to use our words and taught us some of theirs. And although Black Whale and I thought our Massasowet looked comical wearing the bright red coat they gave him, they gave something they valued.

Elisabeth

A day later, Winslow and Hopkins finally returned from Massasoit's village with Attitash and her husband, but without young Billington. They brought only one great kettle of corn.

Attitash put down her pack, obviously weary from the

long walk. I brought Attitash a dipper of water. She drank deeply, thanked me and stood to stretch. Her lean body was exposed, and I noticed a small mound pushing her naval. Putting my hand on my own flat stomach, I asked in my own words if she were with child. Her laugh of delight answered.

"Only one kettle of corn?" Governor Bradford asked, as Squanto and Master Winslow told us about their journey.

"Do not despair," Master Winslow said. "Massasoit has promised more corn from his stores in another village."

Much of what Master Winslow and Master Hopkins told us was so strange, I could scarce believe it. They'd met Governor Massasoit at one of his homes and spent a sleepless night on the same bed as the Indian governor and his wife.

"How did your father sleep?" I asked Constance.

She laughed. "Who could sleep in the same bed as savages, though their sleeping platform was as big as two or three beds? Even when they were traveling, the Indians kept Father and Master Winslow awake by singing themselves to sleep." Constance scooped a dipper of corn and added it to her basket. "Not a pretty song, more like wailing." She laughed again, then lowered her voice. "Mother says Father should not speak of sleeping in the same bed. People will talk."

20

Elisabeth

I woke with my lower belly feeling like I had swallowed a writhing snake. My need to piss was too strong to take time to dress and go outside. I lifted my shift and sat on the piss-pot. When I finished, I dressed and took it out to the muck-heap. Pouring it out, I saw little strands of blood floating in the yellow piss. Fear swirled up in me like cold sea water. The curse had spread to my most private place! Shaking with sudden chills, I twisted my skirts up so I could see my legs. The dim light of early dawn showed streaks of blood running down each leg. Wiping out the piss-pot with leaves, I tried to collect my wits.

"What's troubling thee, child?" Mistress Brewster stood at the doorway.

My face flamed "Nothing."

"Have ye taken ill?"

"My belly hurts...down here." A cramp in the region I indicated made me wince. "Hurts bad."

"Have thy monthly courses hit thee?" Mistress put her arm around my shoulder.

I remembered the excited hushes when my sister Rose became a woman. "Could that be? There's a bit of blood in the piss-pot, but I didn't think..."

"Methinks ye have become a woman. I made extra clouts for when ye'd need them."

I wondered what Mother would say, then remembered her face bearing a confusing mix of fear and gladness when Rose became a woman. I could hear her voice saying to me, "Already?"

The clout felt like I was riding a cloth goat. The waist band lacings were either too tight or too loose and the clout slid about chafing my thighs. I wondered if John Howland could tell from my awkward carriage that I had become a woman.

My nightly prayers were that my blood would wash away The Cur's curse. I also included thanks to God for being free of young John Billington. However, I feared his absence would end with dire consequences for me. What if he'd been killed by a wild animal—or one of the many Indians hostile to Massasoit as well as to us? Would I be held responsible for his running off because I did not turn aside his approach more courteously? My courses ended within a week, as Priscilla had told me they would.

No more corn had been brought to us though it was promised. Humility's and little Samuel Eaton's hunger nearly put the Billington boy out of my mind. Always, I prayed for food.

This last prayer was answered when Tokamahamon—another Indian who spoke some English—delivered several more kettles of corn. He also brought a message that young Billington had been rescued from the Narragansetts and was with some Wampanoag who lived along the Cape. He would be returned to us. The rescue party would go by shallop.

We cooked up the new corn into bread to send with them. There was plenty now to keep our own bellies from aching. I prayed constantly for John Howland's safe re-turn, and sometimes prayed that he would have revenge on John Billington. The days were slow and the nights crawled.

Near the end of the third day, William Latham dropped his hoe and hollered, 'Look to sea! The Shallop's com-ing!" Seagulls seemed to be leading the little boat, shriek-ing as they wheeled and turned around it. With little wind in its sails, it came slowly with the incoming tide. All of us ran down to the water to wait for the shallop. Francis Billington was at the water's edge with his mother, so I stayed back. As the boat drew near, we could see young John Billington, standing by Master Winslow in the bow of the shallop. I waved to John Howland, and then went back to his house to prepare food.

The corn bread was ready and goat cheese on the table when William Latham burst in. "We have him." John Howland came just behind William.

I composed my face. "How does he?"

"Scared, tired. Not as hungry as we are." John picked up a piece of corn bread, without sitting down or waiting for it to be blessed.

"And where was he?" I handed John a beaker of ale.

"Halfway 'round the Cape! We stopped at Cummaquid first, and they directed us next day to a place called Nauset. The long and short of it is the Indians at Nauset brought young Billington." John gave me a grin that more than hinted revenge. "The boy has a bit of a bruise on his face."

"Did the Indians punch him?" William Latham asked.

"Nay, we figured he'd caused us such trouble that we'd not wait til we got home, and Governor Bradford could deliver the rod on his back. This new bruise he got in the boat." John was enjoying himself.

I turned away so William and Master Eaton would not see my pleasure.

"Why had they kept him there so long?" Francis Eaton asked. "Did the boy not want to return home?"

"Some of Massasoit's people found young John half dead in the woods. They were bringing him here when Narragansetts attacked and took the boy to bargain with us." John lit his pipe and blew the smoke out slowly. "King Massasoit's people at Nauset rescued the boy back from the Narragansetts."

"The heathens are fighting with each other?" William's brow knotted.

"Just as we Christians do." John made a wry face. "Think how it is at home! French against English. English loyal to the king's version of religion against English loyal to God."

"Well done, John!" Governor Bradford arrived and clapped John on the shoulder. "Survived the storm, negotiated with the Indians, and returned the prodigal son to us!" He sat down by John, and I handed him some ale. The governor took a quick drink then set the beaker down carefully, as if he were using it to compose himself. "I admit I kept thinking of my own son back in Holland, and how it would be if he were ever to get lost."

"What will happen to the Billington boy now?" I asked in a tight voice.

"I told his father I would mete out the punishment myself for the boy running away, since we risked our lives to find him." Governor Bradford turned to me. "We'll eat supper later tonight; I must take the boy to the Common-house to give him the rod first."

"Then the punishment will be just; not an ungodly father's revenge." John spoke carefully, still looking at his hands.

"At least his father won't feel a need to impress the rest of us with his punishment to cover the shame of an untamed boy," Governor said. "But I venture that he'll still feel compelled to give his own when he gets the boy alone."

For several days, young Billington skulked about with a permanent scowl, keeping his distance. His mother scolded our governor for not finding her son earlier. Goodman Billington cursed his son loudly, proclaiming he'd chastened his boy sufficiently with the rod to make him obedient. "The Devil had hold of him, 'twas my wife's left hand that petted him too much when he was a lad, passing her fiendish ways on him."

I shut my ears to worrying about the Billington household. Within a week, when Isaac Allerton came to have a drink of ale with our Governor, I was put into a cauldron of troubles that made young Billington seem a trifle.

"How old is Elisabeth?" Isaac Allerton asked. Flecks of tobacco clung to his light brown mustache, and the smell of his pipe smoke rose from his clothes. I brought the flask of ale to the table, but he ignored me.

Governor Bradford glanced at me with raised eyebrows, and I drew myself up tall. "She's standing right beside thee, Isaac, and can speak for herself."

Master Allerton did look at me then. I felt as though I were a horse up for sale at the fair. I was tempted to ask Isaac Allerton if he wished to know how well I'd breed, but held my tongue, as my neck and face flushed hot. "I was baptized August, 1607, Sir."

Master Allerton's brow knit as he calculated my age. "Ah then, she is fourteen years—the age when orphans can choose with whom they will live." I looked to John Howland. His jaw was clenched. He was holding his tongue until our governor and Deputy Governor Allerton settled on where I would spend the next seven years slaving for my keep. Master Allerton shook his thinning hair out of his pale blue eyes. "Orphans with financial means, of course, and the age when those without are taken into servitude."

Servitude! I held onto the ale flask with both hands so I wouldn't drop it. In my suffering at the loss of my parents and then the Carvers, I had not thought of this consequence of their deaths.

Master Allerton held out his glass and I poured carefully, using my right hand. He again addressed Governor Bradford, with no glance to me. "Will she be indentured with the Brewsters or thee, William?"

Governor Bradford waved his hand in dismissal. "Brewster's agreed to assume her care until she turned fourteen. When Elisabeth came to cook for us after Jane died, we made no arrangement for her future."

"She is sorely needed in my house before we begin harvesting," Isaac Allerton said, wiping ale off his mustache. Fatigue showed in the dark pouches under his eyes. "I am the only man here with three motherless children. 'Twill be at least next spring before a ship might come and I can get a new wife."

"Are you proposing servitude or wedlock, Isaac?" John asked the question that was crammed in my throat. Seven years working for Allerton was prison enough—marriage to that man was unthinkable.

"Servitude. Under my oversight, Elisabeth could be washed clean of her afflicted left hand." Allerton glanced casually at my hands. I hid them under my apron. "We all heard Goodwife Tilley try to break the child of Satan's hold on her hand. I can be much firmer with the rod." Master Allerton held out his beaker but I went back to the fire, restraining my wish to dash the precious last bit into his eyes. "She can sleep on the floor with my daughters. I'll keep my son in my bed to be certain Bartholomew does not bother her."

Bartholomew is not the bother, I thought, his father is.

"Not only do I need her now, but 'twould be far easier for me to find a bride if my home offered a maidservant."

"Surely we need no reminder that many of us lost our wives," Governor Bradford said with a trace of bitterness. "However, my own child remains in Holland so I have not thy burdens, Isaac." William Bradford squared his shoulders. "With so many men and so few women, however, we all have need of help."

Master Allerton clenched his pipe with white knuckles.

Governor Bradford finally spoke into the silence. "Pray

God a ship will arrive soon—with willing women and necessary goods." He lit his own pipe, puffed on it, then at last turned to me. "I had not realized that ye had reached fourteen years, Elisabeth. 'Tis time ye begin thy servitude. I'll speak to Father Brewster."

I drew a breath to keep my tongue civil. "Excuse me then, Sirs, while you determine my future." I grabbed a bucket to collect mussels and ran out the door.

Isaac Allerton's daughters, Remember and her little sister Mary, were helping Mistress Brewster in her garden. Truth be told, both girls did sorely need a mother. I had not thought until then about my particular situation. Desire and Priscilla had their own wealth. Constance had a father and two servants as well as a stepmother. Mary Chilton was already claimed by the Winslows. I alone was in need of being kept by a master. *Merciful God*, I prayed. *Do not deliver me to Isaac Allerton.*

Desperate for solace, I ran to the seashore. As I hoped, no one was there but the little shorebirds. They ceased their pecking in the sand as I came, and flew up, gathering into a cloud that puffed big and small as they circled. Weighed down by my prospects, I sat on a rock and considered my lot. Whether I was in servitude to Allerton or Bradford, within a year there would be a new mistress for me to work under. Whoever either of them married, she would not likely be as kind as Mistress Carver or Mistress Brewster.

The fright chilling my blood would not let me sit. As I rose, the shorebirds flew up again with a whoosh and formed their undulating banner, waving back and forth as though they were connected to each other. Moved by their freedom, I whirled around as though I could shake off the invisible bonds that held me. The birds screeched, and their banner moved over the water. I turned to see what had startled them and met John Howland. He came quickly toward me and sat down without speaking, his eyes holding mine.

"I confess I did not see this coming." John clenched a stick so hard it broke. "I thought thy family left thee enough goods for thy keep until ye were old enough to wed."

"'I did not understand this...this consequence myself!" Fighting my despair, I looked to the east, where the vast sea separated us from England. I had assumed Brewsters would keep me after I was old enough to work. But they had not the means the Carver's had. "My father was a cloth maker. We had little to spare when the cost of wool or flax was too great or the price of cloth too low." I paused, thinking of my sisters and brothers back home wedded, with families, and oblivious to my plight. "Father assured us the Lord would provide in this Promised Land. He spent all he had saved to come here." I looked past John to the birds, searching the shore for food. "Never did it occur to me I would be in servitude. Now I am like these birds, scrambling to survive!" I turned away from the birds on the shore and looked up at an eagle circling high.

John threw the broken pieces of his stick into the water, startling the birds again. "If ye are willing, I'll speak to Elder Brewster."

"What could ye say? That ye would be my master?" My dread gave a harsh edge to my voice. "There's naught for me but to accept that I'll spend seven years indentured to Master Allerton, doing whatever he wants day and night."

The birds settled down again, their long bills pecking in constant motion. John took my hand. "Elisabeth, I must tell thee. For some time I've had tender feelings toward thee. Ye were so young, I thought I was like an uncle to thee, but ye've bloomed and ..."

I ducked my head to hide my tears with my arm. If I

cried like a little girl, I could not expect him to treat me like a woman.

His long strong fingers linked tight with mine. "When young Billington tried to have his way with ye..." He saw me flinch, but continued. "I knew then that I was not like an uncle to ye." I tried to speak, but John silenced me with his eyes and took my other hand. "I've fallen in love with thee, Elisabeth. Ye are young, but might ye love me someday?"

"But I love thee already, John." I took my hands back and crossed my arms around my body. How would I tell John I was too damaged by Satan's snare to ever be a man's wife? "But ye could not wait seven years for me! Ye...you need a wife and children. You are long a grown man and can get a wife from England."

He flinched, the hurt showed in his eyes. I had not thought to injure his feelings by calling him "you," but to acknowledge the distance we could not cross.

"'Tis not my intention to wait seven years nor is it to get another wife!" He took hold of my shoulders and locked his eyes with mine. "I will wait 'til ye are ready to be a true wife, but I'll wait for thee as thy husband."

My confusion overwhelmed me. "Stop speaking in riddles! What would ye say to Elder Brewster?"

"I would tell him we want to be married now!"

Stunned, I pulled my hands from his. "But I'm only fourteen! I'm too young! Too young to face the peril of childbirth!" Wild thoughts whirled in my mind, bumping into each other.

"Just as I was saying!" He grabbed my fluttering arms. "I would not ask thee to consummate our vows, until ye are ready." He held me at arm's length, and his eyes were as dark green as the depths of the sea. "Trust me, dear one. I would not force thee. Ye would continue to sleep at Brewsters' until ready to be in my bed."

My heartbeat seemed to slow as if I had just been covered with a warm cloak in the midst of a chill wind. I took a deep breath and blew it out. I wanted to accept this balm for only a blessed minute, even though I was obligated to reject it.

John bent his head and kissed me quickly. "Think on it, my love. Pray on it. Elder Brewster would receive some of my small wealth to cover thy care."

I stepped back, my tongue searching for an excuse to cover my secret shame. "Do not think ye must offer me this out of pity."

He reached for me, but I pulled away. To hide my deception, I turned to the rocks where the mussels lodged and began collecting. My fingers were almost as numb as my heart. I peeked back and saw him standing, his hands clasped to his head. Leaving my bucket, I ran along the shore until I reached the rocks that formed a wall. I had not crossed over it before, since it was the barrier between our village and Hobbamock's homesite. My need to be out of sight of anyone in Plimoth drove me to pick my way over, scraping my arms and ankles. I sat down by the two large rocks that leaned against each other like "A-for-Adam." While my breath slowed, I reviewed the startling turn of events. Was John truly in love with me or only offering to wed because of his kind heart? Even if he loved me, he would not wed me if he knew how impure I was. And if I did not tell him, I would forever fear my dreadful secret would be discovered.

Peeking back through the triangle formed between the A-for-Adam rocks, I saw a small figure in the distance. John was still waiting. As I watched, he turned and trudged out of sight.

A whistle startled me out of my reverie. It was not a bird, but Attitash. She gave me a small smile as she came to sit near me. I wondered if she found it too bold of me to come to her side of the rocks.

"Esapett." Her eyes questioned mine while she wiped her own, as if they too held tears. I longed to talk to her, but had so few words. I felt like a babbling babe.

Attitash reached and took my hands. Mine looked chapped and red next to her brown ones. Her hands carried solace.

"Netop," she squeezed my hand.

"Ne-top?" I repeated.

"Ahhe, Esapett—Attitash." She took our clasped hands and moved them toward me, then back toward herself.

"Thank ye, ca-taba-tash—," I responded, wondering if 'netop' meant sympathy, worry, or kindness.

"Esapett no smile." The openness in her face warmed my closed-off soul. My secret had been kept for nine long months, now it was pushing through the scars, tearing me open.

I tried to force a smile, but my mouth was stiff. Closing my eyes to stop the tears, I drew a deep breath. "I have trouble—worry."

"You want baby?" Attitash patted the slight swell in her own belly.

"Nay—matta!" But that was a lie. I did want a child. "Yea, ahhe. I do want. But a bad man…," I put on a mean face and made the vulgar motion for man I'd seen her use, "…touched me here." I placed my hands over my bosom. "I can't suckle with unclean breasts and soul." My empty arms began rocking my ribs.

The shock on Attitash's face showed she understood at least some of my meaning. She looked up the shore, touching her eyelids. "Jon-owlan not…see?"

"Nay—matta." Sobs broke from me unhindered. She embraced me until I quieted, then lifted my chin.

"Attitash help Esapett." She made motions, waving her hands in the air, then bringing them to her nose as if breathing in fresh air. Stroking my face with both hands, she smiled and I comprehended she was offering me healing. Attitash had helped us grow crops when none would grow and she had given John Howland a medicine that made him well. Whatever she offered, I would accept. If God would use a heathen's potion to heal me, I could not question His ways. If this was not God's work and I was not healed, I was destined to carry my hidden shame and live as a servant.

Summoning my courage, I whispered, "I will. Ca-taba-tash."

Attitash counted on her fingers, showing me three. After she pointed at the sun, she made three circles in the sand.

I nodded. Three circles of the sun, three days until she would try to rid me of the shame upon my body. If her potion worked, my hollow place would fill with warmth again. With that hope, I could become betrothed to John Howland and be spared from going into servitude. With her healing and God's continued blessing, I might be pure enough to be John's true wife in a year.

The sunset was bouncing my shadow against the rocky shore. Afraid I'd lose my courage if I hesitated, I ran so fast I stumbled several times, puffing hard when I rounded the point of the shore and saw my Jack's dear figure coming my way. I could not hear what he called over the crash of waves as the tide came to shore, but I did not need to. His face was filled with concern. Heedless of the cold in my hollow place, I stood before him and put out my hands. He gripped them tightly and asked me over and over what was wrong. I could not speak.

At last John released me. "Ye worry me, running away like that. I would not have thee choose me to avoid servitude—only if ye truly wish to be my wife."

"Ye would be willing to wait for me?"

"Better for me to wait a year for thee, than to see ye drudge seven years for another man and his family." He stroked my face. "I must wait. I could not take another woman to wife. None other would be as wise. None as beautiful. None as strong."

I looked down at my clenched hands, gathering courage for what I must say. "John, I cannot give thee an answer until after the Sabbath."

"It's already Wednesday, do ye need more time?"

"Truth be told…" But the truth could not be told. Only some of the truth. "I have an ailment."

"Ye are ill? Ye looked a bit peaked, but not truly sick."

"It's ….it's an ailment young maids suffer."

That stopped him. Face flushed deep red, he opened his mouth and closed it again.

"I think it can be cured," I said. That is, there seems to be a remedy." My words spewed heedlessly out, so fast he looked more confused. "If the remedy does not work, I would not be able to bear children, and ye do want children."

John rubbed his face with both hands then dropped them at his side."Yea, I mean, pray God I would have sons."

We sat down together, wordless in our need to understand each other.

"So ye believe ye could be healed soon?" He sat just close enough to me that I could feel his heat.

"By Sabbath day. I'm told it takes four days." I was certain he would not tread into the secret world of women and maids.

"Elisa—dear one," he finally murmured. "I can wait four days. I said I'd wait for thee a year. If ye heal, and will consider my offer, ye must believe I did not propose marriage as a mere attempt to save thee from Isaac Allerton."

"Be assured, Jack, I confess I had dared to dream ye might someday."

"I know this is not how ye dreamed of receiving a proposal," he interrupted.

"I always dreamed my husband would be like thee." I could say this truthfully. "Someone with a kind heart, clever with his mind and his hands." I moved my hands to feel the muscles in his arms. "Strong, and if good looking, all the better."

He kissed me. I dared not open my lips and taste him.

"God will surely make thee well."

"Wait until Sabbath. If Providence gives me this grace, ye will wait to bed me."

"I want thee now, but I will wait. And I will pray." John touched his lips to my hand.

My own prayer that my twisted soul would heal without ruining his, was silent but fervent. I dared to hope God heard it.

When I entered Brewsters' house, I stepped softly on the fresh laid rushes. Humility and Priscilla were already asleep. I touched Humility's rosy cheek. Pray God John Howland would father a child for me.

Sleep would not come to anyone so filled with contradictions. 'Twas true that whether I went into servitude or became a wife and mother, I might still die young. And only God knew where I would spend eternity either way. When exhaustion overpowered me, I vowed to forego Attitash's cure. Even if she were my friend, her cure might guarantee my eternity in hell. Then reality clothed me with despair. If I did not go to Attitash, I would never be John's wife. I would be Isaac Allerton's maidservant, and when he married, I would serve his wife. My red-brown curls would turn gray, my strong firm body become bent like my mother's had been, and remain unmarried. Rising from my bedding, I swallowed my fears. I would risk my soul to my heathen friend.

Attitash

"How do Strangers say netop?" I asked Papa, remembering the uncomprehending look on Esapett's face when I used the word.

Papa tested the point of his spear with his finger. "Winsow said, 'fa-rends,' when he talked about our people joining together against enemies."

I went over to mother at the drying fire. "I must see her soon, she needs a healing ceremony—she needs to be cleansed." I spoke softly, wanting only my mother to hear my suggestion. Mama carefully composed her face, stood and led me to the moon lodge.

"You cannot heal a clothwoman," Mama's nostrils flared. "Esapett would not want it, even if she needs it."

"She wants it, she told me."

"Told you? You can't even make her understand 'netop.'"

"Her face is frozen with trouble." I remembered Esapett's unmoving eyes. "I took her hands and her bones cried out. She suffered from a bad man, worse than I suffered from the Narragansett." The bitter taste of anger thickened my tongue. I licked my lips. "She is afraid to lie with a husband. She'll never have children."

Mama's mouth lost its tight line. Her face took on sadness she rarely let show. I'd seen it when my brother was born too early and did not live to be named. She squared her shoulders. "Their gods killed so many of our Wampanoag. It's their Gods that made the man do this, her own people must cure her."

"Isn't that why her people can't heal her? Their gods do not want her healed. We must try, Mama. She saved Little Fish."

Mama sang a low prayer, closing her eyes to listen. When she opened them again, she looked at me as she had when I wanted to bury Yellow Hair. "You must tell no one. You will be either a strong leader or the cause of big trouble, Daughter. This could bring her Gods' destruction to our people."

At dawn, on the third circle of Nippa'uus, I waited for Esapett on the shore where we'd last met. There would be no healing if she could not open her heart and accept the sacred offerings. When the first rays lit the top of the trees, the space between Leaning Rock showed her coming. I went back to our path, knowing she would follow me at a safe distance. At the edge of our homesite clearing, I paused to make certain Tisquantum was not around. When we entered the moon lodge, Mama had sweet grass burning in a small bowl and partridge berry leaves floating in warmed water. Mama pointed to a fur for Esapett to sit on and gave her a cup of warm water. Esapett looked shocked when Mama and I removed our one-shoulder dresses. I gave her my warmest smile, gesturing to her own body. At last, she took off most of her cloth, still wearing a thin layer. Her arms and shoulders were bony and sickly white. I placed my hand protectively over the slight swelling over my navel.

Mama began the healing prayer singing softly and I joined in. Esapett's Eyes-Like-Quiet-Water were huge, but she kept her face still. Mama gently waved the sweetgrass smoke to her own face, breathing deeply. She offered it to me and I did the same. Mama then presented it to Esapett, whose jaw was clenched and her eyes squeezed shut. Esapett waved her hand, but not to the sacred smoke. As Mama directed it to Esapett's tight face, I sang softly, clapping my hands like songsticks. Finally, Esapett breathed the smoke in and coughed. Mama took off Esapett's cap, brushing the curls from her forehead. Keeping her eyes on Esapett's, Mama slowly pulled Esapett's dress down below her little breasts. Esapett inhaled sharply, but did not push Mama's fingers away. Mama sang as she traced Esapett's body with the sacred smoke, and then repeated with the sacred water. Esapett began shaking and called out in her harsh tongue. I put my arms around her and pulled her against me. My own voice trembled a little, but I reached deep and filled my throat until my song was strong again.

Esapett slumped in my arms. Her face smoothed and her jaw relaxed. She began a very quiet humming, like the birds sing just before dark.

Elisabeth

I had expected a medicine to drink, or a poultice. It took all my strength to hold myself straight when Attitash's mother exposed my body. Attitash's wild singing made it difficult to keep still as her song went up and down and did not ever find a pretty note to rest on. The pungent smoke I was forced to breathe was not the smoke in our pipes. Despite my efforts to remain aloof, when the warm water sluiced over my breasts, I lost my composure and began to convulse. More water, then more smoke and I forgot where I was.

> *Mother took my face between her hands. "Be careful, Elisabeth." She led me to get water from the spring. But the path was crowded, filled with so many people that I lost Mother. I cried out, "Mother! Why did you leave me? I'm so alone. It was The Cur. It was The Cur. The Cur!" John Howland was astride a horse, holding a small child in front. I was now riding in a cart, surrounded by many children of all ages, an infant at my breast.*

Someone was holding me. A friend was holding me, singing the wild song into my ear. Attitash. Her song released the bitter turmoil in me, though I knew not how I was cleansed. My head felt as though cold water had been sprinkled on it. "Ca-ta-ba-tash," I took Attitash's hand in mine, and nodded my thanks to her mother who opened the flap for me and I ran.

When I'd climbed over the A boulders and reached the mussel bed, I let the sea wash over my feet. A bubble of laughter welled up from my belly; finally I was able to feel pleasure again. Bare feet appeared by my basket and I looked up to see Remember and Mary Allerton. Remember's face was so flushed that her freckles stood out. Her smile was tight and fake; my hand tingled with the need to rub those freckles off her face. Little Mary greeted me politely, but Remember took her sister by the hand and pulled her splashing back through the tide's curl to their father's house. Had they seen me at the Indian women's hut? No matter, I was free to accept John Howland's love and avoid Isaac Allerton's house.

With my cleansed heart singing beneath my activity, I hurried about the endless Saturday tasks.

21

Elisabeth

"Priscilla, will ye marry John Alden?" I asked. "The two of you have been cooing like nesting birds."

"Are ye the last one to notice?" Priscilla showed her dimples with the smile of an innocent maid. "We hope to wed in early fall. John will build us a house as soon as he can." She neatly tucked her hair back into her coif and took up her pestle again, swiftly pounding the corn into meal for the Sabbath.

"I am happy for thee," I said with sincerity, although a tinge of jealousy made my words sound flat.

Priscilla's smile faded. "One thing troubles me, Elisabeth. My mother and father would not have wished for me to marry a cooper."

"But he has the skill and strength to properly build and seal a barrel, so our ale will ripen instead of rotting. Is that not worthy in a husband?"

She sighed. "He is not gentry like my family."

"We are in a new world now, Priscilla."

"Yea. If only they could have known how glad John Alden makes me!" She beamed her dark blue eyes on me. "I would hope to be happy for thee, Elisabeth. If Governor Bradford does not send thee to Allerton, where will ye be?"

"God alone knows."

Sabbath morning the men marched to the meeting house, followed by women, maids and children. During the hymn, John looked across at me on the women's side, but I kept my face a mask. Edward Winslow stood to read Scripture, announcing a passage from the first chapter of the gospel of Mark. I had given up listening to him and was praying for the Holy Spirit to fill me, when his voice cut through my prayer.

A man with an unclean spirit..cried out...and Jesus rebuked him, saying 'hold thy peace, and come out of him.

I stole a look across the aisle at John Howland. His face was peaceful, calm. No doubt, John believed Jesus could call an unclean spirit out, but he might never believe God would use a barbarian to cleanse me. I would tell John that I was healed, but I could not tell him how.

We did not eat Sabbath supper until sundown. I had the meal nearly ready when John came in with a load of wood. He stood rooted when I turned, and I could not pull back the love from my smile. Before I spoke, the smile on his own face told me he knew my answer. I was glad no one else was in the room to divine my feelings.

William Latham came in the door with the yoke and two full buckets of water and looked at me with surprise. "Are you so glad then to be going to Master Allerton's?" he asked.

"Put the water down, William, and get to the table." I commanded as if I were already a mistress. Little Samuel Eaton toddled in with his father, and I set him on a chair with a biscuit.

Once I had laid out the food, Governor Bradford blessed it, and then turned to me. "Elisabeth, John How-land said ye have an opinion on thy placement. Are ye willing to go to Master Allerton's or do ye wish me to find thee other servitude?"

"Yea, I do have an opinion, but not about servitude." I could not help blushing.

Before Governor Bradford could respond, John spoke. "Elisabeth will not go into servitude if Elder Brewster agrees that she shall be my wife."

Governor Bradford's face flushed. "Ye may wish to prevent her servitude and get thyself a wife, John. But we cannot allow such a young maid to be brought to the marriage bed. We are not like the gentry in England who marry off young maids to secure wealth."

"Do I strike you as a man who would do so!" John slammed his beaker on the table, sloshing ale.

"John, John." Governor Bradford spoke as to a young boy-servant. "Take thyself outside and cleanse thy temper. Then we can have a civil discourse."

John rose and stalked off, but stopped at the door, his voice back to its usual timber though his fists were still clenched. "My apologies. However, you must know that, should Elder Brewster agree to my proposal, I would provide for her keep. Elisabeth would remain in Brewster's house 'til she's woman enough to become a true wife." He left the door open as he went out and I could see him pacing about the garden.

Little Samuel started to wail, and I picked him up to shush him while I formed a response. After coming through hellfire and finally being cleansed, I would not let all my hopes end with the small matter of my tender years. Little Samuel subsided to a whimper and I addressed our governor. "You are right, Sir; I am too young to marry, but I trust John to treat me with respect."

Governor Bradford's eyes softened. "Ye would not rush to the marriage bed, Elisabeth?"

"Nay, Sir." I gave Master Eaton his son and got the kettle to pour more tea. Facing our governor again, I took a deep breath. "You must trust me also, Governor. Neither John nor I wish to let our love lead us too soon to bedding. But, these are awful times, Governor. I would accept his legal care and his offer to contribute to my necessities."

Governor Bradford took a big spoonful of the pottage, swallowed it as if he had nothing on his mind but food, then went to the door and called John back in. "We'll go together to speak to her guardians, Howland. If Father Brewster agrees, I will inform the assembly ye are betrothed." Governor Bradford did not wait for John's reply, but sat to take a long drink of tea and eat the remains of his cornbread. "She's learned to cook well for such a young thing. If her guardians agree, John, I believe ye would get thyself a good wife."

'Good wife,' I thought happily to myself. *Goodwife or Good Mistress, but no longer 'good maidservant.'* John met my eyes, and the warmth in them made me think that if I were truly cleansed, one year might be too long for us to wait.

There was a brief discussion with Elder Brewster to which I was not privy. He came to the house and without much ado, took my hand and gave it to John. Our betrothal was accomplished. John kissed my hand quickly. We both stood smiling at each other, until Elder Brewster laughed and walked me back to his house.

Mistress Brewster waited until next morning to counsel me. "Ye are too young to be brought to childbed. This scheme to avoid thy servitude depends on a lusty young man like John Howland allowing thee to be wife in name only." She set the kettle to boil and blew up the fire. "Can ye hold him off?"

"Yea, Mistress!" I bit my lip. "Truth be told, I fear being brought to childbed too young."

"Fear is a strong defender of maidenhood." Mistress measured out a bit of tea. "See that he does not touch thee below the waist."

I stiffened, at a loss for words. Did she know that I'd been foully touched already?

Mistress glanced up and saw my discomfort. "Take care. My granddam gave me that advice when I first met William Brewster. I was in love *and* pure when we married." I wondered if she ever wanted badly for her husband to touch her. Since my cleansing, I had felt afire whenever John was close. But I was uncertain if that meant I was still not pure or was now free to love.

As we collected our harvesting baskets, Desire spoke to me with urgency. "This will get thee out of servitude, Elisabeth, but John is more than twice thy age! If he changes his mind before ye consummate the marriage, he might annul it."

"Change his mind?" I was so agitated I babbled. Did Desire believe John could be forced to disown me? "Why would that happen, Desire?"

"John's done with his own apprenticeship and has Carver's worldly goods," she said. "He could get a mature maid for wife on the next ship." She saw the fury in my eyes. "I don't want to upset thee, Elisabeth. It's plain he does care for thee. But I want thee prepared for the ways of men."

"I know ye've cause to distrust men, and so have I." I tried to keep my voice gentle, but firmness underlay the soft tone. "But my John is different."

She looked away from me. Knowing Desire could not forgive her mother for sending her away—treating her own daughter instead of the new husband as the problem—I pondered how to replace her festering bitterness. A gift occurred to me. "If God blesses us with a daughter, we would name her for the desire of the Lord, just as you were."

Desire did not respond as a coughing fit caught her.

"If ye hold our little Desire, God willing," I continued, "ye would know her father's and mother's love is as strong as thy father's was for thee."

Desire conquered her cough but was silent as we continued walking to the fields. We had already begun picking corn when she burst into sobs. I put down my basket and went to her.

"Forgive me, Elisabeth," she burst out. She opened her arms and we wept together.

Though I still carried secrets, I was free of Satan's hold—ready to take John Howland's name. I was a bit lightheaded from an overwhelming happiness, such as I had never known. Surely the same Divine Providence which brought John Howland out of the sea would now provide a bright new future for me.

It seemed the day would end as well as it began. As we returned from the fields late afternoon, the men sighted a flock of geese and took their fowling pieces out. By the time supper was on the table, my newly betrothed had brought me three geese. As soon as I'd cleaned up I took them back to Brewsters' garden to pluck. Mistress had taught me how to reach under the heavy feathers covering the breast and find the softest down for my bridal pillows. When too many of the downy feathers blew away in the breeze, I became exasperated. Mistress Brewster laughed at my attempts to grab the floaters, reminding me to spend my efforts plucking.

When my bag was full at last, I left the bare-skinned geese covered with cloth and went along the path toward the seashore, floating like goose-down myself.

In the days since Attitash cleansed my soul, it had become our evening habit to meet at the shore. I would cross the rocks which served as barriers between our communities and we would sit unseen. Just being in her presence calmed me, the clouds parading their evening shades, water slapping, birds wheeling, manatees cavorting, a small whale cutting too close to shore. Some evenings, when the sand was not too wet from rain, I wrote the mark for my name. She would then draw pictures for me. Our ability to speak with words was limited, but that did not prevent us from communicating with knowing glances, smiles, and occasional laughter. We did not linger long. By common understanding we would part before the western light turned lavender.

John rarely came down before sunset, so that night as I approached the shore, I was startled to see him there, conversing with Edward Doty, Hopkins' manservant. 'Twas the set to John's shoulders that stopped my going forward—not an easy stillness, but an angled cant to his head, set on his neck as if misplaced.

I took a few steps nearer and spoke his name quietly. He turned to me without speaking. Doty's mouth quivered as if he'd just swallowed raw mussels and he strode away without so much as a nod in my direction.

I swatted at my skirt, now sodden with sea mist. "What did Doty want?"

John now bent over as if by a strong wind. "He wanted to warn me."

"Warn thee?"

"Warn me I should not marry thee." He watched Doty walk away but I feared he simply could not bring himself to face me.

My heart squeezed like powerful hands had hold of it. Cockeyed Edward Doty had said this? Mayhap he only saw me with his possessed eye. I tried to remember our conversation at the goat-pen nearly a year ago. All I could recall was Doty's revelation of Stephen Hopkins' blasphemous demand—and sneering at us "puritan-separatists." Was Constance's father behind this?

John was talking, but I only heard his slow cadence, like he used when quieting Rogue. I concentrated and heard, "Doty's allegation carries no weight with me." His words should have calmed me, but his demeanor was not calm. I could see his jaw muscles clenching and his fingers so tightly pressed together the knuckles were white. "He must have said something to make thee listen to him." I cast about in my mind, considering several possibilities, and chose the least dreadful. "What did he offer as persuasion—that I am too young?"

John looked down at his hands for too long a moment. I attempted to staunch the chill seeping through my body. When he raised his eyes to mine, they were dark green and moist.

"Doty says he has evidence that ye are—ye are a witch."

Witch! The word reverberated in my head. My fingers crossed of their own will, desperate to fend off Satan's fiendish new assault on my life.

I remembered the witch back home, or so we called the sour old woman who chased us with a stick. Mother gave my sister Rose and me the rod for doing so, along with a lecture. "A witch is someone who's given over her entire being to Satan," she had said, picking up my left wrist, "not just one hand." She then told us again about the young maid burned as a witch before I was born. "She was fair to look at, but there was firm evidence. But ye have nay evidence on this poor old goody." I'd not asked then what the evidence was.

Now questions spewed out hot, quick, and incoherent. "What did Doty...? Why...? How could he...?"

John reached to take my hand, but I twisted away and jammed both fists under my armpits. How could he repeat this shameful charge?

John's lips curled in a grimace. "Doty said he'd not want my sons to be born of a witch."

The hideous accusation gripped my throat. When I could speak again, I demanded, "Do ye think I am?"

"Nay!" John answered too quickly. He ran his strong fingers through his hair. "I need to prepare our response, but I must know what he claims is the evidence."

I clung to John's use of "*our* response," needing every scrap of hope I could gain. Closing my eyes, I prayed my beloved would not desert me.

"He'd only begun to list the sightings when ye came upon us." John took me gently by the shoulders. I trembled like the shore reeds in a gale. "Look at me, Elisa." He waited until I could open my eyes and look into his. "Do not fear. 'Tis just one hot-headed servant. Most likely it is his attempt to distract attention from rumors that his own eye is possessed. I will speak with him again tonight. If he comes up with any plausible accusations, we will dispute them." John leaned and briefly kissed each of my cheeks, as though I were a little girl.

Pictures were colliding in my mind: Mother giving me the rod for using my left hand; Remember Allerton seeing me just after my cleansing, and her disapproving looks when I wrote in the sand with Attitash; Isaac Allerton speaking with Edward Doty a few days past. Were all my hopes to be crushed now? "Must we now wait to wed?"

"Nay." John put his arm about me and led me toward our houses. "We must take the most essential step to show Doty I will not heed his wild rumors. I will ask Governor Bradford to marry us tomorrow evening."

"God willing," I whispered to myself. How could I have believed so easily that my life would change for the better?

John may have thought I'd go inside, say my prayers and sleep but I knew I had to find Constance. I had no intention of revealing Doty's foul accusation to her yet, only to find out if her family was involved. I found her alone in her garden, throwing supper's scraps into the muck pile. Her face showed no guile, only confusion when I asked her where Edward Doty was.

"What's the sudden interest in that hot-headed servant?

John Howland just came looking for him also. They've gone off somewhere."

"Just so, I'm looking for my John and heard he'd be with thy manservant."

"Do ye want me to help thee find them?" When I did not answer, Constance looked closely at my face. "Whatever is troubling thee? Thy face is paler than goat milk!" She took my hand and pressed her warm fingers into my cold ones. "Tell me."

But I could not say the dreaded words. "Just a little spat, Constance. Edward criticized me and my John is trying to…to find the source of thy manservant's venom."

Constance waited, obviously expecting me to tell her the details of the criticism. I realized venom gave her far more to worry about than mere criticism. "Dear friend, come to me if ye hear Doty or thy father repeat words against me."

"My father? Surely ye don't think…" Constance bit her lips, thinking it over. "Well, Father did say that I must not think of marrying too young, like thee."

"And of course ye are not in need of avoiding servitude, Constance." It sounded like I was accusing Constance of something—like having a family or worldly goods. Needing to flee the tangle of my own words, I sputtered my good-evening and fled. My steps slowed as I approached Brewsters. Could Mistress see how exposed and raw my heart felt? Mistress was lifting the cloth from the plucked geese. Reminding me that they had to be cleaned before we retired for the night, she began stropping the butcher knife, prattling about how easily Humility had gone to sleep. I pushed up my sleeves and reached in to remove the organs. The kidneys came first and I set them in a kettle to fry with other sweetbreads. The heart was small and bloody, and I gulped to keep mine own quiet.

Mistress stopped sharpening. "Ye must have cleaned

fowl before. What's troubling thee?"

What indeed. "Just a small issue John Howland and I need to resolve."

"Well, John Howland can wait, the geese can't." She began carving up the bird I'd cleaned and we worked in silence 'til all the birds were simmering over the low night-fire in a mixture of water, sorrel, and greens. Priscilla joined us after her sweet goodbyes to John Alden—more thorns in my heart.

We were all sore weary, but I lingered at the fire as she crawled into our bedding. I pretended to plait my hair but I was actually tending to my fearful mind.

Attitash

White Flower wanted to come with me to the shore that night. She signaled to the little whales as if they could understand her. White Flower was still a young girl, but she was getting taller and her body was beginning to show curves. Esapett had looked like that when I first saw her. She'd filled out during the summer.

"Why do you miss the young clothwoman?"

White Flower's question startled me. "Who said I do?"

"You keep looking beyond our rocks."

Caught, and not even aware myself I'd been doing it. Why did I watch for Esapett? I could still see the look of relief and wonderment on Esapett's face when she rescued Little Fish; the way she tenderly gave him back to me. I missed hearing her low laugh, but I couldn't explain that to White Flower. I missed the thrill of beginning to understand her words and watching her draw her funny pictures. It was not like missing Black Whale—not a deep gnawing pain—but I did want to see her again. "We trade picture signs in the wet sand. Hers are easier to make, mine are prettier. Her picture of Nippa'uus made it look like a snake, not a warm ball."

When the shadows were growing long and Esapett had still not arrived, I went around the rocks to see if she was coming. She was walking away with Jon-owlan and did not have the light step I knew—she clung to him as if she'd been injured.

I was trying to imitate Esapett's' pictures in the sand for White Flower when I saw something from the corner of my eye. As I waited, the young girl with faint brown spots sprinkled on her face came to the rock boundary with her little sister. I'd noticed these girls other times, watching Esapett and me. The spotted-faced girl and her little sister were standing by the rocks that mark our homesite shore from the Strangers. The little girl put her hands over her eyes, but her big sister showed no respect for me at all. She looked straight into my eyes, then turned and wiggled her finger; a cloth-man came out from behind the rock. I'd seen him with Hop-kins. Of course, I would not look into his eyes, but in the brief moment before I lowered mine, I saw his eyes had special powers—each looked in a separate direction.

The spot-faced girl pointed to my picture in the sand, a scowl on her face.

I stomped over my drawing. Calling to White Flower, I turned my back on the intruders, and we left quickly.

Elisabeth

My ears were alert for John's footsteps outside, but all I heard was the soft crackle of the low fire, the goose pottage simmering, and the sleeping household's heavy breathing. My dire thoughts would not quiet in such close quarters. Seeking fresh air for my mind, I opened the door slowly so it would not creak. The moon was nearly full, flitting between clouds. Then movement near our garden gate made my heart flutter. I wondered if Doty was spying on me.

"Elisa?"

I rushed to him. "How long have ye been out here?"

John did not answer, just pulled me tight against him.

I was so full of questions—what had Doty said? Did a servant with a bad eye carry any credibility? Had Governor Bradford given us his permission to marry? Had John even asked for it? Fearing all the answers, I blurted out a diversion. "I plucked the geese ye brought—for our bridal pillows."

He chuckled, which I considered a good sign. "I'll need to shoot a lot more to fill two pillows." That was a good sign too.

"So ye found Edward Doty?"

John released his tight hold on me. "I did. Ye may be too sleepy to delve into this rot."

That was not a good sign at all, but I drew myself up, chin high. "Give it to me now. Sleep won't come to a mind full of questions."

He led me to the bench in front of the house. His voice barely above a whisper, he began listing the "sightings" Edward Doty had given.

The first was expected—use of my left hand despite Mother's attempts to cure me. The rest were all under the banner of "Consorting with Satan's favorite handmaid." There were several "sightings" to prove this: seen with a witch's familiar posed as a bear the day Samoset arrived—that would have been Attitash wrapped in her furs, of course; attempting to force Mistress Winslow to use the heathen maid's remedy; engaging in heathen methods to grow crops before our rightful leaders had decided to do so; allowing Hobbamock's women to bring their heathen corn to the children of our settlement. With each new piece of "evidence" my neck got warmer, but John kept hold of my hands and continued the foul litany: offering a savage ointment to our sick; appearing as a witch's familiar myself—a wolf, whose howling voice sounded like mine.

This last accusation nearly made me laugh, but coming with other true events interpreted by ill intent, I could not.

"Doty said he'd been given evidence that ye engaged in a wicked rite with the savage women in a satanic hut. And, lastly, that ye are learning secret satanic signs and teaching evil to the heathen Hobbamock's daughter."

These final accusations left me numb in mind and voiceless. I waited for John's comment. His silence brought back my voice in a wash of fury. Flinging my hands out of his grip, I punched air. "Tell me why anyone should believe this slander, John!"

"This can't all come from Edward Doty." His voice carried as much anger as mine.

"Even with his need to divert attention from his cock-eye he could not dream all this up himself. Someone else is using him. Wicked people will tell any lie that's useful to them."

"To defame me?"

John drew a ragged breath and offered me his hand again. I took it. "Ye are not the true target, Elisa. Someone wants to make himself look pure, or more powerful."

"Someone else is doing Satan's bidding." I had vowed not to weep, but I barely got the words out before my wrath yielded to tears. John gently pulled me to him and I muffled my anxiety against his chest.

"I haven't yet asked Governor Bradford to set our wedding date," he said softly. "He was already asleep tonight. Tomorrow I must lay out to him what Doty's saying."

"Must he be told?" I could not bear to think of my name being so muddied.

"Yea, he must. He will ensure that no one will interrupt our ceremony with reason why we should not be wed."

We parted with promises to sleep well. Needless to say, I did not. My heart was cleansed, but my mind dwelt on the possibility that Remember Allerton—Or someone else?—knew I'd been revived through a heathen ceremony.

Attitash

Still wondering if Esapett had been injured, I watched their field the next morning as we worked to gather squash. She was walking slowly, but with no hesitation. When she took her water jar to the brook, I went to meet her.

We exchanged our usual greetings, and she smiled, but her face was not lit from inside. I took both her hands and looked into her eyes. Esapett kept her eyes down for a few beats of my heart. When she did look at me, her eyes were not like quiet water. They were like roiling water below the beaver dam. I tried to reassure her with my touch and our few common words before we parted.

As I reached our weachimin field, I heard voices and stopped. Tisquantum and the man Papa called "al-a-ton" were examining the Strangers' weachimin. They had pulled an ear off and stripped it, running their fingers over the kernels. Tisquantum said my name to Al-a-ton. I quietly walked toward them and both men jumped when I greeted them. Al-a-ton spoke too fast for understanding. I asked Tisquantum to translate, but he laughed. Then he said something to Al-a-ton and they both laughed. These men were too much alike. They both would bring trouble, for our people and for Esapett's. It was time to throw Tisquantum's betrayal back into his face.

Rushing to our field, I met Black Whale. "Tisquantum and a Stranger, Al-a-ton, were laughing at me." The fury in my voice did not surprise my husband. I felt my new life kick, as if it too were angry, and I wrapped my arms over my little bulge.

"Ahhe, I was watching you. I heard their derisive laughter." Black Whale pulled me into his shoulder. "When do you want to confront Tisquantum? Take care we don't wait too long—before he's brought too many bad spirits to our own."

Before I could answer, Mama arrived. "Hobbamock was going to the fish weir earlier, and found Tisquantum talking to that man-with-two-looking-eyes and Al-le-ton." She rubbed her temples. "He did not understand everything, but they said your name and they said the cloth-girl's."

"Did they say anything but our names?"

"Hobbamock asked Tisquantum what they talked about. He laughed at your father too, saying Al-a-ton claims you were sending bad spirits to Esapett. Al-a-ton said his daughters told him you make evil pictures."

Before my protest was formed, Mama shushed me. "Of course we do not believe Tisquantum—or if he is telling the truth we don't believe those Cloth-men. Tisquantum is like the rotting fish left on the shore when the tide ebbs. I think it's time to confront him."

Mama picked up my little brother. "We will stop Tisquantum. But until he's silenced, stay away from the Strangers—even Esapett. We know she would not harm us, but they could use Esapett as their excuse to do so. We must protect our family. "

I put my hand on New Life, feeling a flutter.

Elisabeth

"Ye look like ye've been caught with thy hand in the butter churn, child. What's upsetting thee?" Mistress Brewster's lips were a straight line.

I told her what occurred at breakfast. John had asked Governor Bradford to marry us that very evening. When our governor questioned the sudden need, he looked to my belly as if we'd broken a Commandment. John quickly explained it was an accusation of a different kind that brought about this request. Our governor shoved aside his plate and rubbed his brow. "It would look like something was greatly amiss if ye marry suddenly. We must address this accusation quickly, and keep it a small matter. John Alden has asked if he and Priscilla Mullins can wed in a week. If both couples wed at the same time, there will be less meat for gossips to chew."

"John and I will be wed as soon as 'a small matter' is settled," I concluded.

"Ye must be forthright with me, Elisabeth. A 'small matter' would not cause such a furrow in thy brow." Mistress's soft eyes could still carry a captain's glare.

"Doty told John Howland I'm a witch," spewed out of my mouth like bad meat coming up. I met her eyes with fire in my own. "Governor Bradford says we must staunch the flow of gossip before we wed."

"Oh, the wickedness of idle mouths!" Mistress smacked her hands on her cheeks. "What is William's—I mean, the governor's—plan? I insist on being an advocate for thee."

That cheered me, William Bradford always listened to his foster mother. But the lift in my hopes was tempered by the realization that Mistress herself might believe some of the accusations were sufficiently true.

As Mistress led me to a quiet spot within sight of our field, my mind struggled with what would be acceptable. "Doty reported sightings of me as a witch's familiar. It's all in his imagination." I paused. "He also claims I have been seen 'consorting with the devil!' By that he means my meeting Attitash for simple lessons in each other's ways."

"Never—do hear me—never become so close to the heathen that ye would believe their ways are our ways." She let go of my hands and wiped her eyes. "I must pay more attention to thy ways. I will assure our governor—and thy betrothed—that ye will have my Christian love watching over thee. That ye understand now what danger thy soul was exposed to." Mistress rose and led the way home.

It was made clear to me, before our wedding was approved, that it was my duty to avoid provoking new accusations. Nothing further would be said to Edward Doty, Governor Bradford declaring that Doty's tattling tongue would not be dignified with a response.

I had revealed to Mistress Brewster my fear that Doty— or whoever had fed him this "evidence" would come forth as one who had reason to believe the marriage should not take place. She assured me that no manservant would dare to speak out at a wedding where "Our governor and I myself would proclaim him a slanderer."

A week later, Constance, Mary Chilton and Desire helped Priscilla and me prepare for the brief ceremony.

"We don't have vain weddings, with fancy clothes and excess of food and drink," Priscilla informed Constance, when she asked what we would wear.

Constance looked at my worn muslin clothing "Thy church does not even allow decent clothes?"

Having calmed my snarling curls somewhat, Desire fastened my hair with a comb. "Look in Mistress Carver's trunk."

I opened the trunk and Desire lifted out the garments. The lavender scent Catherine Carver had worn wafted out of the garments.

Priscilla picked up a linen shift and helped me into it, then held out Mistress Carver's stays. "Oh, these are lovely. See how cleverly the whale bone is stitched into the pockets! It doesn't even bulge or show, just holds one in."

Desire took the stays from Priscilla and stroked the smooth fabric. "Catherine Carver looked so beautiful in these. They made her look young again." Desire handed the linen stays back to Priscilla, whose own stays were already tightly laced. "Help Elisabeth put these on."

"I have little to hold in. Do I need them?" I looked at the shadow of my ribs showing beneath my pale skin. My own muslin stays were worn and loosely laced.

"Ye are surprisingly endowed, for one with so little meat on her bones," Mary said.

I held my breath while Priscilla wrapped the fabric around my middle, pulling the laces in back until they cinched in my waist. She continued lacing, and the sewn-in bones held the stays up to my nipples.

"I can't breathe," I complained. I looked down to see only the tops of my breasts peeking above the shift.

"Mother always tells me, 'Beauty doesn't hurt,'" Constance giggled. "She wants me to wear tight shoes, tight corset, and two petticoats in hot weather."

"It does seem to me that being able to breathe is more important than being attractive to a husband who has promised to postpone making me a real wife," I protested.

Priscilla laughed. "I'll loosen thy laces a bit." I let out a big breath as she did so.

"We don't have to sacrifice all comfort, just to please a man," Desire said. "And comfort helps keep randy goats like Isaac Allerton from panting too close." Desire pulled a dark green waistcoat made of fine wool from the trunk. "This won't be too warm for a fall evening." It was only a little long, hanging a bit below my navel. I pulled on Mother's best dark blue skirt, and Mary found a clean white coif to cover up my hair.

"Don't be vain, but thy cheeks glow, and ye look beautiful." Priscilla gave me a quick kiss.

"And so do ye, Priscilla. Beautiful enough to be a true wife," I said quietly.

Priscilla touched my hand. "I am more than three years older than thee, Elisabeth." She did not add that she also possessed her own small wealth, and could thus choose her time to wed. Their wedding was not perceived by anyone to be a liaison dangerous for John Alden.

As the two bridegrooms arrived in the evening cool of

the Brewster garden with Governor Bradford, they both looked a bit nervous. My John's hair was neatly gathered and tied, his cheeks shaven, and he wore a clean linen shirt.

When he saw me, however, he raised his eyebrows in delight. "Ye look a fair woman," he whispered to me, as we stood by Priscilla and John Alden with the Brewster household gathered.

Governor Bradford solemnly read out the marriage ceremony. When he came to, "whoever dost know a reason why either of these couples should not be wed, speak now," I held my breath. I saw John glance toward the road, no doubt looking to make sure Edward Doty was not about.

All was blessedly quiet and Governor moved on to our vows "to have and to hold from this day forward." John's voice was strong when he repeated his vows. His eyes, a warm green, held mine. I feared my voice would shake, but I took a deep breath and spoke bravely.

"I now pronounce thee man and wife," Governor Bradford declared.

A layer of regret held back my tears of happiness. Our wedding was tainted with suspicion. I had always imagined Mother with me, as well as Father, my sisters and brothers. I also expected my wedding day to bring the intimacy married women blushed about with pride.

John kissed me on the lips in full view of the household. Then he wrapped his arms about my waist and was pulling me closer when Governor Bradford put an arm on his shoulder.

"Steady there, Howland!" our governor admonished. "Ye've a long time 'til ye be husband in more than name." John laughed wryly and relinquished me.

Mistress shook her finger at him playfully. "Now, John. Ye promised to keep her maidenhood intact for another year."

He responded by kissing my hand, held at arm's length. After congratulations and conversation, the wedding party dispersed to homes and John left with William Bradford to sleep alone. I had only Humility to sleep with me.

Brewsters had given up their well-curtained bed for Priscilla and John Alden. Rustling and whispers came from behind the curtains, followed by thumping, giggles and finally a faint cry. I tried to picture my husband with me wrapped in quilts on the floor, but could imagine only his warmth.

The long winter would arrive soon. Only when leaves grew new would we share a bed, and then only if the rumors we were trying to quell did not rise up again. Many a fire that's been doused comes back to life.

22

Attitash

Leaves were turning color and evening fires were needed to keep out the night chill. Black Whale kept an eye on Tisquantum while Papa ran to fetch my clan uncle, Red Hawk. They returned with Our Massasowet's approval of the plan.

The nearly full moon was sinking over the western hills when we went to Patuxet. As we watched from the woods, Tisquantum came out of the Stranger's neesh-wetu for men and sat facing the Big Salt Water. He tried to keep a foot in both worlds, I thought, living with the Strangers, but still praying to Kiehtan. Maybe that's why he was hollow; he was split inside from such a wide straddle. Facing the Big Salt Water ourselves, we said our own prayers silently.

As the first streak of Nippa'uus rose above the water, we moved out of the woods. Black Whale, Papa, and Uncle grabbed Tisquantum and held him as he writhed helplessly.

"You sold our daughter to the Narragansetts." Mama spat on Tisquantum. "She would have been lost to us, a wife to our enemy."

"You believed Attitash?" Tisquantum snarled.

Grabbing his topknot, I pulled his head back while Mama gagged him with a leather strap. Uncle Red Hawk twisted Tisquantum's arms behind his back and Papa bound his wrists. I could see the muscle in his neck shudder and fear in his eyes.

"We will not harm you now, because you are Wampanoag," Papa said. "But you will not betray our daughter again, and you will not betray any of our People."

Tisquantum was trying to talk, but the leather was too tight.

"We have told Our Massasowet." Papa continued. "He knows you tell some of the lies about Attitash. If you betray us again and tell more lies, you will not live."

Tisquantum narrowed his eyes and strained against the gag.

Papa pulled Tisquantum to a sitting position. "Tokamahamon will speak for Our Massasowet now," Papa said. "He proved he has enough of the cloth-men's tongue to speak when he brought more weachimin for them. Do you understand?"

Mama loosened the leather gag while Uncle untied Tisquantum's wrists.

As we walked away, he called out in a ragged voice. "Attitash lies!"

I laughed, but it was not sweet laughter.

"We know who to believe," Mama's voice was like the mother bear's roar. "Our People know who lies and who tells the truth."

Elisabeth

My John tried to reassure me about Doty's rumors. "Just stay away from the Indian girl and it will all go away," he had said. He did not sound convinced of his own assumption nor would he agree to go with me to the shore at eventide. I yearned to let Attitash know why our friendship could not be openly enjoyed and I argued to no avail that his presence would keep the gossips from misinterpreting an encounter. My situation was so fragile that I stopped looking for Attitash

Nor did I feel like a true wife. 'Twas difficult to rejoice

with Priscilla. She blushed constantly, taking the felicita-
tions of our company with a pretty smile and hanging on
John Alden's arm.

However, my Jack did feel free to give me luscious kisses and embraced me tenderly before he left me to sleep at
Brewsters each evening. I felt a great relief that his atten-
tions did not bring back memories of my tormenters. But
his loving actions did both sooth and disturb me—stealing
my sleep with dreams of the marriage bed.

"So Howland saved Elisabeth from servitude." Goody
Billington was saying to Constance, knowing I could hear.
She probably spoke for all, but at least she'd not openly
accused me of witchcraft. Constance had revealed she'd
heard Doty say Master Allerton was rightly concerned
his daughters might be sullied by someone in our midst.
Constance insisted that this caused no damage to my own
reputation, but I knew she protested mightily because she
feared the opposite.

Hemmed in by gossip, I had to find some way to clear
my name. Desire was most likely to be direct and honest with me. When I posed the question of who could
be encouraging Doty's accusation, she took my question
seriously.

"Elisabeth, ye must think of who considers thee an ob-
stacle to their own gain—and thus whose conduct shows
jealousy of thy husband's worldly goods and thy own de-
sirable appearance."

I protested that a thin young maid such as I could not
be viewed as attractive, but she said that with so few maids
amongst so many men that anyone who'd reached womanhood appeared beautiful. So much for thinking I was
pretty.

When I also protested that we had a compact for "The
Common Good" and shared the new land equally, Desire
laughed. "That will only last until a harvest fails. And

when another ship brings new settlers, they might not agree."

Desire commenced to consider all possible names. "Doty himself is leading this charge. And his cocked eye draws endless gossip about his own possession by Satan. Since he is a servant who has not inherited a late master's wealth, he is no doubt envious of John Howland. He may be attacking thee on his own to get thee away from Howland."

"But Constance prattles about Doty and Leister both wanting to court her. Surely he is not yearning after me."

"Yea, prattles," she said and we both giggled.

"If true, however, then he may be a willing accomplice for someone else," Desire said.

We next considered Isaac Allerton. My husband's recent wealth had denied him of my servitude. And his oldest daughter was left trying to cope with all the household chores and the care of her little sister Mary. This gave cause to why Remember Allerton was joined with the accusations. Whether she also felt envious of my good fortune or not, she had to resent my escape from becoming her family's servant.

We then talked of young John Billington and all the Billington family. Due to my rejection of him, young John was obviously angry and probably jealous too. In addition, the punishment John Howland gave him for his assault upon me, and the beating our governor gave him for running had shamed his family. They would no doubt enjoy seeing me blamed.

Desire then mentioned Mary Chilton. This name surprised me indeed. Mary was fair to look upon and well situated in Master Winslow's house. Desire argued that we should leave no stone unturned, and that with an identical loss to mine—youngest child losing both parents—I now enjoyed a better status than Mary.

"What of Susanna White Winslow?" Desire then said. "Mistress Carver was her cousin and perhaps she hoped to be given some of the Carver..."

"Is there anyone you would not name, Desire?" I interrupted before she could list everyone I loved and trusted. Desire paused with her mouth still open in mid-sentence. Finally closing it with a wry smile, she took my hand. "How could ye think that? I assure thee, dear, that leaves almost our entire company—and I don't believe that even those we named are all part of this conspiracy. I only list them so we do not miss an essential actor in this dismal drama."

"Then let's not mention Mary and Mistress Winslow again—unless we find nothing in any of the others' actions."

"Agreed." Desire took a sip of her tea, stifling a cough.

STEAM ROSE FROM the wet bed sheet as Mistress Brewster and I shook it out in the cool air. I could tell she was troubled. After some time she gave words to her worry.

"Some of the rumors about thee persist and must be answered before ye become more intimate with thy husband." She reached into the tub with her laundry stick to pull out another sheet. She kept her eyes on the sheet—not on me.

I had taken hold of the hem of the sheet she'd pulled out, but now dropped it back in the water. "Do you believe vicious hearsay?"

"As thy guardian, concerned for thy soul as well as thy husband's, I must know what caused the rumors." I did not answer. She continued, her face growing stern. "How much of the story is true that you participated in a satanic ceremony with the Indian girl?"

"Who told you this, Mistress?" I wanted to find Remember Allerton and hang her by her heels.

"It does not matter. The rumor must be rooted out."

"The truth is that I did go in the hut Hobbamock's wife and daughter use for womanly cleaning."

"And why would ye not come to me?" Mistress's retorted.

"I went because Attitash invited me."

"A heathen invited ye? And ye went?" Mistress held my eyes firmly with hers. "There is talk that dark secrets were involved. Edward Doty told my husband yesterday that on the voyage over a seaman bragged thy carriage towards him was forward. And Doty said later ye were seen coming from topdeck after dark. What really happened?" She continued to hold the wet sheet on the stick. "Ye must be honest with me, and with thy husband."

I picked up my sheet again and began to shake the water off as a diversion. Once we'd spread it over the fence, I sat down, my head in my hands. Mistress sat next to me.

"You're right, Mistress. I was desperate to be rid of awful memories of…of the seaman. I'd only gone topdeck to retrieve a shawl. He forced me…he tried to take liberties with me. " I rubbed my arm where the memory lay of the Cur twisting it.

She gasped, then cleared her throat and drew a deep breath. "Did he succeed?"

"Nay, but my soul was soiled." I expected accusations, but Mistress Brewster's silence gave me some courage. "I did pray, Mistress. Attitash and her mother prayed too."

"Did ye give thy soul to Satan?"

"Oh, Mistress!"

"Do ye love God?"

"I do love God, I do!"

"Elisabeth, ye are so young, coming to this new world and losing all thy family has left thee without the understanding needed to discern God's will. Wait while I fetch my Bible."

She handed the open Bible to me, her finger on a verse in Luke. "Can ye read this?"

I slowly read the part promising that power to rule would be given to Jesus if he worshiped the devil. My voice broke when I finally read the words I'd used so many times, "And Jesus answered him, 'Get thee behind me, Satan'." I'd used those words when Satan used the Cur, young Billington, and Allerton against me. But the devil had never promised me power. "What do you think Satan is offering me, Mistress?"

"Dear child, he is offering you false power over thy husband. Satan is tempting thee to continue the deceit, tempting thee to believe ye can enjoy young Howland's love and devotion while yet sparing thyself the pain of revealing what happened. Only if ye reveal every trace of deceit and beg his forgiveness can ye be a true wife."

I thought Attitash had given me back my ability to be a true and loving wife. Now I would have to once again face the fragile nature of that gift. I could not endure the emptiness of life without John Howland. My only hope was that my husband would accept that God had used the heathen to release me. But first I would have to reveal The Cur's heinous act.

My mind was consumed with trial attempts to tell my husband of my deceit. I still had not found the right words—or even the right thoughts—when John came to me in Brewsters' yard.

"I wanted to find thee alone." His eyes were a warm, deep, green. "Mistress Brewster told me we might be allowed to bundle soon."

"Jack." My throat closed and I tried to draw a deep breath.

"Do ye need water?"

"Nay, but I need to tell ye something—something I should have told thee long ago."

"Then we should find a quiet place." John led me out the gate and down to the shore.

It was windy and cold. We huddled by the big rocks, near to where I met with Attitash. I slowly told my dreadful story of the Cur—wanting John to feel my fear, my anger, and my confusion. He remained silent, his eyes on the heaving waves. I finished with the cat's timely interruption.

"Why did ye not tell me? Especially after young Billington assailed thee?"

"I don't know; I was afraid." I wanted to fly up with the shrieking gulls. To be where no one could see me, hear me, touch me, smell my despair.

"Afraid of what?"

"Afraid of what has now happened—afraid my reputation would be ruined." I jammed my fists into my eyes. "Afraid I would never be able to love."

"Ye did say ye love me."

"And I do! Oh, Jack, if ye could only know how much I do love thee—and desire to be thy true wife." I stood up, bracing myself against the wind, and walked a few steps toward the crashing waves. Prayer filled me. Not words, but desperate hope. Hope that God would show John my fervent soul, yearning to be a loving wife. I turned back to him. "No matter how I prayed, I could not free myself of the fear—I could not wish for thy loving caress. That's why I went with Attitash. She knew I needed cleansing."

"How could a heathen cleanse?"

"God must've given her some of His love! Even if her people don't know God, He knows them." Hearing the words of my mouth out loud sounded blasphemous, but I persisted. "God gave them healing plants. When Attitash's mother poured the medicinal water over me—I felt washed clean."

"So, the rumor is true." John stood and walked toward

the waves, his back to me. He stood with rigid shoulders, fists balled. When he turned back, his face was closed. "Come, it's time to eat. Governor Bradford and the rest of my household will be waiting for their meal."

"I can walk by myself."

"Nay! That's what ye cannot do, wife." His voice carried strong over the crashing waves and noisy birds. "Everyone is watching thee."

If I were a witch I would have changed myself into a familiar—perhaps a small fish—to swim out of sight. "Do ye think I'm a witch?"

For a few beats of my heart I thought he would answer "yea." Finally he looked at me, his eyes filled with such pain they were a bright green. "I do not think ye are a witch, but I swear by God, I do not really know thee."

I could not speak. I scarcely knew myself. I was no longer the young girl who boarded the Mayflower with her parents.

John took my arm stiffly, as if he were escorting a stranger. I nearly tripped on my petticoats keeping up with him.

When we reached his house, he let go without a word. My hands prepared the food for our noon repast as if they belonged to someone else.

The rest of the day went by like a reflection in a muddy pond. I saw myself cleaning up, taking down the laundry, fixing supper and cleaning up again. When I returned to the Brewster's, I answered Mistress's whispered question with a brief nod. She did not ask me more.

When Humility was asleep, I pulled her close to me, her blissful ignorance a comfort.

The room is filled with young maids dressed in their night clothes. One of them has no right hand, only a left one. I look at my own hands and realize I have no right hand. Another maid creeps toward me, crawling like a large cat. I am inside that maid looking out.

My body was frozen stiff with fear when the dream woke me. I rubbed my hands down my arms, traced my breasts, my ribs, my thighs. I was there, alive and whole. Pushing off the covers, I saw candlelight. Mistress sat in her chair, reading the Bible.

She looked up and met my eyes. "Come, read this."

I tucked the quilt around Humility and pulled on my shawl. Taking the Bible from Mistress, I looked at the name in large letters at the top of the page. "John?"

She smiled. "Yea, ye do know that name." Pointing to the first few verses, Mistress told me to read aloud. It read like a song. "*In the beginning was the Word. And the Word was with God and the Word was God.*" ..."*And the light shineth in the darkness; and the darkness comprehended it not.*" I puzzled over it, reading it aloud again. "What does it mean?"

She took the Bible back and closed it. "It means that God gave us His son to be our light. And the darkness cannot overcome that light." Mistress took my face in her hands. "Elisabeth, God gives thee light. Ye can be what God wants thee to be. No matter how much darkness has been visited upon thee."

Her words felt like the water Attitash's mother washed me with. She continued. "Keep Satan behind thee. Thy deception is darkness. Ye must ask John Howland to forgive thee for deceiving him."

"I did tell him about the Cur. He said he doesn't know who I am."

"So it was the Cur," Mistress murmured to herself. Putting her arms around me, Mistress said, "Give John Howland a little time to understand why ye've not told him before. John is a grown man. I doubt John remembers whether he revealed his troubles to the upgrowns when he was but fourteen."

If I dreamed the rest of the night, the dreams fled

before I could remember. Attitash must have been in them, as she was on my mind when I rose next morning. Had she already gone back to their winter village without knowing my tangled situation? God loved Attitash and I need not put her behind me. I felt an urgent need to see her before she left—just what my husband and Mistress Brewster were insisting I should not do. I smothered my wishes by remembering John Howland's closed face.

When I arrived to cook breakfast, I found Mistress conversing with John Howland in the garden. I went about my work quickly. Today my hands belonged to me. John sat down with Governor Bradford and Master Eaton and gave me a near smile.

When the men had finished eating and I was dishing up the meager leavings of cornmeal stew for little Samuel and William Latham, John put his hand on mine. "Will ye walk to the field with me?"

We walked side by side until we were away from the houses. He stopped, rubbing his neck. "It will take time for me to know thee better."

"I understand." Was he next going to suggest our marriage be declared void? Gone before we'd consummated it and he'd truly known me, as the Bible says.

"I mean—there's more to ye than I thought. Mistress reminded me of how young ye were then—when the evil was done to thee."

"I am trying to understand myself, John," I replied. "But I must ask thy forgiveness. I should have told thee my...my history...when ye first proposed."

"I'd still have married thee, though I would have been angry."

My face went tight, pulled by the anguish in my heart. "I would not have thee marry me in anger."

"I'm not angry at thee! I'm angry at the Cur!" His eyes were now a hot, dark green. "Remember how fierce with anger I was when young Billington tried to kiss thee?" He rammed his fist into a rotting tree, scarcely wincing. "If only I'd known what the Cur did to thee before he died! I would have smashed the man's face—or kicked him between the legs."

I could not think how that would have made me feel any better now. Nor could I think of how to tell him the cleansing healed me—to make him understand God's light shone on me through a heathen rite. I could at least offer him truth. "As thy wife, I promise to be honest with thee." I would be, when I found the right time and the right words.

He took my hands. "And I will be honest with thee."

"Do ye know me better yet?" I lifted my face to his. He brushed his warm lips to mine.

LOOKING INTO THE FIRE after supper, our governor took a long swig of ale, then talked about the growing worry in our little settlement that no ship from home had arrived. John and I could only nod in agreement. As the harvest progressed and the October days grew short, our predicament weighed heavy. Many were hopeful that clear directions to locate us had been sent back with the Mayflower. Others were convinced that the Mayflower itself had been lost; in which case we were doomed.

John was, of course, with the hopeful group and began to use his arguments with our governor, but Bradford cut him short.

"Howland, this is not about when a ship will come." William Bradford's face flushed and he carefully set his ale mug down. "A leader in our company declares we are stranded here because God's righteous anger does not suffer the worship of other gods."

My mouth was so dry it felt like I'd eaten brown cornsilk for supper. John took my hand and looked Governor

Bradford in the eye.

Governor Bradford took another swig of ale. "His accusation is directed at this maid, for turning her back on God and embracing the heathens'."

John's grip on my hand was so tight I felt it all the way up my arm. "The 'maid' you speak of is my wife."

"Yea, 'twas Elisabeth he accused." Governor Bradford still did not look at me.

The October chill reached my bones. "Did he say I am a witch?"

Governor Bradford lowered his eyes. "Yea, Elisabeth, he did."

John dropped my hand and clenched his into fists. "You cannot believe this!"

"Nay, I do not." Governor still did not look at us.

"Is this 'leader' your deputy governor then—Isaac Allerton?" John asked the question, and though I knew the answer, I studied William Bradford's hooded eyes.

"He is." Governor Bradford glanced quickly at John. "I must live with this—this relationship. He was elected lieutenant governor ye recall when John Carver died. I was quite ill myself and could not take on the duties alone."

John and I had said we'd face together those who would speak evil against us. But now we faced a friend.

"I have thought about this all day and talked with Elder Brewster. I must keep the peace among our people. I must keep up their hopes that we will be found." Governor tapped his cold pipe. "I insist, Elisabeth, that ye have absolutely no contact alone with Hobbamock's daughter. Ever."

I bit my lip. Ever?

"There is no need to be with them, my dear," he continued. "Winslow and I have sufficient communication with Hobbamock. They take care of their women. There's not a reason in God's world why ye should mingle with them."

Mingle? Did Governor Bradford believe that saving us from starvation was mere mingling? Of course Bradford did not realize the benefit of this "mingling" as we'd kept undercover and used Squanto to save the planting.

He turned to John. "Howland, I've given my blessing to you, and married you to this young maid. Now you must show your mettle as a husband. She may not live to be your true wife if you cannot control her. That should be easy; today Hobbamock takes his family back to their home with King Massasoit."

If Attitash was leaving, I might never see her again. That would end the threats against us both, but another crisis was bound to demand response by her people and mine.

John studied his hands as Governor Bradford continued.

"Losing her as a true wife, is the least of it. If she is charged with witchcraft, the strength you show her might save her life."

Cold gripped my spine. I made a mask of my face so as not to reveal my vivid memories of Mother's voice describing the screams of witches being consumed by the flames.

23

Attitash

Not knowing when I'd see Esapett again made leaving Patuxet difficult. However, Papa had to be at the Green Weachimin celebration, as the Pniese were meeting with our Massasowet. I was very eager to be with Grandmother and our Otter clan. When we'd said goodbye to Grandmother in the time of new leaves, she'd given us strong warnings that Papa was taking us to a cursed place with bad spirits and we would die. There were times I thought the prediction would come true. Now we were returning and not only had we survived, but if my new life arrived safely, we were increasing.

"Grandmother will see I carry new life," I told Black Whale, watching him prepare his quiver with fresh arrows. "And we'll reach our Trees-in-Love in one day's walk." I wondered aloud if I should try to find Esapett before we left.

"Every time you're around her, something bad happens," Black Whale said. Before I could respond, Suki and Mowi's barking alerted us to a visitor.

A moment later Win-sow came into our homesite. Black Whale was courteous to him, having learned to trust Win-sow when he stayed at our camp as a hostage during the treaty negotiations. After the welcoming words, Win-sow looked toward our home and asked about our preparations for the journey, then said something about "Mistress Elisabeth Howland."

"Talk to Esapett–I say fa-well," I said in the Clothman's tongue.

Win-sow then gave Black Whale a small flat stone—their wampum. The surface was carved with a man wearing a weird headdress.

I prepared a small bag of the black willow powder and gave it to Win-sow. "For Esapett."

"Catabatash," Win-sow said politely. He shifted his shoulders uneasily. "Elisabeth not come to you."

Black Whale nodded with satisfaction.

"Not want to?" I asked Win-sow.

He shook his head. "Elisabeth want, but—" He couldn't find our word. He didn't need to. Esapett was still in danger. I resolved to keep my ears open when we arrived at the Poanoke.

Elisabeth

Governor Bradford's words brought terror to both John and me. John willingly followed our governor's admonition to control me, reminding me next morning not to go near Hobbamock's homesite, as if I'd not heard our governor's demand. I did not respond to him, and worked furiously all morning, shucking corn as if each ear were Isaac Allerton or Edward Doty.

Priscilla's basket of corncobs was half full and mine nearly topped when she convinced me to explain the source of my anger. I revealed Governor Bradford's edict.

"What would ye have our governor do, then?" Priscilla asked.

"I can't think of what Governor Bradford should do. But my husband should trust me." I tossed my last corncob into my basket and reached for more.

Priscilla started to answer, but covered her mouth as Master Winslow approached. He greeted us both politely then handed me a leather pouch.

"Hobbamock's daughter asked me to give you this, Mistress Howland. It's willow bark powder. The Indians use it for healing."

I could not speak; my hands reached for the bag.

"She sends her farewell," Master Winslow said.

At last I found my voice. "Thank you kindly, Master. But how—why were you talking to Attitash?"

"Didn't your husband tell you?"

I lost my voice again and Master Winslow smiled.

"Mayhap he wanted to surprise you. John Howland asked me to visit Hobbamock's family; he said you wanted to say farewell, but you did not want to raise concerns by going yourself." Master Winslow glanced back toward our fields, filled with men picking corn. "Some of our company do not understand that the Indians saved us from starvation." Edward Winslow nodded to Priscilla and me and went on his way.

Priscilla dimpled and reached for the un-shucked corn I'd taken from her pile. "Let me finish this. I know ye want to find thy clever husband."

I was running towards the field where John was pulling up the empty cornstalks when Constance called, "Elisabeth! Come with me. My father's man-servants are fighting a duel!" She grabbed my hand, pulling me toward our meeting house while telling me what little she knew. Daggers and swords had been used. One Edward was injured in the hand, the other in the thigh. Both Edward Doty and Edward Leister knew that dueling was against the law. Captain Standish was pressing to have them whipped and tied up. "Father is trying to keep them from being killed in the process—they are indentured to him for at least five more years!"

As we drew nearer, John caught up with us. We could see both men lying on the ground on their sides, bent backward at an extreme angle with their feet tied to their heads. They were so contorted, it was almost impossible to view them as still alive.

A crowd mocked them."How does it feel? Like hunters
have ye trussed up and ready to carve? Now ye can settle
the score—nose to nose!"

I had no connection with Edward Leister at all—save
his presence in Constance's household. But a small cruel
part of me rejoiced to see Edward Doty tormented. My
hand moved over my mouth so I should not cry out some
rude insult to him.

"So, Master Howland. Is this the Christian way?" said a
voice from behind. We spun around to see Squanto standing a pace behind John. He turned and left.

Attitash

Papa did not allow Tisquantum weapons while we remained at Patuxet. But he was allowed to be on his own
during the day until we left for the harvest gathering at
Poanoke, our winter home. Green Weachimin was always a reunion for our people after spending the summer months in our small wetus scattered along the coast.
Now, my pleasure was mixed with anxiety over dealing
with Tisquantum. Black Whale and Papa kept Tisquantum
between them on our journey.

"You should walk behind your wife, Black Whale,"
Tisquantum objected. "The cloth-men might come up
behind your women and snatch them."

Papa dismissed Tisquantum's nonsense with a flick of
his eyes. We were well on our way up the high ridge that
separated Poanoke from Patuxet bay when we paused to
eat and rest. Mowi and Suki both growled low in their
throats and planted their feet when Tisquantum reached
for the water cask Mama held out. Tisquantum snarled
back at the dogs, then drank long.

I knew Black Whale was chewing over Tisquantum's
taunt. Though I tried to warn my husband to let words fall
on deaf ears, he spoke to Tisquantum now. "They respect

our women more than you do. And we no longer need you to speak for us. We have a treaty and Win-sow entrusted me to carry a gift to our Massasowet."

Tisquantum laughed. "Black Whale, you should know not to trust a treaty—or trinkets. They had two of their own men trussed up like the deer we catch. What do you think they'd do to you?" He glanced at my swollen belly then to White Flower. "Or to the not-yet-ripe one?"

With only a glance to indicate their resolve, Papa and Black Whale grabbed Tisquantum's arms while Mama and I gagged him.

We reached a stream running into the Big Salt Water and I realized we were close to where we'd buried Yellow Hair an entire circle of the seasons ago. Tisquantum was a sharp quill pressing into my side. If I were to trip him, we could wrap a rope about his neck, pull it tight and leave him here for the wolves as he'd wanted to do with Yellow Hair. I pulled back my vengeful thoughts and told myself to keep walking, take care of New Life, and go home to Grandmother.

Elisabeth

My initial satisfaction at seeing Edward Doty suffer had faded as they cried out for mercy. The contorted position took its obvious toll on their bodies. Both Edwards continued to moan, their voices cracked from straining against the rope on their necks. Still, I knew the punishment was just.

"God's truth, the men must be punished. But we'll all be punished if no one finishes the field work." Mistress Brewster gathered us to walk with her. As we neared Brewsters' house, Mistress Susanna Winslow asked me to bide a moment in their garden, explaining to Mistress Brewster she needed a quiet word with me. She leaned against Brewster's garden gate, glancing about until certain we were alone.

"Elisabeth, I must tell thee something my husband discovered." Mistress Winslow's face seemed friendly. I tried to imagine what was coming next, and nothing friendly came to mind.

"Last night as my husband left Governor Bradford's, he overheard the two Hopkins men-servants teasing each other as they sat in Hopkins' garden—imbibing in their master's ale no doubt. Edward Leister was taunting Doty that he was obsessed with thee."

I thought that was the truth but waited to hear her out.

She took my hand. "I must tell thee, my husband does not want this known—to preserve thy reputation."

"Doesn't want what known?"

She lowered her voice. I leaned close to hear. "Leister was tormenting Doty—telling him he'd not lose thee to Howland but to the witch's fire."

I rubbed my eyes, trying to extinguish visions of flames searing my body while my mind and soul lived. Trembling with the attempt to control my fears, I prayed that Master Winslow could keep this vile quarrel hidden.

"They are ignorant, wicked, stupid men!" The heat in Susanna Winslow's voice startled me. "Their argument blew up like fat on a fire. Leister accused Doty of being in Satan's snare himself, evidenced by his bad eye—possessed by devils so it sees only evil." She handed me her fine linen handkerchief, and I dabbed my eyes. "Pray, Elisabeth. The men have been bound up more than an hour already. Governor Bradford needs to hear from those of us who pray for all mankind that the punishment has been sufficient. Mistress Brewster and I will be visiting him soon. If ye come with us, it will cover thine own role in this duel. It would not seem likely that the woman who is the object of the duel would seek the Lord's mercy." She glanced at the sun high in the south. "Mistress Brewster and I will go to see our governor when we've finished eating."

I hurried to fix dinner for the Howland household of men. As they sat down, William Bradford addressed Master Eaton. "Get started building some stocks, Francis. Never thought I'd need them so soon, but we must not be reduced again to trussing men up."

I struggled for a deep breath. I could be bending my head and sticking my arms through the stocks. Yea, better than being trussed, but painful indeed. As soon as I set food on the table I excused myself and ran to the Commonhouse.

Captain Standish sat near the collapsed men, eating a turkey drumstick. "Mistress Howland," he greeted me between mouthfuls. "See how they suffer?"

As he spoke Edward Leister began to howl, "Craaaaamp."

Standish gave me a steely look. "Make certain you don't end up like this, Miss."

Clenching my stomach tight to control my words, I moved close to the tangled pile of men, talking to Standish over my shoulder. "I know not what you allude to, Captain, but let me look closer so my mind will carry the dreadful impression." I leaned down so Doty could see me with one eye. Whispering so soft I was not sure even Doty could hear, I said, "Mark my words, Goodman Doty. I would seek your release from this hell, but you must promise me your gratitude will allow you to see my pure heart. And you must cease your false accusations."

Edward Doty took a deep breath and with a strangled voice answered me. "I am sorry—truly sorry. 'Twas—'twas Satan's snare fouling my words."

I stood quickly, sensing Standish looking at me. I had one last question for Mistress Winslow and Mistress Brewster before we talked to our governor.

"Why do you think God turned Doty's eye over to Satan?" I asked the two women.

"It might not even have been something Edward Doty

did himself," Susanna Winslow said. "Mayhap 'twas something his mother did while he was still in the womb—gazing on some terrible evil, or letting her husband embrace too passionately after the child was quickened."

Mistress Brewster nodded. "His mother may have resisted giving birth and his eye got stuck against her bones. In any event, the men have suffered enough, don't ye agree?"

And so I joined the other Mistresses to persuade Governor Bradford it was time to release the duelers. It took little persuasion. Later, John found me working in the garden.

"How did ye find the heart to give Doty mercy?"

"Truth be told, it was not only mercy. We were sick of their cries."

"They will not duel again." John put an arm around my waist. "But ye must understand, ye may have need of mercy thyself."

My waist tensed against his hands. "Because I have broken a law?"

"Nay, never." John stroked my back lightly. "Because others break God's commandment to be truthful. And His commandment not to covet a neighbor's wife."

I smiled at that—a small smile, but my first that day. "There is no fodder for Allerton's accusation with Attitash gone."

"But she may be back," he said. "As soon as the crops are reaped, Governor promises a true Harvest Home celebration. He has invited Hobbamock."

My anticipation at seeing Attitash soon was tempered by fear that we would be back in the cauldron of Satan's accusations.

Attitash

Our Massasoit kept Tisquantum under his eagle eye during our Green Weachimin and not once did I see my betrayer being anything but subservient.

Black Whale did well in the betting games and races. There was a lift to his shoulders I'd not seen while we were in Patuxet. When we escaped to our Trees-in-Love, Black Whale's eagerness was as wild as when we first made love. When I collapsed in Black Whale's arms, my new life shifted. "Listen to your papa breathe," I said. Black Whale's chest rose and fell slowly, like the sea at low tide. I traced his curved brow, marveling again at the strength of bone beneath my finger. Sinking back, I nuzzled into his shoulder with his strong hands resting over New Life's little bulge.

As we returned to Patuxet for their harvest celebration, I wanted to keep savoring that memory, as well as Grandmother's face when she felt my new life and Wind in the Rushes' new swelling. Most of all, I wanted to keep the comfort of being with my own people—where no one might be plotting against Esapett and me. Watching Black Whale walk ahead of me towards Patuxet now, I saw his shoulders had returned to their stiff posture. I wondered if Esapett was well and safe and felt my own shoulders tense.

Elisabeth
No hint of further taunts reached me, but night terrors woke me and I huddled under my quilt waiting for sleep to return.

About a week after the duel, I woke from a dream about witch hunting. Wrapping my cloak over my shift, I went into the garden to shed my dream in the full moon, shining down like spilled embers on the sea. I opened my eyes to its light, willing it to fill me and wash away fears. When a twig snapped, I froze. Then I heard my name, spoken with the timbre and pitch I knew deep in my body. John came to me and enveloped me without a word. For a long moment he held me tight against his chest, my head tucked under his chin. Finally he asked, "What keeps thee awake, dear heart?"

Muffled against him, I whispered, "the moon." I looked at his face and realized that fear also kept him awake. "No, the moon did not wake me, but it may help me sleep."

John looked up to the moon. I could see the pulse in his neck and his eyes drinking in the light as mine had. "What do ye fear?"

At first so many answers tumbled into my mind I let them rattle about—the terror of stocks, hanging, and fires was too terrible to speak out loud. Living frightened me too, if it were without my beloved. I put my finger gently against his pulse and felt it echoed in mine. "I fear I will never be thy true wife."

"That will not—cannot happen!" He took me by the shoulders, his eyes bright in the moonlit air. "It is not just protecting thee I desire. I need thee. All I want is to touch thy face, look into thy eyes." His lips grazed mine lightly and I responded by opening to taste him. His kiss filled my mouth.

My fear ebbed like sand beneath the tide. "I too long for thee—to be with me at night when I sleep and there when I wake up in the morning."

"And ye shall have me." He traced my face, resting his finger on my lips. I have already begun to plan my house, so next spring we can live together as man and wife."

My smile met his. The sound of the wind whipping up on the sea intruded. The accusation of my witchcraft was in part due to the failure of a supply ship to return to us from England. "Jack, what if a ship does not come?"

"Trust in God," he answered with his usual aplomb. "We have enough harvest to get through the winter. Next spring the trading ships will come. God does provide, sweet wife." He gave me a quick kiss and turned me toward the door. "Now, get thee to bed before Mistress Brewster finds us about in mid-night."

24

Elisabeth

Mistress Brewster tested the board secured down the middle of her bed and turned to us. "Howland, strip off thy breeches afore ye get in so they don't soil this clean bedding. You'll have to climb over this to sleep and let Elisabeth have the outside." She beamed at me. "I'll be within a hand's reach, Elisabeth, if he tries to turn bundling into a wedding night."

Priscilla shot me an encouraging smile. She and John Alden had also used Brewsters' bed to bundle a week before they were wed. Desire gave her bed to Mistress Brewster, and snuggled with Humility on floor blankets. Her head was under the covers, preferring to ignore our situation through the pretext of lulling Humility to sleep. We could hear Master settling into the loft hammocks with his sons. I shook out my apron as John put his breeches on a chair, the tails of his long shirt hanging to his knees.

We pulled the curtains and the bed was filled with John. Sitting with my back to him and my bottom against our bundling board, I spoke quietly. "Mistress says ye will help me with the laces of my stays."

"Yea, she gave me many admonitions to tend to thee. But 'tis not easy in the dark."

John was not as quick as Priscilla or Desire, but I relished the feel of his lingering hands and made no complaint "Do men take lacing practice like they do the arms exercise?" I asked softly. Not soft enough; laughs and guffaws came from outside our bed-curtains.

"My fowling piece is far easier to control than these laces and for less fair a purpose." John's voice was not at all quiet, and drew more laughs from the household.

"Hush!" I whispered, looking over my shoulder. I could just make out the curve of his smile in the firelight that glowed through the curtain. "If ye would tell the entire household what's behind the curtain, I will sleep with Desire and Humility on the floor."

John moved his mouth to my ear, kissing my cheek on the way. "Beg pardon, but I'm just throwing sops to stay their curiosity. If they hear nothing, they'll be all ears."

Catching his intent, I called out for the benefit of the household, "Let me do it myself." John loosened the last lace. I pulled off my stays and leaned back against him as he stroked my cheek and asked in a soft whisper if I remembered my sister's bundling.

"Little indeed. I was eleven when Rose bundled and so embarrassed I hid my head under the covers." Even through the muslin shift, my blood sang and my nipples tightened.

"Have ye need of a candle, Howland?" John Alden called.

"Nay, I'm fine in the dark," my husband replied as he released me to the safety of my side of the board. To provide a safer topic for the eavesdroppers on the other side of the curtains, as well as to quench my surging feelings, I asked John to tell me of his boyhood. We turned to face each other over the bundling board as he described his brothers, the horses and even dogs he'd loved.

His voice was still low, but there was a fervor that would carry to anyone listening. "Do ye remember the day Samoset walked into our village?"

"I shall think of it 'til the day I die." Listening carefully, I could hear the heavy breathing of everyone in the household. It seemed we were the only ones still awake. "I did envision Attitash in a dream before we landed," I said in a faint whisper.

"A dream?" John asked. "Was that how ye understood her so easily?"

"Understood her? She was pure mystery to me. "

"I do know that if ye had not become friends, we would have starved by now." He took my hand. "And I might have succumbed to the fever. 'Tis cruel that ye are now pushed apart."

A warm rush filled me—he understood my heavy regret. I closed my eyes to hold in the emotion, and whispered into the dark, "She will be brought to childbed this winter. If she safely delivers, God willing, I would be desperate to see her babe."

"Ye shall see thy friend and her babe, Elisa. I will find a way." Before I could ask, he hushed me. "When the new ship arrives—as it shall—all will know the rumors about ye are false." He took both my hands, leaning across the board to speak into my ear. "We will be truly wed and ye shall once again see Attitash." The board was little hindrance to his kiss. I opened my mouth and tasted him. He tasted like he smelled—sea salt, pinewood, and ale.

"Even if ye could not arrange this, Jack, thy willingness to try assures me of thy love."

"How could ye not believe so? Do ye remember hearing Solomon's Song? *Many waters cannot quench love, neither can the floods drown it.*"

"Desire read some to me, but not that part."

"This is our love, Elisa. It cannot be quenched, and I shall make thy heart happy. *Set me a seal upon thine heart... for love is strong.*"

"*I am my beloved's and his desire is toward me.*" I repeated the part Desire had read.

"Ye do know Solomon! And yea, my desire is toward thee. Will ye let me touch thee?"

I said nothing, but untied the drawstring on my shift. His hand moved slowly, pausing for silent permission. My yearning sighs were answer enough, and he reached beneath my shift 'til he gently held my breasts. I gasped for air and when I did not resist he moved a finger slowly 'til he touched each nipple.

"Does this trouble thee, Sweet?"

"Nay, truth be told, it delights me. Mistress said only that ye must stay above my waist."

His fingers slid to the tip of my navel. The yearning of my body struggled against fear that I could not control his passion. He reached further, then withdrew his fingers, saying softly in my ear, "Even if Mary Brewster would not know what I'm doing, I must keep my promise to treat thee gently."

As he removed his hand, I took it and held it to my cheek. "Ye know I want thee too."

"I do know." His voice was husky with emotion. "I live for the time ye'll find me in thy bed every morn."

It seemed a long time after he'd settled on his own side before I could sleep. I dreamed of holding a babe with John's green eyes. My babe played pat-a-cake with a black-eyed babe as Attitash laughed.

ALL WEEK MISTRESS BREWSTER supervised the cooking, as we prepared for the Harvest Home celebration. I spent most of the day frying up the birds John Howland handed back from their fowling expedition. His eyes shone as bright as the ducks' green plumage when he brought them to me.

"If I had known the delight of a good shot and ducks in hand awaited me here, the decision to leave England would have been easy."

"So ye only left England so ye could shoot?" I felt the fat breast of the bird beneath its feathers.

"Yea, and squeeze the cook." He made bold to lay

hands on my hips. His hands were strong, but felt gentle on my body. I slid from his grasp, giggling.

I tried not to think on the heat in John's hands as we marched that evening to the Commonhouse for our weekly Thursday Thanksgiving service. The Harvest Home celebration would follow next day. Our little settlement made a fine stream of people, the men marching behind as usual with their muskets on their shoulders. The colors of the trees were such a brilliant red and orange, it would have been impossible to describe them to my family back in England. The bright leaves fell and dappled the road as we walked, as though we were royalty being honored with flowers tossed in our path. When we arrived at the Commonhouse, I found a seat in the women's side across the aisle from John. He was especially handsome in John Carver's fine black coat. I wore Catherine Carver's dark green waistcoat for the first time since the day we were wed, and over it, Aunt Agnes' light green shawl. It still carried her scent and I breathed it in, remembering how lovingly she and Uncle Edward gazed at each other. All our assemblage wore their best, though it felt vain to notice.

I closed my mind to such worldly thoughts as we sang, *His mercy ever is the same, And His faith unto all ages.*

When the singing ended, Master Allerton stood to prophesy. He exhorted us to praise God for granting us this new land of milk and honey. He did not observe that while Moses had found plenty of manna, our dear ones died because they had little to eat.

I wanted to call out, "This land is not so much milk and honey as meat and corn. God used the Indians to provide food for our survival." If only I could reveal that Attitash had convinced Squanto to teach us how to plant. It was Governor Bradford and Master Winslow, not Master Allerton, who agreed to change our ways so the corn would grow. I thanked God fervently for sparing me from becoming Isaac Allerton's servant. I thanked God for purifying my fouled soul through Attitash. Glancing across the aisle I saw tension in John's straight mouth and stiff shoulders. John could no more hear the Lord's goodness in Master Allerton's words than could I. When the service ended at last, Priscilla and I hurried to Brewsters to check the simmering stews.

Attitash

Papa put on his finest shells and feathers so he would make a dignified entry to the feast with our Massasowet. Our leader would have Tokamahamon speak the cloth-men's tongue at the feast. Tisquantum would be watched carefully. Black Whale and the other hunters were still out hunting deer and would join us later.

Mama and I greased our bodies against the chill. We draped our shoulders with furs, making sure our breasts did not peak through. White Flower helped us put feathers in our hair and wampum strings on our necks and arms. She took Little Fish by the hand and Mama and I carried the pots of oysters and eels to the village the Strangers called Pli-mot.

25

Elisabeth

Mistress Brewster shooed us maids about as if we were chickens, exhorting us to have all the food ready. The smells of cornbread, corn pudding, stewed plums, and pottage mingled with those of the herbed fowl and mussels. By the time the men had assembled tables in the village square, Mistress's efforts were amply rewarded.

As the men marched to the meadow to exercise their weapons, Governor Bradford remained to greet the Indians. Massasoit arrived with Hobbamock, Squanto, and the new translator Tokamahamon. More Indians arrived. And still more! So many men I could not keep count. They filled up the grassy area surrounding our Commonhouse. The smell of their bodies contradicted the savory scent of food. I searched the path, but saw no sign of Attitash or her mother.

"How will we feed them all?" Mistress Brewster asked. Our governor did not answer her.

As men began to return from their drill, Governor Bradford and Massasoit stood at the head of the tables filled with food. The Indians sat down on logs, rocks or even the ground. Their bare chests gleamed with grease with no sign of chill.

Humility pulled on my skirt, almost making me drop a bowl of corn chowder. "Elisa-buss, see baby!" Attitash's little sister held her baby brother by his hand, followed by Attitash and her mother. Their hair was strung with shells and feathers. Though the sun shone thin and the sea breeze was strong, they wore only leggings, skirts and ponchos—Attitash's baby-belly barely visible. Their furs hung loose from their shoulders.

"Welcome…ka wee," I greeted, as I made room on the table for their bowl filled with eels, mussels, and delicious smelling oysters. Attitash's smile in return was questioning. "Ca-taba-tash. I am fine," I assured her; my smile telling her more than my words. It felt so right to see her again. "And ye?" I caught eyes staring at us and we moved apart.

Captain Standish called to Mistress Brewster as he came striding between us. "Do the women have all the food out? There's not enough!" He paused and looked directly at Attitash. "Well met, these heathen wenches are comely and fruitful. How are we to breed as well as the savages with so few maids of our own?" His face the same height as Attitash's neck, stared rudely at her body. Smacking his lips, he turned to young Bartholomew Allerton, who was ogling Attitash. "Stay thy lust, lad. They do display their wares too boldly."

Isaac grabbed his son's ear, laughing. My nails dug into my hands. Attitash's eyes met mine, her own tightening in caution as she turned her head to follow the noisy figure of our Captain sashaying down the table, inspecting the many bowls and pots. His fingers hovered over the food and stopped above the bowl of oysters. "Bless this food so we can eat." he called out to Elder Brewster.

"Then tell your men to hurry, Captain," Master Brewster replied, pointing toward the field where the men were cleaning muskets.

When John and the rest of the men finally arrived, Elder Brewster blessed the food. As he carried on, Attitash's little brother took a piece of meat from the bowl and popped it into his mouth. No one did anything to admonish him. Attitash took a piece of corn bread and handed it to him. Naturally, Humility began to whine for some. I put my hand over her mouth to muffle her noise. My own stomach growled, as I inhaled the succulent smell of the plates of hot bread, oysters, and the wild fowl simmering in a pottage. At last Elder Brewster finished praying and the men began helping themselves. When we had refilled all the serving platters and made sure Attitash and the other Indian women had plenty, Mistress Brewster finally gave us leave to fill our own trenchers. Mine was heaped with corn pudding, corn bread, eels, and goose pottage. Even though I had taken no lobster or cod, I had not eaten so much since we left England. I glanced at the sea, hoping to see the white sails of a ship from home in the horizon. As always, there was only the dark blue of the sky. As I sat down by John, a wet nose bumped my leg. Rogue laid her head on John's knee and was rewarded with meat.

Attitash
Mowi and Suki ran around us, all noses and lolling tongues, sniffing for tidbits from my bowls and whining for a share. When they got none, they trotted to where the Strangers' dog begged from Esapett and Jon-owlan. No taller than I, Jon-owlan had gained some flesh and looked strong. Although he seemed nearly as old as Papa, Jon-owlan's glances at Esapett were too tender for an uncle. I had been watching their touches, and they reminded me of Black Whale's before we were joined. Esapett glanced at me, and leaning her head against her man's shoulder, smiled at me. Cautious of the many eyes watching us, however, we made no attempt to converse. Nippa'uus was low in the west when Mama and I set the water-pot on three sticks over a small fire. The water began to seethe and I used my forked stick to take the hot water off the fire, setting it down carefully on stones. As I reached into my bag for the

dried wintergreen, the little girl peeked at me from behind Esapett's skirts, but would not return my smile.

Elisabeth

Humility would not cease clinging to me. Mary Allerton finally lured her out from my skirts to play "all fall down." Then screams cut through the chatter. Humility waved rosy little fists in the air, the over-turned kettle at her feet. Mary frantically shook her bright-red fingers.

Attitash rushed to Mary. I picked up a screaming Humility.

"Stupid girls!" I yelled. "Why were ye playing near boiling water?"

Attitash gently lifted up Mary's left hand, exposing swelling blisters. Taking a bowl of raw oysters from her mother, Attitash handed one to me. I held the cold oyster against Humility's hand, bringing a stop to the babe's cries. Attitash put some on Mary's fingers and wrapped it in sorghum moss.

"Fie, Elisabeth!" Remember Allerton pushed through the crowd. "Will you not keep our little ones away from your heathen friend?" Mary's sobs escalated to plaintive shrieks. Remember picked up Mary's switch from the ground. "Did ye not use this to keep the babe away from the savages, Mary?" She took Mary's left hand and tore off the moss and oysters. "See what happens when ye use thy left hand, Sister?" The child wailed louder and stuck her blistered fingers in her mouth.

Attitash backed up a step, her face mirrored my own fury. Hobbamock's wife fixed her eyes on mine. She clearly expected me to stop Remember Allerton's insults.

I grabbed Remember's arm. "How dare ye speak to me in such a manner? Ye don't know anything about these heathen friends, Child!" My fury sharpened my tongue. "Do ye want us to starve to death? Or be attacked by other

Indians?" I lowered my shrill voice. "Attitash's remedy would heal thy sister."

Remember's freckles stood out on her face. "Father says having a treaty with barbarians doesn't mean we allow their tainted hands to get familiar with us." She yanked her arm away and glanced back through the crowd, obviously hoping her father would come to her rescue. "You let the savage touch my little sister! Now her left hand is marked by Satan."

I had to clap my hand over my mouth to keep from insisting that little Mary's left hand was as innocent as her right. It would be more fuel for her father's gossip against me.

Attitash and her mother turned their backs on us and the crowd made way for them. They ignored Goodwife Billington's sign of the cross to ward off any hex.

Picking up Mary, Remember pushed through the crowd to where Master Allerton was posturing, nodding his head like a hypocrite while Governor Bradford thanked God for our heathen friends. I could not hear Allerton's words in response to his daughter's tale, but if he called upon the Lord, 'twas in vain.

Attitash

I began to make my way to Our Massasowet when Black Whale's hand on my back stopped me. "Wait, Attitash."

"Did you see what happened?" I asked.

"Trouble always happens when you and Esapett are together."

The spotted face girl and her little sister were both crying. I glanced back at Esapett. Jon-owlan held her wrist tightly.

Elisabeth

"Does this discussion involve thee?" John whispered low.

I gave him a brief version of the sudden event. "Doesn't Mary's father realize Attitash will not harm, but heal?"

"He only cares what the crowd thinks," John answered. "Isaac Allerton is too consumed by his ambition. He seeks every opportunity to prosper."

I swallowed hard. There would always be hostile eyes watching us everywhere.

"Governor Bradford is beckoning." John kept his hand on my wrist. Everyone was looking at me though the bustle of chatter, plates clattering, and children shrieking had resumed. Surely a remedy for a child's burn did not justify burning me at the stake. But it could be a successful culmination of Allerton's efforts to keep me from being John Howland's true wife.

Attitash and Black Whale were also going to the head table, where our governors and her parents awaited. Priscilla called out my name quietly as we passed her but I could not respond. All my effort was focused on keeping my face from revealing my thoughts.

"Our desire must be to keep the peace, Elisabeth," Governor Bradford said, when we stood before him. "We must continue to have King Massasoit's people defending us. The allegations about Hobbamock's daughter and you give fuel to those of our company who would rip up the treaty."

Attitash

All the Strangers sitting about the planks-on-trees put down their food and gawked at Esapett and me. Tisquantum stood a few paces away, talking with the rude man called Cap-tan.

Our Massasowet spoke to me while Sachem Bad-ford spoke to Esapett. "We must keep the treaty with these Cloth-men. You have done much to help the Strangers survive. But some of them see bad spirits when you are with their clothwoman. When you return to your grand-mother's fire, there must be no accusations that the cloth-woman used you to carry their bad spirits to us."

I looked at Mama. Her mouth was grim, but her eyes told me to accept his decision. We both wanted Our Massasowet to demand respect from the Strangers, but we knew he could not change who they were. I folded my arms across my belly. New Life would be safer at Grand-mother's fire. New Life was our people's future.

Elisabeth

"With Hobbamock's daughter back in King Massasoit's village ye will have an easier time keeping thy wife from danger, John," Governor Bradford said. "Now go enjoy the rest of thy dinner. Tomorrow we will have a shooting competition with Massasoit's men."

I stretched my ribs to fill my body with air again. At-titash stood silent. Our governor had said Attitash and her husband would live with her people, as they'd done before Hobbamock was brought to live near Plimoth. I flicked my eyes at her as she cast down her own.

Taking a deep breath, I addressed our governor. I'd prepared his meals since Jane died, surely he had enough Christian love in his heart to hear me out. "I would have a moment to say farewell to my friend. She has shown kind-ness to me, and to all of us." Seeing his doubt, I added, "It's almost dark. Mistress Brewster could take us to her house. No one would see us."

"We must keep you safe." Governor Bradford spoke quietly. "There is little I can do to restrain Lieutenant Governor Allerton's will." He beckoned to Mistress, "Mother Brewster, would you take Elisabeth and Hob-bamock's daughter to your home?"

As I started to walk with Mistress Brewster, Governor Bradford called to my John. They spoke briefly, and then

John caught up with me. "I must stop at home for a moment, Elisabeth. I'll join thee in Brewsters' garden."

Attitash and Black Whale followed me to Mistress's garden. I wondered if I should give Attitash a parting gift. I felt the warmth of Aunt Agnes' shawl, but it carried too many memories.

My husband arrived, holding a leather bag that I recognized as Governor Bradford's. John opened it and took out the little Indian bow and arrow. Attitash gasped and her eyes tightened.

"Governor Bradford wants you to have this." John held it out to Black Whale, who kept his arms folded. "We found it in a grave when we first came to this land one year ago. If your wife delivers safely, your babe can play with it."

Attitash

Black Whale glanced at me, then at his handiwork. It was discolored, but someone had polished off the dirt.

"Do you know what he said?" Black Whale asked me. "All I understood was Bad-ford."

I shook my head. "That's all I understood too." Jonowlan and Esapett had been smiling, but now their mouths closed and their eyes searched ours. "Maybe they want us to return the bow and arrow to the grave."

"It's too late for the little boy's spirit journey." Black Whale still didn't reach for the bow and arrow. "It's been a whole circle of the seasons since we buried him."

"The Strangers don't put anything in their graves," I said. "They don't understand."

Black Whale slowly held out a hand and Jon-owlan gave him the bow and arrow. Esapett and Jon-owlan were both smiling again. Mis-tess was too.

"Catabatash," I said, elbowing Black Whale. "T'ank you."

"T'ank t'ank, catabatash," Black Whale echoed, gathering the gift into his journey bag. I took a pretty feather from my hair and a string of wampum from my arm and gave them to her. "Netop."

"Netop." Esapett responded. She removed her long cloth-cape and took off a soft-cloth blanket from her shoulders. Pointing to my swelling belly, she cradled the blanket then gave it to me. "For babe."

I looked down at her gift of the cloth colored like spring leaves. "Ahhe." I draped the cloth so it covered my new-life belly and patted it. "Baby." I took her hands.

Elisabeth
Mistress Brewster's prayer intruded into the circle Attitash's hands made with mine. "Father in heaven, I thank Thee for using the heathen to help heal our children. Now we seek safety for our dear Elisabeth. And for the heathen maid. Keep them from Satan's snare. Let each live in peace with her own people."

Attitash twisted the ends of Aunt Agnes' shawl that I'd given to her on impulse. Her eyes were warm—dark brown; gold firelight caught by tears.

HARD RAIN PELTED the grounds where we'd feasted and the rain smelled like snow. I pulled Humility close to me at night, needing all the warmth her little body could give me. Soon, we women would be spending most of our time inside the dark house, mending what was left of our worn-out bedding and clothing. John helped Master Eaton work on new houses, splitting the logs into boards with the wide bladed adze. He hoped to have our little house framed before the ground froze. Sleep brought dreams of next year in a house with my true love.

26

Attitash

During our journey home to Poanoke I thought of all the work to do when we got home. The sliced squash, beans, wild fruits and herbs were drying. Now we would brew medicines. Black Whale and Papa would hunt the small whales. After they returned, we'd butcher them, dry the meat, pound the whale fat into dried weachimin, and store it for winter body-grease. By the time New Life arrived, our home would be settled with most of my work done.

We were still one day's journey from Poanoke when we returned the little bow and arrow to the disturbed grave. It was too late for the little boy, but we honored Jonowlan's intention to make right their theft. We walked for a long time before we bedded down that night.

Waking to a promising light wind the next morning, I left my sleeping family and went to pray. I reached the ridge just as Nippa'uus appeared on the rim of the horizon, making a golden path on the gray-green Big Salt Water. Something caught my eye. At first I thought the white bobbing was a low lying cloud. Then it became clear. It was the white cloths of a big wind canoe. A new wind canoe filled with more Strangers. Pale clouds gathered, hovering above the horizon. Nippa'uus turned blood red. The rim along the sea glowed orange and purple, as though Mother Earth had been wounded. My sweat chilled on my shoulders and neck. Esapett's big wind canoe full of Strangers had also arrived on a cold moon, and stayed.

This big wind-canoe would stay too. New Strangers in our midst! A weak feeling spread from my ribs down through my legs and I puffed hard to catch my breath. Beneath my fur-covered belly, New Life kicked.

Black Whale came running up the path, pointing out to Big Salt Water. He stood behind me as we watched the big wind canoe continue toward Patuxet and Esapett's people.

"They could break the promises in our treaty." Fear pitched my voice high. "What if the new Strangers take our weachimin and our fields?"

"Our friends Jon-owlan and Win-sow will help Badford keep the treaty," Black Whale said. "The new Strangers must listen." His voice did not have the reassurance his words intended.

But would they? Or would they listen to Tisquantum's bad talk about Esapett? My hands remembered Little Fish slipping from me into the water. My heart remembered Esapett, handing my brother back to me. I covered my belly with Esapett's cloth gift. Behind my eyes, I could see her raising her arms in prayer for me. I began to sing a prayer to Kiehtan to bring my our child safely to the light. Singing with me, Black Whale put his arms over mine. Together we enclosed New Life.

Elisabeth

A cannon boomed in my dream. I opened my eyes to sunrise cracking the gaps in the clapboard.

"The alarm has sounded!" John Alden called from outside. "There's a ship in the bay!"

John opened the Brewsters' door, letting icy wind into the house. "It may be the French." He picked up his musket and adjusted his bandoliers. "If it is, there'll be a battle."

My bones were like water. I pulled on my skirts and

threw my cloak over my shift, praying it would not be the French come to invade us; praying God's hand kept our ship safe; praying that supplies, letters and Christians had arrived, proof that He had not punished us all because a heathen cleansed me.

Elder Brewster stood by the door, his spyglass in his hand. "The flag—'tis—the King's! 'Tis our own ship! They have found us!"

Laughing and crying, I ran outside. Everyone was pouring out of their houses and running to the shore. A year ago I was the one arriving—a young girl with a mother, father, uncle, and aunt. I ran up the hill to where silent graves looked out over the sea. The new ship was anchored and the longboats were already being lowered amid great shouts. The sun was above the sea, warming my face.

On the Mayflower we had sailed toward the setting sun, and so I'd thought of this new world as a sunset world. But one morning, Attitash and I watched the sunrise. She patted herself, saying "Wampanoag, People of First Light."

"Wampanoag, Wampanoag," I whispered, realizing I now lived in a world of First Light. Reaching into my pocket, I took out the feather and shells Attitash had given me. Holding them to my cheek, I could smell her scent and feel her fear at the sight of new people coming with the sunrise. With both excitement and dread, I went down to meet the new arrivals.

Notes and Acknowledgments

Historical Fiction: The characters in *Strangers in Our Midst* are fictional, but use the names of historical people. This is true for all of the Pilgrim characters and some of the Wampanoag. Events involving entire groups are based on historical incidents; all of the actions of the two young women are fiction. I attempted to write what is plausible in relation to what is known.

Records reveal: The Mayflower Pilgrims settled on a former Wampanoag site called Patuxet, where the fields had been cleared, corn grown, and homes built. A few years before the Mayflower arrived, everyone in Patuxet had been captured or killed by Europeans, or had died of new diseases. Following the signing of the treaty of mutual protection, the Wampanoag asked Hobbamock to live near the new settlement to ensure the English followed its terms. The record describes Hobbamock as bringing a large family with him.

The historical Elisabeth Tilley was baptized in England on August, 1607 and came on the Mayflower with her parents. The historical John Howland was born in England in 1592. He was Governor John Carver's servant—probably his clerk. His fall into the ocean during the voyage is described in the primary accounts, including his rescue after grabbing a halyard.

Most of the deaths portrayed in the story are based on historical events, from the fifty Mayflower passengers who died the first winter to the yellow-haired body found with a small Wampanoag child when the Pilgrims desecrated a grave.

Fiction based on research: Although English records do mention interaction between the Pilgrim and Wampanoag men, nothing is mentioned of women. In fact, English records of that time mention very little about their own women beyond their birth, marriage and death. Likewise, we know little of Wampanoag women and, thus, the character Attitash is pure fiction, as are her mother, siblings, aunts, uncles and Black Whale.

The cross-cultural experience between Elisabeth and Attitash is also fiction. When I first began writing, I was uncertain how close the two could become; then I recalled amazing friendships I've enjoyed. Many of these had also seemed impossible when we first met. Neng Xiong was one of the first Hmong grandmothers to come from Laos to Minnesota. She spoke no English in 1976, but communicated with tears and smiles. Ten years later she greeted me with sobs, a great hug, and "too long, too long!" My co-madre, co-abuelita Edda Torres, held my hand while we waited for the birth of our first nieto. Deepest gratitude is to my late friend, Ethele Martin, whose two children are now our adult godchildren, Tamera and Shay-Glorious. Ethele (Tudy) transformed from a young African American mother who would not look me in the eye, to an intimate friend. Without Tudy, I could not have believed in Elisabeth and Attitash.

Resources: The idea for this story began with reading the primary sources written by the colonists, including *Of Plymouth Plantation 1620-1647,* by William Bradford: "Those prudent governors...began both deeply to apprehend their present dangers and wisely to foresee the future and think of a timely remedy...of removal to some other place. Not out of any newfangledness or other such like giddy humor by which men are oftentimes transported to their great hurt and danger, but for sundry weighty and solid reasons."

I relied on contemporary books about Wampanoag and other Indigenous people, including *Facing East from Indian Country, a Native History of Early America,* by Daniel Richter: The new arrivals from the east changed life for the Indigenous people, whose "world (became) every bit as new as that confronting transplanted Africans or Europeans' in the same period" and "most eastern North American Indian probably heard mangled tales of strange newcomers long before they ever laid eyes on one in the flesh, and when rare and novel items reached their villages through longstanding channels...they discovered European things long before they confronted European people."

Religion was total immersion for the Pilgrims. Understanding their view of predestination (pre-destined to heaven or hell) and finding the appropriate scripture was provided by the Reverends: my sisters Julie Christensen and Anita Cummings, the legacy from our father, Rev. Howard Osborne; and the Reverend H. David Stewart. My grandmother, Julia Jones Osborne, left me her well-worn King James Bible, which I used for all the biblical quotes.

The ten stages for Puritans are described by William Perkins, including the humiliation as the fourth stage, found in *Visible Saints, the History of a Puritan Idea,* by Edmund S. Morgan. Bridget Martin provided details on English weather, seasons and on Shakespeare sonnets, including the quote for John Howland, "Rough winds do shake the darling buds of May."

Wayne and Martha Denniston shared their life today in Plymouth and their sailing experiences on Cape Cod.

My ability to imagine daily life for Elisabeth and Attitash was helped immeasurably when I visited the Plimoth Plantation living history museum at Plymouth, Massachusetts—with Pilgrim Village and Hobbamock's Homesite. The role-players in Pilgrim Village portray the Pilgrims in 1627; the Wampanoag people remain their contemporary

316 NOTES AND ACKNOWLEDGMENTS

selves while demonstrating Wampanoag life of the time the Europeans first brought families to live in Wampanoag territory. I learned from their answers to questions posed by bold school children and searching tourists, and from the researchers on staff who replied patiently to my own questions. Each of my five visits produced more answers and more questions. The culmination of my search to understanding Wampanoag life today and in Attitash's world, was my interview in May, 2013 with Bob Charlebois (Abenaki), Researcher, Director of Wampanoag Indigenous Program, Plimoth Plantation. Bob was most generous with his time, his spirit, and his stories. Any mistakes in telling this story are mine alone.

It was clear to me that as a non-native person, I would have difficulty understanding the meaning behind Wampanoag ceremonies and rituals. My Native friends here in mid-continent advised me to ask the Wampanoag, "What can you tell me?" This approach gave me many details of daily life for Attitash and her people. When a ceremony is private to their culture, I imagined details, hoping they would be consistent with Wampanoag beliefs. The cleansing ceremony and coming of age ceremony were written in this manner.

Many Native friends continue to teach me: Elona Street Stewart, a Lanape now living amongst Ojibwe and Dakotah, brings global experience with Indigenous people and cross cultural connections. Elona has never wavered in leading me and remaining my friend. Thanks to friends at the St. Paul American Indian Family Center for patience and sage advice. Nora Murphy and the Dakotah Listening experience at Fort Snelling provided a glimpse into the Dakota world and language. I'm grateful to the Sisseton/Wahpeton Tribe for its Wacipi (pow-wow). This year will be the146[th] at their reservation near my husband's hometown.

Language: I have attempted to use enough language of

that time—Wampanoag, Algonquin, English—to give flavor without confusing the reader. There was no standard English spelling at that time, but I have tried to keep my selected spelling consistent. To distinguish the imagined character from a historical person, I spelled the character based on Elizabeth Tilley, Eli*a*beth.

The spelling of the Wampanoag Poanoke sachem's title is *Massasowe*t in Edward Winslow's writing and *Massasoit* in Bradford's. This word is a title meaning "honored" or "revered". The Pilgrims referred to Massasoit as "King" because he appeared to be so in their eyes. The Sachem acts as spokesperson for the council of grandmothers, which reaches decisions through consensus, and for the warriors' council, the Pniese. Bob Charlesbois described Massasoit as "a great orator and beloved leader, but not the decision maker."

Please visit: *www.fortypress.com* for more *Strangers in Our Midst* resources and links.

Thanks: All of the above is basis for the historical aspect of *Strangers in Our Midst*. I could not have written this as fiction without help from a great number of people.

Thanks to Loft Literary Center teachers, David Housewright, Mary Carroll Moore, and Mary Gardner, my simple story began to take shape. Laurel Yourke's class, "Revising the Novel," at the University of Wisconsin at Madison was worth repeating several times. Under Laurel's brilliant and tough guidance, the draft manuscript was revised into a novel.

Three writers from my first Loft class, Rosemary Jensen, Barbara Schue, and Peter Arnstein, read every word weekly and have given me priceless advice and encouragement. They have my lasting gratitude. I was fortunate to have astute readers in addition to my writers' group. Marie Hart Mattison read and provided copy editing for the first manuscript. Charlotte Landreau referred one of her high school history students, Sarah Pumroy, to me who read an early version and kindly told me which scenes kept her reading. Jerry Hendrickson, reading partner in Gardner's master class, gave far beyond expectations. After much revision, Charlotte Landreau, Anne Anderson, Terrie Brandt, and Anita Cummings, read the manuscript and provided valuable insight and encouragement. Carolyn Berman, Hannah Berman, Lynette Risch Johnson, Cheris Kramerae, and Joan McDermott, read excerpts and gave helpful responses.

Subtext Books owner Sue Zumberge read the manuscript and became a promoter and friend.

Sue gave me a copy of the yearly literary calendar, *Saint Paul Almanac*. Thanks to publisher Kimberly Nightingale, for this community forum which also provided the opportunity to read my poems publicly with other St. Paul writers. Ruthena Fink listened weekly to details about life in 1620s and kept me motivated.

Sue also alerted me to the magnificent Forty Press! Great thanks to publisher Joe Riley, attorney and author Kelly Keady, and editorial director, Nick Dimassis, whose insight, skill and guidance made editing inspiring work.

None of this story would have been written without my extraordinary family; Thankfully, I married Jim Vellenga—a man who would react honestly to all my drafts and is everything a husband, and father, should be. Our three adult children and their families: son, Tom Vellenga, who kept me faithful to political life; daughter, Charlotte Vellenga Landreau, whose enjoyment of historical fiction got me started; daughter Carolyn Vellenga Berman, author of *Creole Crossings*, who gave constant and sage advice. Their dear spouses, Julie Schmid, Carlos Landreau and Greg Berman shared their expertise. Their unions brought us the gift of six awesome grandchildren: Stefan and Ian Landreau, Aidan and Brendan Vellenga, and Hannah and Milly Berman—all unique descendants of the millions in Elizabeth and John Howland's twelfth generation descendents.

CPSIA information can be obtained at www.ICGtesting.com
Printed in the USA
BVOW08s0001091013

333231BV00002B/29/P